The Pictograph Murders

The Pictograph Murders

P.G. Karamesines

Signature Books
Salt Lake City ✣ 2004

This work contains short quotations and references to "Maggie May" by Martin Quittenton and Rod Stewart; "A Prayer for My Daughter" by William Butler Yeats, first published in 1921 in *Michael Robartes and the Dancer*; "The Shooting of Dan McGrew" by Robert Service, first published in 1907 in *The Spell of the Yukon and Other Verses* (New York: Barse & Hopkins, 1907), 45-49 (PS 8537 E7256 1907A, Robarts Library); "Ode to Joy" by Friedrich Schiller, written in 1785 as *An die Freude* and given its famous score in 1823 by Ludwig van Beethoven in his *Ninth Symphony*; and a takeoff in chapter 28 of the poem, "Mending Wall," first published in 1914 in *North of Boston*, with apologies to Robert Frost. The plotline and characters in *The Pictograph Murders* are unique, fictional creations from the imagination of P. G. Karamesines. Any resemblance to any other work or actual person is unintended and would be coincidental.

Cover design: Ron Stucki

Cover photograph: Saul Karamesines, *The Watchers*, 5.5 x 5 inches, 2004

The Pictograph Murders was printed on acid-free paper and was composed, printed, and bound in the United States of America.

http://www.signaturebooks.com

09 08 07 06 05 04   6 5 4 3 2 1

Library of Congress Cataloging-in-Publication Data
Karamesines, P. G. (Patricia G.)
    The pictograph murders / by P. G. Karamesines.
        p. cm.
    ISBN 1-56085-182-1 (pbk.)
    1. Women archaeologists–Fiction. I. Title.

PS3611.A73P53 2004
813'.6–dc22
                                        2004056567

For Ruby
You good dog, you.

*Then First Man called another ... being [and] said that
he should be named ma'i, the coyote. But the coyote got
angry and said: "Such a name!" And he declared that he
would not have it; and that he would leave; but First
Man called him back and told him that he would also be
known as Atse'hashke,' First Angry. After that the coyote
felt better. He thought that he had a great name given
him, and he went happily away, for he was told that he
would know all the happenings on the face of the earth.*

— Sandoval, qtd. by Aileen O'Bryan in
Navajo Indian Myths

One

Coyote yawned, scratched his chest, and gazed at the gallery of god figures standing there staring in that way they did. It peeved him how they stood apart from him, just staring. After all, he was one of them.

"I don't like my name," he said, feigning boredom so he might better play the game.

At this announcement, the figures communed in language sounding like gibberish. The air filled with rustling like wind in cottonwood leaves.

In his head, Coyote said, *They think I'm not one of them. I am! In my own way, I am as powerful as any one of them.* Maybe he couldn't understand what they said, but he knew he had made an impression.

One of them, called Man Counting, addressed him, this time in real words. "What's not to like?" he asked. Bone beads on his chest rattled lightly.

Coyote delayed answering, controlling the conversation through silence. Then he said, "It doesn't say anything. What does that mean, *Coyote?*" He picked up a rock as long and wide as his hand. To show the gods they meant nothing to him, he sat down right there—right in front of them.

"It means Coyote," said Ghost Eye.

"Coyote is Coyote," agreed Man Counting.

"It's not enough!" he snarled. "Give me a new name."

Two Dogs Laughing, his hollow eyes ever mocking, said, "You will never have enough names."

Looking at the rock, Coyote chuckled. He scratched its soft surface with a single claw. *Ch-ch-ch* went his claw. "The more names, the more power," he said. "I will keep Coyote—it could come in . . . hmm," he searched for a word, "useful. Yes, and that other one—I'll keep that too. But as I said, it's not enough."

Two Dogs Laughing said, "Have you thought that if you have a lot of names, the chance that someone will get power over you grows fat?"

"Such a cliché," said Coyote, yawning.

The rustling began again, incomprehensible. This time it sounded like cicadas singing behind leaves. Man Counting said, "It's a true belief. The more names you have, the greater the risk a clever enemy will guess one. Then you will be in his power."

Coyote scoffed. "I have no enemies whose cleverness exceeds mine."

Two Dogs Laughing addressed the figures standing around as if Coyote was not there. He said, "That Coyote, he thinks a lot of himself." The rustling began again, sounding suspiciously like laughter.

Coyote took a breath to hide his anger so they would not see it in his face. But on the inside, it spread in a searing flash and he savored it. *Ch-ch-ch* went his claw. *I will show them,* he thought. "The name," he insisted. "Give it, or I will take one of yours. Then we will see how true is this true belief."

This time the rustling was charged with astonishment. Coyote smiled at his success, showing his perfect white teeth.

Two Dogs Laughing said, "We had better give him his name. He is an angry one, this Coyote."

"His anger is precious to him," said Ghost Eye.

"It comes first," said another figure, the most imposing, surrounded by women as chary as deer. "It comes before the holy powers." As if casting a scrap to a dog, he said, "He is First Angry." Then he turned his mind to other things.

First Angry, Coyote repeated in his mind. *First Angry, First Angry. Ch-ch* went his claw. He looked up and smiled. The women turned away, disgusted, but he thought, *they all want me.* He knew he had won.

"He likes it," said Two Dogs Laughing. "Maybe now he will go away."

"I will go away," said Coyote, now also named First Angry. *Ch-ch-ch, ch-ch.*

"Get your own place," said Man Counting.

"Yes," said First Angry. "I will get my own place of power, better than this." With his eyes, he indicated the great theater where the gods lived.

"Don't hurt anybody doing it," said Ghost Eye.

"I hurt no one," said First Angry. "They all hurt themselves, then blame me. You know how it is." *Ch-ch.*

"Hey," said Two Dogs Laughing, "what is that you're doing with your claw?"

"I was wondering," said First Angry, "if the gods know what they look like."

"Gods don't care what they look like," said Man Counting.

"So they might say," said First Angry. "What I am doing here is making a picture of the gods, a few of you standing there." *Ch-ch.*

"Are you going to show us?" asked Two Dogs Laughing.

First Angry turned the stone around to reveal the portrait he had scratched into it. He really did have skill as an artist even if he said so himself. The gods gazed on it in silence. Then First Angry laid the stone in the sand, portrait side down.

"I give it to you as a gift," First Angry said. "And now, I'm out of here."

As he walked away, he heard Man Counting say, "I thought we were bigger than that."

First Angry laughed, the noise of it echoing off the canyon walls. He trotted out of the gods' gallery into the rising day. Light flowed past on all sides, its warmth raising beads of sweat on his skin. Ah, the light felt so good, so focused on him and yet indifferent to his significance. Darkness had its own intimacy, as he well knew, but desert light—there was nothing like it! It separated his soul from the crowd. It caressed him with an impersonality he thought might drive him mad. Sometimes he felt the urge to drop to the ground and roll in it like a dog in a deer carcass—it inspired in him that kind of rapture.

Some consider the world to be safe in the light of day when light reveals the hidden. But First Angry knew how dangerous the light can be. Because it appears to banish shadowy business, it disarms the onlooker. A good hunter knows how to take advantage of the light, how to use it to creep closer to prey that believes it sees all there is to see.

First Angry grinned ear to ear. What he needed now was

what they said—his own place, a piece of significant ground. Being something of a god, he knew a little bit about everything. He understood how thinking of such a place leads to its creation.

Two

Alexandra McKelvey slid off her backpack, twisted around to lower it to the ground, and spotted a big coyote standing not thirty feet away. Something keen and rabbit-like in her froze. Backpack half on, half off, she stared. Yes, there really was a coyote standing there. But was she in danger? No. Coyotes didn't attack people—not even in the movies. Gripping the pack, she straightened, eyes fixed on the animal.

The coyote's coat seemed watery and illusory like a mirage, a shimmer of black-tipped grays and sand browns. It was the eyes that anchored it to its place and time. Alex followed the coyote's line of vision and realized it was staring, not at her, but at Kit, her Siberian husky, its eyes alight with—what? Fascination? Contempt? Something.

So, she wasn't the one who had caught his attention. It was Kit who had brought him in. That probably meant the husky was coming into heat. But the coyote could be sick, maybe rabid. Alex looked for signs.

Ears set smartly in Kit's direction, mouth shut tight, gaze

intense, the coyote didn't look at all like a sick animal. No foam around the mouth, no snarling. He just seemed ... fascinated. Maybe that was it—he was so smitten with Kit that everything else in the scene had faded to unimportance.

She glanced at Kit, who faced away, sampling the canyon breeze. The dog had missed the fact that she was being watched. *But she could turn at any moment, and then? ...*

Alex's gaze slid back to the coyote. This time the animal flinched at the touch of her look. His eyes flitted in her direction, then he faded into brush at the campsite's edge. When Kit turned a split second later, he was gone.

Alex had heard stories of coyotes luring their domestic cousins into the wilderness and killing them there. She didn't know if it was true but decided not to find out by calling Kit's attention to their visitor and risking the life of her companion of two years. No doubt the wild creature had high-tailed it anyway, putting as much distance between himself and them as he could.

"He's good and gone" she said with a sigh of relief. But as she hiked up-canyon along the natural thoroughfare of the dry wash bed, she looked over her shoulder. There was the coyote following a short distance back. Up ahead of Alex, Kit worked her way along the wash bed unaware.

Once again, Alex decided to keep the coyote's presence to herself and see how the affair would play out. After all, she had no weapon or other way of controlling the situation. She had a leash, but Kit hated being leashed in the desert. If she tried to leash her, the independent gray-and-white husky would fight her, then complain endlessly. Also, she doubted that leashing Kit would solve the problem. Probably the coyote would just keep following. Anyway, wasn't this what she had come to the desert for—these unexpected moments when perspective shape-shifted to form a new body of experience?

In a breath, morning's shadow raised off the canyon floor and daylight flooded Vision Canyon—Alex's name for this special place. Stones all around swelled with light. Yucca flowers that had hung cool and quiet transformed into bells of clamoring light. All the vegetation in the canyon began to spark and glow—wild rice grass, sage, bee plant, red penstemons, white clusters, yellow puffs. Here and there, heavy-blossomed daturas puckered against the bitterness of the sun. But most plants were thin and wiry—waterless or fat on a few drops.

As the coyote followed them into the clean daylight, Alex remembered the warnings friends and family had given her about wandering the desert alone. Naturally, you had to be careful. But with Kit alongside, Alex had an advantage. Kit could be as fierce and sharp as any wild animal.

Alex looked at the husky, still oblivious to the coyote's presence. Oh, well. She supposed everyone was allowed at least one coyote moment. As far as she knew, Kit had never seen such a creature. Never having seen one, how could she be expected to be on the lookout for one? Coyotes could be difficult to anticipate—harder still to get a fix on. In the West, they surpass foxes as icons of opportunism. Sheep and cattle ranchers consider them arch-villains, while Native Americans grant them demigod status via their folklore.

Suddenly there was a sound, the snap of a twig breaking. Kit heard it and whirled sharply. Catching sight of the coyote, she lit off after him, her body language expressing a purity of purpose that Alex had witnessed send dogs twice the husky's size scrambling out of her way. The coyote spun in mid-stride and dodged off through the sage. Alex stumbled after them, terrified she was about to see the coyote-teasing-away-dog drama play out before her eyes.

"Kit! Get back here! Kit!" she yelled. Now she, too, felt a purity of purpose. *Hang unexpected moments,* she thought. *I want my dog back in one piece!* She lost sight of the coyote as he disappeared into the brush and stones ahead, Kit's fluffy white tail following. Then the coyote re-appeared, scrambling up a nearly vertical cliff face.

Alex stopped to watch. The coyote climbed fifteen feet, then pulled himself onto a rock outcrop. He turned and looked down at Kit on the canyon floor. However small the toe-holds he had used, Kit would find them and make her own way up. Alex hurried to reach the rock wall before the husky did just that. The coyote looked from her to Kit. He seemed reluctant to leave but finally turned and disappeared up a slit in the wall.

Breathing a sigh of relief, Alex caught Kit by the collar and led her back to the wash. In the shade of a cottonwood, she swung off her day pack and took out a water bottle. She drank briefly, looking down to see Kit's ice-blue eyes fixed on the bottle. She cupped her right hand and poured water into it, letting it overflow her palm while Kit lapped. Then they continued their hike up the canyon, Kit looking everywhere for coyotes, especially behind her. She wasn't about to be caught off guard again.

They had not gone far when three ravens joined them, their black plumage standing out against the red and tan stone walls and bright blue sky. Hopping and sparring with each other, whirling in little flights of dance and duel, the three kept just ahead of, above, or just behind Alex and Kit. The birds cracked the silence with occasional hoarse croaks.

The ravens' loose companionship combined with wild-flower fragrances pooling in her path to bring Alex bliss. Heat built in the wash bottom as the sun climbed toward its zenith, but shade still stretched along the canyon walls. Here the rock was cool and refreshing to the touch.

She and Kit hiked past shady and sun-gashed alcoves, all of which were familiar to Alex from previous hikes. Today she headed for the canyon's main attraction, that creation that raised the beauty of this particular crinkle in the desert above the many other wonders in the Utah drylands. She rounded a bend and whispered, "There they are!" Ahead of her in an al-cove, the sunlight revealed a crowd of painted figures. She had arrived at the pictograph panel called the Theater of Gods.

Presumably some isolated band of Archaic Indians had produced this series of pictographs. Strange and phantasmal, the most impressive images had massive, trapezoidal bodies, wide at the shoulders, narrowing at their bottom ends or wisp-ing away. Disproportionately small heads crowned many of the great torsos. Some towered above Alex's five-foot-six stat-ure. Most lacked arms and legs. Between the more ornate im-ages, evaporating spirit bodies of dark brown paint seemed to undulate like smoke in a breeze. Herds of bighorn sheep or pronghorns stood broadside, further texturing the panel's high design.

Directly above Alex loomed one of the largest trapezoids, jagged lines of dark and light pigment streaking its body. Two gaping dog shapes faced each other across the chest, one over each breast. Another large image wore what looked to be an abacus on its chest, and on its head, a halo—a pale corn-tassel crown.

Scattered around the large figures were smaller, slanted bodies that appeared to be women, their shoulders dropped and rounded in softer lines. Alex's eyes slid off these to another string of painted mountain sheep, then over to a few of the more anthropomorphic figures. Arms and legs taut with energy, two men leaned aggressively into each other. One held his spear as if to plunge it into the other's body.

Alex had noticed these figures before but only incidentally, and they had seemed out of step—a flash of impending tragedy quavering on the brink, surrounded on all sides by images of poise and potency. Today they captured her full attention.

Near the Warring Ones, as she decided to call them, two skull-headed Watchers stood, their slightly inclined postures and wide eye sockets suggesting that they were interested in the conflict. But lacking mouths, they couldn't influence its outcome. Like ghostly judges, they waited for the moment when the decision would come, when the spear, driven by motive and strength of arm, gouged the victim's life out of his body.

As Alex studied the scene, the spark she had felt ignite when she had first arrived cooled as if a chill wind had suddenly brushed by. *But … Spear Man might hesitate, lower his blade, and shudder at the thought of what he'd nearly done. Maybe he would let the other go and sulk off, overcome by shame and horror. Then the skull-headed watchers would dissipate, their moment passed. It could go either way—couldn't it?*

She frowned. She felt no relief that Spear Man's arm remained frozen aloft, caught in the act of a murderous thought. She had so little experience with death in general, she had difficulty believing in it. And murder—unimaginable! The offspring of haggish lust and misshapen rage. But here it was—an Ancient's testimony of the reality of such events, a centuries-old record of the outbreak of tragic emotion acting also as a forecast, a premonition in paint that played on her mind as a warning.

Alex had seen many pictograph panels, but this one never ceased to surprise her. During her first trip three years earlier, she had stood stricken before it. Without even realizing, she had spoken aloud: "I've been wrong, I've been wrong about everything!" She felt herself dissolving, and when she had come out of it, she was surprised to find her flesh intact, the only evidence of her meltdown being a slick of tears over her face.

She had returned to the panel several times, craving more. Each time, she had allowed herself to be confronted by it, and each time she had felt the same valence, a provocation that revised her world. But now, she saw in it cold ghosts, an aura that rose from the stone surrounding the Warring Ones. She shook her head to clear it of the unwelcome impressions. "Stop it!" she said. "Go away."

Kit trotted up and looked at her, blue eyes questioning.

"Not you," Alex said, patting the dog's head. "Go back to whatever you were doing."

In a doggy version of a shrug, Kit lowered her head, looked away, and trotted off.

Alex thought what she needed now was something to put her back on track, something that would restore the enthusiasm with which she had first approached the Theater of Gods that day. Words welled up from D. H. Lawrence: "That I am part of the earth my feet know perfectly, and my blood is part of the sea."

Alex wondered if it mattered that the people who had painted these pictographs had never seen the sea. Torrents of stars rushed over the canyon at night and the sun flooded it by day. The wind drove down canyon at the people who had lived here, cataracts of tumultuous air. And when the summer thunderstorms broke on the mesas, flushing liquefied earth down the canyons, the red sinews of flash floods had filled their nostrils with the odor of churned minerals. The creators of this pictograph panel knew these things, so they knew something about the force and form of the sea and the power that called together the elements in such ways that they echoed each other.

Alex sat down hard on a rock and turned her eyes from the panel to cool her mind. At her feet lay a smattering of stones that in the course of erosion had come to rest at the alcove's edge. Among them lay one flattened on top, suggesting the same about its bottom, but one never knew with stones embedded in sand.

Without knowing why, she picked it up and turned it over. There on its smooth, flat underbelly, some pilgrim like herself had scratched out a portrait of some of the theater's most powerful ghosts. How long had it lain there before she had picked it up? She stared at it and indulged in a powder-flash connection with yet an additional anonymous other, someone who might have been there yesterday or last month or last year.

She replaced the rock, artwork down, back in its cradle,

taking care not to damage the etching. Then she stood and left the alcove, feeling the stretch of a smile across her face and blinking back tears. The death-to-be scene tugged at her one last time. She banished it, letting the emotion she felt in response to the rest of the panel flood it from her soul.

Kit appeared from nowhere and took her usual position ahead of Alex. They walked past a dead, sun-bleached cotton-wood snag where the three ravens perched, looking like iridescent black ornaments among the bare and seasoned branches.

Three

Coyote, also called First Angry, traveled light. He prided himself on his ability to satisfy all needs along his way. A morsel here, a feast there—somehow, it all balanced out. An expert opportunist—that's what coyotes *are*—he knew in his blood he would at least survive and usually do better than that. It was his charisma. Irresistible, he was.

The world loves a coyote, he thought. *It leaps into my hands to satisfy me.* What he meant was that he was a cunning thief, gifted at sleight of hand and distraction by flattery.

However, the First Angry part of him raised the Coyote part above the status of a charming, if aggravating, clown by providing a dangerous undercurrent. Coyote loved the feeling of being dangerous—delicious! It was like a profound mystery only he understood or knowledge of a secret identity—the thing that set him apart from everyone else. Coyote also called First Angry smiled. Getting the new name had changed everything.

It was while he was thus trotting along smiling over his secret that he stumbled across Grandfather Rattlesnake. The angry buzz of the snake's rattle startled First Angry. He leaped into the air with a yelp.

"Oh ho!" laughed Grandfather Rattlesnake. "Wiped that toothy grin off your face, did I?"

Coyote didn't like Grandfather Rattlesnake much. The fact that the serpent had caught him unawares only worsened matters. *Grandfather Rattlesnake is so smug. He has great confidence in the venom that pools in his head and drips in his great curved fangs.* Coyote decided that he hated Grandfather Rattlesnake and vowed to do something about it. *I will show him that Coyote also called First Angry is not to be trifled with!*

"Grandfather Rattlesnake, I have cause for high spirits," he said.

"So you say."

"Perhaps you have not heard. Oh, excuse me—of course you haven't. You have no ears!" Coyote knew that Rattlesnake did not appreciate anyone calling attention to the fact he had no ears. The snake's forked tongue flicked in and out warily.

"Has some big thing happened?" Rattlesnake asked.

"Only the gods giving me a new name," Coyote said.

"Let me guess," said Rattlesnake. "Is it Mad Dog? Is it Rolls in Carrion?"

"It is First Angry," said Coyote, ignoring the insults.

"First Angry, eh?" said Rattlesnake. "Hmm ... I was pretty close with Rolls-in-Carrion."

Rage began building behind Coyote's eyes. "Grandfather, you never like anything I do!" he said.

"You never do anything I like! And I'm not your Grandfather. You and your new name! You're just foolish Coyote with no relations who would claim you and no future. Just a common thief with a good coat and big teeth—that's all you are."

These words enraged Coyote. He sprang at Rattlesnake, but Rattlesnake was ready. The sight of Grandfather Rattlesnake drawn into a striking coil, his lidless eyes measuring Coyote's every move, struck fear into Coyote's heart. And in that lipless mouth, two curved fangs waiting, loaded like hypodermics. Coyote didn't need to be reminded of the pain and suffering—yes and death—they could inflict. He checked his spring and stumbled, then sat on his haunches, licking his lips.

"You're right," Coyote said. "I'll never amount to anything, of course."

"Of course you won't."

"Now, if you'll move aside, I'll go on my way."

"Hah! I will not move aside, you go around *me*," said Grandfather Rattlesnake.

"Yes, yes—of course. Good day to you, Grandfather."

"Good day indeed! And I am not your grandfather."

With that, Coyote stepped off the path and walked around Rattlesnake, thinking, *Every snake must shed, and when he does I'll be there to help him out of his skin!*

Behind him, he heard Grandfather Rattlesnake say, "Now if that Coyote was a snake like me, he might actually have some backbone."

Four

Alex shooed away the bugs whining at her ears—the dreaded no-see-ums, tiny winged mouths gaping after flesh. Since they were too small to withstand even a puff of wind, any breeze would have sufficed to drive them off. But on this day all breezes frolicked somewhere other than in Big Wash Canyon.

"Ugh! Too bad," she said.

Kit stood staring at the shovel whose handle Alex gripped. The husky expected that in the course of digging, Alex would unearth small rodents. After all, that's what happened when *she* dug.

"Go dig up your own mice!" Alex said.

With that, Alex began her second year with the Deep-pockets Project, an archaeological dig run by Brigham Young University, by excavating the first of the camp's two latrines. It was not glamorous. When she could move, she made a hard-to-strike target for bugs. But as the pit deepened and she was forced to jump down inside it to work, she could move her arms less and less. The insects attacked with a vengeance.

Furthermore, when it became obvious that Alex was not going to turn up any mice, Kit trotted off for better prospects. Alex watched her go, envying the dog's freedom from chores—other than those associated with being a dog, that is. Kit was an eccentric animal, but a dog all the same. With a sigh, Alex went back to digging.

"If anyone had told me that joining the Mormon church would lead to digging latrines in a remote canyon in southern Utah, I might have had second thoughts," she said. She smacked a no-see-um mired in a trickle of sweat. *Actually, it wouldn't have made a bit of difference.*

When the missionaries ran into her three and a half years ago, they had had her attention pretty much from the start. One of them had felt inspired to raise the subject of eternal progression. The idea that an individual could increase her intelligence through the exercise of free will flew in the face of everything she knew about I.Q. tests and the images of a static afterlife on which she had been raised. Raised? Hah! *Threatened with* was more like it. She thought the idea that anyone could progress or regress according to choices made along the way was not only sensible but poetic and inspiring.

She accepted their invitation to be baptized. The ceremony took place in a Tucson chapel with only a few people witnessing the event. Alex liked that. Her family was scattered throughout the Southwest and was indifferent to her decision to join a church. No matter; she had been independent since she was seventeen.

On the other hand, her boyfriend, Michael, was incensed. But then, anything might and often did incense Michael. She wasn't sure why she had stayed in the relationship except that she really did like him and thought that her faithfulness to him might eventually dull his perpetual anger. Now she realized that he had been in the early stages of alcoholism. Even before she'd known about his illness, she was vaguely aware that their relationship was a dead end. She had had it with his abuse. When he refused to change, she broke it off and that was that.

She transferred her college credits from the University of Arizona to Brigham Young University and began graduate work in English literature in folklore studies. Some of her classes took her into the anthropology department, where she began mixing with archaeologists. One of them, Rennie Ross, told Alex about the field school project opening in the southeast corner of the state. "Want to *really* get a taste of western folklore? Try archaeology. You'll spend your days working where the Ancestral Puebloans told each other the old stories."

Such a compelling pitch caused Alex to drop everything and enroll in the field school. She enjoyed it so much, she decided to do it again. This year she went down two weeks early to help set up the field camp. Her trip to Vision Canyon had been to help her make the transition from university student to desert dweller.

That was how she had come to be up to her elbows in a latrine pit, chipping away at a caliche layer with a horde of tiny assailants drilling for her blood. Sweat rolled into her eyes. Blinking against the sting, she took off the bandanna tied at her throat and twisted it into a headband, knotting it beneath her dark hair in its braid. She stopped to gulp warm water from her water bottle, sighed, and went back to work.

After finishing the latrine pit, she helped the four crew chiefs and the project director, Dr. Benjamin Hanks, erect the mess tent—a monstrous heap of heavy green canvas fifty feet long. Alex's arm and back muscles strained as she heaved on the rope in a team effort to raise the tent onto its poles. Finally the old army tent hulked beneath four big cottonwoods, occupying the most concentrated piece of shade in camp. It would serve as kitchen and dining room as well as work area and lecture hall.

After that, the men—Mike Greaves, Taylor Cormack, and Danny Wyborn, project crew chiefs and all veterans of the previous field school season—built tent platforms for the two-person Springbar tents used for housing. As Alex helped Rennie carry one of the platforms out to a tent site, a big red ant crawled up her pant leg and nailed her on the thigh. Later inspection revealed a throbbing welt the size of a quarter. "Goes with the rest of your collection," Rennie said, nodding at Alex's arms covered with bug bites.

The following day, they erected shower towers, one on the male side of camp and one on the female side, and hung canvas privacy screens around each. Outside of the mess, they dug a pit to supplement the propane-fueled refrigerator's cubic storage space. The pit was deep enough to reach the cooler soil, and the big cottonwoods shaded it nearly all day. Its cool chamber would preserve vegetables and large cuts of meat.

Finally only a few details remained such as adding finishing touches to the solar-heated showers. Dr. Hanks took the van north to visit his family and transport this year's crop of field school students back down to the camp. He was a counselor in the bishopric in a Pleasant Grove ward and had duties there that demanded his attention. He took Mike Greaves to drive the pickup and water trailer on the return trip. They would be back in three days.

Alex, Rennie, and Kit walked the road leading to the artesian well to scout its condition for driving the truck and water trailer over. The road was sound, but as they crossed the bed of Big Wash, they were swarmed by dozens of deer flies. Scrambling out of the wash, they were glad for their jeans and long-sleeved shirts that protected them from the flies. Kit's double fur coat protected her, but she had to defend her tender ears. She whirled this way and that, biting at flies. Rennie and Alex made a point of telling the other crew chiefs about the flies since once the field camp officially opened, the wash would become a popular hangout.

That afternoon, the kitchen help arrived—Todd Dodie, a thirteen-year-old Navajo. Alex knew him from the year before. Short and barrel-chested, he swept his black hair off to one side. A pair of brown, mischievous eyes flashed above what Alex could only describe as powerful cheekbones. Alex thought the boy even better looking than he had been last summer. Todd's family were not traditionalists, so he spoke only a smattering of Navajo, mostly native insults, Alex suspected.

The bad news came later that day when the cook arrived. At first sight of the cook—usually one of the most revered individuals in field camp—the crew was discouraged. Bill Wiggins was a big, beefy fellow, a good sign in a cook, but where experienced field camp cooks present a clean appearance and a particular and sometimes snappish temperament, Wiggins slouched into camp looking sleepy, disoriented, and unwashed. A pair of thick lips frequently and without perceivable cause slid into a dull smile. His watery blue eyes returned a look without any hint of connection having been made. But when he caught sight of Kit, his eyes lit up with interest for the first time.

Alex lost no time in telling him not to feed the husky kitchen scraps. "And don't allow her in the kitchen. She understands the command, 'Get out of the kitchen!' Don't let her fool you."

"Not even a little?" Wiggins whined.

Alex blinked. She realized that Wiggins was still back on the "no scraps" part of the conversation. "Not even a little!" she said. "Not a crumb. Don't even give her water from the kitchen. If you notice she needs water, get it from the jug over there." She gestured at the table set up out in the open air, but the cook's attention had long since lapsed. Alex reiterated the no scraps rule.

"But why?" he asked.

"Because she's a thief." Alex exaggerated this point but only a little. "If you encourage her at all, she'll pick you clean. And she's on a special, high-quality diet. If you interfere with that, it will upset her digestion and you'll end up with a mess on your hands."

Alex deliberately framed this threat in language she hoped would convey an alarming image. But the expression on Wiggins's face told Alex that she had failed utterly in making an impression. "It's a camp rule!" she asserted.

"Come 'ere, doggy. Come 'ere, girl!" Wiggins coaxed in a whining falsetto.

"She'll use you," Alex persisted. "She'll use you and still won't be your friend!"

Kit trotted smartly to the cook and leaned her sleek body

into his legs, throwing her head back to blink her startling blue eyes at him.

"That'sa good guuurl," Wiggins crooned.

Alex threw her hands up and stalked away.

. . . . .

As dusk approached, Todd, Taylor, Alex, and Danny lounged under the cottonwoods. Alex and the two crew chiefs had been students the year before and their camaraderie had carried over to this field season. Kit lay off to the side in a nest she had dug down to cooler dirt, curled up like a doughnut, napping lightly. Occasionally she flicked an ear to bat away a bug. Nobody talked. Like long-time residents sitting on the porch of the town mercantile, they rocked back or leaned forward in their chairs.

Wiggins's tent was set up near the mess for access to the kitchen. It had slumped into silence in the late afternoon heat, its occupant presumably asleep. Now it began billowing with activity. Wiggins emerged carrying a towel and wearing a pair of ragged tennis shoes and swim trunks. Rolls of exposed flesh jiggled atop one another.

Alex hoped she could rid herself of the memory of such an apparition when it came time to eat food prepared by his hands. After a moment of noisy but purposeless activity, he shuffled out of the tent toward the road that ran to the well.

The paint on the fifty-five-gallon shower barrels was still drying. Tomorrow they'd be lifted on top of the towers that Taylor and Danny had constructed, but they couldn't be filled until Dr. Hanks and Mike Greaves returned with the water trailer. Until then, the only water available for washing, drinking, and cooking was out at the well across the wash. The foursome watched Bill Wiggins shuffle in all his glorious vulnerability onto the road.

"Should we tell 'im?" Danny asked.

Alex shifted in her chair, avoiding Danny's eyes. Taylor stroked his mustache, his look distant. He seemed not to have heard the question.

"Tell 'im what?" Todd asked. He hadn't heard about the flies. He got no answer, but seeing a look pass between Alex and Danny, he sat back to wait.

Kit trotted out to the road as if to follow the cook, but when she saw where he was going, her upcurled tail drooped. She walked back to her nest and flopped down in the company of those who had wisely remained behind.

At most, the distance to the wash could be covered in five minutes. These minutes glided by, marked only by ticks and creaks of various pieces of equipment and tent materials and as their molecules shrank together, cooled by the rising breeze.

"Ahh! Awahhh!" Two startled shouts rang from the wash. Vap! Vap! Vap! Heavy running feet slapped against the road's dirt surface. As the footsteps approached, Alex, Danny, and Taylor looked up. Wiggins burst through the greasewood, towel flailing over his shoulders as he barreled into camp, his red face twisted with revulsion.

The territorial deer flies would not have followed him far from the wash, but Wiggins was sure they were pursuing him still. Scourging himself furiously, he ran past the group sitting motionless in their chairs. His tent bucked at his entrance and sputtered as faltering hands zipped shut the door netting.

Alex felt a sense of guilt, but it was a light, heady guilt. In fact, she was surprised how pleasant it felt, as she sat there sharing it with her two cohorts in the shade of an easy desert afternoon.

A few minutes later the tent unzipped. Wiggins emerged wearing long sleeves and long pants. Like a bear testing the air, he raised himself erect. Satisfied that he had lost his tormentors, he strode past his audience and began preparing supper.

The show had not been hilarious exactly, but something about it had been satisfying. Alex concealed her giggling while Danny tried to hide a grin.

Taylor remained seated, glaring at the cook. A stickler for good hygiene, he had taken an instant dislike to Wiggins, as he had already told Alex. "Before you touch anything in that kitchen, wash your hands!" he commanded.

As if responding to a voice in his head rather than to a real, live Taylor Cormack sitting a few yards away, Wiggins crossed to the jug on the open air table, washed his hands, and shuffled back to the kitchen. Taylor watched, stern and unamused. Alex looked at Danny. Danny looked at Alex. Eyebrows lifted and mouth corners twitched.

Todd Dodie's dark eyes flitted from Alex to Danny and then took in the stern look on Taylor's face. His gaze rested on Alex, questioning.

"It's the deer flies," Alex said. "Their ... *humor* ... is biting."

Todd smiled. "Their cousins, the yellow jackets, are the same," he said. "Though some might describe their humor as stinging rather than biting."

"It's a fine line," Alex agreed, trying to suppress laughter long enough to get out of the cook's earshot. Not that Wiggins would necessarily make the connection if she had let out a good guffaw.

five

When First Angry walked into the village, some of the old women cast suspicious glances at him. He tried to be polite to one of them.

"How are you, Grandmother?" he asked, smiling.

"I'm not your grandmother," the woman said. Her eyes flashed, and she turned her back to him. This did not discourage First Angry. To most people, he was nothing unusual. He could walk among them in the light of day.

Of course, the young women thought him attractive. *So I am,* he thought. *What do I care what the old toads think?* But as a skilled opportunist, he could not choose quarry haphazardly. The world turned a certain way. He had to work with that. Everybody did.

By the afternoon of the fourth day, he had already met three women. One was too young to be of any use. She behaved like a brat and didn't know anything useful. Also, she had family nearby watching her. He bought her a soda and excused himself.

The second was older and on her own but had thoughts of

changing him. He smelled it in her words, saw it in the way she looked at him. Change *him*, First Angry! He hated that sort of thing. He told her he was married.

He saw the third woman when he was sitting in a mini-mart chewing on a stale sandwich. The moment she opened the door, he smelled blood. He looked around until he spotted the woman and knew her to be the source of the blood odor. His senses sharpened and he sat up in the booth to watch, nostrils flaring. The sandwich lay forgotten on the table like an old bone.

The woman moved through the store with her head down, taking care to avoid all eye contact. She looked every bit the outcast, like someone who kept to herself to limit risks. Sun-bitten, she wore a striped tank top that showed freckles spattered across pink shoulders like stars in a scorched sky. At a glance, First Angry knew that some of the freckles would turn to disease. The sun treated her harshly, yet obviously, she spent a lot of time in it. Her eyes were dark and spooky and showed the pain and fear of a domestic dog that has been repeatedly beaten. *Clearly*, First Angry thought, *clearly this one is wounded and will not run far.*

He licked his lips and began to whistle low and sweet, a single measure he repeated three times. On the third time, the woman looked up and around the store, searching for the source. Their eyes met. The touching of their gazes startled her, and she looked down for a moment. In that moment, First Angry licked his lips again, this time to polish his smile.

Six

Alex sat under the army surplus tent looking at the new faces. The five students, four men and a woman, practically doubled the population of the desert campus. Dr. Hanks settled the students in the mess tent right off for a no-nonsense recitation of camp rules.

Alex didn't know any of the newcomers. All were young—senior undergrads. She doubted a single one had worked or lived in the desert for any length of time. Probably this would be their first taste of the blood, sweat, and tedium of fieldwork.

But there was something else that Alex had learned about working in the desert—something less obvious than the perils of buggy, hundred-degree-plus temperatures but with effects just as serious. Last summer, she had experienced for the first time the amazing effects intense desert sunlight had upon the soul. In moderate amounts, sunlight affected human beings positively. But that flood of pupil-shrinking, body-piercing rays that began when the sun crested Colorado's Sleeping Ute Mountain took a steep toll on the psyche. The light danced in the air one breathed, provoking everything from mild irritability to migraines and full-blown anxiety.

Alex had spent time in the desert light before but never for weeks on end and never so fully exposed. At first, she couldn't figure out what was bothering her. Then one day she succeeded in untangling the angst it caused from the usual field school stresses. She nearly laughed out loud. *It's the light! The mind-altering, skin-changing, soul-filtering light.*

Dr. Hanks's voice jarred her back to the present. "Everyone—this goes for crew chiefs, too—is expected to abide by the university's honor code." He directed a meaningful glance at the chiefs.

Mike Greaves, the survey crew chief, stamped his foot in a "doggone it!" gesture. But the other three sat quietly, expressions serious. While Dr. Hanks was the formal head of the project, it would be their responsibility to keep the excavation on track. This would include teaching the students the basics of excavation as well as controlling huge amounts of information unearthed during the digging.

"No loud music in camp, and no music at all after eight p.m. ..."

Alex heard Caedyn Hoyt, a golden boy whose looks practically screamed *look out for me*, whisper to another student named Chris Jolley, "I *knew* I shoulda brought my MP3 player!" The two snickered.

During introductions, Caedyn and Chris had announced they were cousins from Mesa, Arizona. They looked like pioneer Mormon stock. Alex wondered what it was exactly—physical or cultural qualities? Probably both, as well as a certain lack of awareness of their surroundings that Alex had seen in middle-class America in general. Still, it never ceased to amaze her how some multi-generation Mormons appeared to keep to the surface of all the wonders they had been taught to believe in since childhood. At times she felt as if any movement, any word, might stir the substance of being.

Feeling herself watched, she turned and met the gaze of the only female student, Marina Angeles. Marina was pretty with large brown eyes in a round face framed by long, straight, black hair. She seemed to have noticed Alex taking measure of Caedyn and Chris. Alex and Marina acknowledged each other with smiles.

"... to keep a clean camp for obvious reasons, one of them being that this land belongs to someone else, and if we want to be invited back next year ..."

Kit walked into the kitchen, but a look from Alex sent her back out. Just outside of the dining area, the husky flopped onto her side with a grunt.

"... the usual schedule: everyone rises nice and early at five-thirty, gathers for breakfast, packs their own lunches, and is ready to go so we can be on site by seven. This way we get as much work in as possible before the heat ..."

And the light, Alex added mentally.

"... gets intense. At two-thirty we return to camp, shower, make a water run ..."

"Water run?" asked Caedyn as if the words were in a strange language.

"The camp gets its water from a well three-quarters of a mile that way." Dr. Hanks waved his hand at the desert east of camp.

"Is that safe?" Caedyn asked. Chris supported him by throwing Dr. Hanks a look of concern.

"It's been laboratory tested. These folks have been drinking it for two weeks with no adverse effects. Right guys?" Dr. Hanks looked to his chiefs for support.

The students turned to the crew chiefs and Alex. Mike Greaves sat grinning and scratching the two-week beard growth that dominated his face. Next to him sat Taylor, his slightly bleached-out hair and mustache giving his tanned face glints of sun-turned hardiness. Alex's and Kit's tentmate, Rennie Ross, was tall and imposing, and while they had been building camp, she had become quite rough around the edges. Alex wondered how *she* looked. Glancing at her arms, she could see that her slightly olive skin had gone quite a bit darker, and when she lived in the desert like this, she abandoned make-up use. Last year at camp someone had told her that she looked like a feral house cat with scary green eyes.

Danny Wyborn flashed Dr. Hanks a dry, twisted grin. "Well, Taylor has this Dr. Jekyll/Mr. Hyde problem," he said. "Other than that ..."

"Hah! I've noticed that *you* glow in the dark," Taylor shot back at Danny. Then Taylor's eyes rested on the cook working in the kitchen. He pointed at him. "Now that fellow there—he's been drinking the water for just two days. You should have seen him the day he arrived. You wouldn't believe the improvement!"

Mike Greaves guffawed and Dr. Hanks fixed Taylor with a stern stare. "All right, that's enough," Dr. Hanks said. Turning to the students, he continued: "Now, any questions?"

"Will we have free time?" asked Hector Stoddard, a tall, skinny young man who wore thick, black-rimmed glasses.

"Yes, free time. Thanks for reminding me. After clean up and camp chores are finished, you're free to wander the canyon. There are lots of sites with petroglyphs and a few pictographs nearby."

Rennie said, "Just watch out for the rattlesnakes."

Marina's eyes widened. "Rattlesnakes?" she asked.

"And don't pet cute, furry animals," Mike Greaves advised.

"That's right, because if you can get close enough to touch them, they're sick," Dr. Hanks said.

"Sick with what?" Caedyn asked.

"Perhaps *Yersina pestis*—the black death," Hector said. "Although there's also the hantavirus, of special concern to us because we'll be digging into the burrows of rodents which may or may not be carrying the disease. Biting insects like mosquitoes transmit tularemia and the West Nile virus. Then, of course, there's Valley Fever contracted, not from animals or insects, but from airborne mold spores."

"What! What is this, a third world country?" Caedyn blurted out.

"Hector's right," Dr. Hanks said. "All those things are real threats. That's why insect repellant was listed in your class syllabus as a required personal item. Wear your repellant, avoid all furry creatures who appear too friendly, and you should be just fine. If any of you do get ill, I want to know about it right away."

"There's also rabies," Hector added. Everyone looked at Kit.

"She's been vaccinated," Alex said. "And she wears a flea

collar. However," she added, "under no circumstances is she to be given people food. That's a camp rule."

"That's right," Dr. Hanks said. "We don't want trouble with the dog begging."

"Begging? *Stealing,* more like," Alex said. She raised her voice so that Wiggins would be sure to hear. "No matter how cute she looks, don't feed her or you'll be sorry."

"One more thing before I forget," Dr. Hanks said. "Friday afternoons after we knock off, we return to camp, get our laundry, and drive into Blanding to the laundromat."

"*Launderette,*" Taylor interrupted.

Dr. Hanks stared blankly at Taylor. "What?"

"Launderette," Taylor said. "*Laundromat* is a trademark. Launderette is the proper generic word for a commercial, self-service, laundry facility."

"I didn't know that!" Danny Wyborn said, feigning appreciation. "Gosh, if you hadn't set us straight, I might have gone the rest of my life calling launderettes *laundromats,* and who knows what might have happened."

"Yes, Mr. Cormack," Dr. Hanks said. "Thank you for that vital insight. Where was I? Oh, on weekends I'll be leaving to go north. Anyone who wants to can come, but you'll need to be back at the museum ready to return at three p.m. Sunday."

"Field trips," Rennie said.

"Field trips," Hanks echoed. "Occasionally we go on field trips that last into Monday. All students are required to attend—no exceptions. Right, anything else? Get settled, then. Mike, show them to their tents."

Mike stood up, shuffling papers. Alex watched Jack Reed, the only student who had remained silent during the orientation, approach Mike. Mike grinned at him in friendly fashion, but Jack's look remained guarded.

Then came Hector Stoddard. Hector had a classic *geek* look about him but wasn't shy. In fact, Alex thought he radiated intellectual cockiness.

Caedyn and Chris blustered forward, pushing and shoving each other like fifth graders in the school lunch line. Both were broad-shouldered, solid, and attractive, although—Alex winced as she thought it—they seemed terribly young for their ages. Marina brought up the rear, restlessly braiding and unbraiding her hair.

Kit rose from her patch of shade and walked into the group, accepting attention from the newcomers. But Alex suspected there was some doggy panhandling in the making. She caught Kit's eye and shook her head. "No," she mouthed.

The husky yodeled an insult at Alex and followed the students as they grabbed their gear and trailed Mike into the greasewood.

Dr. Hanks turned to the other crew chiefs. "We've got a water trailer now and showers to fill, right?"

"Right!" Taylor said crisply. He and Danny made for the truck and water trailer.

Alex filled two cups with water from a container in the kitchen and carried one to Rennie. Handing her the cup, Alex raised hers. "Here's to an eventful field school." The two touched their cups in a toast.

"Not *too* eventful," Rennie said.

"What would that be?" Alex asked. "Flash floods cutting us off from the site? Skinwalkers hexing and vexing us?"

Slapping shut her notebook, Rennie leaned back in her

thirty-five

chair, pushed her auburn hair off her forehead, and adjusted her glasses. "Hah, if it doesn't go further than that, it'll be a banner season," she said.

Curious, Alex sat down. "What *are* you expecting?"

"That's just it. We don't know. We've got a wild card in our deck."

"Ah, you mean Harry."

The field school was set up on land owned by Ernest Brock, a rancher who lived in Big Wash Canyon and ran cattle there. Four years ago, he had decided to sell off some impressive Anasazi ruins on his property. His hope was that the mystique of Indian artifacts would lure a well-heeled investor to his door. Enter Harry Hoskers—an actor who played bit-part characters in television dramas. Nobody knew exactly why Harry had wandered off the concrete and asphalt turf of L.A. into the Four Corners region, but by one twist of fate or another somebody had introduced him to Ernest Brock. It was not long before Harry was the proud owner of a genuine Anasazi Indian site

But Alex had gotten the uneasy feeling that Harry's sense of ownership extended into the uninterrupted vistas on all sides: to Sleeping Ute Mountain reclining on the eastern horizon; north to the Abajo Mountains, blue-shadowed mother of local storms to the north; and west and south across the desolate mesas and empty desert sky. This in spite of the fact that along the edge of the property ran the northwest fence line of the Navajo Nation.

"By golly!" he had said to the field school students at the Deeppockets campfires last year. "You people don't know what you've got here." Trust him, he said, he knew a good movie set when he saw one. Why, danger was everywhere—in the tense cultural mix where hostilities and delicate balances abounded; in the brew of illegal activities, ranging from drug running to pot hunting; and in the desert itself, with its poisonous denizens and flamboyant runs of temper. Harry told the students that he had "worked with female co-stars with similar qualities." Then there were the nearest towns, Bluff and Blanding, thirty and forty miles away: "Two little nobody nowhere towns with potential for the person with the right vision," as Harry had put it.

He bought a house in Bluff but preferred living out of his truck and trailer. He talked to locals, exploring regional myths and taboos. It was rumored that he parleyed with antiquities dealers on both sides of the market.

But the project's roots lay in events that had happened three years ago. On an early spring morning, Harry had rented a D-9 Cat out of Cortez, put it on a flatbed, and driven it into Big Wash Canyon. He maneuvered the machine across the wash, up the bank, and across the flood plain onto the archaeological site. Alex could just picture the black puffs of smoke streaming above the greasewood and hear the machine's roar rake across the surrounding mesa walls. Harry drove the Cat to the nearest obvious feature—a crumbling pueblo. With the gusto of a gambler staking it all on one roll of the dice, he drove the Cat into it.

As Harry told the story, he was engulfed in his work and didn't know he had company until he paused to consider his next move and felt the barrel of a gun press into his skull, "right around the brain stem region." Old Russell Redhorse, the Navajo rancher from a mile away, had come to defend the spirits of his grandfathers and grandmothers. Not his *specifically*, but in his mind, all ancient ones were relations, the sanctity of their resting places his personal responsibility.

Harry wisely refrained from arguing property rights with the old Navajo and his two sons. He dismounted with his hands up. Russ Redhorse said nothing, and as soon as Harry got down, the old man left. As Alex understood the Navajo Way, Russ, a strict traditionalist, knew that many Anasazi—now called Ancient Puebloans—lay buried on the site. He would not have wanted to risk attracting the attention of any lingering *chindi*, evil ghosts capable of bringing illness and bad luck. All reverence being due the Ancient Ones, their ghosts were pure trouble.

Avowing a change of heart, Harry went to see a local archaeologist, Sam Rafferty. Raff offered to pull some strings to see if the university would be interested in managing an excavation of the site. Then the thing would be done properly. Harry liked the idea. He raised funds among his Hollywood pals, for whom taking part seemed like a politically correct gesture. Money in hand, Harry extolled to university officials his profound desire to add to the scope of information about the Anasazi Indians. The university accepted, and the Hoskers Project was born. Students gave the project its unofficial name, Deeppockets, because of its copious funding. The name spread to the faculty and then stuck fast.

But simply getting a big project up and running hadn't been enough for Harry. He proposed adding Deeppockets to the National Park system with Chaco Canyon and Mesa Verde. The archaeologists were noncommittal about this, but that was okay. Harry still thought his project was going *mahvelously*.

"Harry's worse than skinwalkers, hm?" Alex asked.

"You know the score at field school. It's all about control of the site, control of the provenance, control of the excavation schedule. It's a balancing act, and I get the feeling Harry's cutting the tightrope and slicing holes in the net."

"How?"

Rennie ran her hands through her hair. "Oh ... I don't know. He's an ... an outsider. He doesn't grasp what that means in these parts. He goes off for hours, sometimes days doing heaven knows what. He reminds me of a kid banging a stick along the fence to make the dogs bark, all the time thinking the fence will protect him. Then one day he bangs on the fence and finds out somebody has left the gate open."

Alex winced. "What can you do? It's out of your hands."

"You're right! It's *his* site—a fact he likes to remind us of. I suppose we just have to hang on until something happens, if it does. But I don't like some yahoo jeopardizing my work."

Alex chuckled. "A yahoo wearing two-hundred-dollar Timberland boots and tight jeans."

"You've noticed."

Alex nodded. "I've noticed. But a well-dressed yahoo is still just a yahoo. And like you say, maybe nothing will happen. Meantime, it's a beautiful evening. How about a walk?"

"Can't. Got to set up these notebooks. Thanks, though."

Alex stood up. "Sure?"

Rennie picked up her pen and opened a notebook. "Yep. See? This is me, working."

"Okay. Then I'm gonna find m'dawg and take off." Alex stepped outside the big tent and whistled shrilly. Kit trotted up looking expectantly at her.

"Want to go for a walk?"

Without missing a step, Kit changed direction and headed for the dirt road that ran by camp. Alex followed, absorbed in thought.

Rennie was right. Elements of the stories about Hoskers showed that he liked to play close to the edge. Deeppockets was isolated, and sometimes that was enough to prevent trouble from spreading. But the desert was volatile. Step on somebody's territorial, ecological, or spiritual toes and the response could be swift and dramatic.

Then there were the local pot hunters, some of them legendary for their macho survivalist ways. In some cases, extended families engaged in illegal pot hunting, lending a clannish element to it. The antagonism between pot hunters and archaeologists ran deep. Pot hunters saw archaeologists as competition, the only difference between them being that they worked opposite sides of an inequitable law. No doubt, the interested pot hunting parties knew about Deeppockets and were watching.

Alex shook her head. In a situation where control and diplomacy were all too important, Harry was, indeed, a big fat ticking time bomb.

"Oh well," she said to Kit. "All *I* want to do is live the desert life, wake and sleep by the sun and moon, and watch you climb seemingly unclimbable cliffs. Now if something were to happen to prevent my doing that, ... well, that *would* be annoying."

But Alex guessed that whatever Harry was up to would take time to set into motion. Until it really got going, she would keep excavating in paradise right along with everybody else.

Seven

First Angry, also called Coyote, couldn't believe his luck. *Not luck–genius.* No such thing as luck, especially in his case. He had been so *out there* that, without knowing who the woman was, he'd chosen true. It couldn't have worked out better if he was all knowing, which he admitted he wasn't. Even he, Coyote, knew cleverness had its limitations. He could accept that. Who wanted to know everything? At least a quarter of the fun lay in not knowing what would come loping, or limping, down the trail in your direction. A full one-half of the good time lay in improvisation.

Unfortunately, the fun began to wane in the dénouement. At the hunt's end, there was nothing left to do but feed. Satisfying in its way to the Coyote part of his soul, disappointing to the First Angry part. Being insatiable, that part of him smoldered like an ember hiding among the ashes waiting for the next rise in the wind.

The active element of a superior mind is contempt, and First Angry's contempt for this woman knew no bounds. Oh, she had ducked her head, tried to avoid him, made a half-hearted attempt to flee, but in the end she turned and walked straight toward him of her own free will. She had made it almost too easy with her desperate attraction to punishment. Her awe of his terrible beauty caused him to feel both pride and disgust, which would make it easier for him to give out the bad treatment she craved when the time came.

He lay beside her watching her sleep, his lip curled in a sneer. It was nothing personal, really. She could never be more to him than a means to an end. But such weakness, such wounds! She begged for misery. Completely susceptible to his spells *and* key to his plans for that place of his own he had been making his way toward since leaving the gods' gathering place! It was almost too good to be true. *He* was too good to be true.

The woman stirred and startled as if his designs upon her had touched some part of her subconscious, some corner of the old brain that remained alert. He quickly changed his face, putting on one of his most beguiling masks. In the beginning, the big trick was to act the gentleman. Be nice. Make gallant gestures. Appear harmless.

She stared at him wide-eyed as if she didn't know where she was. Then she sighed and lay back, running her hands through her sun-stripped hair.

"What are you looking at?" she asked.

"You," he said, smiling. He watched to see what she would make of that.

"Oh," she said. She started to get up, then hesitated. "Oh," she repeated. "Do I look a fright?"

"You look frightened," he answered.

She looked away but made no reply.

"Why don't you let me treat that sunburn?" he asked, rising.

forty-two

"Oh ... uh, no ... it ... seems like it's always there," she said.

"You should protect yourself better," he said. "Against the sun. The light out here is dangerous, even if inspiring."

"Inspiring?" she asked.

"Doesn't it inspire you?" he asked, moving off to one of his packs. He rummaged through it. "It's everywhere, like the air. I wonder, when you inhale on an exceptionally bright day, do you breathe in light like, say, the bouquet of a wine? The intensity is really quite remarkable."

She didn't smile, didn't even look at him. He wondered if she was taking anything at all from their association. He had hoped it would give her *some* pleasure.

"Ah, here it is," he said. He took the container to her. "Turn over," he told her. As if giving in to the inevitable, the woman rolled onto her belly. Coyote, also called First Angry, gazed with satisfaction upon the damaged skin of her shoulders, evidence of the woman's penchant for punishment. He opened the jar and the air in the room filled with the odor of the unguent.

"What is that?" she asked.

"Aloe vera," he said, "a plant that drinks in the light and produces a remedy for it." He dipped his fingertips into it and touched them to her burn. She shuddered. "That is, for those who need a remedy, which you do. My dear, you weren't made for the desert light, nor the desert light for you."

"Can't avoid it," she replied. "My job takes me out into it." She flexed her shoulders as he worked the salve into her skin. "It's cold," she said. Then she sighed. "Feels good."

"Then you should keep your skin covered. Exposing yourself like this, you're just asking for trouble."

If she caught his double meaning, she didn't show it.

"Speaking of my job," she said.

"I'm keeping you from it, aren't I?" he asked.

"It's not your fault," she said. "Reminds me of a song." She sang, "*It's late September and I really should be getting back to school.*"

Coyote knew the one. It was a dismal piece and a little too applicable to the situation. Maybe she was more aware than she seemed. He decided to make a play. He stopped working the aloe into her skin, drew back, and in an injured tone asked, "You think I'm using you?"

"No, no!" she said. "But I don't know what you're doing ... with someone like me." She didn't turn over to look at him when she said this. She remained on her belly, her chin resting against her arms folded on the pillow.

Again he was struck by her terror of eye contact. Such evasion was typical among animals trying to avoid being attacked by dominant members of their kind. He knew something about living with such fear, but in his case, it had made him strong. He resumed applying aloe to her burn.

"I think it's obvious," he said.

"What?" she said.

"What, as you say, I'm doing with someone like you."

"It's not obvious to me," she said with a sigh.

Coyote chuckled. "Then perhaps it will be," he said, "soon."

Eight

Deeppockets' crew chiefs sat around the mess area fire pit enjoying their last moments of leisure. Alex walked by on her way to the water jugs to fill her bottles for the night. She saw Kit sitting among the chiefs. The dog glanced sideways at Alex as she passed but Kit made no move to follow.

"Some faithful companion," Alex muttered as she filled her bottles. When she passed the fire again, Kit lay in a Sphinx position staring into the flames, her long, white front legs crossed primly at the ankles. Alex shook her head. Kit's eccentricities never ceased to amaze her.

Caedyn Hoyt stepped into the firelight and gave Kit a rough pat. The husky acknowledged him briefly then returned to her meditations or whatever she was doing.

"Mind if I butt in?" he asked, sitting down before anyone answered.

"Not at all," Taylor replied.

Alex saw Danny flash one of his time-for-a-good-joke grins. She hurried to her tent, set her water bottles inside, closed the flap she had left open, and hurried back to the fire. She didn't want to miss anything.

She returned to find that Hector, Chris, and Marina had all joined the fire circle. The quiet student, Jack Reed, was just walking up. Hector was pushing his glasses up on his nose and looking skeptical. Something was happening, all right. Alex sat across from Kit, who was now accompanied on both sides by students. Kit looked at her through the fire but didn't join her.

"That's what they want you to think," Danny said. "It makes things easier for them."

Hector said, "I've never seen any reliable report on such phenomena that didn't account for these events by establishing their coincidence with perfectly normal related incidents."

Such language was too much for Mike Greaves. "What did he say? What did he say?" he asked.

"He said he don't believe us," Rennie said.

"Oooh! *That's* what he said!" Mike said.

"*Heckler* here doesn't believe in ghosts or even in ghost *drums*," Taylor explained.

Alex took her cue. "*I've* heard them." Heads swivelled in her direction. "Last year out on the site. A flash flood cut us off after we crossed the creek for the day's work. People could wade in and out but we couldn't risk the vehicles. Someone had to stay with them, so Rafferty, Rennie, and I spent the night. I remember the mosquitoes were really bad and I couldn't sleep."

"Did you get tularemia?" Caedyn asked. "West Nile? Rabies?"

Alex ignored him. "I was startled awake by a sound of

drums beating slow and steady. The noise came from far away yet seemed to surround me."

"What did you do?" asked Marina.

"Nothing," Alex said.

"Weren't you afraid?" Marina asked, wide-eyed.

"Strangely, no," Alex said. "In fact, their soft, steady beating lulled me back to sleep."

Everyone expressed appreciation of the story except Hector. Brow furrowed, he appeared to read a series of calculations in the air. His eyes lit up. Again he pushed his glasses up on his nose.

"Obvious," he said. "The Hoskers site is just west of the Navajo reservation, isn't it?"

"It is," Danny said, "but the nearest home site is nearly a mile away."

"Doesn't matter," Hector said. "The fact there was a flash flood during the day indicates instability in the weather. While it's unusual for the wind to blow from the east in this area, it's not impossible, especially if there are remnants of the storm cell lingering. A microburst could sheer downward on terrain to the east and deflect sounds from the nearest home site west to the excavation. Navajos hold ceremonies in which drums play important roles. Some require activity at night. Obviously, what you heard were not the ghost drums of long dead Ancestral Puebloans but the real drums of a Navajo ceremony over at that homestead. A good breeze could have carried the sound a mile over open ground, especially given the resonating features of geological formations in the canyon and the vibratory qualities of the drumbeats themselves."

Alex was impressed. In fact, except for the detail in Hector's explanation, this had been her own conclusion about the experience. For the sake of the story, she had omitted one element from it. When she had sat up to look for the source of the drumming, her eyes had focused on a distant yellow twinkling over at the Redhorse place. Her guess had been that the twinkling was a fire and that the old Navajo was holding some kind of to-do.

Mike Greaves broke the silence. "Well if it ain't Sherlock Holmes!"

Marina picked up a stick and poked at the fire. "You're no fun," she grumbled.

"You can't go around explaining everything!" Caedyn said. "You spoiled the story."

"What a dweeb!" Chris threw in.

Hector leaned back from the storm of criticism that had unleashed itself. Only Jack remained uninvolved.

Danny broke in. "People like you are always the most surprised when the skinwalkers get them."

Alarmed, Alex looked around, frowning.

"What's the matter?" Marina asked her.

"I'm just making sure Todd's not around," she said.

"Why?" Caedyn asked. "Is *he* a skinwalker or whatever?"

"No," Taylor said. "It's just that talking casually about skinwalkers in front of a Navajo is bad form."

"There's no such thing as casual talk about skinwalkers," Alex said.

"What are skinwalkers!" Caedyn, Chris, and Marina demanded.

"They're a kind of witch," Alex said.

Hector rolled his eyes.

"It's important to know that there *are* such people," Alex said. "Other cultures consider the witches among them to be a real and obvious problem."

Taylor broke in. "You guys know Dr. Brownlee, don't you?"

"He ran earlier field schools down here, didn't he?" Marina said.

"The same. He's a bishop, you know," Taylor said. Well, on a night just like this one, he was out on McCracken Mesa looking for a site. He left his truck parked on the rim and walked down into a canyon. He was gone ... two and a half, three hours at the most. When he came back, a full moon had risen. By its light he could see something wrong with his truck. Squinting in the dark, he saw that the driver's door was standing wide open. Then he realized that he could see clear through the truck!"

"The other door was open, too!" Marina exclaimed.

"Right! He walked to the truck, listening. Nothing—dead quiet. Then he switched on his flashlight and saw his geological survey maps scattered all over the cab like a tornado had gone through. He leaned across the seat and shined the flashlight on the ground, then he saw them ..." Taylor paused dramatically.

"What?" Marina asked.

"Footprints."

"What kind of footprints?" Marina asked.

"Strange ones, because ..."

Caedyn reached over, grabbed Marina's arm, and yelled, "Boo!"

Marina jumped and screamed. Everyone laughed. "Caedyn!" she yelled, punching his shoulder.

"Ow! Hey, you were like a little kid just asking for it."

"Do that again and you'll see how like a little kid I am—I'll kill you."

Caedyn held up his hands. "Okay, okay. I'm sorry." He turned to Taylor. "So, what happened next?"

"Where was I? Oh yes. The footprints weren't human. At least, *those* ones weren't."

"What ones?" Caedyn asked.

"Caedyn, keep up!" Marina said. "Don't stop for him—go on!"

"The footprints on the passenger's side of the truck were made by large canine paws," Taylor said.

Marina gasped.

"But that's not all. On the other side of the truck, Dr. Brownlee found prints made by bare human feet."

"That's just a stupid werewolf story except it's set here instead of Europe," Hector said.

"Not at all," Danny said. "Werewolves don't want to transform but they can't help it. They're victims. Skinwalkers aren't victims."

"They're victimizers," Alex said. "They change because they want to, and always for some evil purpose."

Taylor leaned forward, the firelight enhancing his air of mystery. "By the way, there's something over by the site that you all ought to know about."

Alex and Rennie glanced at each other. Rennie shrugged.

"I was climbing the mesa at the edge of the reservation and happened to glance over on the reservation side of the fence and saw this ..."

"What?" cried Marina.

"This ... structure."

"You mean like an old sheep pen?" Mike asked.

"No," Taylor said. "More like a hut or small shelter." He hesitated, then said, "Never mind—forget I brought it up."

"No way! You *gotta* tell us now," Chris said.

"Well, it's just that it was ... strange ... because it was decorated with human bones and colored feathers."

Alex couldn't tell if Taylor was teasing or not. Something about his tale rang true, but the human bones seemed a bit much.

"You sure it wasn't old cows' bones or maybe from deer?" Danny asked.

"They were most certainly human," Taylor answered.

"Really?" Marina asked. "Is there really something like that over near the site?"

Taylor went stiff with formality. "Do you think I would make up such a tale?"

"Maybe it's some kind of shrine," Mike said. "I gotta see this!"

"It's on the reservation side," Rennie said. "We can't go there."

"Who's to know?" Danny asked.

"Yeah, who's gonna care?" Caedyn asked. "Let's go tomorrow," he said to Chris, who nodded in agreement.

"Don't try sneaking over," Rennie said. "Around these parts, you never know who's watching."

Heaving a sigh of impatience, Hector pushed his glasses up and stood. "Don't we start work on the excavation tomorrow?" he asked.

"That's right, Hector," Taylor said. "Best if we all turn in now. Early start to the day tomorrow for everyone." He stood abruptly, picking up his chair to take it back to the mess tent. Rennie stood, too. "That's right—we get up at five-thirty tomorrow ..."

"Ugh!" Caedyn exclaimed. "I better go crawl into my bag. Come on, knucklehead," he said to Chris.

"You're the knucklehead!" Chris said, grabbing Caedyn around the neck and grinding his knuckles into his scalp. Slapping and punching at each other, the pair retreated with Jack following. Marina stood and dusted off her shorts.

"Those were good stories," she said. "Tell us more later?"

"Count on it," Danny said.

"Good!" Marina said. She smiled at the chiefs, then headed toward her tent.

Mike grinned at Danny, Alex, and Rennie. "Well, I guess I better get my beauty rest too! G'night." He disappeared into the greasewood.

The trio stared morosely into the fire. "Well, that sure backfired," Danny said. "That Hector kid's wound tight!"

"Maybe we just stepped on a pet peeve," Rennie suggested.

"Obviously," Alex said. "But as far as archaeology is concerned, there's a lot to be said for his adoration of the scientific."

"Right," Rennie agreed. "He's already a convert!"

Alex looked around for Kit. Sometime during the storytelling she had walked off. "Speaking of 'pet peeves,' I've got to find my dog, then I'm going to—how did Caedyn put it? Oh yeah—'crawl into my bag.'"

"I'll come with you," Rennie said. "I just have to put away a few things."

Danny said, "Good night, ladies," and disappeared into the darkness.

Alex whistled. After a moment, Kit materialized out of the gloom. She trotted into the path, as usual looking right into Alex's face. It was always a surprise the way Kit made eye contact straight across as if she considered herself to be on equal ground with Alex, perhaps a little higher. It was one of the things Alex really liked about the husky—that she thought so well of herself. Rennie and Alex walked through camp, talking softly.

"Danny was right," Alex said.

"About the hazing backfiring?"

"Yeah. Mr. Wizard just sort of took it over."

The two women laughed as they unzipped their tent and stepped in with Kit, who flopped down on an old poncho spread out on the tent floor.

"But what's that story about a shrine?" Alex asked. "You think it's for real?"

"You never can tell with Taylor," Rennie said. "But yeah, I think he found something."

"Human bones and all?"

"Human bones and all. Think about it. If there isn't any such structure, we'll find out soon enough, and ... well, he's not going to say something that would undermine his authority."

"No," Alex agreed, sitting down on her cot to undress. "But then, why didn't he say something about it before?"

"You know Taylor," Rennie said with a sigh, pulling off shoes and socks. "He moves in mysterious ways."

Rennie and Alex paused at the sound of a car engine approaching. It slowed near the field school turn-off, stopped, then turned down the road that led to the camp.

"Who's that?" Alex asked.

"Don't know."

Several minutes later the murmur of voices announced that two people were approaching the vacant tent on the other side of Alex's and Rennie's cottonwood. One voice was Dr. Hanks's; the other belonged to a woman. Rennie looked out the back window flap as the voices passed behind them. "Must be Heather Barton. About time! She was supposed to be here last Friday."

"Who's she?"

"She'll manage the artifacts—cataloguing, washing, labeling. She's on loan from a site in New Mexico."

"You know her?" Alex asked.

"No," Rennie yawned. "None of us do. But I guess we will."

"Yep," Alex said. Closing her eyes, she listened to the shuffling sounds from the other tent and the occasional watery rush of a breeze through the cottonwood. Just as she started to drift off, she heard a coyote howl.

"That sounded close," she mumbled.

"What did?" Rennie asked. But Alex had fallen asleep and didn't hear the question.

Nine

The dirt beneath Coyote's feet crumbled. Stones pattered down the cliff face falling toward the ground eight hundred feet below. Coyote thought the rush of dirt and pebbles sounded like a sigh of gratification. He had *arrived*. On the mesa top under cover of night, he surveyed his new territory and heard the shadows around him twitter, *he is here, he is here!*

Yes, I am *here.* Coyote didn't worry about that swish and ping of falling dirt—no one could hear it. Nor did it bother him to perch like a hawk on the rim of the ledge or that the boundary between solid ground and thin air crumbled each second he lingered.

He bit his lip, lifted a pair of binoculars, and looked through. His eyes followed the black line of the creek, fluffed out by dim clouds of cottonwoods, willows, and tamarisk. The canyon wound between the mesa where he stood and the one across canyon, then suddenly opened onto a floodplain. There—down there! His place of significance, of potency. Coyote clicked his teeth together. This is the place he had seen in his mind when the gods in the great theater told him to leave.

"This is the place." He chuckled at his little joke. He swung the binoculars to the far left and focused on a wavering light in a grove of cottonwoods—a campfire. The roofs of a few vehicles sitting in a makeshift parking lot gleamed faintly with starlight and the pale tops of scattered tents stood out on the greasewood flat. He could make out a shadowy figure walking away from the center of camp toward the furthermost tent. He knew it was *her*, the woman with limp, heat-killed hair and skin that flinched if he but breathed on it. *Perfect! Everything's going just as I imagined.*

What did it matter to him, Coyote, if somebody else already occupied his Promised Land? How many stories were there about such things, about people displacing other people? Many old stories and some that were not so old. Some were only now emerging like butterflies from secret cocoons, beating their wings to dry them, and when they fluttered off, there was no putting them back. He imagined the world filled with such butterflies, poignant testimonies of the fragility of one's situation. Pretty, yet telling. Meanwhile, his own manifest destiny stoked hot in his heart.

His heart was also where the deep mysticism of thievery dwelled. Birds fly, fish swim, coyotes steal. He knew all the tricks—how to steal without anybody noticing, how to pinch with one hand while accepting a victim's compliment with the other. Even how to prompt the gullible to offer up their best in exchange for a stone in a sack. It made no difference if it were something small like a coin or big like a tract of land. Calling upon the powers of the world—powers he, Coyote, had by birthright—he could slip the earth out from underneath their feet without stirring a hair on anybody's head. It would leave them breathless wondering how he did it.

He lowered the binoculars and stepped back as a chunk of earth tore loose and fell with a great clatter, picking up other debris until the landslide cascaded with a roar onto the stones below. His nostrils filled with the fine, dry dust that swirled up. *Yes, timing is everything!*

The sound of crashing earth caused the overall silence of the mesa to shudder. Crickets stopped their mindless whirring to consider the mystery of the noise. If anyone down in the camp heard the racket, perhaps they would think the moment had come for that particular patch of dirt. The god of erosion had spoken. In response, zealous earth had thrown itself from the heights. Interesting, but no cause for alarm.

He shook his head at the beauty of it all. Meaning belonged to the strong, interpretation to the winner. He could make the future what he wanted it to be, and the present only *he* knew. Those pitiful creatures down there had no idea. They really, truly believed they knew what lay ahead. They thought they were there to do archaeology. They were thinking that tomorrow, we will do this; the next day, we will do that. *How absurd!*

Tomorrow, he—Coyote—would begin to pick apart the carcass of their world. *Ha, ha! They didn't even know they were dead!*

That's it! They were dead already. Their beliefs were dead, their expectations were dead. Everything would crumble before his higher purpose. Nobody would be able to do a thing about it. Imagine—to be dead and not even know it! Yes, indeed. While they did their work among the dead, he, Coyote, would begin his work among them.

Ten

Mike Greaves tramped through Camp Greasewood banging a wooden spoon on the bottom of a cast iron skillet. "Wake up, my little rosebuds!" he called. "Rise and shine!"

Alex and Rennie heard him coming. By the time he reached their tent, they were already dressed. "We hear you! We're awake!" Rennie snapped.

"Just doing my job!" he said, laughing. He walked into the greasewood forest toward other tents, banging away.

"There's got to be another way," Rennie groaned.

Alex scoffed. "Just be grateful there isn't a garden hose within thirty miles."

The two dressed and shuffled toward the mess tent, Kit trotting ahead toward the odors of bacon and eggs. Most of the men were sitting down at the tables already. Several heads bowed as blessings were asked over the food. Alex happened to look at Taylor just as he ended his prayers. She saw him raise his head and cast the cook a defiant glance.

Hardly anyone spoke. It was just too early for talking. Kit

patrolled the border of the tent for pieces of bacon or other goodies that might have gone astray.

Dr. Hanks appeared. "Okay, troops," he said, looking at his watch. "You've got thirty minutes. Finish eating, pack your lunches, then let's go."

Bill Wiggins and Todd Dodie cleared away breakfast and put out lunch fixings. Groggy students made sandwiches and selected from an assortment of chips and fruits. Crew chiefs followed suit, then loaded equipment into the van and pickup truck. Alex and Marina each grabbed a handle of one of the full-sized coolers with the lunches and loaded it into the back of the van. Dr. Hanks got behind the van's steering wheel and Mike assumed pilot's position in the pickup. Alex glanced around, hoping to get a look at Heather Barton, but the artifact crew chief was nowhere in sight.

Just before getting into the van, Alex turned to Kit. "You stay here," she commanded. She had no doubt Kit would obey. Last year, the husky had found her way to the site in the heat of the day and spent the entire time crammed beneath a pitiful sage trying to extract relief from its shade. The experience had proved a deterrent and she never followed them to the site again. She recognized the routine and knew well enough where they were going.

Of course, Alex knew that Kit didn't always stay right in camp. She figured the husky followed Wiggins or Todd around or, when the mood struck her, headed out on some adventure of her own. But Kit was a good desert dog with an excellent internal clock; she would be in camp to welcome them when they returned later.

Alex climbed into the van with Dr. Hanks, Rennie, Marina, Hector, Jack, Caedyn, and Chris. Taylor and Danny sprang into the back of the pickup and rode with the equipment. The pickup and the van roared out into the canyon as the first light began to flow over the mesas.

Arrival at the site was marked by excitement as Taylor and Danny rousted a sleepy rattlesnake from the parking area. Dr. Hanks had no love for snakes; he went after it with a shovel before Alex or Rennie could intervene. They watched in disappointment as the unfortunate snake, sluggish from the morning chill, was hastily dispatched. Headless coils writhed and twitched as the shock of death exploded through them.

sixty

Dr. Hanks caught the two women's disapproving stares. "Had to think of the students," he muttered. "Don't want any of them to end up in the hospital from snakebite."

"Ri-i-ight—better that the snake wind up dead from peoplebite," Rennie said.

Caedyn said, "Cool. Can I have the rattles?"

Taylor grabbed another shovel and dug a hole. With a quick movement, he swept up the head and tossed it in the hole and then buried it.

"Hey, what did you do that for?" Caedyn demanded.

"The head is still dangerous," Hector said, pushing up his glasses. "One puncture from a fang may result in an injection of venom into the bloodstream, even with the head decapitated ... in that manner."

"Huh!" Caedyn took out his knife and began sawing at the tail. The crew chiefs watched silently but did not intervene. When Caedyn finished, Taylor buried the rest of the snake.

"Mike," Dr. Hanks said, "you, Taylor, and Danny hurry up and empty out the truck. Then go back and get that other latrine and bring it out. Marina, Jack, ..." He looked at the two students. "Ready to do some digging?"

Thinking they were going to excavate, the two answered, "Sure!"

"Then grab shovels and follow me. Rennie? You get the ramada up, keep these others busy."

Alex smiled as Dr. Hanks marched Marina and Jack out into the greasewood beyond the furthermost boundaries of the site. She knew the two students were being put on latrine duty as she had that first day of setting up field camp. She was relieved that she didn't have to supply that particular kind of talent again.

So yet another field season on the Deeppockets site began with the building of the barest facilities for those who would be spending many long, hot days there. The students cleared the ground next to the parking lot for the ramada. Caedyn and Chris helped Taylor and Danny unload and roll the four cement-filled tires with steel poles set in them to the right spot. Then Mike, Taylor, and Danny returned to camp to collect the latrine.

Hector insisted on doing a little calculated clearing of the path between the parking spaces and the ramada while Rennie and Alex adjusted the position of the tires and poles. Next came the green tarp. With everyone stretching and pole-adjusting, they attached the tarp by its steel fasteners to rings embedded in the poles. Rennie and Hector set up a card table and chairs beneath the canvas.

Alex looked up to see Dr. Hanks making his way back through the greasewood. Marina and Jack labored in the distance, their forms distorted by heat waves rising from the earth. Gnats were already beginning to swarm, both the opportunistic buffalo flies, which hovered about waiting for blood-drawing injuries to occur to hosts working in the thorny greasewood, and the maddening little no-see-ums, which made their own opportunities. Some of the students slicked themselves down with baby oil to drown the no-see-ums when they landed to bite. Having been bitten to a fare-thee-well a couple of weeks before during her turn at latrine duty, Alex seemed to have become immune. Once the swelling went down, she no longer reacted to the bites. In fact, the little monsters found her unpalatable.

Mike, Danny, and Taylor returned to the site with the latrine. Dr. Hanks started Alex and the students clearing greasewood over the rubble piles of pueblo room blocks, then supervised the moving of the latrine over to the pit Marina and Jack were digging.

By 11:30 a.m., the tired, sweaty, bug-bitten students and crew chiefs assembled under the ramada for lunch. Water flowed freely—into mouths, over heads, onto clothing. Hector's pale skin showed obvious signs of burning. He accepted Marina's offer to apply sunblock to his face, neck, and arms. Apparently, his previous night's transgression at the fire had been forgiven.

Caedyn and Chris gulped water and attacked their lunches with vigor. Jack maintained his usual silence, retrieved his lunch quietly, and sat at the back of the group. When everyone was well into their meals, Rennie walked up carrying site notebooks.

Dr. Hanks looked over the group, his face showing a mixture of concern and amusement as he appraised his students' and crew chiefs' conditions.

"Everybody enjoying the weather?" he asked.

Caedyn mopped his forehead and neck. "This is like working construction," he said, "but without any pay."

"What about you guys?" Hanks looked in the direction of Marina, Chris, and the quiet student.

"Great," Jack replied. "Never better." In fact, of the whole bunch, only Jack seemed none the worse for wear.

"Better'n the beach," Chris answered, brushing sweat-soaked hair off his forehead. Marina nodded to Dr. Hanks, indicating she was okay.

"Hector?" Dr. Hanks asked.

Hector snapped to attention. "Yes, sir. I can't wait to do some real archaeology, sir."

Hanks nodded. "You need to be careful, all of you. Drink lots of water, wear sunscreen, be sensible. This sort of work can be hard on anybody. Don't want to have to report to BYU that we lost someone."

Lunchtime ended and the students and chiefs continued clearing greasewood off strategic areas and otherwise preparing the site for excavation. Around two o'clock, a pleasant canyon breeze swept off the bugs and provided relief from the rising heat. The students slowed down, removing hats and bandannas to better enjoy the currents of sweat-drinking air. As the first day wound down, Dr. Hanks went around to each group of greasewood hackers and stopped work.

The students began gathering equipment. Taylor and Danny folded up the table and chairs, laid the canvas tarp over them, and laid the ramada poles over the tarp. Except for those items, the site was picked clean. Dr. Hanks took an appraising look around.

"All right," he said, moving toward the van. "Let's get back to camp, get cleaned up and cooled off!"

Caedyn whooped. With a surprising burst of energy, he and Chris ran for the pickup bed and vaulted in. Mike hopped into the driver's seat, put the truck in gear, and took the lead. Catching hold of the pickup's tailgate on the fly, Taylor and Danny pulled themselves up into the truck with Caedyn and Chris. Alex rode in the van with the others.

When the two vehicles pulled into camp, Kit trotted out to greet them, showing an unusual amount of happiness to see Alex. Since Kit was not big on showing affection, Alex accepted it gratefully when it came.

"What have you been up to all day?" she asked as she patted Kit's head and scratched her back.

"Awooo!" Kit answered.

"All right, showers for everybody. Water run in an hour!" Dr. Hanks announced.

As Alex walked past the mess on way to her tent, she saw a woman she assumed to be Heather Barton sitting at a table sorting paper bags, rubber stamps, Sharpie markers, and other artifact cataloging materials. Heather looked up, sort of, as people passed. For just a split second, her eyes met Alex's.

The woman seemed above average age for an artifact crew chief, perhaps in her early thirties. She had a pair of soulful brown eyes framed by bleached blond hair, and a saddle of freckles across both cheeks. Deep facial lines creased the skin around her eyes and mouth.

People reveal more about themselves in a word, a glance, or a gesture than you sometimes want to know about them. Alex figured that such people had been shaped by long stretches of sadness. Heather seemed to be one of these people—a woman who wore not only a much-broken heart but an injured soul on her sleeve. Alex glanced away before her gaze violated the woman's shallowly maintained privacy.

Even as she passed out of Heather's sight, an unpleasant feeling lingered. Mentally, Alex ran through the list of personalities at the field school for one that might pose danger to such a vulnerable person. She was relieved to realize that she couldn't think of any.

Maybe she was wrong about Heather—maybe beneath the sad spaniel demeanor there lurked a female warrior, someone more capable of defending herself than she seemed. But the image of Heather's careworn brown eyes flashed across Alex's mind as evidence that her first impression was probably right. Within her heart, Alex suspected that Heather, with her profound hunger and thirst for peace, was a magnet for trouble.

On her way to the showers, Marina crossed the path in front of Alex, wearing a pair of shorts and t-shirt, a loud Winnie-the-Pooh towel draped over her shoulders. The contrast of Marina's alertness and child-like concern for others and her graceful and animated body comforted Alex. Not every woman who came into this world carried the tattered and painful baggage that Heather so obviously carried—or that even Alex carried.

Let's not go there, she thought. She looked wistfully after Marina. *What must it be like to come into the world with as clear a dancing floor as Marina appeared to have?* Alex shrugged off the specter of loss and isolation that Heather Barton had invoked. Thank goodness she had found the church, Alex thought, or rather that it had found her just in time. *Yep. Another few months and ... who knows, maybe I'd be dead already.* She fetched her towel, made her way to the shower, and sat in line.

She finished showering and made a water run with Taylor, Danny, Caedyn, Chris, and of course, Kit. Kit dearly loved the water runs. It was a ritual of the husky's ego to race the truck to the wellhead. Kit always gave herself a head start, hurtling down the road before the pickup even pulled out of camp. Her strategy for winning was simple. She cut curves in the road by darting through the brush, always taking the shortest course between two points.

Danny drove. They bumped down the road to the well-head, Kit already far in the lead. From her position against the truck bed's wall, Alex could see Kit emerge from the wash, a gray and white streak on the opposite bank.

Once out of the wash, the truck picked up speed. Alex could see Danny's head turn as he watched Kit leap over low sage and dodge through the larger greasewood, then dart back onto the road. He revved the engine and closed the gap.

Kit left the road again as it curved around a rock outcrop. She ran up its side and then climbed onto the boulders, sure-footed as a cat, leaping over gaps between the stones, skidding across the flat surface of one large rock, then gathering herself and leaping to the next. She ran headlong down the other side to come out slightly ahead of the truck. Danny had to slow down for ruts. Kit glanced over her shoulder and pulled ahead.

When they stopped at the wellhead, Alex hopped out and looked at the pool surrounding the well. Churned mud swirled through the water and scores of tadpoles were just settling from a recent panic.

Alex glanced around and found Kit lying on a rock on the very edge of a hill next to the pool. Her white front legs were crossed where they dangled over the edge of the rock. She panted lightly, gazing down on them with that look of superiority that Alex knew so well.

Alex laughed. "Crazy dog!" But inwardly, she was pleased with Kit's prowess.

"She got any wolf in her?" Caedyn asked.

"She's a papered husky," Alex said. "No wolf. Not in the recent past, anyway."

Water poured into the trailer as Taylor and Danny opened the wellhead. Alex crouched at the pool's edge. She loved looking at water in the desert. It was both a mirror and a window. One moment she could look and see its silvery reflection of the day, a slick representation of the sky vault overhead that was itself opaque until stars wore through it at night. The next moment a tadpole swam up, crimping and shattering the image as it gulped air and turned downwards, revealing the congealed atmosphere beneath the surface where creatures finned and stroked. And that delicacy, the water-skin, finer than spider's silk, was a wonder.

She dropped a pebble in the water and watched it wobble to the bottom. The sky buckled, then calmed. Tadpoles scuttled and stopped suddenly and sank as they perceived danger and then sensed that it had passed. Then Kit waded in and completely disrupted the water world, lowering her head and lapping noisily.

Caedyn and Chris took Kit's place on the little hill while Danny leaned against the pickup's tailgate chewing on a grass stem. Taylor clambered up on the trailer and dipped a stick in the tank bung. Drawing it out, he noted the depth and let the water continue to flow.

When the tank was full, Taylor and Danny detached some pieces of equipment and tightened others. Kit leaped into the back of the truck for the ride home, having already proven her superiority. Everyone else piled in after her, Caedyn and Chris complaining as she leaned her wet body against theirs.

"Yuk! Get away from me, swamp creature!"

"Oh, man! I just took a shower! Now I smell like a toad."

Alex grabbed Kit and dragged her over, positioning the smelly dog between her knees as the truck headed back to camp.

The trip provided a pleasant end to a good day; Alex was glad she had gone. Caedyn and Chris hung around the truck and did rounds with Taylor and Danny as they filled the shower barrels. Alex went to her tent and fetched one of the rawhide chew strips she kept hidden in her backpack. She brought it to the mess area and threw it to Kit, who caught it and trotted off to enjoy it in some secret place.

Eleven

After supper, word spread through camp that a hike to Cliff Kiva was in the works and that anyone wanting to go had to gather quickly to make best use of the remaining light. Kit sensed preparations for an outing. Yodeling her excitement, she searched faces for an invitation to come along. Alex scratched the dog's back reassuringly. On these trips, Kit was essential equipment.

In the hours around dusk, rattlesnakes set out on their evening hunts. Kit was a natural rattlesnake alarm—if she set one off, she leaped away and revealed its position to the humans following. When they discovered the husky's special talent during the last field season, Taylor, Rennie, Danny, and Alex had gotten into the habit of following her single-file during evening hikes, greatly reducing their risk of snakebite.

As the sun dropped toward the mesas, the students and crew chiefs—minus Heather—set out on the main dirt road, hiking toward the kiva site. Kivas were important to the Ancient Puebloan culture. In their womb-like structures, the people had held meetings and performed sacred ceremonies just as modern Puebloans do today. But Cliff Kiva was different from most. Rather than being located among the pueblos, subterraneous, it lay hidden high up in the folds of a cliff face eight or nine hundred feet above the canyon floor. It shared the neighborhood of the Deeppockets site and the field camp but existed in a world apart.

The group walked along the road running through the canyon, then veered off and started climbing. At the top of the mesa, they took in the view. Miles of the Colorado Plateau, going golden with the evening sun, stretched into the distance. Overhead, the blue sky ran horizon to horizon with a few cottonball clouds drifting serenely. Less than a mile away, Deeppockets sprawled on its flood plain.

Mike led the group over the mesa until he found the stone cairn that marked the kiva's entrance, then he dropped over the lip. Taylor and Danny followed with Alex close behind. Kit skidded down the slope but had to stop because the entrance posed problems for four-footed explorers.

A crack in the massive sandstone formed the kiva's corridor. The men ahead of Alex moved along it by straddling the fissure on two thin ledges a boot's sole wide. Anyone losing their balance faced a long fall—how long depended on where along the crevice he or she took the plunge.

Behind Alex, Caedyn poked in his head. "Cool! A cave!"

"Are there bats in here?" Chris asked.

"Bats!" Marina squealed. "*Please* tell me there no bats!"

"No bats," Alex shouted back, "but be careful."

Kit thrust her nose in. Frustrated by the obstacles the fissure posed, she yodeled.

"Wait out there if you have doubts," Alex shouted back at her.

Alex straddled the cleft. More than fifty feet ahead, she saw Taylor positioned at the end of the corridor, peering back into the passageway. Behind him the chamber glowed with waning light.

Touching her hands to the walls on either side of the fissure, Alex worked her way along. She'd been here before, but the fissure yawning between her feet still intimidated her. Best thing was not to look down, so she didn't. She waddled along the ledges, moving to one side or the other when either ledge tapered off. Behind her, she heard Marina squeal.

"Caedyn, you're crowding me!"

"Sorry!" Caedyn said, but Alex could tell that he was just barely containing his impatience.

Gaining confidence, Alex moved more quickly. Just before the cleft widened into the chamber, the ledges melded into one at the brink of a deep shaft. It was just a narrow leap, easily accomplished elsewhere, but when only thin air and ragged stone walls lay below, the mind tended to play tricks. Taylor extended his hand and helped her across.

"Thanks," she said.

"De nada," he answered. He turned back to encourage Marina.

"I'm going to fall!" she said.

"No you're not," Taylor said. "Don't look down. Come on, you're doing great."

Marina approached the chasm gingerly, squeaking from time to time as a foot went wrong. Reaching the chamber, she lunged for Taylor's hand. Danny helped pull her across the drop-off. Caedyn followed closely on her heels, avoiding Taylor's and Danny's help and leaping the drop-off without trouble.

Hector came next, looking somewhat put out. He passed through the corridor all right and jumped into the chamber. Chris followed, then Jack, then Rennie, looking uneasy. Her heavy, old-fashioned hiking boots made feeling the way with her feet difficult. Out of deference to her rank in the field school, Taylor and Danny didn't attempt to encourage her, as they had the students. They knew Rennie well enough to understand she would not respond to cajoling or coaxing; in fact, these tactics might actually distract her.

"Thanks, guys," Rennie breathed as they helped her across.

"That everybody?" Mike asked as he strode around the chamber.

"Not a soul lost," Danny said.

Just then, Taylor leaped away from the drop-off. "Look out!" he called. Kit's silhouette came hurtling down the corridor, ricocheting off ledges and walls as she shot through to the chamber. She made a grand leap across the drop-off, landing in the soft dirt, tail up-curled, tongue lolling. The expression on her face said, *Did you see what I did?* A few people clapped.

Jack Reed whistled low. "Now, that's a *dog*!" he said.

"Not to be outdone by inferior two-leggeds, are you?" Alex said as she patted Kit.

Kit "woo-woo-wooed!" and spun in the dirt, crouching in a play bow. Alex kicked at her front feet and she danced away.

"What an amazing place!" Marina said, gazing up at the roof that arced high overhead. The chamber ended in a boulder-rimmed balcony that opened onto a sheer mesa wall. Alex walked to the edge and peered down at the ground. She had forgotten how high up they were. Across from the balcony, the broad stone wall blushed with amber glints of sunlight. Kit jumped onto the boulders at the rim, leaping from stone to stone.

"She won't fall, will she?" Jack asked, eyeing her.

"If she does, she'll land on her feet like a cat," Alex said.

Jack peered over the edge and looked doubtfully at her.

"She hasn't fallen since she was three months old. Down the side of a snow-covered mountain. Rolled like a snowball." Alex chuckled. "I didn't think she would stop, but she finally did, then climbed back up as if nothing had happened. Wouldn't accept any help. I think she vowed that day she would never fall again."

"Don't know if everybody's noticed," Mike said, "but over on this wall, there are pictographs."

"What's that guy got on his head?" Chris asked, pointing to a pictograph of a man with an object balanced on his skull.

"It looks like a duck," Caedyn said.

"Hah! Was that the Anasazi fashion?" Chris exclaimed.

"A lot of people have wondered what that is," Mike said. "Maybe it's a basket or a headdress."

"I think it's a duck," Caedyn said. "What do you think, Chris?"

"Definitely a duck."

"Hey, where does this go?" Hector asked. He was at the back of the chamber near a hole in the rock wall.

"Why don't we go see?" Taylor replied. Approaching the hole, he backed up to it on his hands and knees and disappeared from sight.

"Well, who's next?" his disembodied voice called.

Caedyn seemed interested but wanted to see how it went for the others before he tried it. Jack shook his head and backed away.

"Not me," he said. "Can't stand that kind of thing."

Alex got down on hands and knees and slid through. Danny followed, then Caedyn and Chris, but those were all the takers for this leg of the adventure. Even Kit thought better of following.

The hole opened into another corridor that was narrow and jagged. Light filtered in from above where the rift cut through to the mesa top. Walking on the floor or climbing along the walls where the path narrowed, the five made their way through the passage. Alex followed Taylor, who rounded the corner ahead of her and disappeared. Turning the corner, she stumbled into him standing at the rift's dead end, staring up at the top of the fissure. Alex followed his gaze. A large, black wing hung over the edge of a rock shelf, stiff in death.

Few things aroused the wonder of Alex's flightless soul as did wings, although sometimes she flew in her dreams. One such dream had been so real, she could still recall the emotions it evoked. She had flown over a field of wheat stubble, following a winding stream. Sunlight played on the stream's riffles. Vividly colored frogs leapt from grassy banks into the water as Alex's shadow had glided over. The dream was elaborate, following a wonderful rationale consistent with the overall idea of human flight—of *her* flying.

"What is it?" she asked Taylor. "A hawk?"

He climbed up to the carcass and peered over the ledge. "It's a buzzard."

Taylor left, and Caedyn came around the bend. The wing caught his attention right off. "Hey, what's that?"

"A dead buzzard," Alex said.

"Really? Wow!" He began climbing to the ledge where the buzzard lay.

Suspicious, Alex asked, "What are you doing?"

"I'm going to get me some of them big black wing feathers," he answered.

Irritated, Alex asked, "Why do you collect souvenirs of death?"

Surprised and a little shocked by the question, Caedyn stopped climbing. "Isn't that what archaeologists *do*?" he asked.

Deciding not to dignify his question with a reply, Alex abandoned Caedyn to whatever choice he made. Danny and Chris climbed up on the wall to let her pass.

She hoisted herself onto the little dropoff at the entrance, lay on her belly, and wormed forward until she cleared the hole. Then she stood and brushed herself off.

"Find anything interesting?" Mike asked.

"There's a dead buzzard at the end of the passage."

Mike tipped his head to one side. "Huh! That's neat!"

Rennie stood looking out past the balcony's edge at the fading light. "We're losing light," she said. "Let's move out while we've still got some."

On the edge of the balcony, Kit lay stretched across a rock like a postcard panther. As Alex and Mike moved toward the corridor's entrance, the dog guessed their intentions and jumped up to take the lead. Alex called for Mike to wait.

"Let's send Kit through first since she needs to go so fast," she said.

Mike nodded. "Good idea."

"Okay Kit, go!" Alex said. Kit leapt the drop-off and flew down the corridor, using the same rebounding motion that she'd used to get into the chamber.

Mike followed, then Alex. Now the corridor gaped gloomily. In one way, the reduced light proved to be an advantage—the cleft's shadowy depths weren't so menacing and one's body did not feel as inclined to fall. All the same, Alex moved carefully, emerging into the early dusk of a desert evening.

The day's warmth clung to the rocks by the kiva's entrance. Alex leaned against a rock and let its heat soak into her back. Kit scrambled across the slope looking, as usual, quite pleased with herself.

Marina emerged from the entrance, looked up at Alex, and smiled. "What's next?" she asked.

"What's next!" Alex said. "By the time I get back to camp, I'll be ready for bed. You will too, I bet."

Caedyn emerged, his look defiant. Alex noticed the three long black feathers protruding from his shirt pocket, then returned his look. They stood there like that a moment, then Caedyn walked past Alex and scrambled up the slope.

"Yeah, okay," Rennie said after everyone had gathered on the mesa top. "We're almost certainly going to connect with some snakes. Everyone follow the dog!"

"Follow the dog?" Chris said. "What good will that do?"

"That dog's our rattlesnake alarm," Rennie explained. "Jump when she jumps and we won't have to carry anybody out."

This statement impressed the students. They formed up behind Kit, who had already begun crossing the mesa on the exact trail the group had taken coming up. Her white rump and plume-like tail reflected the evening's glow and made her easy to follow in the fading light.

Alex watched Kit pick her way across the mesa. *An amazing soul, that dog.*

Caedyn's voice by her ear startled her.

"What did you mean back there," he asked. "What's wrong with taking a few feathers from some dead bird?"

Alex looked at his feathered pocket. "Apparently nothing."

"Look, if you've got something to say, say it!"

Alex wondered if it was worth it to debate higher matters with someone as thick-skinned as Caedyn. She decided to do it for fun.

"Those feathers—the rattlesnake's rattles—when you take things like that, you remove them from their genuine context."

Caedyn's brow furrowed. "From their context—from their context," he mused.

"From their *genuine* context."

Alex received some unexpected support from Hector. "It's like pulling a tooth that shouldn't be pulled," he said.

"You're kidding," Caedyn said. "What's pulling a tooth got to do with taking a few souvenirs?"

"Context is important in archaeology, too," Hector said.

"That's right. Artifacts taken out of context destroy the story," Danny said. "After all, we're trying to figure out what the big picture is. Why these people lived here, how they used the canyon, what their day-to-day life was like."

"Really?" Caedyn said. "I thought we were here to dig up fancy pots!" This was meant to be a joke but provoked a moment of chilly silence.

Alex drew on ideas she knew would throw the boy but might stick in his mind. She said, "Have you heard the one about Coyote and the anthropologist? Well, there was this anthropologist who went to the reservation and heard a Navajo grandfather telling Coyote stories. The old man talked for hours until everyone had left or fallen asleep. When only Grandfather and the anthropologist remained, the anthropologist started asking questions—Why did Coyote do this, why did Coyote do that? The old man stopped the anthropologist and said, 'Are you studying to become a witch?'" Alex stopped to let the punch line sink in, but the look on Caedyn's face was so steeped in confusion, she had to laugh.

"The anthropologist evoked the dark powers by trying to take things apart," she said. "That's what witches do."

"Back to witches," Hector said.

Just then, Kit triggered a rattler and skittered away from it. Danny shined his flashlight on the ground. In a moment he found it—a little one. It lay stretched out, gazing at the group. Without a hint of panic, it crawled to the nearest rock. Putting its back against the rock, it wound itself into a striking coil and lay at the ready, tongue flicking.

"So that's what a *live* rattlesnake looks like," Marina said, glaring at Caedyn.

"*I* didn't kill it!" Caedyn said. "Stupid snake didn't need its rattles anymore."

Everyone had a good look, then trickled after Kit. They reached the road and broke out of the snake line, spreading across the dirt and gravel surface. Alex reflected on the different personalities making up the group. Although things had already happened that evoked a wide range of responses, the students still formed a coherent group and showed interest in each other.

Although, that Caedyn ... Alex stared at his back. As if he felt her gaze, he turned around. Through the twilight, she saw him put three fingers behind his head like feathers in a headband and waggle them.

The first stars appeared, sharpening on a whetstone of slate blue sky. A canyon breeze puffed and rolled, flowing down from the Abajos. Off to the east, a sudden riot of hoots and growls erupted, then stopped as suddenly as it had begun.

"Was that coyotes?" Chris asked excitedly.

"Yep," Taylor said

"You mean there are coyotes this close to camp?" Marina asked.

"Probably closer sometimes," Danny said.

"What a *cool place*," Caedyn said. "You never know what's going to happen!"

"That's right, so look lively," Taylor said.

"Yeah, or something might eat you," Chris said, elbowing Caedyn's ribs. The two boys started wrestling in the road. Kit ran back and fastened her teeth on Caedyn's pant leg, tugging and shaking her head like a terrier whiplashing a rat. Caedyn broke free and darted down the road. Kit shot after him, hurtling herself into the back of his knee just as he was throwing his weight on it. It buckled and he went down on the road with a grunt.

"Hey!" he yelled, swiping at the dog. She yodeled, dodged his swings, and danced in and out, nipping at his shoulder, back, and thigh. Then she lost interest and trotted on, leaving Caedyn sitting in the dirt.

Alex had been the victim of that same knee maneuver many times. Feeling vaguely guilty, she offered Caedyn a hand up. He took it grudgingly. Alex braced as Caedyn levered himself up from the ground.

"Did she do that on purpose?" Caedyn growled.

"Don't feel singled out," Alex said. "She's done it to me, too."

Twelve

Coyote had a dream. That was strange because usually when Coyote rested, he fell into dreamless oblivion and awoke feeling half-smothered rather than refreshed. Some nights he slept not at all.

But tonight something roused him from his accustomed oblivion. The blackness cleared. He thought his eyes were open. Before him stood a spirit, erect and odd, with the head of a fawn, the body of a lamb, and the tail of a mouse. If Coyote had not been so surprised, he would have sprung upon the creature and devoured it, it aroused such hunger in him.

The spirit pointed with its lamb's hoof. Coyote, also called First Angry, looked and lost his appetite to terror. Boiling waters of a monstrous flash flood rolled forth, consuming the world. The grinding red torrent exuded hunger even more ravenous than Coyote's own. Something told him that he was to blame for the torrent, but he didn't know how he could be responsible for something so *huge*. As it churned toward him, devouring all in its path, the flood waters turned darker red and the waves rose higher.

"I can't swim!" Coyote cried—another strange thing, since in reality he could swim quite well. He looked around but could not see an escape.

He turned to the spirit to beg its help, but the fawn-lamb-mouse thing had turned into a hollow log standing on its end. It protruded from the waters up into the sky. Coyote knew this log was his only escape. He entered it and climbed up, up into the sky through its hollow passageway, which turned out to be surprisingly roomy. When he emerged from the log, he found himself in another world, one strange to him but thankfully dry.

"This will do," he said. A path led through the rocks. *Where does that go?* He shook water from his fur and went down the path, heading ... somewhere.

Soon he forgot the terror he had felt at the sight of the flood. His appetite returned. As his hunger grew, he looked for something to eat. What should he see but a rabbit nibbling grass beside the path. *A rabbit–my favorite prey! I will catch this rabbit and fill my belly!*

From the distance, it looked like a small, common, brown rabbit and easy to catch. But as Coyote crept closer, he noticed that it had some unusual features. First of all, it was not brown at all but had a beautiful silver coat that shone like the moon. Coyote had never seen anything like it. Its ears, long like a hare's rather than a rabbit's, were tipped with jet and turquoise. It used its paws to pull down the long grasses it nibbled just like a person uses hands.

This rabbit has strong blood, he thought. That made him want it all the more. He crouched near the rabbit, preparing to spring.

Then a wolf appeared near the rabbit, white as snow, with eyes as blue as the turquoise on the tips of the rabbit's ears. Coyote could tell from the way the rabbit acted—as if the wolf's presence was no big thing—that the two were together. Coyote hesitated. The wolf looked right through him, then trotted away.

That look the wolf gave Coyote enraged him. It made him feel as if he were nothing, and that sort of disrespect always aroused his anger.

The wolf gone, Coyote turned his attention back to the wonderful rabbit, only to find it looking at him with great green eyes. *I have never seen a rabbit with green eyes,* he thought. It will be almost a shame ...

Unlike the wolf's eyes, the rabbit's eyes saw him, and he suddenly realized that it wasn't a rabbit at all, but a woman. His body jerked and he awakened gasping for breath. His eyes filled with light from the full moon hanging overhead. He lay on his back, staring at it.

"Who was that?" he asked, panting. He sat up and yelled, "*Who* was that?" Echoes bore his question off to the stars.

Thirteen

The rest of the field school's opening week passed smoothly. Mike took Jack and Caedyn out on survey to finish recording sites near Deeppockets that had not been mapped the summer before. At the site, Rennie opened a test trench on the outside of the pueblo block Hoskers had plowed into with the bulldozer to investigate a peculiar arrangement of stones, recruiting Alex and Hector to help. Danny set to work removing rocks and dirt in a kiva depression near Rennie's excavation. He had only Chris to help in this tough job until Jack and Caedyn came off survey. Taylor set up in the midden at the southeast edge of the site. Dr. Hanks assigned Marina to work with him.

The midden was the settlement's trash heap, the area where the Ancient Ones, while the site had been a going occupation, had placed the residue of their lives. Usually located east and a little south of a settlement, middens teemed with artifacts.

Unlike modern landfill where people deposit their cast-offs or to-be-forgottens, Anasazi middens gathered into their layers broken housewares, waste materials, and the beloved. Along with burned bone, corn-cob laden ash, and intricately painted shards, the Ancient Puebloans laid to the earth their kin, arranging them as carefully in their resting places as they did the complex patterns that bent and curved across the surfaces of their black-on-white pottery.

Often, unique grave goods or items thought to be favorites of the deceased accompanied a burial, perhaps for use in the next life or in final acknowledgment of the loved one's connections to those who remained behind. These grave-goods, usually artifacts of the highest quality, drew pot hunters, who knew from experience where the "good stuff" was to be found.

Upon examining an arroyo running along the midden's edge, Dr. Hanks had seen in the stratigraphy what appeared to be the exposed edge of a burial pit. He put Taylor in charge of the midden excavation because Taylor had a special skill for and interest in excavating burials.

Only two events disturbed the field camp routine that first week. On Friday morning, Alex left the breakfast table and saw Bill Wiggins behind the mess tent, Kit standing at attention in front of him. As Alex watched, Wiggins fed Kit one, two, three, four leftover pancakes. Alex stood waiting to see if he realized he had been caught in the act, but no. Oblivious, he patted Kit's head, then wiped his hands on his apron and re-entered the tent, a smile of satisfaction on his face. Alex stewed a moment but decided not to confront him. If Kit's pattern of behavior held, the repercussions of the cook's actions would bring the event into the open soon enough.

The second event occurred out on site the same morning. The field school members arrived and divided into their respective work areas. The first person to make a trip to the latrine was Chris. He came bounding back to report that poised on the top of the latrine's back-dirt pile was an animal's skull. A single red feather dangled from its eye socket. Excavation screeched to a halt as everyone fell out to inspect the omen.

"It looks like a goat's skull," Rennie observed.

"It looks like someone's put a *curse* on us," Chris said, scowling in the direction of the reservation. All faces turned that way except for Rennie's, Danny's, and Alex's. They looked at Taylor, standing part way up the back-dirt pile, one foot resting against it in classic pose. He stroked his mustache thoughtfully as he regarded the skull.

Feeling their gazes, he looked up. "What?" he asked.

"Wouldn't *you* say it's a goat's skull, Taylor?" Rennie asked.

"Oh, it's a goat's skull all right," he agreed. "The question is, what does it *mean*?" He glanced in the direction the skull pointed—west—toward the base of the mesa where the so-called shrine stood.

"What do *you* think it means?" Chris asked Taylor.

"Don't know," Taylor replied. "Never had a curse put on me before." He left the mound and trotted back to his excavation. Marina followed, turning to shrug as she trailed through the greasewood in his wake.

"I'll bet *someone's* put a curse on him before," Rennie said. "He just never noticed."

. . . . .

That afternoon, the field school students and chiefs returned to camp, showered, washed and labeled artifacts, ate, then grabbed their laundry. Dr. Hanks insisted they take the van to

Blanding even though he needed it to drive to the Provo-Orem area. "Better gas mileage," he said. "Just hurry it up."

Everyone piled into the van. Talk of root beer freezes, mail, and phone calls filled the vehicle's interior. Mike and Dr. Hanks stayed behind in camp along with Heather Barton, who remained routinely apart from the group.

As the van crossed the reservation's boundary, Taylor directed everyone's gaze down a faint path to a structure tucked against the mesa's foot. If he hadn't pointed it out, its natural camouflage would have made it hard to see.

"Is that the witch shrine?" Caedyn asked. He'd been out on survey when the skull had been discovered, but Chris had told him all about it with a few embellishments. "Stop! Let's go see!"

"Not now," Rennie said. "Laundry."

"Chores before childish indulgence in superstition," Hector muttered.

"Hector, you're so charming," Marina chided.

"Bad choice of words," Alex said, laughing.

The route into Blanding crossed Navajo lands, BLM lands, and the state highway. The van's occupants indulged in austere sightseeing to while away the thirty-five-minute trip. They passed Hardy Smith's trading post, a working store located practically in the middle of nowhere. The trumpet-vined building stood in a small oasis of grass, tall trees, peacocks, and a few head of cattle.

In stark contrast to the paradisiacal glory of the trading post, widely spaced Navajo hogans and home sites stood dry-boned and dusty looking. Near one hogan an ancient Navajo grandmother astride a horse followed a herd of goats and sheep along the banks of a wash. The van slowed to push through a free-ranging herd of pinkish horses and passed the usual assortment of ravens perched on fence posts and potgut squirrels sitting upright by the roadside or rolled flat on its pavement. To the south, the jagged pinnacle of Shiprock and the spires of some of the northernmost geology in Monument Valley spiked against the horizon.

Settled in 1905 by pioneers from the San Juan Mission town of Bluff thirty miles to the south, Blanding sat upon the broad back of White Mesa. In the late 1800s when the Bluff pioneers faltered in the face of hardships such as flooding of the San Juan River and repeated crop failures, Latter-day Saint leaders did what they had done in Mormon colonies scattered from one end of the territory to the other. Via letters and personal visits, the leaders encouraged settlers to stay put and not return to Salt Lake City or to the towns of Escalante and St. George, from which many had come. The church authorities—among them Joseph F. Smith, Erastus Snow, and Brigham Young Jr.—promised progress and development in the area and prophesied great things regarding Bluff's future. They also told the Saints of the San Juan Mission that they would fulfill their spiritual callings by expanding their influence in the region.

To some pioneers already interested in the white-rimmed mesa to the north, this last assertion was like the firing of a starting gun. They scouted the mesa and undertook irrigation and settlement projects there. A few changes in the local economy, such as switching from farming to an economy based on ranching, and Blanding was born.

During this time, "gentile" cattle companies jostled the local population for control of water and territory. Along with some trouble from local Navajos and Utes, the hostile competition from the cattle barons left Blanding residents uninspired on the subject of "outsiders." It was especially bad if the outsiders happened to be archaeologists. A dissatisfying relationship with an archaeologist had started a bad tradition decades ago, and since then, field school students were among Blanding's least favorite visitors.

It was during the town's fledgling days that an archaeologist came into the area offering money for pottery or other significant artifacts residents could prize from the mesas and washes of San Juan County. Searching out such treasures and handing them over for rewards became a popular way of supplementing household incomes.

Then the Antiquities Act of 1906 passed. While not addressing the problem of desecration of Native American graves, it did require that anyone intending to work a site apply for a permit. The intent of the Antiquities Act was to eliminate pot hunting and to track excavation in general. But suddenly residents of southeastern Utah towns that had built an artifact-scavenging facet into their cultures found themselves shut out and on the wrong side of the law. After securing the required permits, archaeologists had nearly exclusive access to the wondrous reservoirs of native cultural artifacts. Whenever the locals engaged in what they perceived to be the same activities as the professionals—activities they felt to be their right as residents of their little corner of the Colorado Plateau—they were penalized for it.

The archaeologist who paid the Blanding residents to find artifacts left. The sometimes arrogant archaeologists who flooded the area in his wake flaunted their unrestricted access to the same resources of the land from which the locals struggled to make their livings. Feeling betrayed, exploited, and unnaturally restricted by the law, some—not all, but enough to make an impression—continued foraging the desert for artifacts. The pot hunters turned to the black market to re-establish the old relationship between antiquities and cash, only with a twist: pot hunting became an outlawed activity and a way of gadflying the uppity strangers who invaded nearly every year with their precious permits.

And that is how archaeology students became *personas non-grata* in the predominantly Mormon town of Blanding, Utah, and its surrounding lands. This held even though the students were from the same church, maybe especially if they were.

During the previous field season, members of the Deep-pockets field school had endured stares and taunts about pot hunting from the locals, even during church meetings. Local merchants prominently displayed T-shirts embossed with Anasazi pots and the town's unofficial motto, *Raiders of the Lost Art*, where field school members would be sure to see them. Tongue in cheek, Rennie had bought one.

Jack, Danny, and Marina finished their laundry and set out on foot to find pay phones and pick up mail. When the rest of the crew finished, they re-loaded into the van and Taylor drove it to the gas station/mini-mart to refuel. As Alex stood at the counter waiting to pay for lip balm and a quirky new bandanna, the mini-mart door flew open and in strode Harry Hoskers.

"Just the folks I was looking for!" he said. Clad in his usual expensive jeans and crisp T-shirt, this one advertising the *Holly-*

wood Hard Rock Café, he swaggered up to Taylor and Rennie. A grin accentuated the lines of his chiseled jaw. With both hands, he smoothed down his glossy salt-and-pepper hair. "How's it going out at my site?" he asked.

"So far, so good," Rennie said.

"Except somebody put a curse on us!" Caedyn bellowed from across the store. Harry looked at Rennie and Taylor.

"What's this about a curse?" he asked.

"Nothing," Taylor answered. "Probably just a prank."

"Oh hey, I was wondering about tomorrow for a tour of pot-hunted sites. Weather looks good. Rafferty's free."

"You've already talked to Raff?" Rennie asked.

"We were planning to drive out to camp tonight, but you guys came in, saved us a trip." He folded his arms across his chest and rocked back on his heels. "Well?" he asked. "What do you say?"

Taylor and Rennie looked at each other. After a quick search of each other's faces, they nodded.

"Good!" Harry said. "What time should we rondy-voos?"

"How about ten-ish?" Rennie proposed, looking at Taylor to see if he agreed.

"Perfect," Taylor said.

"Mr. Hoskers?" Caedyn said, stepping forward. He balanced a pile of Twinkies and Snoballs on his left arm and extended his right to shake Harry's hand. "I'm Caedyn Hoyt. I saw you in an episode of *Blue Man's City*. Awesome! Stoked to meet you."

Harry shook Caedyn's hand absentmindedly. "I'm looking forward to this," he said to the two crew chiefs.

"I'm sure it will be interesting," Taylor said.

"See you tomorrow, then!" he said, turning to leave. He stopped as another thought struck him. "Have I ever shown you these?" He reached into a pack he wore over his shoulder and drew out a handful of what looked like newspaper and magazine clippings. He unfolded one and showed it to Rennie and Taylor. Alex looked over their shoulders.

"That's me," Hoskers said, pointing to a picture of himself in a tuxedo escorting a glamorous woman along a red carpet. "This is me, too," he said, unfolding an entire tabloid sheet. The pictures were at least four years old, dating back to Harry's Hollywood heyday. He unfolded page after page with pictures of him escorting mildly famous women to one entertainment industry function after another. Alex rolled her eyes and withdrew to pay for her items.

Harry said, "If it wasn't for the site, I'd be up in Aspen right now snorting my brains out with the rest of the beautiful people!" He laughed and folded the papers again and stuffed them into his pack. "See you tomorrow! This is gonna be great!" He looked at the students gathered around. "Very educational!" he added.

He pulled a set of keys out of his pocket and tossed them into the air. When he caught them, Alex glimpsed an expensive ornament attached to the ring—a sterling silver replica of an Ancient Puebloan pottery shard. Very eye-catching, the sort of thing Alex pictured herself buying someday when she had the money. Her admiration was cut short when in the next moment Harry whisked himself through the door and was gone.

Alex saw Rennie and Taylor look at each other wide-eyed, startled by the encounter. Careful not to say anything about the site owner and benefactor in front of the students, the two crew chiefs finished their business in the store in silence. Danny, Jack, and Marina rejoined the group at the gas station.

"Mail call," Danny said, waving a handful of envelopes.

"Too bad!" Caedyn said. "You just missed the famous Harry Hoskers!"

"Really?" Marina said, disappointed.

"Don't worry," Hector said. "You'll get another chance tomorrow. He's taking us on a tour."

"What kind of a tour?" Marina asked.

"A tour of sites hit by pot hunters," Alex said.

Danny searched Taylor's and Rennie's dismayed faces.

"What's going on?" Danny asked. "You guys look sick."

Taylor and Rennie moved away from the group, drawing Danny off with them. Alex followed. "Hoskers just told us that having the Deeppockets site is better than using cocaine," Taylor said. "Not reassuring somehow."

When the van arrived back at camp, the group saw Dr. Hanks waiting by the mess tent, his laptop case slung over one shoulder and duffel in his hand. "Took you guys long enough!" he said. "I've got to get going."

The crew chiefs gathered around him. "We ran into Harry," Rennie said. "Tomorrow, we're going on the Harry Hoskers Righteous Indignation Tour of Pot Hunted Sites."

"Good," Hanks said. "Well, I've got to get going."

"He said something interesting," Rennie began, but Dr. Hanks walked away from her, threw his bag in the van, and climbed after it. Rennie followed, trying to explain.

"When doesn't he?" Dr. Hanks said. "You, Taylor, and Danny can see to it just fine. You're a responsible bunch."

"Raff's coming," Rennie added as Hanks started the engine.

"Even better," Hanks said. "See you Sunday."

Rennie stepped back while Dr. Hanks backed the van out of the sandy lot. As he pulled onto road, he rolled down his window and shouted, "Did I tell you I'm bringing volunteers on Sunday?"

"I assumed you would," she said. He wound the window up and drove away.

"You guys are my witnesses," Rennie said, her voice cool with frustration. "When something happens and he gets all bent out of shape, you let him know I tried to tell him."

. . . . .

In the middle of the night, a wind rose, blustering down from the Abajos. It started as a pleasant flow, sweeping in through the tent windows and cooling Alex's sleep, then gained strength until the tent's sides began to ripple and billow. Alex woke to the flup-flup-flup of canvas snapping against the nails anchoring it securely, she hoped, to its raised plywood platform. In the distance, thunder rumbled. Alex looked over at Rennie's dark form, already dressed and pulling on shoes.

"Sounds like the canyon's clearing its throat," Alex observed sleepily.

"That's because it's gonna sing."

Alex sat up and dressed. The clock on Rennie's milk-crate read two a.m.

"It figures," Alex said. "The one day we get to sleep in."

"Go out to Marina's tent," Rennie said. "Help her get secured. The storm's traveling fast."

Marina's tent sat on the greasewood flat several yards away from Rennie's and Alex's. Kit anticipated her destination and darted ahead.

"Always gotta be first," Alex muttered as she watched Kit disappear into the greasewood. Overhead, thick clouds rolled like ethereal boulders across the sky. The temperature began to drop. Alex shivered. She roused Marina. They checked the tent over to make sure it was secure.

Marina turned to Alex. "Now what?"

"You could stay with your tent," Alex answered. "Or head for the mess tent. They'll be rolling its sides down to keep out the rain."

The sky went silver with lightning, washing the canyon walls with an electric glow. Then came a low, growling boom. Alex looked up at the clouds. Just to the north, the canyon was beginning to blur. Big rain, coming fast.

"I'm not staying here by myself, I'm heading for the big top!" Marina exclaimed. She ran down the path to the mess.

Alex glanced around for Kit, but the dog was nowhere to be seen. "Fine," Alex muttered. "You're on your own." Fat raindrops kicked up dust at her feet. She ran for the mess.

Except for flashlights darting about, the big tent was dark. Nearly everyone had taken refuge there except for Mike, who had chosen to ride out the storm in his tent, and Heather evidently doing the same. Wiggins had gone home for the weekend, as had Todd. During a lightning flash, Alex glimpsed Kit lying on the mess tent's dirt floor. Kit lifted her head and looked at Alex slyly, triumphant that she had found a way to defy the no-dog-in-the-mess-tent rule. Alex shined her flashlight on the husky.

"You *scoundrel!*" Alex said. Kit flopped her tail twice, raising a puff of dust.

The storm crammed the canyon with wind, rain, and roaring thunder. The mess tent's walls heaved in and out as if it were gulping great droughts of storm wind. Around the tent the ancient cottonwoods switched back and forth. A loud crack and a thump behind the tent turned all heads that way. Taylor, Danny, and Caedyn ran back and opened a flap to peer out. Just inches from the mess tent lay a big, dead limb.

Taylor made his way through the kitchen area. "Firewood!" he said, his voice light with excitement. Then, "What the? ..."

"What's wrong?" Caedyn asked.

Taylor shined his light over a large metal tub sitting on a table. "Unwashed dishes!" he exclaimed. "He left a whole tub full of unwashed dishes just sitting here!"

Rennie made her way back to have a look. Reflected light illuminated the pair's disgust. Rennie began searching through the kitchen and Taylor rolled up his sleeves. Meanwhile, the heart of the storm passed, beating out its thunder and firing bolts through clouds and between heaven and earth. Rain-washed air gusted through the tent, cold and clean-smelling.

As Taylor and Rennie heated water on the two propane stoves, the storm loped down canyon. Alex stepped through the tent flaps to have a look around.

The roar of downpour had turned to a light pattering. The air was moist and sweetened; it flowed over Alex like water over a river stone, raising a prickle of goose bumps. Closing her eyes, she breathed it in. Curious to see how the storm had transformed other parts of camp, she walked toward her tent.

As her eyes adjusted to the desert night, the canyon emerged to her view in a layered nightscape. Through the clouds, moonlight and starlight cast a powdery glow over trees and sand. The Milky Way shed a soft, simple, grainy luminosity that the canyon took up as an optical echo. Silver-glazed greasewood and sage lay all around. Rainwater drip-drip-dripped in the branches. The storm had pressed the sage leaves, which had released their oils into the air to mingle with odors rising from wet sand and rain-slicked rocks. The whole complex of scents tingled in Alex's nostrils.

A short distance ahead she saw the star-bathed form of the big cottonwood that stood over her tent. A breeze straying after the storm flowed past her and entered the tree, transfiguring it with a long shuddering sigh. Alex's eyes widened. It seemed she could see each leaf catch the pale lightfall on its fluttering tip. A sweet watery music rose and fell in waves of leaf-whisper.

Alex sucked in her breath, the pleasure she felt stretching her lips in a smile. She walked toward the tree, unconcerned about trespassing into this domain of instant beauty. Beauty was everywhere. If she stopped each time it blossomed in her path, she might never take another step but become rooted in some paralysis of wonder. Then maybe she'd change into one of those columns of stone she saw standing sentry alone or clustered around little gardens of beauty. It was as if some sudden coming together of elements and events had so spellbound wayfarers who happened upon such bewitching splendor, it had brought the poor, petrified souls to a standstill.

Fourteen

Morning of the next day was pleasant, courtesy of the pre-dawn storm. The desert air shined from the scouring. Small clouds scudded on gray bottoms across the blue. The field school Suburban, along with Harry, Rennie, and Raff in Raff's pickup and Heather Barton in her Subaru, crossed the reservation's trickling washes without incident. At the state road, the Suburban and Raff's truck parted company with Heather's Subaru. She turned toward Blanding bound for parts unknown while the other two vehicles headed out across the vast mesas and back roads of a lesser known Canyon Country.

Monument Valley appeared and disappeared as the road undulated beneath the vehicles' tires, then Raff steered his truck onto a graded surface marked by a red, white, and blue San Juan County road sign. Alex couldn't help but be amused by those signs even though they stood as evidence of a heated war waging between the residents of the local, mostly conservative Mormon population and "environmentalists." At news that environmental interests wanted to close roads in the county that were not obvious public rights-of-way, San Juan County made an end run by re-grading or otherwise establishing a presence on the many off-road trails crisscrossing the canyons and mesa tops right down to the faintest four-wheel dirt track a mule wouldn't climb. They branded these paths with patriotically flavored signs.

Alex had to hand it to the locals. They were fighters, that was for sure, and they were smart enough to play the common law that English peasants had used to defeat kings: the ancient public access law. So far, it was working.

Kit sat upright in her seat next to Alex. She had been allowed to come on Alex's assurance that Kit's delicate sensibilities would prevent awkward scenes with artifacts or human remains. Pleased to have been included, Kit struck a human-like pose as she rode with her two-footed colleagues. Eventually, though, she fell to standing in Alex's lap so she could stick her nose out the window.

"Hah!" Alex said. "See? You're just a dog after all."

The group arrived at the Burned Kivas site. Access to the top of the steep mesita would have been a challenge had it not been for the graded siege ramp stretching two-thirds of the way up the side and the dozer cut that wound from there to the top. Students and crew chiefs stared at the ramp in awe. Hoskers gestured left and right as he posed his interpretation of the evidence of assault.

Alex wasn't interested in Hoskers's insights. While Danny, Taylor, and the students listened to him prattle, she followed Rennie and Raff to see the facts for herself. The extent of the damage staggered her, not to mention the level of determination the siege ramp evidenced. How had the pot hunters gotten a big D-9 Cat into this remote location? How could they operate so brazenly? This was no hit-and-run operation; this had taken all kinds of thought and planning.

"Why do they do this?" she wondered, at the same time realizing she knew why—*they did it for the money.* All the same, not everyone desecrated grave sites, scattering peoples' bones for the money. Not everyone robbed 7-11s either, but some people did. Some people destroyed elephant populations to harvest a single part of their bodies. Ore extraction companies strip-mined. Tobacco industries strip-mined too, leaving behind illness and death after reaping from highly profitable addictions. Alex's own father had died at sixty from heart disease resulting in part from his two-pack-a-day habit. What was profit for some became expense for others.

Pot hunters might argue that the dead no longer needed those treasures that had once been housewares. They could no longer drink from those mugs or cook in those pots or inspire admiration with their pretty ornaments. After all, many heirlooms ride the generational waves, passing from survivor to survivor. Sometimes such items had a broader value as a reflection of cultural identity and were bought and sold for great amounts of money. Alex had seen the PBS shows where experts assigned value to such treasures. Yet, they were merely the daily stuff of life.

But dead people, pot hunters might say, don't have anything more to lose, and they certainly don't wonder about their cultural identity. So where is the wrong in profiting from outcroppings of a deceased civilization? Wasn't it more or less the same as harvesting Spanish gold from the wreckage of a hapless treasure ship?

Hoskers and the students were catching up now, and Kit was way ahead of everyone. In spite of Alex's assertions about Kit's sensibilities, she knew the dog needed watching. She hurried along the dozer cut.

Catching up with Rennie, she gestured at the siege ramp they were climbing and said, "These guys are real blue-collar types—hard working, sweat-breaking, machine-wielding Americans."

"So they say," Rennie replied.

On top of the site, potholes peppered with cast-off shards and broken pots gaped like miniature abandoned mine shafts. Alex did not see any human bone. Raff and Hoskers had done a good job of re-burying any that had been turned up in the harrowing. Raff led everybody over to perhaps the most striking feature of the site—the burned kivas. These, too, had been dug into. Charred timber and ash lay scattered across the ground.

No one said much. Caedyn and Chris, uncomfortable with the scene confronting them, started wrestling. Hector viewed the destruction with his usual scientific objectivity. Marina walked along with her arms folded across her chest as if to ward off a chill. Jack took in the scene in absolute silence, his face still, as if with impassivity. Hoskers walked back and forth over the site, gesturing this way and that, his voice echoing off surrounding canyon walls.

After they had spent an hour at the site, Raff herded everyone down the siege ramp and into the vehicles. They visited another ravaged ruin, this one in a farmer's field. Although privately owned and therefore susceptible to the owner's wishes concerning it, the site had been potted out without the owner's knowledge or permission. Skulls and other human bones lay strewn about, of absolutely no value to those who had exposed them to the light of day.

And so it went. The tour took in another site that was in some ways the most dramatic. It was a deep alcove scooped out of the sandstone by persistent winds and the patient grain-by-grain work of water. A smooth wall protected the alcove from the new stream course below it. The students clambered up a rope that appeared to have been permanently installed.

Once up the rope, Alex looked down the eight-foot wall at Kit trotting back and forth at the bottom, searching for her own way up.

Raff stood on the bank, watching her. "Sorry, mutt. You've been abandoned."

"Wanna make a bet?" Alex asked.

"She can't climb that," Raff said. "*Can* she?"

Alex shrugged and walked deeper into the alcove. The heat of the day had come up along with an intense glare, but inside the cellar-like cave, tons of rock turned back the heat and offered the visitors relief, just as it had its previous residents.

The alcove's soil lay deep and heavy and cool. As she walked through the sand and stagnant air, Alex felt as though she were pushing her way through thick draperies. Even the deepest shadows made her think of old, dusty fabric. A few granaries with sandstone masonry furnished the alcove with yet darker cavities. But here, too, along with centuries-old cobs and kernels, lay stashes of ancient dry air.

The alcove's stone mouth framed a bright landscape. A breeze had sprung up and cottonwood leaves and cloud-dappled blue sky shivered and tumbled in the rush of breezy, earth-spinning, time-altering light. Alex had the sense of watching a time-lapse film from the stillness of another place that was not moving nearly as fast.

Hoskers led the group from one spot to the next, calling attention to pot hunting damage. They gathered around him to stare into the deep holes. Kit appeared from nowhere. Alex glanced over at Raff, who pretended to collapse from surprise. Then Kit wandered to the other side of the cave.

"I first visited this place late last fall," Hoskers said. "It was virtually untouched—pristine, some would say. Later I came back and found the place had been given a tossing. Word is, they got baskets out of it—nice ones. Talk varies on how many, but someone said the baskets fetched thirty thousand dollars on the black market." Hoskers's voice deepened with indignation. "Came out again a few weeks ago, and it had been hit again, probably by someone who had heard the news and came hoping to find something the first guys missed."

"Hey, McKelvey, what's your dog up to?" Raff asked.

Everyone turned and stared at Kit at the far end of the alcove. Her behavior puzzled even Alex. The dog stood in an alert posture with her muzzle pointed at something in the sand. Her head cocked first one way, then the other. She made a strange sound, a cross between a growl and a whine. She pawed at the sand in front of her, jumped back, cocked her head again, and looked at Alex as if asking for help with a problem.

Thinking the dog might have found a snake, Alex hurried over. Kit danced to one side, yielding the matter into Alex's hands.

Next to Kit was a pothole. Something Alex took for a piece

of gnarled wood lay partially exposed in the sand. As the others gathered around, Alex crouched for a closer look.

"What's that?" Caedyn asked. "A hunk of dried meat or something?"

Marina startled everyone by gasping a sob of shock. In that same instant, Alex understood what she was looking at. Startled, she lost her balance and fell backwards.

"I'll be," Raff exclaimed quietly, crouching at the rim of the hole. "It's a mummified infant."

The tiny form lay on its face in a head-down position. Its rigid body seemed to have been cemented into stillness until someone came along, chipped it out, and threw it back as something useless. The group stood quietly around it, staring in shock and wonder.

Alex couldn't take her eyes off the little feet, so delicate and detailed, so undeniably human. She felt fascinated and repulsed at the same time.

"Is it an Ancient Puebloan infant?" Hector asked.

"I'd say," Raff replied.

"Did some animal dig it up?" Chris asked.

"Some animal dug it up, all right," Raff said, "but not the four-legged kind."

"What other kind of animal is there?" Caedyn asked.

"He means the two-legged kind," Chris whispered to his cousin.

This took a moment to sink in. A strange combination of disgust and wonder dawned in Caedyn's face. "You mean someone dug 'im up?"

Raff looked at Hoskers. "I doubt this has been here long.

Something would have come along and chewed on it. Did you see it when you were here last time?"

Hoskers shook his head. "I wouldn't have missed something like this!" His voice had the tinge of something that sounded like admiration. Alex saw Rennie glance at him, a slight frown creasing her brow.

"Then somebody's been back again," Raff said. "I think this kid was probably buried in a basket and whoever found the burial dumped the kid out and took the basket, happy they'd hit pay dirt."

"Well," Taylor said, "let's get this child taken care of, shall we?"

As the archaeologists began preparing for the burial, Alex looked around to check on Kit. The dog lay stretched out regally at the very edge of the rock face, white legs sticking out into the sunshine. Marina sat next to her stroking her silky coat. Feeling the re-burial to be archaeologists' business, Alex joined the woman and dog. Kit looked over at her, her pale eyes slitted and winking against the light.

Another sound of denim rasping across stone and Jack sat on a rock to Alex's left. Alex glanced at him briefly, then did a double take when she noticed a flush to his face. In a jolt of intuition, Alex understood that what had just occurred, while affecting everyone deeply, had some special meaning for Jack.

Unaware of Alex's scrutiny, Jack shook his head, drew up a knee, and rested his chin on it. He breathed a sigh—or was it a snort? Alex wondered if that was anger she sensed brewing inside him. Feeling her gaze, he glanced at her, turned to toss a pebble out over the edge of the alcove, then looked back.

Alex sensed guilt and frustration in the young man, but its

relationship to what had happened in the alcove wasn't clear. She smiled at him reassuringly, though what she was trying to reassure him about she didn't know. He flashed back a wry smile, then continued throwing pebbles into space.

Caedyn and Chris walked to the alcove's edge. Alex took this to mean the re-burial was over since she couldn't imagine Caedyn leaving before the ritual had ended. He sat and dusted off his hands, looking down the line of people. Nobody seemed in much of a mood to talk, but that didn't stop Caedyn.

He said, "I've never seen a dead person before."

Marina looked up at him, her eyes angry. "So, Caedyn, what did you collect?"

"What do ya mean?" Caedyn asked, confused.

"Rattles from snake, feathers from bird ... you know, what did you take?"

Caedyn's jaw dropped as he caught her meaning. He turned on Marina fiercely, but she had walked behind him. Danny saw her head for the rope and hurried over to help.

"*I* didn't kill the kid!" he yelled. "What're you blaming me for?"

Marina ignored him and concentrated on Danny as he gave her advice for getting down. After a split second of invisibility, she reappeared below, heading toward the vehicles parked across the wash. As Alex watched her, she once again admired the young woman's gift for forthrightness.

But she had stung Caedyn good. Alex tried to help. "She's just in shock," Alex said.

"Huh?" Caedyn said. "You probably think the same thing she does."

"C'mon, Cade, chill out," Chris said, laying a hand on his shoulder.

Caedyn threw off the hand. "This is stupid. What did we come here for?"

Nobody replied and no more was said. Kit came over to lie beside Alex, pressing her back against Alex's thigh.

"Okay, troops, let's go," Raff said, moving to the edge of the alcove.

Taylor attempted to lift the group's spirits by jumping from the top of the wall into the soft sand below. He took off running through the brush. Excited by his leap, Kit slid part way down the sandstone and leaped out, falling onto a shoulder as she landed. Unable to resist either a race or a chase, she righted herself and set off after Taylor. Danny, Caedyn, and Chris followed, leaping down into the sand like sailors abandoning ship. Even Hector made the daring leap from the alcove's mouth, staggering off wildly. Jack followed, apparently deep in thought. Rennie and Alex did the conservative thing and used the rope. Raff and Harry Hoskers came last, sliding down the sandstone on their backsides.

The group re-assembled at the Suburban, flinging open its back doors and dragging out the coolers. As everyone ate a late lunch, Kit made her rounds looking for crumbs in the sand, but she knew better than to beg outright while Alex watched. Taylor sliced a watermelon, handing it around. Its icy sweetness was a success, the day having turned hot.

Lunch ended with a watermelon seed-spitting contest, then everyone packed up, cleaned the area, and re-loaded the Suburban. Raff turned his truck around and leaned out the window to suggest a trip to Blanding for ice cream, then a stop at his house to watch videos. Everyone thought this plan good.

In the Suburban, Alex offered Kit her favored position at the window. But this time, instead of thrusting her nose out into the wind, the husky lay down on the vinyl seat and closed her eyes. After a while, she shoved her nose under Alex's hand and pushed her head into her lap. Surprised, Alex stroked the gray-capped skull and the long white muzzle. The husky sighed, then fell into a fitful doze.

Fifteen

Carrying a small sack in one hand, Coyote, also called First Angry, crawled into his den. Wiping sweat from his brow, he sat and dumped the sack's contents onto the dirt floor. An assortment of pottery shards tumbled into the dust—thick, black-on-white Pueblo pottery, stark with its checkered décor and zig-jagging lines, beautiful and significant. Thinner black-on-red pottery, earthy and rare. Then there were the corrugated gray shards, which were not as glamorous, yet when added to the fragmented rainbow before him, they beguiled his eyes.

Wonderful! Wonderful and potent. He picked up a large piece of the black-on-red and licked it. His spit raised the sheen of the glaze and the shard's complicated pattern, a partial sunburst framed by wavy lines. What had the entire pattern been before time, jealous of the secrets the design revealed, destroyed the artisans who had created it, then crushed the bowl and scattered the pieces, returning its ancient spell to the bowels of mystery?

Such knowledge was not meant to fall into the hands of

blundering souls, the likes of which unearthed the sacred matter time had buried. Defiling the holy, raping eternity! That's what they did, like the unfit primitives they were. In the presence of such profundity, a finer touch and higher intelligence were called for. Coyote picked up a piece of the black-on-white decorated with a labyrinth of angled spirals. He alone knew how to appreciate the value of what lay in the palm of his hand. To him alone belonged the right to touch, to hold.

The power is as the dust on butterflies' wings. He turned the piece, and his mind turned with it. *Oh, what had it been like when it had been whole? So beautiful, so laden!* Even a piece of the puzzle felt precious beyond the value of gold.

"Talk to me," he said to the shard. He held it to his ear. "I am Coyote, also called First Angry. You may tell me your secrets."

Ish, said the shard.

"What?"

Ah, said the shard.

"I hear you! You're talking, talking to me!"

Ish, repeated the shard.

Coyote scowled. What did the shard mean by these sounds, *ish* and *ah*? Were they words from another language or something else entirely? Coyote looked at the shards lying on the ground. He picked another up and held it to his ear.

Or, said the shard. *Gah.*

He picked up another. *La,* it said.

O, O, O, O! said another.

Coyote's dark eyes filled with wonder. Each shard made a different sound, or two sounds, distinct from all the others. One after another, they uttered their unique cries.

"It's like music," said Coyote, tossing the shards lightly in his hand.

Ka, O, ish, hee, la-la, O, O, ahh, buh, la-la, ish, ka, gah, nah, k-ch, k-ch.

"Hmm," said Coyote. Then a thought struck him. Perhaps the sounds were not words, but parts of words, as the shards themselves had been parts of whole pots.

He tried arranging them a certain way, then listened. Nothing—just more inscrutable music. He tried another way—again, nothing. Coyote sighed. Why did everything have to be a big mystery?

"Hmph! What do I care what they mean by these noises?" he said. "I am Coyote. I can make things mean what I want them to. What's the good of having power if you can't impose your will—make your own mystery of things?" With that, Coyote picked up the shards and put them back in the sack. "Come, my beauties! I have a plan for you."

"Ohhh," sighed the shards. "Ahhh."

Sixteen

When Bill Wiggins returned to camp, he seemed puzzled by the bottle of green dishwashing liquid festooned with flagging tape sitting on a freshly disinfected tabletop. The cook picked up the bottle, turning it 'round and 'round. Stowing it under the table, he shrugged and began his ritual of cacophonies as he set up his kitchen for tomorrow's breakfast. Rennie, Taylor, and Alex sat in the dining area watching.

Taylor leaned on the table, chewing his bottom lip. In a low voice, he asked, "Do you think our culinary miscreant took the hint?"

Alex and Rennie flashed him looks of doubt.

"Perhaps you're right," Taylor said. "Perhaps stronger action is called for."

"No lynching," Rennie cautioned.

"Lynching would definitely be against the honor code," Alex said.

"Lynching?" Taylor said, looking up to appraise the suitability of various cottonwood limbs overhanging the mess area.

"I was thinking a snipe hunt, but a lynching—brilliant!" He got up as if to proceed with preparations relevant to their discussion and stepped away from the tent. "As for the honor code," he said, "once Standards reviews this particular case, I'm certain they'll be lenient."

Marina approached the mess tent. At the sight of her, Taylor whipped off the towel he wore around his neck and motioned for her to stop. "One moment, milady!" With a gallant gesture, he spread the towel over the duff at the tent's border. Marina watched his antics in bafflement. Satisfied with his arrangement of the towel, Taylor stood back and, with a chivalrous bow and sweep of the arm, gestured for her to cross.

"Why thank you, kind sir!" she exclaimed, both embarrassed and charmed. She walked gingerly across the towel.

"Think nothing of it," Taylor replied. With that, he picked up his towel, shook it out, bowed, and left.

Marina sat down with Rennie and Alex. "He's kinda cute," she said. "Isn't he?"

"Oh, he's *cute,* all right," Rennie said.

"Is he seeing anybody?"

Rennie shrugged. "Hard to tell. For all any of us know, he's married with two children."

Marina's eyes widened. "You mean you think he's secretly married?"

"No ... it's just that Taylor keeps to himself about personal matters," Alex said.

Marina stared hard at Taylor's back as he disappeared into the greasewood. "You know, you're right. I can't tell from looking at him either."

"You ... thinking of going after him?" Alex asked.

"No. I just think it's best to know status of the people around you. Seems to me it's the responsible thing to do."

Alex tilted her head as she thought about this. She decided to try something. "Hmm. What about Jack? What can you tell about him?"

"Oh, he's married," Marina replied.

"You can tell that by looking at him?"

Marina giggled. "No, I overheard a phone call he made last Friday."

"Gee, I didn't notice a ring," Alex said.

"He doesn't want to lose or damage it while he's digging and moving rocks. I asked."

"That's interesting," Alex said. "I wouldn't have guessed. I mean, obviously he's been on a mission ..."

"He's got garment lines," Marina added, matter-of-factly.

"Uh, yes," said Alex. She, too, had noticed the telltale "garment" hem pressing through the fabric of his clothes just above the knee. The undergarments were indicative of an adult LDS member's mission service or married status. "But he wears those knee-length shorts, too, so one might guess."

"He does, but I always look for those G-lines to be sure. Habit, I guess."

"For some reason, it didn't occur to me," Alex said thoughtfully.

"And he acts it anyway," Marina said with a wave of her hand, dismissing the obvious.

Rennie asked, "What about Caedyn? He seems like a ... well, a ..."

"A fairly typical immature male?" Alex suggested.

"Yeah, that's it," Rennie said.

Pressing her hands between her knees, Marina said, "Been there—done that."

"You don't mean *you* dated Caedyn!" Alex said.

"More than that. We were almost engaged."

Alex and Rennie looked at each other, wondering whether or not to probe further. They couldn't resist; besides, such knowledge might prove important later on.

"*Almost* engaged? Mind if I ask, ..." Alex began.

"... what happened?" Marina said. "Go ahead and ask. I'm sure you already know."

Alex thought a moment, then said, "He tried to cut off your rattles."

"Pluck your feathers," Rennie added.

Marina nodded. "Something like that. He's such a ..."

"Souvenir collector?" Alex asked.

"Repressed big game hunter?" said Rennie.

"He didn't get it. He hasn't changed one bit since we broke up, either."

Alex looked at the pretty, long-lashed, brown eyes, lowered now as they recalled some fairly recent pain. To her, Marina seemed the essence of unconfused womanhood, the eternal female, Venus rising from the water.

"I guess I just didn't have what it takes to get through to him," she said.

"Don't do that," Alex urged. "It's not your fault."

"How do you know?" Marina asked her.

"Huh!" Alex exclaimed. "You're at least a thousand years older than he is!"

Marina smiled demurely. "Danny—he's got someone, doesn't he?"

"Yup, up north. He'll start going there on weekends once camp's settled."

"And what about you two?" Marina asked. "Have you got ... um, significant others?" She smiled and waggled her head.

Suddenly Alex felt the conversation had gone too far. It had been a long time—since just before her conversion—that she had kept any male company. Time had shown her the relationship she'd had with Michael had been a cruel disaster. Joining the church had all but required she end it, and once she did, she went on a long sabbatical from any romantic entanglements partly to get over the bad taste still lingering in her mouth from that last one.

But she hadn't felt comfortable doing that, either. The church accosted her at every turn about marrying and raising a family because *the man without the woman is not perfect, neither is the woman without the man.* One bishop tried to set her up with a "nice Mormon boy." Given her family, a complicated one filled with gypsies and thieves, and given some of her own adventures prior to joining the church, *nice Mormon boys* seemed somehow underdone. They weren't very interested in her either. She didn't know what it was, really. At twenty-six, she was already nearly four years past the average age for Mormon women to marry. Yet, she felt completely uninspired on the subject.

She said, "I don't know about Rennie, but I'm fully dysfunctional in these matters."

"Really? But you get along with the guys pretty well, and you're interesting."

Interesting? Alex cringed. She knew what Marina really meant by that. She meant that the fact that she was a convert showed through. Already sensitive to the idea that she was not a "real" Mormon, one either born in the church and bearing all the signs of it, or a convert who, like St. Paul, was fully born again in the Word, she had struggled with feeling like a second-class citizen. She had been patient with her new social circumstances and served to the best of her ability in any church position church leaders called her to, from Sunday school teacher to church librarian. All the same, in her experiences before she had joined the church, she had gained some forbidden knowledge and that had set her apart from the third-, fourth-, or more generation Mormon crowd she had joined when she moved to Utah. *Interesting?* In the course of her new religious life, Alex had tried to forget just how *interesting* she was.

As she groped for a way to change the subject, the sound of an engine whining toward camp caught her attention. Saved by the approach of the van, Rennie and Alex stood up, effectively ending the discussion.

"Sounds like Dr. Hanks arriving with his first crop of volunteers!" Rennie said with exaggerated interest.

The van pulled into the lot and stopped in a cloud of dust. For a moment everyone inside sat still as they took in their surroundings. Then Dr. Hanks got out and began helping volunteers unload their gear. Rennie went to assist.

Alex looked at Marina. "Well, I better go help," she said. With those words, she set the boundaries beyond which Marina was not welcome to venture.

Two men and two women had come to sample the archaeologist's life for a couple weeks. The women were a pair—two older women, one widowed, one divorced. One of the men was a former machinist for the Coast Guard, late thirties, tall, with a manual-labor formed physique and a lean, angular face. He introduced himself by a nickname he seemed very proud of.

"They call me 'Sharp,'" he said.

His last name? "Spikes." He laughed at the expected response. "Yep! That's really it—that's my name!"

"I'll bet you got that name in the Coast Guard," Rennie said.

"Yes, ma'am!"

The fourth person was a high school honor roll student from Idaho named Josh McCray. His parents had arranged for this trip as an experiment in independence. He had a wry smile and inquisitive glance.

The two women, Doris Harding and Janice Evans, were absolutely taken by Kit. "Oh! Isn't she beautiful! Look at those blue eyes! They're like hearts of ice!"

"They're like the sky at sunset! Siberian or Malamute?"

"Siberian," Alex said, uncertain yet which woman was which.

"Oh, she's just exquisite! We put our own dogs in the kennel before we came," the taller woman said. "They're just little dogs, house pets."

"Didn't want them to get eaten by coyotes!" the shorter woman exclaimed ominously.

"Or desert dogs," Alex quipped.

"Ah," the two women exclaimed, "an alpha female!"

"Yep," Alex said. "That's Kit!" So the conversations went. The veterans of camp walked up and joined in welcoming and accommodating the newcomers.

· · · · ·

Later that evening, Heather Barton returned, but she made no attempt to introduce herself to the new arrivals. When she noticed strangers, she ducked her head and hurried to her tent.

Alex watched her pass. Heather appeared almost panicked as she kept to the rim of the tent light where the shadow of the roof cut it away. Kit, who out of habit lay on the very border of the tent shadow, watched Heather pass without comment. She was probably the only other creature besides Alex who noticed her arrival.

Alex retired early to find some solitude and to sort out her thoughts. She lay in bed thinking of Heather, of her furtive passage through camp, her shoulders hunched as she attempted invisibility. Alex wondered if Heather's fears were specific or non-specific. Did she fear being seen by someone in particular or was she just plain shy? Could there be something she didn't want anyone to notice—was that why she avoided the crowd under the light?

Alex rolled over and looked out her back window at Heather's tent. A gauzy, green glow showed through the canvas as the beam from a motionless flashlight penetrated the tent wall. No sound, no movement issued forth. Alex lay back down.

Was Heather clinically shy? Was she misanthropic? Or was there some other reason she kept her distance? Hm, maybe Heather was like Alex, *interesting,* only in a different way. Something in Alex wanted to approach the woman with a flag of friendship, but instinctively, she understood that the chasm between them was so wide it could not be bridged during a few weeks in the desert. Maybe the best thing was to leave the woman alone, let her do her job with the artifacts that came out of the site, and keep all concerns to herself, although ... something about the woman really bothered her.

Seventeen

Dawn of the next day promised a new high in the canyon's temperatures. Out at the site, Alex took up her work with Rennie and Hector. Dr. Hanks added Josh to their crew. Caedyn and Jack had exchanged their places on survey with Marina and Chris. Danny snagged Jack and Caedyn for much-needed help removing rocks and fill from his kiva excavation. Taylor acquired the two "isses"—Doris and Janice—to help with what had indeed turned out to be a burial pit in the midden. Sharp Spikes migrated between Danny's kiva and Rennie's excavation as needed.

Just before lunch, Mike Greaves drove onto the site, walked over to Alex, and crouched beside her where she sat mapping an arrangement of stones. "I don't want to make you mad," he said, "but I just stopped at camp. Ol' Wiggins has Kit tied up to the open air table in the mess area."

Alex had gone into a kind of Zen state to cope with the rising heat and light, but at this news, her calm snapped. She felt a strong urge to stand up, march back to camp, and resolve the situation right away, but she repressed it. Without looking up, she said to Mike, "Did she steal something?"

"He says she pinched a roast from the kitchen table."

Alex nodded. "Thanks, I'll take care of it as soon as I can."

Mike nodded back and left the site.

All through lunch, Alex thought up ways to confront Wiggins with how he had broken the camp rule not to feed Kit. She was not at all surprised by this turn of events, but that didn't quell her rising ire over Kit's imprisonment. The sound of another truck engine broke in on her musings as Raff drove onto the site *sans* Harry Hoskers.

Raff got out of his truck, sauntered over, rummaged through the cooler for a soda, and sat down under the canvas as the crew finished lunch. There was a loud *whish* as he popped the can's top.

"Hi Rafferty," Dr. Hanks said. "Where's your side-kick?"

"He's not my sidekick," Raff snapped. "But I, uh ... got a message from him." Raff gave Hanks a coded look.

Worry darkened Hanks's face. "Okay, everybody," he said. "Time to get back to work."

Groans of protest filled the sweltering air under the ramada. Alex looked at Rennie, who showed every sign of remaining there with Rafferty and Dr. Hanks. Taylor and Danny looked as though they knew something was up but walked out to their excavations. Alex left and went back to work. Eventually Rennie appeared, her lips drawn in a thin, tight line.

"Something happen?"

"Oh, something happened all right. Hoskers has landed himself in the hospital at Moab."

"How?"

"He got beat up in Bluff."

"You're kidding!" After Alex thought a moment, she said, "Of course he did."

Danny saw them talking and came over. "Something happen I need to know?"

"Yeah," Rennie said. "Raff came out to tell us Hoskers got beat up in Bluff and is in the hospital in Moab."

"It figures," Danny said, wiping sweat off his brow.

"Raff said he got an anonymous call for 'Tonto to come pick up the Lone Ranger—he fell off his horse.'"

"Oh, that's clever," Danny said. "That it?"

"Yep," Rennie said. Flashing one of his ironical smiles, Danny returned to his kiva.

Minutes later, Dr. Hanks appeared on the rubble piles behind Rennie's excavation.

"Um, I'm headed up to Moab. You're in charge," he said to Rennie. "Pack everybody up at two-thirty."

"Righto!" Rennie said, saluting smartly.

"I expect to be back by tonight, but if I'm not, round up Danny and Taylor and have them help you get things going tomorrow morning."

"Will do," Rennie said.

"Okay, good luck. I'm going back to camp with Raff to clean up and head out."

Rennie nodded and Dr. Hanks left.

The rest of the afternoon passed quickly in spite of the relentless heat. Those who knew how laid their trowels and other equipment in their own shadows, otherwise the tools became too hot to handle. A few observant individuals like Hector and Sharp picked up the trick. Toward the day's end, everyone wore a glaze of dust and sweat-laced grit. Water coolers had been nearly drained.

No way was Alex going to ride back in the dark-colored Suburban, which had been baking in the sun. Mike showed up at the site with the pickup and she hopped in the back with Caedyn, Chris, Josh, Taylor, and Danny, craving the breeze kicked up by the pickup's slipstream. She looked around at the men riding with her. Tans had made significant progress during the day. Nobody's clothes were dry. Taylor and Danny had peeled off everything down to their cut-offs. Taylor wore a fresh, crisp, red paisley bandanna around his bare throat. It was a funny habit—no matter how hot and tired the rest of him looked, he always wore a clean bandanna.

When they arrived at camp, Alex jumped from the pickup and stalked over to where Kit was tied. The husky looked up guiltily. Alex untied the rope looped through her collar and shook her finger at the dog. "You *stay out of that kitchen!*" she said. Kit jumped up and slinked away. Alex went over to the mess tent to confront the cook.

"Don't tie up my dog," she said in a low voice.

"She ... she stole my roast!" Wiggins sputtered, pointing to the spot in the kitchen where the erstwhile roast had been sitting.

"Yeah, and that wouldn't have happened if you had told her to stay out of the kitchen, like I said, and if you hadn't been feeding her!"

"I *haven't* been feeding her!" Wiggins said.

"Yes you have!" Alex exclaimed. "You gave her four pancakes last Friday. I stood here and watched you do it!"

This news caught Bill Wiggins off guard. His eyes rolled

slightly as he thought back. A smile of embarrassment stretched his lips. "Th ... that was the only time!"

"Phah! I doubt it! But it only takes one time, you know, one big fat juicy time to trigger her thieving instincts. Four pancakes is more than enough." She leaned close to the cook, fixing him with an unblinking gaze. "Listen, don't even *think* about tying her up again. You have a problem with her, you come to me. *I'll* handle it. Now that she's started stealing, there's no way you're going to stop her without keeping her tied all the time. But that won't work because she's an escape artist. Sooner or later, she'll chew through or slip the rope. So it's up to me, not you, you ..." Alex caught herself before she finished the thought. "Look, *I'll* take care of this. You just do your part and don't give her any leftovers. Okay?"

Wiggins nodded. "Okay!" he said, raising his hands in front of him. "All right."

"All right." Alex left the mess tent and walked through the small crowd that had gathered to watch the confrontation.

She hated it when she lost her temper. Anger tasted bad, it smelled bad, and it felt absolutely horrible, like some industrial giant had dumped toxic waste directly into her blood. She had found her ex-boyfriend Michael's displays of temper absurd. In the end, it was the very thing that had made it easy for her to walk away from him. Since she spent most of her days in perfectly equitable if thoughtful moods, she didn't understand where in the world her own flashes of aggression came from. Maybe from some deep dark place inside her—some place out of her sight. Could a person have such places and not know about them?

She consoled herself with the thought that as showdowns

go, this one had been pretty tame—no blood shed, no hot language, and the only victim was the roast. Nevertheless, it felt to Alex as if something savage had occurred. Feeling a need for cleansing, she went to her tent, fetched a towel, and headed for the showers. Taylor and Danny pulled across her path with the pickup full of students.

"Come out to the well-head with us and cool off," Danny said. Without answering, Alex threw her towel into the truck bed and climbed in.

Eyeing her, Caedyn said, "I didn't think you got mad, just superior."

"*Shut up,* Caedyn!" Marina said.

Alex fumed in silence. That Wiggins! The fact that he had provoked her into getting angry made her even angrier. She saw Kit appear behind the truck, loping behind the vehicle in its dust cloud, just keeping up.

. . . . .

Dr. Hanks did not make it back to camp that night. Rennie, Taylor, and Danny opened up work Tuesday morning with a business-as-usual manner, transporting everyone to the site.

That morning Sharp Spikes inquired as to the meaning of the skull with a red feather in it that lay on the dirt pile by the latrine. He was informed that it was a mysterious omen that had appeared on site soon after the year's excavating had begun. Caedyn told him about the "shrine" across the road and delivered his theory about how a curse had been put on the site.

Sharp scoffed. He walked to the latrine. Several people witnessed him pick up the skull and hurl it as far as he could, which was a considerable distance. It cleared the cow fence bordering the excavation and landed out of sight in the grease-wood.

Wednesday morning, Hector returned from the latrine and reported that the skull was back, only now, in place of the red feather, there dangled a long, raven-black one.

Eighteen

Later that week Alex and Rennie took a walk down Big Wash. Deer fly season had ended and the heat had killed off the no-see-ums. As they strolled down the shady washbed, Rennie told Alex about her conversation with Dr. Hanks, who had returned from Moab with a good news/bad news scenario of Harry Hoskers's condition.

The good news was that Hoskers had been released following observation for a concussion. He had orders not to drive, operate heavy machinery, or participate in strenuous exercise and to stay in bed for three days. The bad news: Hanks reported that Hoskers seemed intoxicated, almost in ecstasy over the beating. He kept saying, "I must be getting close to something!" He asked repeatedly, "Where should I go with this?"

Rennie reported that Hanks had attributed Hoskers's "enthusiasm," as he called it, to a kind of hysteria associated with shock. Rennie told Alex that she had tried once more to communicate her sense of impending disaster and asked Hanks if he had questioned Hoskers about just what it was he thought

one hundred and twenty-eight

he was getting close to. Hanks said he thought the statement had no meaning at all, considering the man's generally excitable personality and background—being an actor and all. Rennie asked Hanks what he had said to Hoskers when he had asked, "Where should I go with this?" Hanks replied that he had advised him to file a complaint with the local police.

Rennie said, "Let me guess, he said no police."

"That's right," Hanks had replied. "I guess you know our Harry."

"He wasn't talking about reprisal anyway," Rennie persisted. "That's not what he's interested in."

"What do you mean?" Hanks had asked.

"When he said, 'Where should I go with this,' he wasn't asking what kind of official action he should take. He was asking himself what the next logical step was he ought to take."

"The next step in what?" Hanks queried, irritated.

"In whatever it is he's doing!" Rennie said. "Don't you see? He's up to something! He's ... playing some sort of game, and Deeppockets is his stake!"

Rennie said that at this point, Dr. Hanks had given her a *you've been too long in the sun* look. He said, "I hear what you're saying ... I think. Now, let's get back to work."

Rennie admitted she had left in a huff. She just couldn't get past her feeling that Deeppockets was in *beaucoup* trouble, not in any obvious way, but in some intangible, karmic sort of way. She looked at Alex. "You know what I mean, don't you?" she asked.

"Yeah," Alex replied. "Tomorrow's Friday. Want to go camping?"

"What?" Rennie asked, startled. "Where?"

"The usual place—Vision Canyon," Alex said. "I need to consult the spirits."

Rennie hesitated. "Well, ... Hanks is heading home for the weekend ..."

"Taylor and Danny will be here," Alex said. "What's the matter? Don't you think the boys can do as good as you?"

"Danny won't. He's going with Hanks. Duty to girlfriend and all."

"Taylor's a stout-hearted lad," Alex said. "Won't Mike be here?"

"No, he's going, too. Personal business."

"So that leaves you and Taylor ..."

"And you, if you're here," Rennie pointed out.

"Five students, and how many of the volunteers are staying?"

"Spikes is staying. He's down for two more weeks. And the kid from Idaho—he's here for a month."

"Doris and Janice?"

"Leaving. Too hot."

Alex tallied up the sum. "You're right," she agreed. "Taylor might need help. Yeah, you better stay."

"What about you?" Rennie said. "If something happens ..."

"You mean, if *the* something happens? I don't think it's going to."

"Why not? Hoskers will be out of the hospital, and ..."

"Well, you heard what he said. He doesn't know what his next move is ... *yet*. And when he makes it, it should take a while for it all to come together."

"Or fall apart!"

Alex nodded. "Or that. We'll all be back by then."

"How do you know?" Rennie asked suddenly, grabbing Alex's arm.

"What?"

"How do you know it's going to take a while? What if someone gets hurt?"

"I don't know for sure, but chaos takes time." Alex said.

"Oh," Rennie said sarcastically, "that's very reassuring."

Alex laughed. "Just don't panic thinking about it." She recited:

> If there's no hatred in a mind
> Assault and battery of the wind
> Can never tear the linnet from the leaf.

"What's a linnet? Some kind of bug?" Rennie asked.

"It's a bird. A songbird that dispenses 'magnanimities of sound.'"

The two women rounded a bend in the wash. A flock of mourning doves drinking at a puddle burst into flight at the sight of them. Rising, they scattered a few struggling notes like those made by a rapidly plied rusty hinge. Rennie and Alex looked at each other and laughed.

. . . . .

Waking on the rim of Vision Canyon was different from the forced consciousness of the field camp's morning routine. With no wake-up calls to jerk her from sleep, Alex opened her eyes slowly. She blinked at the ceiling of the cargo space in her '67 station wagon until her vision focused. She had left the windows down overnight and the breath of a cool morning breeze moved across her face. Shifting her gaze to one of the wagon's side windows, she took stock of what she could see of the day.

No clouds, no trees, no close mesa walls obscured the view. From horizon to horizon, the sky stretched bare and blushing. Alex got up on one elbow for a better look. As soon as she stirred, Kit, who had lain curled at her feet, jumped up and made known her urgent desire to escape the vehicle.

"Okay, go on, girl," Alex said, the hoarseness in her own voice jolting her. In two bounds, Kit leaped into the back seat and out the window.

Alex took a deep breath. The place had its own perfumery, a fabric of scents she thought she would be able to recognize blindfolded. Partly in a dream state, she pushed away her bag. The fabric rattled loudly. Even her breathing resounded in her head. In an attempt to minimize the racket her every move seemed to cause, she rolled slowly, got up on her hands and knees, slid from the cargo space over the back seat divider and into the seat. Landing on her back, she lay waiting for the disturbance to die away, savoring the sweet, tender air and the naked light. Then she opened the door and put her bare feet down on the slickrock.

Oh! It was as if she had pressed her soles against the flank of a big animal that had been standing all night in the cool air. A shiver of pleasure started at the bottoms of her feet and traveled up her legs as brain and nerve endings sent a storm of sensations back and forth. Sniffing, she straightened her clothes and looked to see what Kit was doing.

The dog busied herself reading the bulletin boards, as Alex called it, checking bushes that the other animals had scent-marked, re-marking them, snuffling the ground where mosaics of tracks cross-stitched the sand.

Alex pulled her keys from her pocket and walked to the

back of the car. She inserted one into the keyhole to release the crank, wound down the back window, and pulled out the tailgate. It folded down, providing a good seat for taking in the view.

Early morning had begun to swell with a silvery pink light low on the horizon, changing in its ascent to a mercurial blue. It seemed to Alex that beside herself, Kit, and some birds, the only thing moving in the immense silence was the crescent light, and that slipped into the sky noiselessly.

She knew she had to get a move on before the heat woke up. She fired up her camping stove to heat water for her chocolate and poured some homemade granola into a bowl. She put out some food and water for Kit, then rolled out a Green River melon. She brought her big cutting knife down on the melon and it broke with a loud crack of the rind. Its fruity odor splashed into the air.

Breakfast seemed to last forever. Her senses rushed to every point of stimulation. The cinnamon she put into her hot chocolate caused a taste-bud rush. By the end of her breakfast, she felt transformed. Her blood was aroused, growing sharp in her veins. Down in her lungs she could taste the good of the place.

Shouldering her pack, she called Kit, and they hit the trail heading into the canyon. The upper trail crossed the smooth backs of great rocks, which forced the angles of Alex's feet and ankles to change until all of her lower leg muscles had had a good stretch. Near the end of the trail, the path softened underfoot and she sank nearly ankle deep in sand. She waded through and dropped into the canyon bottom, Kit keeping slightly ahead.

Today she had no intention of visiting the pictograph panel. She turned in the opposite direction to see another place of great importance to her. Like an oyster shell, its external appearance belied the pearl hidden within. She called this place the Water Temple.

The Water Temple was a shallow, water-sliced tributary—hardly even that much—that at its entrance confessed nothing to the passer-by. It looked like a straggly little arroyo holding no promise, especially in comparison to the splendor of the Panel and the other wonders up canyon.

She hiked for about a quarter mile until she found it. She scanned the arroyo for footprints. Other than lizard scrabble, there were none. Whistling softly to Kit to signal her change of direction, she started up the arroyo.

She picked her steps carefully. The Water Temple stood in her mind as a truly tender place. She understood it would be easy to violate its tenderness. Up ahead, Kit crisscrossed the arroyo, nose earthward, blue eyes distant.

A pair of scrub jays took exception to their presence and raked the silence with harsh cries. Alex passed quickly so they might quiet. She walked under what she thought must be one of the oldest and most perfectly formed junipers anywhere. Its dry, sweet, terpene odor dropped on her from the foliage.

Heat built up fast in the canyon, as probably it was doing in Camp Greasewood where Rennie would be trying to cope with the rising angst to which the project seemed to be falling victim. She wished Rennie had been able to come, but she understood why she hadn't. Rennie was highly responsible and duty-bound, which is why Dr. Hanks treated her as the second-in-command at the field school. She guarded the project's interests with ferocity. But if Hanks continued to ignore signs of trouble, her role would be reduced to that of a camp Cassandra. Alex knew that of all things, that would be the most painful fate Rennie could suffer. Ah well, what would happen, would happen.

The wash broadened into a fan of moist sand. The walls, too, widened to form a rounded chamber capped by an azure disc of sky. Just a few yards away lay a shallow plunge pool. Kit waded in and drank noisily. In the talus slope behind the pool, water glittered around three moss-framed, stone-keyed seeps. The wiry and crooked little streams stepped and ruffled down slope to empty into the pool.

Alex sighed. All that existed in the world were the seeps, tinkling like liquid chimes, and Alex, her sympathetic chords thrumming in response. Water in the desert—sunlight's perfect foil. Here were veins of it—capillaries, really—weaving their way singing *Take, take, only enough and no more.*

Out of faith that the seeps would be running, Alex had carried little water in, only one bottle mostly gone now and one empty. The seep on the far left dripped faster than the others. Each time it was different, which one seeped fastest. Choosing her steps to avoid damaging a garden of columbines, she climbed to the far seep.

She propped one bottle under the fastest dripping seep and set a second in the next. Compared to the faucet blasts of modern plumbing, these beads dropped ever so slowly. She guessed that if you depended on a place like this to sustain you, you planned your thirsts. You waited for the water to come to you; you couldn't force it. If she wanted, she could count how many drops fell as they plunked like pearls down broken green strings of moss. All around her, echoes played off stone walls—whispers reciting tonal charms.

Surely this was a deliberate place. Alex got the impression that it had shaped itself by some notion or choice, perhaps even by inspiration. Geologically, it could be considered a happenstance of nature. As some said, in any realm of the great kingdom of Serendipity, elements and natural forces happily and unexpectedly discovered each other in glorious cosmic accidents.

But there are no accidents, Alex thought. Things came to where they were or to where they met through choice. Choice shone as a facet of probability, and probability a facet of—what? Creation? And creation shone in long, illumined and illuminating rays, shafting and fanning from—where? Some said they didn't come from anywhere, they just were: beauty is its own excuse for being.

But as Alex gazed around the Water Temple, she thought that beauty is not its own excuse. Objects or the confluence of events that people respond to for their beauty seize upon the soul, provoking a desire that Alex thought of as a harbinger of *Other.* Alex was irresistibly attracted to *Other,* even though in her experience, encounters with it required heaping dearly held beliefs upon a flame-licked altar. In return, the conflagration yielded generous pay-off. Eye opening and song inspiring, *Other* enfolded the soul into a boundless, native economy, a multiplicity and replenishment leading to both satiety and desire simultaneously. *No,* she thought, *there's a good chance beauty directs the gaze to something beyond itself.*

Alex had read or listened to words from others like herself who adored Nature and spoke of preserving it. Some pilgrims, stricken by visions that the earth and her skies conjure, seemed to try to make it a lover, a parent, a goddess. Alex suspected that at least a few who sought to defend Nature from the ravages of humankind in turn exploited it on other levels by forcing upon it imagery and intentions shaped wholly upon fixed self-images, sorrows suffered, innocence lost. Then in such cases, and to varying degrees, perhaps it was themselves they were hastening to defend, salvage, or preserve.

But then ... maybe that was exactly right—voices of the earth speaking loss and longing. Parts of the earth mourning over exploitation suffered, struggling to survive. Yes, Alex mused, it was possible: being of the earth, people shared its fate right down to the cellular level and all that trouble raised voice in these ways, crying out.

But as Alex crouched beside the seep, it seemed to her that the earth traded life and light across an eternity of being. If that was so, then perhaps Nature could take care of itself. Maybe beauty, the kind that shakes mortal understanding by the scruff of its neck, is inviolable. Through cataclysms of renewal, it will return and reclaim its ground.

"More to the point, what about me?" Alex asked. "Am I capable of renewal like that?" She had made changes, of course, but like she imagined it might be done, on a grand scale, elements a-swirl, crossing corridors in an *Augenblick*, taking on new names? *No! Yes!* "Not just at this moment."

She gazed around the chamber like a fledgling that sees the edge of the nest with an eye suddenly wide to the peril in its own wings. Below her, the plunge pool lay flat, its silvered surface bending back pale images of cliff and sky.

Water in the desert was both mirror and window. And the

sky overhead was a blue-backed mirror by day, hemming in our consciousness and our image of the present, and an open glassless eternity at night filled with rippling and eddying times and events of light and fire—the pyrotechnics of *worlds without end.* Water and sky, Alex thought—our torment and our relief as they intimate that we are not self-sustaining, nor is the present an end unto itself or all that could ever be.

Nineteen

Coyote kept watch over the comings and goings of the camp from a place high above. Also, he had Burnt Woman to tell him everything. Burnt Woman! At the thought of her, First Angry grimaced in disgust. Such a pale, pitiful thing—so easy to manipulate, he almost didn't need to think. A cruel word here, an ambiguous one there—a sharp blow, then a caress—and she fell down worshiping. Worshiping in her tormented way, as so many worshiped whatever terrifying power it was that held them in subjection. Little people with shriveled souls. Why such common, witless creatures clung so desperately to the ankles of life, he didn't know. In the case of the woman, had she been a dog, he would have put her out of her misery long ago like the Coyote he was.

The gods did not name me First Angry for nothing! He scoffed. He was through watching. He had seen enough. Each day, a complete picture came together in his head as he saw all there was to see and heard all there was to hear. He understood perfectly what was going on down there, both in camp and out at the site—*his* site, *his* ground—better than they did. Every few days, after they had gone, he slipped down and studied their work and appraised the damage. He gathered more shards to add to his collection, which was by now a wondrous construction of partial stories and songs—the sacred means of conveyance, of getting knowledge across. Forbidden knowledge, to all except ...

Suddenly he heard a sound, that familiar buzz. He knew who it was and he felt annoyed. "What is it now, Grandfather?" he asked.

"You think a lot of yourself, you with your great brain," the old rattlesnake hissed.

"What of it? What is it to you what I think?"

"I can't believe the depth of your delusion," the snake said. "You, Coyote! If anyone around here is pathetic, it's you."

Coyote faced the great rattlesnake. "And what about you, crawling across the ground on your belly, you old worm?"

Grandfather Rattlesnake stared. He had never before heard words from his grandson dripping with such venom. Being a connoisseur of fine venom himself, he knew the quality of that which he smelled distilling in Coyote's brain. He saw in Coyote's eyes a new spark. He couldn't help but admire it. That was why he had to put it down, kill it right away.

"So you want to be a snake now?" he said. "You aren't even a real coyote! Look at you, collecting trash, hoarding it as treasure. You're no better than a waif in the city, gorging yourself on throw-aways. The same with your women—all of them! You take up with such losers, shattered cast-offs you find on the trash heap, because they're the only ones who will have you. Especially this latest one, the one that's half-dead! You have no pride. Anything will do for you, no matter how putrid."

"This from the toad-eater," First Angry said. "This from the frequenter of rat dens." He had gone cold inside. *Nothing the old snake says can touch me. I am about to take my destiny into my hands. The old snake is nothing.*

"At least my prey has life to it. You seek out the dead!"

"The dead have secrets. The dead have knowledge. What do your toads and jumping rats have? Stinking fear and bulk to fill your belly. That's enough for you, but not for Coyote. Go away, old worm. Crawl off to your hole, go rob eggs from a dove's nest."

"What? Show some respect! I am your grandfather!"

"You said you weren't."

"When it's convenient, I pretend not to be. You can understand that—pretending to be or not to be one thing or another, depending on what's called for. But you and I both know how deep the relation between us runs."

"Leave me," Coyote said. He turned his back on the old snake. "If we meet again, I will kill you."

Grandfather Rattlesnake's tongue flicked in and out as he considered what to do. He decided to crawl away. "If we meet again," he said, "we will see who will kill who."

"Whom," said Coyote.

"What?"

"We will see who will kill *whom.*"

"You think you are so smart!" Grandfather Rattlesnake said. "We will see how smart you are. We will see."

Coyote did not bother to answer. *I have won and now he will leave.* He listened to the sound of Grandfather Rattlesnake's scales scraping the ground as he departed, but did not turn to watch. Instead, he gazed down on that insignificant hive of busy bees below. He heard the sound of an engine coming down the canyon and saw an old-fashioned station wagon approach from the south.

That's one of them. He watched the car turn up the road to the camp. As he did, he thought of the man, the one who believed he possessed the site. *Wait 'til they find out what he's up to now—wait 'til tomorrow when they see! Tomorrow they'll be thrown into confusion just as if someone had thrust a stick into their humming little hive.*

"It's time," he said. "Time to go down and walk among them when they'll be so distracted they won't pay attention. Time to get them used to me, to Coyote-also-called-First-Angry, walking in their midst." *Timing, timing, timing! It is everything–or nearly so.* "Tomorrow I will take the next step."

Sure of himself, Coyote trotted over the hot ground to his den, where it was cool inside, and added his latest gleanings of shards to his cache of half-secrets. *Soon,* he crooned to the shards. *Soon it will be the day.*

Twenty

Rennie was right. As soon as Harry Hoskers was physically fit for it, he made his move, and it was a shocker.

Monday morning of the third week promised more intense heat. By 10:00 a.m., the soil around the excavations was too hot to stand on barefoot, which was how Alex preferred to work. She and Rennie reached a compacted soil floor surface in the test trench in their excavation. Rennie grabbed her notebook and climbed onto a rubble mound to bring her notes up to date. Alex took advantage of what was left of the morning light to photograph the stratigraphy in a slice of the exposed earth in the trench and then draw a matching profile in her notes. She sat with a Munsell chart draped across her thigh, struggling to match real shades of earth to the ones in the chart.

A shadow fell over her. From the clean-cut silhouette and two shadow-twists of cloth standing out from the otherwise bare neckline, she knew it was Taylor's. Without looking, she said, "What do you think? Is it sandy beige or light tan?"

Taylor squatted down, shaded his eyes, and peered at the profile. "I'd say it's burnt almond."

"Or maybe butter brickle?" Alex asked.

"Or double turtle sundae delight."

"Stop it!" Alex said, giggling. "You're making me crazy!"

The whir of a truck engine laboring up the road to the site drew their attention. Rennie, sitting on top of the rubble mound, looked up. "It's Raff," she said. She closed her notebook and walked to the ramada where Dr. Hanks sat with books, notebooks, and his laptop piled around.

Other workers in Rennie's area included Hector, Josh, and a new volunteer—Lenore Hanson. Danny was engrossed, sitting on the edge of his kiva keeping notes. Sharp, Chris, and Caedyn were working down inside its well-like cavern.

"Yeah," Taylor said. "Science makes a gallant effort to standardize data, yet it all comes down to how your researcher in the field colors what's in front of him."

"That's profound, Taylor," Alex said.

"Yep," he said. "It's all comes down to what we think we see."

Uh-oh, Alex thought. *This is leading somewhere.* She shaded her eyes and looked up.

"Take Marina," Taylor said.

At the mention of Marina's name, Alex knew what was coming. "How is the sweet child?" she asked, taking up the game.

"Fine, fine," Taylor said, glancing in the direction of his excavation. "She *is* a sweet child, isn't she?" he asked.

Alex nodded sagely.

"Easily misled," Taylor continued.

"Oh?" Alex asked. "How so?"

"She seems to have gotten the impression from somewhere, can't imagine where, that I'm married and have two children, all very hush-hush."

Alex's face was all shock and surprise. "No!"

"Yes. Odd, isn't it?"

Alex nodded. "*Very* odd," she agreed, squelching a guilty smile.

"Where do you suppose," he rolled his hand to prompt her, "she could have gotten such an idea?" He raised his eyebrows as if pleading for advice.

Alex shrugged. "There's no accounting for some people's thinking."

"True. Still, I can't help but be a bit concerned. One could consider such gossip about one to be disparaging."

Alex nodded sympathetically. "Scurrilous," she said.

"Uncalled for."

"How about contumelious?" Hector offered from over at the screen where he stood sorting through the dregs of a bucket of dirt from Rennie's excavation.

"What does contumelious mean?" Danny asked from over at the kiva without looking up from his notes.

"Contumelious?" Caedyn asked from inside the kiva. "Did someone just make up that word?"

"Well," Taylor said in a low voice so that only Alex could hear, "I'm sure I can count on your good judgment to quash any further rumors on the subject."

"I shall defend your honor vigorously," Alex said. "Secretly married with two children. The very idea!"

At that moment Rennie reappeared at the top of the

mound, face drawn. "Brace yourself," she said to Taylor. He scrambled up the mound to meet her. Danny set aside his notebook and joined them. Rennie drew them off in order to be out of hearing of the students and volunteers. Alex returned to her struggle with the profile. She heard Rennie's voice rise, pitched with frustration, but she couldn't make out her words.

Soon the little band of crew chiefs broke, Taylor trotting back to his burial. Rennie sat down beside Alex, shaking her head.

"What's going on?" Alex asked.

"Raff came to warn us that Harry's on his way with Jep Randall."

"Randall," Alex said. "Of the Randall pot hunting clan?"

Rennie nodded. "Yep. Arvard, the really infamous one, is his uncle, but it's more or less the whole family's favorite pastime."

"So," Alex said, "Harry Hoskers, owner of an Ancient Puebloan site clear out in the middle of nowhere, is playing host to a member of a notorious pot hunting family."

Rennie nodded. "That sums it up."

"How soon are they getting here?"

"Raff guesses he left Blanding only twenty minutes ahead of them."

"Pot hunters coming to afternoon tea on an excavation site," Alex said. "Weird!"

"I don't know how I'm going to endure this."

"Hey, it'll only be for the day, maybe even for an hour. You know Hoskers—short attention span."

But Jep Randall's visit to the site wasn't for an hour, nor was it only for a day. When Harry Hoskers introduced the new "volunteer" around, he announced that he and Jep would be coming out to the site every day that week. Jep, Harry explained, wanted to see firsthand "how them archaeologists do it."

Among the crew chiefs, the change in mood was severe, Rennie's being the worst. To her, Jep Randall's presence made the site vulnerable. Not having any say in the matter frustrated her and increased her sense that the excavation could spin out of control at any time. Loss of control was an archaeologist's worst nightmare. A lot of time and energy went into keeping control over every movement of the excavation. But it was becoming increasingly obvious that Hoskers had a different idea of what controlling the site meant.

Over at the burial, Taylor greeted Jep with cheerfulness whenever he came around. But his overall silence at other times suggested that being polite was a strain.

Attempts were made to keep Jep away from Taylor and the midden area, a pot hunter's usual target, and over on the opposite side of the dig at the pueblos with Rennie and Danny. But Jep didn't feel himself to be under the usual constraints of site visitors. Often he stopped work and without explanation wandered over to Taylor's excavation like iron filings drawn to a magnet.

"Geez!" Rennie said through gritted teeth as Jep embarked on another of his migrations to the burial. "Let's just let the coyote have the run of the lambs."

"What's Hanks thinking?" Alex asked.

"That it's good P. R., potentially educational for the pot hunter. He says to mind our manners and make old Jep feel like he's at home."

"And Hoskers—what's he up to?"

Rennie shrugged. "Who knows?"

On the third day of Jep's and Harry's visit to the site, Jep crossed the line. As he poked and scraped in Danny's kiva, his boredom with the whole business erupted. "You guys are wastin' your time here," he said as he climbed out of the kiva and stood on its edge. "That over there's where the good stuff is." He indicated the midden with a jerk of his head.

"Some might think so," Rennie said with just a touch of sarcasm in her voice. "I suppose it all depends on why we're here, doesn't it?"

Jep took off his hat and scratched his head, a twisted grin spreading across his whiskered jaw. "Ma'am, you and me—we ain't so different," he said in a falsely good-natured tone as if acknowledging some secret understanding.

"Then you must think we're pretty dumb," Danny said, "spending so much time over here where there isn't any good stuff."

Jep laughed, looking toward Taylor's excavation. "You gotta do what you gotta do to make it look legit, but come on now, 'fess up."

Alex decided to keep out of this one and began excavating a square of fill.

"This place must be loaded," Jep continued. "Plenty for everybody!"

Rennie's notebook slammed shut.

Alex caught her attention. *Careful!* she mouthed. *Don't let him get to you.*

Just then Dr. Hanks came over the rubble mounds with Harry in tow. As if he were hosting a cocktail party, he greeted everyone cheerfully. "Well!" he said, a hopeful grin lighting his face. "How's it going over here?"

That did it. Rennie stalked off her excavation, heading, Alex assumed, for Rafferty, who made a point of coming to the site every day Hoskers and Randall were present.

At lunch later that morning, Rennie and Rafferty were conspicuously absent. Dr. Hanks sat with furrowed brow as if puzzling over a mystery. As the students and remaining two chiefs broke to return to work, Hoskers and Jep Randall left the site, citing "pressing business" but promising to return the next morning.

"Having a great time," Hoskers said as he loaded himself and Jep Randall into his truck. "I *love* this place."

As Alex left the ramada, Hanks stopped her. "Hey McKelvey," he said gruffly.

Alex turned and looked at him.

"Think you can handle Ross's excavation 'til she gets back?"

Alex shrugged. "I guess so," she said.

"Appreciate it," he said.

"But remember, I'm an English major, not an archaeologist!" She laughed and took a few steps in the direction of Rennie's excavation.

"Uh, McKelvey?"

Alex stopped again and turned around, eyebrows raised.

"Am I ... did something ... happen out there this morning?"

"You have to ask?" Alex replied.

"Uh ... well, what was it, if I may ask?"

"There's a pot hunter on the site, imported by the man

who took us out on a tour of pot hunted sites not two weeks ago. Hoskers and his pet pot hunter have been here three days, more than enough time to worry your crew chiefs, who feel like the project is being set up big time. Said pot hunter has been getting the red carpet treatment, being permitted to wander the site at whim." She paused. "What's wrong with this picture?"

"Did this guy say something to Rennie?" he asked.

"He said it to everyone," Alex said. "Rennie just had the strongest reaction."

Hanks's face lit up with understanding, but only for a moment. "She walked off the site with Raff," he said. "Why didn't she come to me?"

"She *has* been coming to you," Alex said. "Now excuse me, please, but there are a bunch of scorched students loose over there with shovels and trowels."

"Carry on, McKelvey," Hanks said. Alex trotted over the mounds to the excavation.

When she arrived, Danny asked, "Where's Rennie gotten herself to?"

"AWOL with Rafferty, apparently," Alex replied. "Hanks is sitting under the ramada without a clue."

Danny shook his head. "Who's managing these roustabouts?" he asked, indicating Rennie's crew. "Me?"

"No, me. Dr. Hanks appointed me temporary crew chief." Alex saluted.

"Good for you!" Danny said, then more mutedly, "At least Hoskers and Randall left. Did you tell Hanks what happened?"

"He got the picture."

"Then maybe he'll fix it so they don't come back."

"Don't count on it. Hanks is at Hoskers's mercy, too, you know."

"Hey!" Spikes called from down inside the kiva. His head popped up and he looked around for Danny. "Come see what I found, Boss Man!"

"What is it?" Danny asked.

"Bones! A skeleton of ... something!" Everyone went over to peer down into Danny's kiva.

"Wow! Great!" Danny exclaimed. "Chris, run over and get Taylor." He looked up at Alex. "Rennie isn't here and bones aren't my forte."

"It's some kind of animal," Sharp said. "Maybe a bird?"

"Maybe it's a turkey," Caedyn said. "We've been finding all this turkey bone. They raised turkeys, you know."

"Not in the kivas they didn't," Sharp said.

"No, wait! I see a paper coming out of this," Caedyn replied. "Exposing the terrible mistake archaeologists have been making all these years. Kivas are not religious structures after all, they're turkey pens."

"Well that explains what you're doing down here," Spikes said.

"Maybe it's an eagle skeleton," Mrs. Hanson suggested.

"Nah," Sharp said. "I've been up close and personal with eagles, and these here bones ain't big enough."

"Maybe it's a turkey eagle," another voice said.

Everybody turned to look at Hector. Sharp staggered comically.

"We-e-ll!" he exclaimed. "The professor just made a joke! First time, son?"

"Actually," Hector said, "yes."

"Sounded like it," Sharp said.

· · · · ·

Rennie returned to the site half an hour before quitting time, looking as if some of her burden had been lifted. Alex informed her of the find in Danny's kiva. She hurried over to have a look.

"Taylor said it's probably some kind of hawk," Danny said.

Rennie nodded. "Probably red-tail."

"*Buteo jamaicensis,*" Hector said.

Rennie looked at him. "Really?"

Hector nodded.

From down inside the kiva, Danny asked, "What would a turkey-eagle be?"

"Well, the wild turkey is *Meleagris gallopavo* or something like that. As for the eagle half of this mythical creature, I would suggest the golden eagle which is, ah, *Aquila*, uh, *Aquila chrysaetos*, I think."

"So," said Danny, "would it be *Aquila gallopavo* or *Meleagris chrysaetos*?"

"Oh, I like the sound of that second one!" Alex said.

"Me, too," said Rennie.

"*Meleagris chrysaetos* it is, then," Danny said.

Hanks came around to call quitting time. Everyone collected the gear and headed for the vehicles. When they arrived in camp, Alex helped Rennie unload the coolers. Carrying the largest one between them, they walked toward the kitchen.

Rennie said, "What a terrible day. I feel like things just keep getting worse."

Alex had noticed a beat-up, faded blue Honda sitting in

the camp's parking lot. She figured the camp had a visitor, but the distinctive voice she heard coming from the mess tent snagged her attention like a treble hook. She looked for its source. Her eyes rested on a man sitting next to Heather Barton.

As Alex took in the look of him, a bolt went through her, head to toe. She stopped abruptly, yanking Rennie backwards as she did. The mess area seemed to transform. Every foot of dirt, every glint of light seemed suddenly inflamed with significance. Alex had never had an out-of-body experience, but the sight of the stranger jerked her out of the bounds of the moment and sent her reeling to a psychic plane or a place in her soul where she'd never been—someplace incorporeal and energetic or maybe instinctual. She felt a flash of confusion at the sensation.

What in the world? Did she *know* this man? She stared, searching her soul for the source of an impression that felt like a memory. But if she had ever met the guy, she'd remember, wouldn't she? Whoever he was, he had a gloss to him that made Alex think of a polished apple that had fallen from an ominous tree. His black hair, sleek, falling past his collar, had a faint wave to it so that here or there a curl went boyishly wrong. His dark eyes were nearly as black as his hair. His skin, tinted something like Alex's own, reflected a mixed gene pool. He could pass as a member of just about any Middle Eastern or Mediterranean people or maybe even as Hispanic. He had a strong, animated jaw line, and when he smiled—which he often did in a deliberate fashion—he flashed a set of the whitest teeth Alex had ever seen. His bare arms, stretched on the table before him, were long and brown and strung like bows with fit muscle.

Without realizing she said it aloud, she asked, "Who is that?"

Rennie looked. The man sat shoulder to shoulder with Heather, leaning against her, provoking strained smiles and a high blush on her sun- and life-burnt face.

"Looks like a friend of Heather's," Rennie said, her voice grim.

"Some friend!" Alex said.

"No kidding. Looks dangerous."

"Deadly." Alex winced as she said it. She wasn't sure where that had come from. She had no idea what the man was like ... although somehow she felt that she did. Alex sensed that he was aware of her. In fact, she had the impression that he was aware of everything. Was it just her or did he have a palpable presence, an air about him that she could feel, something forceful and unwholesome?

She looked for Kit. The husky walked among the field school students and volunteers, seemingly unconcerned about the newcomer. Rennie renewed her course toward the kitchen, dragging Alex along.

"Alex, it's not polite to stare," Rennie warned. But it was too late.

Twenty-One

The stranger turned to see Alex staring. He nodded and smiled that white, perfect smile—a seducer's smile. On a deep level, Alex recognized it. And the flashing eyes of a predator. Still, his look had a powerful effect. Heat flooded her cheeks. She felt disoriented, as if the world were spinning. His eyes didn't linger, but as though the greeting was incidental, he turned back to Heather. As Rennie pulled Alex into the kitchen, Alex craned her neck to peer between the wooden tent supports for another look.

But now she wasn't staring just at him, she was taking it all in, the whole scene. Heather Barton—shy, abused, faint-hearted —being petted, coaxed, and cajoled by—what was that creature? Alex didn't have a word for it, but on a deep level she understood that Heather was in trouble.

Poor Heather! Alex hoped that the woman's self-defensive instincts would kick in and send her screaming from the tent and the danger courting her there. But Heather's face, anxious though it was as she prepared for the daily artifact cleaning, glowed with something that would have been charming had it been inspired by someone other than the man sitting beside her. Heather's face shone with hope. Alex's mind did back flips in alarm. Whatever it was that the stranger was selling, Heather had already bought it.

Rennie gripped Alex's arm and dragged her bodily from the mess area.

"Wait!" Alex said. "I have to find out who that is."

"No you don't," Rennie said. "You have to pull yourself together."

"Rennie!"

"No, Alex!" she hissed. "You're coming with me."

Reluctantly, Alex allowed Rennie to lead her away. She knew Rennie was right. She ought to hide out and cool off her mind, which felt like it was on fire.

But as Rennie forced her toward their tent, Alex felt drawn back to the mess by a nearly irresistible urge—more than an urge and something beyond a gut response. The sight of the stranger had aroused some old knowledge in her, something in her very core. But what and why? Alex gritted her teeth. Something about him seemed familiar, but—impossible! She was sure they'd never met.

"What's wrong with you?" Rennie asked. "You act like you've seen a ghost!"

"It's that guy."

"Yes, I know—what about him? Alex, do you *know* him?"

"I already said I don't!"

"But you act like you do."

Alex blinked. "I don't, and I don't know what's wrong with me. Something about him just grabs at me. I have to find out who he is."

"You want some advice?"

"What?"

"Stay clear. He and Heather have something going on, although what, I can't imagine. He looks *way* out of her league."

Alex could barely focus on what Rennie was saying. "I've got to go back," she said. She started to turn, but Rennie blocked her way.

"What are you doing?" Alex asked.

"What are *you* doing? Look, do me this favor, okay? Just come out to the tent, sit down, and try to think."

Alex hesitated. "Okay." They walked to the tent and Rennie herded her inside.

"Normally I wouldn't interfere with your *peculiar* inclinations, but I've never seen you like that. Another ten seconds and I think you would have caused a scene."

"Really? Huh," Alex said. She had to force herself to pay attention.

"You locked on to him like a weapons tracking device. What's going on?"

"I don't know."

Rennie sighed in exasperation. "Well, if this is some sort of love at first sight, it's really twisted."

"What are you talking about? It isn't that."

"Then what is it? Alexandra McKelvey, you have got to cool it, whatever it is. We've got a field school to run here."

"*That's* what you're worried about—the *field school?*"

"No, of course not! I'm worried about you. Look, if you're going to do this—this whatever—why don't you just watch him from a distance? Don't slink right up to him and call him out."

Alex chuckled. "I guess I do feel like that—like I want to call him out."

"Yes," Rennie said. "And what has he done to you?"

Before Alex knew what she was saying, she blurted, "It's not what he's done. It's what he's going to do."

Rennie looked repulsed. "Oh ... oh ... that *is* sick!" she said.

· · · · ·

Taking Rennie's advice, Alex managed to keep her distance from Heather's strange boyfriend except during the artifact session when he sat at the table with Heather, Alex, and the students cleaning and labeling artifacts. Alex was struck by how familiar he was with the process. Clearly, he had experience in the field. Alex shrugged. Why was that a surprise? Being an archaeologist, Heather would know other archaeologists, and possibly, sparks would fly, and then ...

But as Alex watched the two of them together, she asked herself, *What's wrong with this picture?* The stranger reeked of practiced confidence while Heather could hardly bear passing scrutiny.

And what was his name? Alex avoided an introduction but listened in on conversations for someone to mention it. Maybe his name would give her some clue as to who or what he was. But nobody said it. Perhaps they didn't know.

Just as Alex began to think he didn't have a name, only a presence, Heather pulled a large shard from one of the artifact bags and said, "Look at this one, Tony."

Tony. Didn't sound familiar. Alex was sure she didn't know a single Tony. The students accepted his presence as they would any other volunteer—except for Marina, whom Alex had come to rely on as a social barometer. She sat watching Tony and Heather with a clear air of perplexity. Once when Alex slipped a glance at Tony, she noticed Marina looking at her with those alert brown eyes.

Tony stayed through dinner and then spent the rest of the evening at Heather's tent. Alex avoided hers. She went for a walk with Kit, and when she returned at twilight, she checked to see if the beat-up Honda was still in the lot. It was.

She glanced around the mess. He wasn't there—probably still with Heather at the tent. And where was Rennie? Back at the site, probably.

Alex sat in the mess tent at one of the outer tables. Wiggins was working in the kitchen and the generator was running. The two bulbs that provided their sad light to the eating area glimmered faintly against the desert night. Kit flopped into the duff—as usual, her body divided in half between the weak light from the bulbs and the darkness beyond the tent, the line being drawn across her body by the shadow of the tent's eaves. Straining to see into the dark, Alex could just make out the back of Kit's head. Her ears stood erect to the front. She panted softly. Even with the generator running, she followed sounds from far beyond the camp's borders.

Wiggins finished cleaning and turned off the generator and retired to his tent. The resulting quiet came as a relief to Alex's ears. Marina and Josh sat together at the fire. Everyone else was either out walking in the canyon or in their tents or the showers.

Suddenly, Kit bent her body around and looked toward the path that led to their tent, where the stranger materialized from the darkness. He paused at the fire to speak to Marina and Josh. A muffled conversation ensued. Alex supposed that Marina, true to her social consciousness, would ask questions to satisfy her curiosity about Tony's presence in camp. Alex had questions too, but for her, finding the answers would require a more probing kind of perception than what the interchange of question and answer could provide. It would be interesting to talk with Marina later, though, to see what her take was on the guy.

His business at the fire over, he walked toward the mess on his way to the parking lot. Alex tried to pull a Heather and go invisible, but Tony spotted her.

"Hello," he said. He tapped his finger to his temple. "Alex—right?"

That voice! Alex thought that if the man wasn't somehow so false, his voice alone could call forth flowers through snow. She barely glanced at him. Why? To put him off or because she didn't trust herself?

"And you're Tony."

"Tony Balbo."

Balbo—Mediterranean, then.

"Mind if I sit with you?"

"It might be hard to find your way out of this canyon if it gets any darker."

Tony chuckled. "Don't worry about me. I know my way around."

Alex risked a glance. In the darkness, his looks weren't so devastating. "I suppose you do," she said.

He sat in a chair two down from hers, leaned back, and put his hands behind his head, taking his leisure. For a few moments he sat there in silence.

Alex waited.

"So," he said at last. "Is Alex short for something—Alexandra, perhaps?"

"Yes."

"A good name, Alexandra—strong, yet obviously feminine."

His point sounded somehow immodest. Alex shivered. She didn't reply.

"I had a friend named Alexandra once. She went by 'Xandra.'"

"How 'bout that," Alex said flatly.

Tony caught her reticence but seemed undaunted. "Have you been with this project from the beginning?"

"I have," Alex replied.

"Are you a student or a crew chief? You must be a crew chief since you appear to have a certain status in the group ..."

Alex cut short the flattery. "I'm not an archaeology student. I'm an English major—not crew chief material."

"Really?" Tony said. "And here all this time I thought you were an archaeologist like the rest of these fine people."

"All what time?" Alex asked.

"This time," he laughed. Again the music. In anyone else, it would be attractive, Alex thought. "Since I saw you when you came in with the rest."

"Mm," Alex grunted.

"You must like it," he said.

"Like what?" Alex was being completely uncharitable, but not without reason. She sensed that assuming what Tony meant would be making a mistake. She wanted him to spell out everything.

"Why, all of it—the physical labor, the archaeology, the heat, the light ..."

Alex snagged on his inclusion of the light. As a matter of fact, the light *was* important to her. She had never met anyone who had even mentioned it. At least, not so appreciatively.

She looked at him with a little more openness. "The light *is* something, isn't it?"

"It is," he said. "It has a presence of its own." His voice was subdued but plush. For the first time, Alex heard something in it that approached sincerity. She decided to take a chance.

"Um, have we met before?" she asked.

Again a peculiar energy charged the air as if she were on the verge of *feeling* his response like a fine mist or the heat of a flame. The sense of familiarity was dizzying. She dropped her eyes and emotionally backed away.

"You think we know each other?" he asked.

Alex winced. That wasn't at all what she'd said. Turning her words like that felt rather like a game play, a strategy—turning her words and answering her question with a question. She decided right then that she wasn't even going to try to like him.

"I simply thought we might have met before," she replied, irritated.

Tony leaned forward in his chair as if regarding her more closely. "Perhaps in another life," he answered. "Or maybe another world."

A stabbing chill ran down her spine and she nearly cried out. A voice in her head said, *Give him no more of your language.* When she didn't respond, he fell silent. Alex thought she had put him off enough that he would take the hint and move on, but he didn't. He sat there in the shadows with her as if he had a world of time on his hands and was waiting for something.

Alex's irritation mounted. *What's he hanging around for? Why doesn't he leave?* Another thought hit her. *What am I waiting for? Why don't I leave?*

Just as she was about to head for her tent, he spoke. "Your Mr. Hoskers was in camp earlier today."

There he was doing it again—presuming. "He's not *my* Mr. Hoskers," she said.

Tony ignored her jab. "He was in the company of a well-known pot hunter. Rather poor taste, don't you think? Bringing a pot hunter to an archaeological dig?"

Alex's interest sharpened. How did Tony know the pot hunter was well-known? "Yes, very poor taste, but ..."

"It's Mr. Hoskers's site."

"That's right, it's his site." She wondered how far she dared indulge her curiosity. She decided to go for it. "You know Jep Randall?"

"Not personally, no. One hears stories. Mr. Hoskers I know slightly better."

"From L.A.?" Maybe that's where Tony had cultivated his slick manner and appearance.

He laughed. "No, never touch the place! I've worked in the Four Corners area, and over the last few years Mr. Hoskers has gained something of a reputation."

"Mind saying as what?"

"Some say ... as an inexhaustible intruder."

Alex had the distasteful impression that, while she was probing Tony for information, he was doing the same with her. Or maybe, she thought, he was trying to cultivate common ground between them on the mutual dislike of someone else. Either way, Alex wasn't going to buy it. "Aren't we all," she said.

"Aren't we all what?"

"Inexhaustible intruders."

Tony chuckled a throaty, lilting chuckle. Once more, he let the silence close between them. After a moment, he leaned forward, squinting into the darkness. "That your dog?" he asked.

"Yep," Alex said.

"What's her name?"

"Kit."

"Ah!" he said, settling back into his chair. "I'll bet she looked like a kit fox when she was a pup, with those big ears."

Alex felt another flash of surprise. Tony was absolutely right. When Kit was a skinny, big-eared pup covered with beige puppy down, she had indeed reminded Alex of a kit fox she had seen in her headlights one night as she drove through the desert. Alex had named her pup after that kit fox. How did he do that—call certain things so closely like a gypsy fortune teller?

With difficulty, she forced herself to sit still and continue her wait. Tony swayed back and forth, trying to see Kit's head. "A beautiful animal," he said. "Hey Kit! Come here, Kit."

Kit flicked back an ear, but no more. When Alex saw this, she went on alert. Now something was going to happen.

"Kit!" He whistled low.

Kit panted lightly, continuing her surveillance of the night. It was as if he wasn't even there.

Tony made kissing noises at the dog.

Again her ear twitched, but that was it.

This time Tony's chuckle sounded a flat note. "What's the matter with your dog?" he asked. "Is she deaf?"

Alex didn't answer.

"Come on, call your dog over, Alexandra! I'd like to see her face."

Alex cringed at the use of her full first name. But she continued to sit without answering.

He tried again. "Kit! Come here."

Alex heard the silk in his voice tear just a little.

"Alexandra, call your dog for me."

Alex didn't respond.

"Call the damn dog," he said, a menacing tone rising in his voice.

The command provoked her. "No," she said.

"What do you mean, no? *Call* her."

Alex stood. Looking Tony full in his shadowy face, she said, "If she wanted to come, she would come." She turned her back on him and walked away from the mess tent. Kit rose and trotted ahead of her.

Well, *that* had gone nicely! In spite of her promises to proceed cautiously, she had, after all, called the man out. And why? She had no idea!

Behind her, Tony Balbo sat in startled, angry silence. Alex could feel his rage flaring up in the darkness at her back. An interesting artifact of the man's complicated gestalt, she thought. But what did it mean? *It means,* Alex thought, anxiousness burning in her chest, *it means I've started something I don't know how to finish.*

· · · · ·

Friday dawned, generous in its heat. Harry Hoskers and Jep Randall had taken Thursday off but were there bright and early Friday. Having gotten a rise out of Rennie two days earlier, Jep harried the crew with his "You guys is the same as us" theme. To make matters worse, he didn't leave after lunch with Hoskers as he had in the days previous. Waving Hoskers on, he said he'd get a ride into town with Rafferty.

Wondering whether or not Tony Balbo's faded blue Honda would be in the parking lot when they returned to camp, Alex paid little attention to the pot hunter riding shoulder to shoulder with her and the students in the Suburban. As they pulled into the camp, she saw with a mixture of relief and disappointment that Tony wasn't there.

Jep waited in the mess area while Rafferty, Dr. Hanks, and the crew chiefs had a pow-wow in the big tent. Jep had just asked Caedyn where the latrine was when Mike Greaves swung the pickup into the parking lot.

At Mike's request, Jack had gone with him to help tie up details in the survey work. Jack had proven useful out on survey, showing a talent for noting even the sheerest lithic or tiniest pottery fragment that might indicate a site. Whether or not Jack had heard about Jep's presence at Deeppockets that week, nobody knew. He kept to himself enough that it was just possible that he hadn't. Alex happened to be in the mess tent to witness the scene that unfolded.

Jep looked up to see who had arrived. His face brightened in surprise when he saw Jack and Mike walking toward him. The two were talking and weren't aware of Jep's presence until he announced it.

"We-e-ell! If this ain't the darndest thing! If it ain't Cousin Jack walkin' into this here archaeological camp like he lived here!"

At the sound of Jep's voice, Jack looked up. His face paled.

He stopped short, staring at the pot hunter with what looked to Alex like absolute horror.

"We-e-ell!" Jep said again, striding over to him. "Baby Jack! You haven't gone legit on us, have ya?" He drew even with Jack and slapped him hard on the back.

Jack looked around as if to gauge the damage Jep was doing him, then gave up, swallowed hard, and endured it. "What are *you* doing here?" he asked, his voice tight.

"I'm gettin' me an ed-u-cay-shun like you, Cousin!" Jep answered jovially. "Courtesy of the Lone Ranger."

Jack swallowed hard again and shook Jep's arm off his shoulder. "I've got to go take a shower," he said. He took a step forward, stopped, looked around camp at half of the field school staring at him, then plunged through the greasewood toward his tent.

"I'll bet you do, Little Jack," Jep called after him. "Hop on into the shower and scrub yourself down real good. See if it makes ya any cleaner." He put his hands on his hips and brayed out a laugh. Then he turned to the stunned group staring at him. "That there's my cousin, John Randall Reed, Uncle Arvard's little sister's youngest. He used to go out with us when he was just a little 'un. That boy there—he had the touch."

Rafferty exited the mess tent and grabbed Jep by the arm. "C'mon Jep. Time we headed to town."

"Wait, wait!" Jep said. "I've got to use the can."

"We'll stop along the road. Get in!" Rafferty ordered. He led him to his beat-up truck and opened the door. Jep started to climb in but stopped to take a parting shot.

"Don't think this is it!" he shouted. "I think I like it here—I think I like it a lot!"

"Shut up, Jep!" Raff said, shoving him the rest of the way into the truck. Then Raff got in, slapped his truck into gear, and tore off down the road.

After a few stunned moments, the buzz started. Someone said, "Jack's a pot hunter? He's so *quiet!*" Alex looked over at the crew chiefs. All three were staring at Dr. Hanks.

"Don't look at me!" Dr. Hanks said. "How was I supposed to know?"

Alex smiled. Her mind went back to that day in the alcove and Jack's strong response to the discovery of the mummified infant. Tony and the machinations of his soul might be a mystery to her, but *this* ... this was something Alex figured she *did* understand.

Twenty-Two

Coyote felt out of sorts. He had stalked Rabbit but she had kicked up her heels in his face and leapt out of reach. She'd surprised him and his anger had erupted, but after only a moment, it was pacified. He saw that she had not gone far, which as much as said, "You there, you Coyote! You try again."

"I *will* try again," Coyote said, chuckling. "Yes indeed I will."

Coyote had forgotten the dream about the Rabbit with turquoise ears, but when he saw this Rabbit, it all came back. This was that same Rabbit, wolf and all. *That insulting wolf who ignores me! But then, Coyotes have always had trouble with Wolves. And what sort of Rabbit keeps company with one?*

"Yes, what sort of Rabbit?" he whispered. He felt put out by the question. He prided himself on knowing things, but something about Rabbit vexed him. It wasn't just that she'd gotten the better of him. Oh, that had stung, but the sting had in turn given way to fascination. Down to the last drop of blood in his veins, he knew her. After all, Rabbits were Coyote's favorite prey.

On the other hand, she seemed to wear ornaments of some deep mystery. What mystery? What mystery could possibly exist that Coyote did not know? And what Rabbit could carry such things so lightly?

Coyote remembered his dream of Rabbit's turquoise and jet tipped ears. Those earrings she wore when they saw each other in the camp—simple turquoise and jet disks set in the smooth and delicate lobes of her ears. *Hmm.*

The dream Rabbit had silver fur. This Rabbit had been wearing a light gray shirt with white shorts, showing, when the light hit her skin in a certain way, long, gleaming ivory thighs. *Hmm.*

Those green eyes! Oh, Coyote remembered those, all right— remembered them from the dream. *The eyes that saw me, yet didn't turn away! Oh, she'd sprung out of my reach, but that's not the same. She had leapt away, but it had been a display of her power, not a flight of fear or revulsion.*

For the first time in his life, Coyote, also called First Angry, felt something that was not hunger, though it resembled it, and something besides anger, though it had a similarly intoxicating energy. He would have to see about this Rabbit, see what she had in mind.

Really, he thought, *I am beginning to have too many women on my hands! But the other ones are mere game pieces. This one is an altogether different game.*

He looked down on the camp. "You there, Rabbit! We shall see about you," he whispered.

Twenty-Three

Just before dawn, a coyote chorus at the edge of camp rattled everyone awake. The noise ceased. In the silence that followed, clouds that had slipped in overnight absorbed glow from a sun lying below the horizon. The sky turned bright pinkish red.

Everything, foliage to tent canvas, blushed. Field school members' skins tinged sallow pink. Suddenly, the sun appeared over the mesas and morning soared fully fledged out of the east.

Taylor and Danny stood just outside the cottonwoods, gazing up at the conflagration. Alex joined them, Kit in tow. "Red sky at morning ..." they recited together.

Once the sunrise died, the heat rose rapidly. Before ten, a hot wind had kicked up, pelting the residents of the tent town with sand. The camp had planned a field trip to Hovenweep National Monument. But as the morning's unusual weather pattern unfolded, the crew chiefs grew uneasy. Dr. Hanks had departed the night before on his weekly migration north, so they were in charge.

"What d'ya think?" Rennie asked as she joined Danny and Taylor. Alex sat nearby, petting Kit. "Do we need to secure the site before starting out for Hovenweep?"

Taylor cleared his throat. "I'm almost through excavating. If a storm blows in, she could be damaged." By "she," he meant the adolescent female whose grave Hanks had discovered eroding into the arroyo.

Danny said, "The kiva's covered, but under the right conditions, it'll turn into a swimming pool. I don't know if the plastic will hold against a big blow."

The sound of a truck engine roaring toward camp broke off the discussion. Rafferty swung his pickup into the lot. "What a glum looking bunch," he said, approaching the chiefs.

"We've got a trip planned to Hovenweep ..." Rennie began.

"No such luck!" Rafferty said. "The weatherman says there's a whole raft of monster storms rolling your way. The site ain't dressed for it. You need to get out there. Probably nothing you can do to save every little thing, but maybe you can control the damage."

"How long have we got?" Danny asked.

"They say till evening, for what that's worth."

The crew chiefs sprang into action.

"Hold it!" Rafferty said. "There's more. According to Hanks, your camp looked pretty beat up after the last storm. Compared to what they say's coming, that one was just a whelp. I think it might be a good idea to evacuate."

"Evacuate!" Rennie exclaimed. "What is this, a typhoon?"

"They say it's tropical moisture from the Pacific with its punch still intact. Tucson and Phoenix reported seven deaths, a couple of missings, and lots of injuries. The National Weather Service has issued a severe thunderstorm warning for the Four Corners area. The flash flood threat is extreme."

Rennie nodded. "All right. We can't take chances with the students and volunteers. We need a plan."

Raf and the crew chiefs decided that Alex, Danny, and Taylor would run out to the site and secure it, maybe even doing a bit of pre-storm excavation. Mike and Rennie would handle the evacuation of camp. Rennie would drive the students, volunteers, and their gear into town where all could crash at Raff's till conditions improved. Taylor and Mike would remain behind to guard camp.

Rennie and Alex passed the word to the students and remaining volunteers, who included Sharp Spikes, Josh McCray, and Mrs. Hanson. Everyone broke to gather his or her belongings and secure the tents. Heather Barton, who had hung back at the edge of Raff's chat with the crew chiefs, walked through camp with an armload of belongings, loaded her Subaru, and drove away without a word to anyone.

Rennie watched her go. "Oh well," she said with a shrug. "At least she's consistent. You know what to expect—which is nothing."

Alex packed her stuff, including Kit's dishes and food, and set everything on her cot. She decided she'd leave Kit at camp while she went to the site with Taylor and Danny. Grabbing the site notebooks, she helped the men throw extra Ag-Bags and visquine into the pickup. She and Danny sat on top of the plastic sheets to prevent their whipping up in the truck's backwash.

As Taylor backed out of the lot, Alex surveyed the activities in camp. People were loading their gear into the Suburban.

Others were helping Mike carry tables and equipment into the mess tent. Hanging back at the edge of all the activity was Jack Reed.

Since his identity had been revealed, Jack had gone incommunicado except for a short conversation with Dr. Hanks. Hanks had then gone off in his characteristic rush without confiding to his chiefs the nature of the talk. The chiefs assumed that since Jack had not been expelled from the field school, Dr. Hanks had received some satisfaction concerning Jep's assertions about "Baby" Jack Reed. The current emergency had turned the crew chiefs' concerns elsewhere. As the pickup pulled away, Alex felt for the young man standing by the cottonwood, clenching and unclenching his fists.

At the dig, the contingent of site securers stretched a large portion of white plastic Ag-Bag over the one already covering Rennie's workspace and secured its edges with heavy stones. Danny's kiva posed a unique problem. The giant wishing-well shaped kiva formed a natural catch basin for water running down the rubble piles behind it. Danny jumped down inside while he and Taylor considered what to do. Taylor suggested getting the stadia rod they'd used to orient the grid last season and place it as a center pole to support the plastic. Hopefully the rod would pitch the cover so rain would run off rather than puddle in and split the plastic. Danny drove to camp to fetch the rod.

While they waited, Alex walked with Taylor to his excavation. Only then did she realize that she had been avoiding the burial. She watched uneasily as Taylor removed the stones anchoring the plastic sheet that covered the young woman's remains.

As the sheet slipped off the remains, Alex averted her eyes. It was as if she were avoiding someone's nakedness and preserving not only the modesty of the other person but her own as well. She lifted her look, but she approached a complete gaze hesitantly.

The woman lay on her side in a fetal position, bones partially embedded in dirt, knees drawn up, skull slightly bowed. She rested in an ovoid pool of earth darker than that of the midden matrix containing her. The weight of the shifting earth had collapsed her ribs inward.

Alex couldn't remember seeing anything so delicate as this final visible signature of being. Unlike the shards that lay on the desert's surface—skulls and femurs of cattle and coyotes—these bones still held the stain of decomposition. Alex felt little jolts of discomfort as if she were looking at a sudden reflection in an unlooked-for mirror. But she also felt fascination and awe.

Above the young woman's skull and off to the side lay an inverted bowl. "Have you seen this?" Taylor asked, reaching for the bowl.

Alex shook her head.

Taylor lifted the edge of the bowl just a crack. A smaller bowl nested beneath it. Alex bent down for a closer look. She could just make out the black-on-white zigzag pattern common to the era. She wondered what relationship existed between the woman and her two bowls. She looked at Taylor. He lowered the overlaying bowl so that it settled perfectly in place.

"I think I'm going to take these out," he said, indicating the bowls. "Just to play it safe." His eyes met Alex's. "I wish I could take the whole burial out."

"But there isn't time," Alex finished for him.

Dust devils began rioting near the site. The snap and rattle of plastic caught their attention as the kiva's visquine sheet spun up into a dervish and traveled over the greasewood.

"I'll get it!" Alex said, trotting off to catch the plastic sheet. The pursuit forced her to scrape through the greasewood still covering much of the site. Sustaining many scratches and gouges, she snagged the plastic specter and made her way back to Danny's kiva.

Danny had returned with the stadia rod. From where she stood at Danny's excavation, Alex saw Taylor jog to the truck, grab equipment and the photo logbook, and trot back to the burial. The small ramada that he used to protect the burial from light and heat went up. Danny walked over for a quick look at the burial and then crossed the site to the kiva.

As Alex and Danny rigged the kiva's cover, movement past Taylor's excavation area caught Alex's eye. She saw a large dust devil carrying dirt and debris crush its way through the sage and greasewood toward Taylor's burial. Alex had just enough time to yell, "Taylor!" He stood and then stared straight at the whirlwind. Before he could react, it struck the ramada full force, snapping around the steel poles. The poles had been cemented into five-gallon buckets, but it made no difference. In seconds the whole structure fell right on top of Taylor, knocking him down.

In the time it took Alex and Danny to run across the site, Taylor had gotten back on his feet. The ramada lay off to the side where he had thrown it. He knelt beside the burial, touching his fingertips to the ribcage of the grave's occupant. His leg and forearm were striped with little lines of bright blood.

"You all right?" Danny asked.

Taylor nodded, his face dark.

"Was there much damage?" Danny asked.

Again the nod.

"Can we help?" Danny asked.

"Let's just take out the bowls, snap some more photos," Taylor replied dryly.

The three set to it, Taylor photographing the burial to document the damage, Alex keeping the photo log-book. They photographed, bagged, and documented the two bowls, then covered the burial and secured the excavation with two plastic sheets, anchoring them with stones.

"Let's finish the kiva," Danny said, "although after seeing this, I doubt it's going to do any good."

They re-stretched the plastic over the pole and secured it with rocks. After that, there was nothing more to do. Returning to camp, Alex was surprised to find that the rest of the field school had already gone. She hadn't noticed when they had passed the site. But she had been so busy and distracted, she could have easily missed the Suburban going by.

Mike walked out to meet them. "How'd it go?" he drawled. "We all tucked in?"

Taylor stood silent. Mike looked at Danny and Alex, raising his eyebrows quizzically.

"We had some trouble from dust devils," Danny explained. "A pack of them. Taylor's sustained damage."

"Oh?" Mike replied, surprised. "The devils did it?"

"One really big devil," Alex said.

"That's really too bad," Mike said sympathetically. "Them devils." He looked at his watch. "Well, it's three and I could use a hand checkin' tents to see they're weather-tight. Wanna come, Cormack?"

Taylor nodded.

The group broke, Danny to pack, Mike and Taylor to finish securing camp, Alex to haul her gear to her car. Kit was nowhere to be seen. Alex worried that she had done something foolish like try to follow the Suburban into town. But when she started the station wagon, the dog burst out of the greasewood and danced about yodeling as Danny and Alex said their good-byes.

Danny said, "I feel like I'm abandoning ship."

"I don't want to spend the weekend in town," Alex said.

Mike said, "It'd be lovely having your company, but we better stick to the plan."

Taylor said, "If you run into Harry Hoskers, maybe you could get him to show you his newspaper clippings."

"Newspaper *droppings* is more like it," Alex said.

The group dispensed "good-byes" and "be carefuls" and then Alex, Kit, and Danny pulled out of camp and started for Blanding. As they passed the site, Alex and Danny looked over. The white sheets of plastic covering the excavations shone conspicuously.

"I don't feel good about this," Danny grumbled.

"I know what you mean."

Three times on the way to Blanding, they nearly turned around and went back. Finally, though, they pulled up behind the Suburban at Raff's place. Alex hopped out with Kit. Rather than worry about her dog roaming the neighborhood, getting into fights with other dogs and making a nuisance of herself, Alex decided to restrain the husky. She snapped a dog cable onto Kit's collar and attached the other end to a fence post. Kit looked at her, sighed, then began exploring the circumference of her territory.

Rennie came out and greeted them. "How'd it go?" she asked anxiously.

"Fine with your excavation," Danny replied. "But I doubt the plastic's going to hold over the kiva. And Taylor's burial took a hit."

"A hit?"

"A dust devil picked up the ramada and dropped it right on top of him and his burial."

"Oh no!" Rennie exclaimed. "Is he okay? Was there damage to the burial?"

"He's okay, and yes there was," Danny answered.

"He seemed incapable of speech afterward," Alex said. "That tells you something."

In the house, Alex noticed several of the field school members missing. "Where's Mr. Spikes and Mrs. Hanson?" she asked.

"They took rooms at the motel. Marina went grocery shopping with Amy. Jack has family in town," Rennie said. At the news about Jack, Alex glanced at her.

"Have you asked Raff about him? Maybe he knows what's going on with Jack."

"Not yet. But I will. How did camp look?"

"Fine," Danny answered. "But we almost turned back."

"Yeah," Rennie said. "I know the feeling."

"So is this where we're crashing?" Alex asked.

"For as long as we need to. Raff says it could be a couple days before we can get back to the site. If we're stuck here that long, we'll field trip Monday to Edge of the Cedars Museum. Then we'll try to make it home."

In the living room, the television beamed dully. Caedyn hogged the remote and ran repeatedly through the satellite channels. Chris and Josh sat talking about skiing. Hector sat in a corner with a sci-fi novel, tuning everybody out. Danny and Rennie joined Raff in the kitchen. Alex followed them.

"I called Hanks, told him what was up," Raff said. "He asked if he oughta come back. I said I thought we could handle it and he should proceed with business as usual."

"Do you think Taylor and Mike will be enough to hold camp?" Rennie asked.

"They'll be busy but fine," Raff said. "Assuming we don't get back for a day or two, our boys will discourage scavengers. And they'll have to undo storm damage."

Danny shifted restlessly. "I feel like I ought to be out there."

"We-e-ell," Raff drawled, "there's a heap o' people here that need shepherdin'. With Hanks gone and two crew chiefs stuck in camp, that leaves you and Rennie."

"Heather's a crew chief, too," Rennie pointed. "She took off and we have no idea where she is."

"Oh yeah, her," Raff said. "I've been seeing her around town keeping company with one peculiar joe."

"Tony Balbo," Alex said. "You don't know 'im?"

Raff frowned. "Name's familiar, but I can't place it."

The first crack of thunder penetrated the walls. "Let's go have a look at that sky," Raff said.

Sam and Amy Rafferty's house sat high on a hill and had a spectacular view. Off to the south, a wave of lightning-threaded darkness heaved toward town, patches of rain bending between clouds and mesa tops. Behind those, a solid, cloud-tearing wall of water.

Raff chuckled. "Huh. Maybe we better find some flashlights."

Alex looked at Kit, wondering what to do for shelter for her. As she was about to put her in the car, Raff said, "Bring your dog in so she doesn't get washed away."

Alex led Kit inside and took her to the kitchen. "You see this?" she said to Kit. "This is the kitchen. Stay out of the kitchen."

Kit avoided Alex's eyes and licked her lips twice in a gesture of displeasure.

Half an hour later, the storm rolled into town. Roaring winds flung down pea-sized hail. Windows rattled. "Oh no! My garden!" Amy Rafferty exclaimed.

The nerve-jangling front moved through quickly, knocking out electrical service for hours. Then came a steady rain that soaked the region through the night.

Twenty-Four

One rainy day as Coyote traveled his favorite trail thinking about Grandfather Rattlesnake and what a problem he was, who do you think he should meet? Grandfather Rattlesnake, of course, lying right in his path. But something was wrong. Coyote, also called First Angry, slowed his pace and looked.

Grandfather Rattlesnake appeared to be ill or perhaps injured. Coyote thought, *I might have said he looked crippled, but you need legs to be that!* He had a thousand little jokes about Grandfather Rattlesnake. He approached the old snake, his senses sharp. Sweetening his voice with concern, he asked, "Why Grandfather, what has happened?"

Grandfather Rattlesnake turned to look at him. "Oh, Grandson, how fortunate for me that you happened by!"

Happened by? I never happen by, Coyote thought. *I am always departing some success heading toward my next opportunity.* He said, "Grandfather, what is the trouble?"

"It was that Badger."

"What has Badger done?"

"Plenty! We were drinking, you see. I admired his fine striped headdress and he said he admired my rattles. I told him I would like to have his striped headdress, but he wanted me to trade my rattles for it. A rattlesnake without his rattles! It simply cannot be. He said no trade, no headdress."

"I see," said Coyote. He thought he knew what was coming. "You are right, of course. Your rattles are worth far more than a headdress, no matter how handsome."

"That's what I thought. So I said to Badger, 'I will not remove my rattles in front of these others. If they see me without my rattles, they will call me 'Grass Snake.' Let's go out back."

Coyote licked his lips. "I'd have done the same," he said.

"So we did. Went out back, I mean."

"What happened then?"

"I tried to take his headdress from him and he tried to steal my rattles! We gave each other a terrible time! He has some powerful claws, that Badger."

"I know. I would never take him on myself, but you are strong in your own way."

"So I thought! We fought for three days."

"You don't say!"

"It's the truth."

"Of course it is. You would never exaggerate. What happened at the end of those three days?"

"Well, Badger said to me, 'Do you remember what we are fighting for?' I remembered perfectly well, but at the moment I thought it best not to say. Badger had gotten the worst of it, you see, and I pitied him. So I said, 'No, but whatever it was, I'm sure we've settled it by now.' Badger, you know, has only one or two working thoughts in his head."

Coyote listened to this tale with great sympathy but focused deeper attention on the wounds on Grandfather Rattlesnake's body. *He's trying to make his discomfort seem no big thing, but those wounds surely hurt, and I'll bet he has other wounds I can't see causing even more pain, or he would not speak to me in this groveling manner. Grandfather Rattlesnake is afraid!*

"What did Badger say?"

"Oh, well—he felt satisfied and went away."

"That Badger! He always was a simple fellow." Coyote chuckled, then licked his lips again. "It must have been some battle, from the look of you."

"Oh, it was! If you think I look bad, you ought to see that Badger." Grandfather Rattlesnake flicked his tongue in and out in the way Coyote, also called First Angry, hated. "But as you can perhaps see, Grandson, I am at somewhat of a disadvantage."

In his dark mind, Coyote said to himself, *Yes, it's 'Grandson' now that I have your life in my hands. It's 'Grandson' now that you are in need of help and at my mercy. You old worm! Not two weeks ago you called me deluded and pathetic. I said I would kill you if we met again. Have you forgotten? I, Coyote, also called First Angry, have not forgotten!*

"If you are in need of assistance," Coyote said, smiling, showing his white teeth, "you may count on me."

Rattlesnake breathed a sigh of relief. "I had hoped as much! Listen, I am too tired to travel, and you know how it is around here, great distances in every direction."

Coyote chuckled appreciatively. "Yes, sometimes that's an advantage, lots of privacy. But at other times it's a nuisance."

"Exactly. Grandson, this is one of those other times."

"I understand! Grandfather, would you like to ride on my back?"

"You would let me?"

"Certainly!"

"Oh, oh, oh! You are too kind."

With some effort and many grunts of pain, Grandfather Rattlesnake climbed up on Coyote's back and coiled in his fur.

"Are you comfortable, Grandfather?" Coyote asked.

"Oh yes! I always said you had a good coat."

So Coyote set out across the desert with Grandfather Rattlesnake riding on his back.

After a while, Grandfather Rattlesnake said, "I'm not too heavy, am I?"

"I hardly know you're there," Coyote answered.

Grandfather Rattlesnake cleared his throat. "Ahem, ahem! You know, perhaps I have been too hard on you. I didn't know you were so good."

Coyote thought, *Good! You don't know how good I am! Better than you and a thousand times better than that old fool, Badger. I am good enough to finish what Badger started. I am good enough to put an end once and for all to your nagging and the drip-drip-drip of your venom.* To Grandfather Rattlesnake, he said, "It doesn't matter."

"All the same, you're not such a bad fellow as I thought."

Coyote grinned. "Why, thank you, Grandfather."

After they had traveled awhile, Coyote said, "I think we both need a rest. I know a good place."

"Suit yourself," Grandfather Rattlesnake said.

Coyote let Grandfather Rattlesnake down.

"This is a nice place," Grandfather Rattlesnake said.

"Isn't it, though? You know, Grandfather, I can see why Badger admired your rattles. You have one of the best sets, if not *the* best. What will become of them when you die?"

"Oh, well, I thought I might give them to Gopher Snake." Rattlesnake didn't know it, but Coyote knew precisely to whom he was referring. "She's been good to me and I would like her to have something to remember me by. But—hah—I won't be dying anytime soon."

At these words, Coyote's hatred for Grandfather Rattlesnake stoked hotter. *Leave them to Gopher Snake who has no use for them? I deserve those rattles! They're mine! Won't be dying? That's what you think, Grandfather. That's what you think!*

Grandfather Rattlesnake had his back to Coyote. Before he knew quite what he was doing, Coyote picked up a rock and crushed Rattlesnake's head. Rattlesnake never saw it coming.

Coyote looked upon what he had done. He had never killed anything before except for a few foolish hopes. But with some people, killing their hopes was the same as taking their lives. He was surprised how easy it had been to go from that to the actual physical destruction of another.

Just what is this I have done? Somehow, I think there ought to be more to it. In fact, Coyote felt a pang. Was it guilt? No! To admit guilt, he would have to admit right and wrong, and to admit right and wrong, he would have to admit to a greater power that distinguished the one from the other. Well, there was such a greater power, but it didn't manifest in "right" and "wrong." *I just feel disappointed it was so easy,* Coyote thought.

He took out his knife and cut off Grandfather Rattlesnake's rattles and shook them over his head. As he did, he danced and sang:

Now they are mine, it is all mine.
Now they are mine, it is all mine.
The wonderful rattles, they are mine
The essence of them, it is mine.
The power of the rattles, it will sing for me,
The power of the rattles, it will strike for me.
I am Coyote, First Angry, the clever one!
I am Coyote, First Angry, the powerful one!

Twenty-five

The following morning rain continued to fall. Alex, Rennie, Danny, and the students attended church services at the local Mormon ward house. The good residents of Blanding persisted in ribbing and jibing the archaeologists at every opportunity, making frequent pointed comments about poached artifacts and pot hunting to the archaeologists' faces and behind their backs. A couple of times, Danny had to restrain Caedyn. But for the most part, the archaeologists submitted to the derision and avoided an incident.

When they returned to Raff's house, they found Sharp inside playing his guitar. Anxious for a diversion, the students gathered around. The singing and joking that followed helped pass time as everyone waited anxiously for word from camp.

None came. The rain stopped, then began again. Not until late Sunday evening did the sky break and stars once more bespeckle the desert night.

. . . . .

Monday morning arrived with still no word from camp. The crew chiefs and students took their field trip to the Edge of the

Cedars Museum. As Alex stood in the doorway to the gift shop, she saw a mud-spattered pickup roar into the parking lot and slide sideways to a halt. At first she thought it was just some local kids fooling around. Then she recognized the project's motor pool pickup, Mike at the wheel. There was something urgent about his manner. Rennie and Danny saw him, too. The three of them met him halfway between the truck and museum.

His normally open and friendly face wore a scowl. "Roads are bad," Mike said. "I got here soon as I could."

"But what's wrong?" Rennie demanded.

"The site," Mike said. "It took a big hit."

"You mean from the storm?" Danny asked.

"Well yeah, that too. But I mean it got hit real bad by pot hunters."

"Pot hunters!" they all exclaimed.

"Yeah, pot hunters," Mike said. "They trashed the midden and stomped Taylor's burial to bits."

"When?" Danny asked.

"Don't know for sure. Me'n Taylor had our hands full at camp. I drove out to check roads this morning and thought I'd look in on the site. There was a flash flood Sunday and the wash was runnin' high. I waded over and found Deeppockets like it was."

"How is it possible?" Rennie said. "How could this happen?"

Alex couldn't keep from chuckling at all the ironies. She said, "Isn't it obvious? Old Harry finally got a response to his excavation-sized personal ad!"

. . . . .

Two hours later, everyone except Jack, who couldn't be found, and Raff, out looking for Hoskers, stood on the muddied surface of Deeppockets, staring in silence at the destruction wreaked by man and storm. Large and small holes pockmarked the middens, their telltale backdirt piles littered with pot shards and bone. Muddy water pooled at their bottoms.

Poor Taylor. His midden burial had been obliterated. Debris from the pot holes had been dumped over on it. Unrelated shards and skeletal fragments now mingled with those of the grave's original occupant.

"Look at the size of some of these holes," Danny said as they surveyed the middens.

"It's a terrible shame," said Mrs. Hanson. "Really an awful shame."

"Could a shovel make holes that big?" Caedyn asked. "And so many of them. That's a lot of digging. Believe me, after digging out the kiva, I know. One person couldn't have done it all. Not by himself."

Sharp scratched his head. "But if somebody brought a backhoe in here, wouldn't the guys in camp have heard?"

"Not with that wind blowing away from camp," Hector said. "However, nothing short of a flood would erase the tracks from such a big machine."

"Yeah, that makes me think," Sharp said. He walked out to the road. He strolled along it, stopping now and then to crouch down and examine the ground.

Danny stared at the potholes. "Would you say these were above average size for pot holes?" he asked Alex.

"I don't know," she answered. "I'm no connoisseur of pot holes—that's Harry's specialty. But a few are bigger than any we saw on the tour."

"And look at this," Danny said. "A couple of them have been back-filled."

"Hmm," Alex said. "Maybe with dirt thrown over from the other holes?"

"Maybe that's it," Danny said. Then he looked up. "Well, we can't say we weren't expecting it."

"No, we can't, can we?" Alex agreed. "And yet, we didn't."

"Yeah, I had a feeling, but I didn't quite picture it happening." He turned to Taylor. "Good job getting those bowls out. They'd be gone."

Taylor didn't respond. He stood scrutinizing his burial like a chess player trying to reconstruct his board after someone had upset it.

Rennie had broken from the group to go inspect her excavation. Now she returned with the news that, other than water damage and a flat rock display of eye-catching shards that had not been there before, her excavation and the kiva were untouched. "I think the best thing is to uncover our areas and start them drying out," she said. "Mike says the camp's a mess—he's working on that end, but we need to fix our living situation first, then get back out here ASAP."

"Might be a good idea to get some photos right away," Danny said. "Keep someone out on site."

"Agreed," Rennie said.

"You don't think they're coming back?" Alex asked.

"Not really," Danny said. "I think someone knew we were gone and took advantage of the situation."

"Everyone in Blanding knew," Rennie said. "We were there for two days."

"So now everyone knows we're back," Danny said. "I think

the site's safe. But I'd still like to stay a few nights. We'll have to work long hours to sort out this mess. It'll help if we can haul out our equipment and just leave it. I'll stay and keep an eye on it."

"I'll stay, too," Taylor said.

Rennie nodded. "Why don't you both come back to camp first. We've got tasks there that'll require some strong arms and acts of derring-do."

"Like what?" Danny asked.

"The storm broke limbs on those old cottonwoods," Taylor said. "One fell and crushed the north end of the mess tent. Others are just dangling. Someone's got to climb up and saw those off so the next storm doesn't drop 'em on us. There are other problems we didn't have time to fix," he said. His face full of regret, he looked at the fragments of the burial.

Sharp trotted over to the middens.

"Find anything?" Danny asked.

"It's a good thing we parked our vehicles on the bank, waded the creek, and cut through the greasewood."

"Why?"

"'Cause we'd have driven right over what tracks there are. Best I can make out, there was one vehicle. But in one place there's a second set of tracks, small ones."

"You just said there was only one vehicle," Danny said.

"It looks like someone was pulling a trailer."

"All the better to haul site-raiding equipment in," Danny said.

"Isn't someone going to get some law out here?" Sharp asked.

"If anyone's interested, Raff will talk to them," Rennie

one hundred and ninety-two

said. "But I'll bet Hoskers is going to have to file a formal complaint before anyone drives out here to help *us*."

Taylor said, "Even then it might take awhile. Lots of folks are going to think we got what was coming to us."

"Wha'd'ya mean?" Sharp asked. "Don't they have to send someone out on account of that grave desecration ruling several years back?"

"Well, the law requires it, but our Mr. Hoskers has been such an annoyance, we might have to wait even if he does file a complaint," Taylor said.

"Right," Rennie agreed. "Thank you, Harry Hoskers." She looked around at the students and volunteers milling over the site. "Let's round everybody up and head back to camp. Hmm ... on second thought, let's leave Marina and Josh out here to do more picking up and help Danny with those photos. That'll put us a little further ahead."

Everyone except Danny, Josh, and Marina walked through the greasewood to the banks of the wash where thigh-high, reddish-brown flood waters still flowed. Pausing to remove shoes, the crew waded barefoot across the muddy flow. Mrs. Hanson decided to wade through in her sneakers this time. When she reached the bank below the vehicles, her white tennis shoes had turned murky red.

As she waded behind Taylor, Rennie asked, "Has Wiggins made it back?"

"No," Taylor answered. "And I'm afraid there's another surprise from that quarter."

"What do you mean?" Rennie asked.

"You'll see."

Alex slipped her flaps on over her wet feet, then walked

around the Suburban to detach Kit's cable from the door and coax her out of the shade. She had thought it best to keep Kit off site while it was in such a bad state. Irritated at being tied up twice in the last three days, Kit ignored Alex's order to get in the vehicle and ran circles around the group. With a flourish, she jumped into the driver's seat and planted herself behind the steering wheel.

"What—you driving now?" Alex said. "In the back with you!"

Kit yodeled a protest but complied. Everybody else squeezed in after her.

A few minutes later, they pulled into camp. Alex could smell the damage before she saw it. The odor of freshly split wood and torn leaves filled the air. Cottonwood twigs and branches littered the ground. Overhead, broken limbs dangled by mere splinters. The north end of the mess tent leaned drunkenly, propped up by shovels and boards.

"Wow," Alex said to Rennie. "I wonder what our tent looks like!"

"Good question," Rennie said.

The pair hurried out to their tent beneath the lone cottonwood. As with the mess tent, limbs and leaves lay strewn over the ground. The tent sagged to one side but seemed otherwise intact. The two women opened the flaps to allow the warm afternoon breeze to scour out the steamy dampness inside. Behind them, Heather's tent seemed equally secure, so they decided to leave it be and let Heather sort things out when she returned.

Soon, sounds of tools chopping and clanging echoed off the surrounding mesa walls. The work lifted spirits and gave everyone the sense of putting things right.

As dusk fell, Ernest Brock's truck passed the camp on the way to the well head. He honked and waved, but after only a few minutes, he returned. Driving right into the middle of camp, he slammed his truck to a halt and climbed out, scowling. Mike and Rennie stepped forward to meet him.

"Whad'you people do to my well head?" Brock said. "Did you run your truck into it?"

"What do you mean?" Mike asked. "Something happen to the well head?"

"Don't tell me you don't know!"

"We don't," Rennie answered. "Please, why don't you tell us?" Sharp walked up to join the conversation.

"The valves are broke," Ernest Brock complained. "You can't get no water out."

Mike said, "Me and Taylor was out there Saturday night, it was fine then. Flash flood came through, cutting us off from it after that. The rest of these people have been in Blanding weathering out the storm."

"That well's our only water supply, too," Rennie said. "We've been taking good care of it."

"Hmph," Brock said. "The creek's down now. You seen anybody else go out there?"

"People come and go, but we didn't see anyone pass by after Saturday," Mike answered. "That doesn't mean someone couldn't have slipped by during the storm or got to it by some other route."

"Ain't no other route," Brock said. "Anybody wants to use that water has to take this road here."

Sharp gestured to Mike to follow and began walking toward the camp pickup. "Mind if we take a look?" he asked the old farmer.

"Go ahead, but don't do it no more hurt," Brock called back. He got back into his own truck. Stabbing his finger at Rennie, he said, "I can't prove nothin', but till I find out otherwise, I'm holding you guys responsible. You'll be get'n my bill." He drove back out to the well, Mike and Sharp following in the camp pickup.

"Lovely," Rennie said. "Alex, could you round up everybody, please?"

Once the crew gathered, Rennie laid down the law. "We just received news the well head is damaged. Since that's our only water source and it's out of commission, the only water available is what we've got in the five-gallon jugs stacked in the kitchen and in the shower barrels. Until this situation is resolved, we're on water rationing. No showers. Use water sparingly—no waste. We don't know how long this problem will last, but we've got at least several waterless hours ahead."

"We might have to move back into town for a while if it's not settled soon," Taylor said.

"Look what happened the last time we did that," Caedyn blurted out.

"Yeah," Chris said. "Total annihilation."

"It wasn't total annihilation, and we'll do what we have to do," Rennie answered curtly. "Now, let's get back to work and see what we can accomplish before dark."

Half an hour later, Mike and Sharp returned to the site. Sharp remained in the truck as Mike walked over to Rennie, where she and Alex were digging out the equipment tent's clogged drainage trench. "Well, we had a look-see," he said.

"And?"

"It ain't that bad. Ol' Sharp seems pretty sure he can fix it. We figger Cortez is the closest place to get what we need, but we're going in to Raff's and make some calls. We'll probably spend the night and head for Cortez in the morning."

Rennie hesitated, wondering if she had the authority to make this call.

Mike shuffled his toe in the dirt. "Hanks might not make it to camp tonight, maybe not tomorrow either," he said.

"Raff will bring him out," she answered.

"Raff's out chasin' after Hoskers, remember? We might not see him for days. Can't you sign the purchase orders?"

After a moment, Rennie moved toward a cabinet at the back of the mess tent. She took out a key and unlocked the doors. "I can't sign them, but Dr. Hanks signed a few in case of an emergency like this." Rennie handed him the purchase orders and looked him in the eye. "No side trips," she ordered. "We need to fix this."

"I know it," Mike said. "You can count on us."

Rennie sighed. "I hope so! We've had just about all we can take."

Mike and Sharp backed out of the lot and took off with a spin of the tires. Rennie slumped down at a table and ran her hands through her hair. "Urgh!" she exclaimed.

Alex sat down next to her. "We're coming up on dinner time," she said. "Want me to see what's available?"

"Oh yeah, dinner. I'll come with you."

It wasn't until they headed to the kitchen that Alex and Rennie noticed a hand-lettered sign taped up on a cabinet, titled CONDEMNED. Alex read the sign aloud:

*By order of the Big Wash Board of Health, these premises are con-
demned pending the upbraiding of the wretch who without regard
for rules of decency and good sanitation routinely and with de-
praved indifference risks the health and safety of residents of these
parts.*

She looked at Rennie. Then they both looked up at Taylor,
who had climbed up into one of the cottonwoods to saw off a
limb.

"Taylor, what does this sign mean?" Rennie asked.

"Check out those black plastic bags in the kitchen," he answered. "You'll see."

Rennie searched the kitchen, halting before two large
black garbage bags stuffed under a table. She opened one up
and grimaced. "Oh, whew!" she exclaimed. "Gross!"

"More dirty dishes?" Alex asked.

Rennie nodded and opened the second bag, with the same
response. "That man is kitchen scum," she said. "Hanks is going to have to do something. We can't keep finding little sur-
prises like this. It's intolerable."

"And here we are without water to wash them," Alex com-
mented.

"Yes," Rennie agreed, "without water to wash them." Then
she brightened. "I know! Let's take them down to the creek
and scour them out there. It's not perfect, but it'll take care of
the immediate sanitation problem."

"Sounds like a job for Caedyn and Chris," Alex said, nudging her.

Rennie laughed. "Good idea!"

Soon, Caedyn and Chris were off to the wash, each with a
bag of fetid dishes slung over his shoulder. Smug smiles on

their faces, Alex and Rennie leaned out from the kitchen and watched the two young men leave camp.

Suddenly Rennie stiffened. "Oh my gosh!" she cried. "I forgot about those guys out at the sight! Taylor, it's getting late. Will you bring them in for dinner?"

"On my way!" Taylor said, swinging down from the tree.

"That poor child Marina," Mrs. Hanson said, walking into the mess tent. "Our tent didn't fare very well. Some of her belongings were completely destroyed—books, papers. I spread our clothes over some of those bushes by the tent. Oh, are you making dinner? Do you need help?"

Alex and Rennie welcomed the help. Neither of them had ever cooked for so large a group. Furthermore, finding their way around Wiggins's kitchen proved a challenge. There seemed to be no logic to his storage system. To complicate matters, many pans, dishes, and utensils had gone to the wash with Caedyn and Chris.

Alex paused for a moment from her kitchen work to watch Hector, who up until now had borne the evils of physical labor with awkward stoicism. A change had come over the budding scholar and scientist. As he chopped wood and stacked it in neat piles at the back of the mess tent, he worked with the grace of a young man enjoying the stimulation of work. Gone were all the frowns of distaste at having to dirty his hands. Now Alex sensed in him a cool determination to get the job done. She understood. Here in the camp, students and crew chiefs alike could fix the damage and experience the sense of power that came from putting things right.

Untangling the mess out at the site would be a different matter. The rough wounds the pot hunters had inflicted would scar Deeppockets permanently, persecuting memory for years to come. Those holes couldn't just be filled in and forgotten. Erasing the damage or trying to weave it into the site's original goals was impossible. The archaeologists, field school volunteers, and students now had to accept the change the attack had made in their plans and turn it into something more than mere violence.

Furthermore, the damage to the well head, occurring at the same time as the attack on the site, suggested that some lively threat lurked for the field school. Alex was willing to bet that whatever was going on wasn't over yet. It seemed to her that someone wanted them out of the canyon.

. . . . .

After dinner, everyone gathered at the fire, which had to be stoked into life with some effort from the wet wood supply. As the crew chiefs and students sat in the firelight, a truck pulled into the lot, a door opened and closed, and the vehicle sped away. Todd strolled over to the fire.

"Hi, Todd," Rennie said. "How are roads coming in?"

"Not good," the young Navajo said. "We had to get out and push twice."

"That settles whether or not Dr. Hanks is coming tonight," Danny said.

Todd looked around at the twilit cottonwoods and sniffed the air. Firelight reflected off some of the limb stumps left behind from Taylor's surgeries. "Looks like you guys have been busy," he said.

"Hah!" Caedyn exclaimed. "You don't know the half of it!"

"Why? Was somebody hurt or something?" Todd asked.

"The site was hurt," Alex said. "Pot hunters got it while we were in Blanding."

"Oh, no!" Todd said, a peculiar light in his eyes. "This is really bad luck," he said. "Very bad luck."

Marina looked up at the Navajo. "Why do you say that?" she asked. "Why is it bad luck?"

"It just is," Todd replied. "Don't you think so?"

"We like to think it's the end of the bad luck," Taylor said. "All good luck from here on out."

"Oh, Todd, we're on water rationing," Rennie said.

"Why's that?" he asked.

"Someone sabotaged the well head!" Caedyn exclaimed.

"The well head!" Todd said. "When did *that* happen?"

"'Bout the same time as the other mess," Danny said.

Todd scratched his head. "You guys got very, very bad luck."

"Why do I get the feeling," Alex said, "that 'bad luck' is a euphemism for something?"

"What's a youfamizzen?' Todd asked.

"Think we ought to send someone out to watch the site tonight?" Josh asked.

"Taylor and I are going out," Danny said.

"You guys going armed?" Caedyn asked.

Even Chris seemed to be wearying of Caedyn's tactlessness. "Come on, Cade," he said. "They're the big boys. They know what they're doing."

Caedyn ignored Chris. "Well, are you?"

Taylor said, "I won't let my trusty trowel out of my sight."

"How long is this water thing going to last?" Todd asked Rennie.

"Don't know. Not long, I hope. Mike and Sharp are on the problem."

The group fell into a momentary silence. Then Caedyn stuck his foot in it again. "Maybe someone from the reservation damaged the well head to get rid of us," he said, seeming to forget that a resident of the reservation was sitting at the fire with them.

Todd's face showed little emotion. "Right," he said. "The Indians cut off their own water supply to get rid of the pale faces."

Marina frowned. "Caedyn, apologize," she said.

"But maybe they did," he insisted.

"That's enough, Caedyn," Rennie said.

"Yeah, Caedyn," Chris said. "If you can't think anything nice, don't think anything at all."

Alex chuckled at the twist on the old cliché.

"So," Josh said, leaning toward the fire, "who *did* damage the well and who *did* hit the site?"

"I think it's pretty clear that pot hunters hit the site," Danny said. "The well head might be an accident that nobody wants to own up to."

"But couldn't the pot hunters have done that, too?" Marina asked.

"The question is," Caedyn said, "what's going to happen next?" The question hung in the air as everyone pondered the possibilities.

"Well, we better get out there," Taylor said at last. "I've got to get a few things from my tent." With a jerk of his head, he indicated that Danny, Rennie, and Alex should follow. They walked off through the greasewood together.

"Look," Rennie said, "don't do anything foolish out there."

"Us? Something foolish?" Danny grinned wryly.

"If we can just muddle through tonight," Rennie said, rubbing her forehead, "Hanks will be back tomorrow."

"What if Hanks doesn't make it back tomorrow or even the next day?" Alex asked. "Maybe we're exposing ourselves to trouble out here. As much as I hate to admit it, maybe we should get off the site."

"Right now, wild horses couldn't drag me away," Taylor said grimly. Danny agreed.

They reached Taylor's tent. The sound of an engine driving toward camp brought them all to a halt. A door slammed, then the vehicle drove away. Leaving Taylor at his tent, Rennie, Alex, and Danny hurried back to the center of camp. A figure walked into the glow of the firelight, Kit following at his heels. Jack Randall Reed had returned to the field school.

Twenty-Six

Jack walked into the wall of silence that greeted him and stopped with a jerk. He looked at the group sitting at the fire, then his eyes shifted to others emerging from the path to the men's tents.

Kit danced around him and gave him a welcoming, "Woo—ooo—ooo!" Without taking his eyes off the others, Jack petted the dog.

"Hi," he said. "Sorry to take so long getting back."

"Where've you been?" Caedyn said.

"What do ya mean? I've been at my grandma's in town."

Hector stood and pushed back his glasses. "Perhaps you ought to provide a full account of your whereabouts and activities," he said.

Rennie stepped between the group at the fire and Jack. "Hi, Jack," she said. "How're the roads?"

"Not too bad," Jack said. "What's going on?"

"While we were in town, the site was hit by pot hunters," Marina said, "and the well was damaged."

The sleeping bag Jack carried under his arm dropped to

the ground. He stooped to pick it up and then nervously re-shouldered his backpack. Quietly, Todd withdrew from the fire.

"The site," Jack said. "You think I had something to do with it?"

"Did you sell us out?" Caedyn demanded, rising to his feet.

"Chill out, Cade," Chris said, trying to pull him back into his chair. Caedyn shook him off.

"Well, did you?" Caedyn pressed.

"I've been at my gram's," Jack said. "I wouldn't ..."

"What's someone like *you* doing at an archaeological field school!" Caedyn said.

"Caedyn!" Marina squeaked.

"Caedyn, stop this," Rennie said. She turned to Jack. "Nobody thinks you had anything to do with what's happened."

"*I* think he had something to do with it," Caedyn said. Fists raised in a threatening manner, he stepped toward Jack.

"Caedyn Hoyt!" Marina squealed. "Don't you dare!"

Danny stepped in front of Caedyn to cut him off. At that moment, Taylor appeared from the greasewood and hung his pack over one of Caedyn's upraised fists. "Do me a favor and carry this to the truck, Cade," he said as he breezed by. When Caedyn failed to respond, Taylor walked to the kitchen, picked up a full water cooler, and added that to his load. "This, too—would you mind?"

"Had dinner, Jack?" Alex asked, tugging the bewildered young man toward the kitchen.

Without answering, Jack followed Alex, his head turned back to watch Caedyn, now laden with the water cooler and

Taylor's backpack. Not until Jack entered the mess tent did Caedyn move toward the truck.

Alex laid out a salad for Jack. "What kind of dressing?" she asked.

"What?" Jack said.

"What kind of salad dressing would you like?"

"Oh, uh ... ranch."

Alex set the dressing next to Jack's bowl and stuck a fork in the salad. He picked up the fork and began eating distract-edly. Alex sat across from him and watched. "How's your wife?" she asked. "Must be hard for her to turn you loose for so long."

"My wife?" Jack said. "Oh, she's fine. Elated, in fact. She just found out we're going to have a baby."

"A baby!" Alex exclaimed. "That's wonderful! I hope the best for you."

"Thank you," Jack answered. He looked at her as if focus-ing on her for the first time. "Thanks!"

Just then, Caedyn trotted back into the mess area and slapped Chris on the back. "Don't wait up," he said to Chris. "I'm going out to the site tonight!" He side-skipped to watch Chris's reaction, then ran toward his tent.

At this welcome news, Alex breathed a sigh of relief.

"We'll see you in the morning," Taylor said.

"Bright and early," Rennie promised.

In spite of his upset, Jack began eating his salad lustily.

"More?" Alex asked Jack.

He shook his head. "No, thanks."

Rennie walked into the tent and Jack went immediately on guard. She picked up a site notebook and settled in to write.

Alex said, "Why don't we go for a walk, Jack. I'll fill you in."

Jack shrugged. "Why not. Let's go."

Alex looked for Kit and saw her sitting in the fire circle with Marina. "Kit!" Alex called. The dog twisted around to look at her. "Come on, we're going for a walk."

Kit sprang up and loped past Alex and Jack to the road. As they walked out into the canyon, Alex told Jack the story of Mike's arrival at the Edge of the Cedars and his news about the site. She described the extent of the damage.

"What about the holes?" he asked. "What can be done about them?"

"Nothing," Alex answered. "Trying to undo the pot hunting damage would only disturb the middens further. As much of the human bone as possible will be reburied."

Jack nodded. "I've always wondered about that," he said. Alex realized that he meant he had wondered about it when he had been an active pot hunter.

Ahead of them, Kit's white tail swayed side to side as she crisscrossed the road, investigating odors and sounds. The Milky Way had begun its roughly north-south flow through the canyon. Jack looked up at it and sighed.

"What about the well head?" he asked. "If there's no water, we can't stay."

"Sharp thinks he can take care of it," Alex answered. "We're on water rationing till then."

"Okay. Where did you get your dog?" he asked.

"A guy in Orem," Alex answered. "I had no clue what I was getting myself into."

"She's some dog," he said, shaking his head.

"I wouldn't recommend the breed to everyone," Alex said.

"Really? Why not?"

"They're headstrong," Alex said. "And they need all the space in the world."

Jack chuckled. "It's amazing how she fits right into the desert while her cousins up in Alaska pull sleds through the deep snow," he said.

Alex said, "Speaking of cousins ..."

His head drooped. Alex waited for him to speak, but he seemed not to know where to begin.

"Did you know Jep was on site last week?" she prompted.

He shook his head. "Hadn't any idea. Who would have expected it?"

"Nobody mentioned it to you?"

"Nobody. If things were said—you know, I might've heard a phrase here or there—they didn't register." He shook his head again. "That Harry Hoskers must be crazy bringing someone like Jep out here."

"That must have been a real surprise to you, seeing him in camp."

"Sure was," he said, then he chuckled ruefully. "But I knew that sooner or later someone would find out."

"Find out that you're from a family of pot hunters?" Alex said.

He grimaced at her bluntness. "Hooh, yeah," he said. "And that I used to be one."

Alex smiled. This was all just as she had guessed. "*Used to be* is the key phrase here," she said. "When did you stop and why?"

As they walked along the road, Jack told Alex the story of his life—how he was born in Blanding to Arvard Randall's youngest sister, Mary Randall Reed. As soon as he could toddle, his dad and uncles started taking him out on pot hunting expeditions. He explained how his mother objected but felt she had little choice but to turn him loose as the men drove off.

All the same, she had high aspirations for her youngest son and began teaching him on the sly about the area's native cultures. She introduced him to the idea that robbing their dead wasn't his future. She encouraged him to break out of the Randall rut and get an education. Jack's father didn't much like the idea of having a son who had more education than he did, but since Jack's going to college seemed at best only a remote possibility, he indulged discussions about it.

When Jack was eleven, his father lost his job. For a while, the men in the extended family went out hunting nearly every night to help Jack's family survive until his dad found work. Jack liked the praise and attention heaped on him whenever he found something valuable, and he developed a knack for locating intact burials in middens. He didn't know how he did it exactly. He said it was as if he could feel the dead down there in the ground. Sometimes he thought he could even visualize them, the way their bodies folded into the earth. "I know that sounds weird," he said.

"Not really," Alex responded. "Who knows what ties run between us and the living or us and the dead? I know I don't understand it all. If we were honest, I think we'd have to admit that no one knows."

"Yes," Jack said. "After awhile, it began to feel like I knew them."

"Wow," Alex said. "Then after awhile, you probably felt that you were betraying them."

Jack nodded. He said that at first he was able to ignore the bones his relatives churned up as they tore into areas he indicated, but finally, along with his mother's unhappiness over the whole business, it began to get to him.

His father got a new job in southwestern Colorado, so his family moved to Cortez. There he had nearly unrestricted access to the famous cliff dwellings at Mesa Verde. As a teen, he visited the dwellings and museum every chance he got, attending seminars and classes. His mother covered for him when his uncles showed up for a hunt. *Out with his friends,* she would say, *staying late at school, visiting a friend in Moab.* Jack became less and less accessible.

He went on a church mission when he was nineteen and ended up in Peru, where he sneaked in a visit to Machu Pichu. That cinched it. Jack decided he wanted to become an archaeologist. When he came off his mission, his mother helped him apply to BYU without his father's knowledge. In fact, his father didn't know about it at all until the day Jack left for college. Taken by surprise, he couldn't think of any objection to his son getting an education, especially since he had gotten a partial scholarship and a job to pay for the rest.

So, Jack went to the university. At his mother's suggestion, he returned to Cortez infrequently. She felt it best if he made as clean a break as possible, at least until he established himself. But when he began following his interests, he found himself in a dilemma: he had to dodge his father's questions about his major and he had to hide his pot hunting past from professors and fellow students.

A year ago he met a sociology major from Montana. She was someone he could talk to about his past and his aspirations, and she encouraged him to pursue his hopes and dreams. But he still felt uncomfortable around his fellow archaeology students and kept to himself.

Then in a bold move, he signed up for the field school knowing full well it was located in the area where he had committed many of his crimes. He and his wife agreed that he needed to confront his past, but he found it worse than he had expected, especially when Hoskers took everyone on the potted sites tour. Jack knew how to read the signs. He recognized telltale items pot hunters left to mark their work and knew who had hit the sites they had visited. When they reached the alcove and found the disinterred infant, it had been nearly too much. He nearly quit the field school.

Alex asked how he had risked going into town with them. Didn't he worry someone would recognize him? He told her he had been away a long time and Blanding had grown so much, you didn't necessarily run into old acquaintances, nor was anyone expecting him. Yeah, he'd had to duck a few, but it had worked ... for a while.

"But by now," he said, "they all know." He stopped walking. "This thing that happened to the site might be because of me."

Alex considered that a moment. "Doesn't *that* throw an interesting light on things!"

"I'll be kicked out of the field school," Jack said.

"For trying to make the big break?" Alex said. "You can't punish a guy for trying to change his life even if somebody else raises a big stink about it."

"I should have told someone," he said. "Maybe Dr. Hanks or Rennie."

"But someone *did* know," Alex said. "Raff knew, didn't he?"

Jack hesitated. "I didn't want to get him into trouble," he admitted.

"Get Raff into trouble!" Alex exclaimed. "That's a good one! If anyone should have told us, Raff should've, but he seemed to think there was good reason not to. "

As they walked back to the camp together, Jack seemed relieved to have gotten everything off his chest. Alex asked, "Could you tell who hit our site by looking at it?"

Jack nodded. "Probably."

"Do you want to?" she asked.

He kicked at the dirt in the road. "I'll have a look," he said. "I'll tell what's to tell."

They walked into camp and Kit trotted to her water bowl and drank deeply. By now, most of the students had gone to bed. Marina sat alone at the fire, looking into the flames. Mrs. Hanson sat in the mess tent reading a book under the generator-powered light bulb. At the next table over, Rennie worked in her notebook. She looked up at Jack and Alex as they walked into camp. Jack picked up his gear and, with a nod to Alex, headed for his tent.

Alex sat down next to Rennie. "I'm ready for bed," she said. "How 'bout you?"

Rennie closed her notebook and leaned back in her chair. "I'm ready but don't think I can sleep," she said.

"Come out to the tent anyway," Alex said. "I'll talk you to sleep."

"I'll meet you there," Rennie said.

Alex left the mess area and clicked her tongue at Kit. "Time for bed," she said to the dog. Marina looked up as Alex walked past her. "'Night, Marina," she said.

"What about ..." Marina began, then stopped.

"What about what?" Alex asked.

"What are we going to do about Caedyn?" she asked.

"Maybe the boys will work him over out on the site tonight," Alex said.

"Very funny," Marina said.

Alex crouched down beside Marina. "Anyone who cares for him and is still waiting for him to change probably has a long wait ahead."

Marina nodded sadly.

Alex went on to her tent. Soon after she had crawled into her sleeping bag and Kit had sprawled on her poncho, the tent flap unzipped and Rennie stepped in.

"Some day, huh?" Alex asked. "No Heather Barton yet?"

"No Heather Barton, no Dr. Hanks, no Sam Rafferty, no Harry Hoskers ..." Rennie said.

"Don't forget dear old Wiggins," Alex added.

"Him too, although it may not be entirely safe for him to return."

"Maybe Hoskers potted out his own site and is at this very moment on his way to the New York black market."

"Or maybe he's just sitting at home listing his heart out in the 'Items of Questionable Provenance' category on eBay," Rennie said.

"By the way," Alex said, "Jack didn't have anything to do with what happened out on the site."

"Says who?"

"Says him."

Rennie sat on her cot and looked at Alex intently. "You believe him?"

"I see no reason not to. He has a good story. I mean, his story not only makes sense but is even inspiring," Alex said.

"So, tell me. I could use some inspiration," Rennie said.

Alex told Rennie Jack's story. Toward the end of it, the two women heard an engine making its way toward camp. Rennie put on her shoes and Alex hastened to get dressed. They made it to the center of camp in time to greet Rafferty as he carried his gear into the mess area.

"Is this a private party or can anyone come?" he asked.

"You can come only if you brought party favors," Rennie said, relief sounding in her voice. "Did you bring any?"

"Only the favor of my company," Raff answered.

"Good enough," Rennie said.

"The storm caused a landslide that blocked up Price Canyon," Raff said. "Hanks can't get through. It's supposed to be cleared tomorrow. In the meantime, got a spare tent?"

"You mean one that's dry?" Rennie asked. "Hmm, that's a tough one."

"What about Hoskers?" Alex asked.

"Neither hide nor hair," Raff said. "Asked around town, went down to Bluff where a neighbor said Harry went to a Park Service pow-wow at Mesa Verde to do his song and dance about getting Deeppockets into the park system."

Rennie slapped her hands against her sides. "Great! So, now what do we do?"

"We do what we gotta do. Greaves and Sharp are in at my place. Is someone out on site? Thought I saw flashlights."

"Taylor and Danny are spending the night there," Rennie said.

"Don't forget Caedyn," Alex added.

"Oh yes, Caedyn," Rennie said. "Our little vigilante."

"How's that?" Raff asked.

"Jack returned to camp and Caedyn wanted to string him up as the perpetrator of the hit on the site," Alex said. "Taylor and Danny took him to the site to get him out of everybody's hair."

"Jack's back, huh? Good. Anyone else missing?"

"Wiggins, Heather, Hanks," Rennie said.

"All right. Then point me in the direction of the tent with my name on it."

Rennie walked out into the greasewood with Raff, then returned to join Alex and Kit at their tent.

As Rennie settled in, Alex mustered a sleepy, "Glad Raff's here?"

"Relieved and delighted!" Rennie said. "I told him about Jack. Of course, he already knew."

"Yeah, I was getting to that part when he pulled in."

"Geez! Somebody could have told us," Rennie said, rather irritated. "It might have saved us some trouble."

"Speaking of which," Alex said, "before I fall asleep, I need to tell you that Jack wondered if the site was hit on account of his being at the field school. Nobody in his family knew he had gone into archaeology except his mama."

Rennie cringed. "Oooh. I'd sure hate to be Jack's mama right now." She paused thoughtfully. "Though, if I were her, I'd be pleased with the boy. So, he thinks this was a message to him?"

"Well, to us, too."

"Interesting," Rennie said, shaking her head. "Interesting."

"You hate this place yet?"

Rennie undressed and eased herself into her bag. "I could never hate this place," she said. "It's like home to me."

Kit made an impatient movement on the floor and growled for silence.

"Sorry, Kit!" Rennie said.

"Oh, don't start apologizing to that dog!" Alex said. "It'll reinforce her superiority complex."

"Anything reinforces her superiority complex," Rennie said.

"Rrrr," trilled Kit.

Twenty-Seven

Coyote had a secret. It was so big, he didn't know what to do with it ... yet. *Give me time,* he thought. *I'll work it out.*

The secret was this: when you took someone's life, you really could *take his life.* Everything he had was yours—his riches, his land, his women. Well, actually, he already had the woman. Coyote chuckled.

Yes, he already had the woman. It had been merely an instinctual move on his part. He had never expended much effort to procure any woman that suited him, and he had certainly never had to kill to do it. Kill for a woman? Bad idea! There was an economy to getting, having, holding, and in that economy, killing for a woman rated as profligate. In fact, until recently, killing for any reason had seemed excessive except in the most abstract sense of crushing people's trust. But Coyote, also called First Angry, knew that if *he* didn't do it, somebody else would. Really, he performed a useful service, helping people get that big shock out of the way. In this wide universe, this anarchy of creation, there was always so much more going on than anybody knew. People ought to thank him for opening their eyes to that fact. What was trust anyway? The most childish of social contracts, a fallacy of innocence! *People ought to just grow up.*

Back to the secret that you could kill to get what you wanted. In the surrounding culture, images of killing propagated until they seemed caricatures of the act. There it was, right under everybody's nose—the big secret! You could kill to your heart's desire in *games*, but did people know what sort of fire they played with? No! Coyote realized that until you did it, you could not know. And maybe even then, even after doing it, some failed to grasp all the implications.

Father, forgive them, for they know not what they do. Yeah, like that.

Coyote's brow furrowed. The truth was, he felt a bit confused himself. He *thought* he had killed Grandfather Rattlesnake, but actually, he had killed a man. How had *that* happened? Well, never mind. The important thing was that everything the man owned had fallen into his hands.

And why not? The fellow was dead! The man's "things" had outlived him, he didn't need them anymore. To let them lie in the dirt would be wasteful. Who *ought* to inherit them? Why, the living, of course! The quick and the strong had obvious first rights of survivorship. In this case, matters of final possession would have to be finessed, but Coyote thought he had everything pretty much under control thanks to little acts of forethought on his part. In the great probate court of life, the strongest and the cleverest always stood to gain. The law of the jungle, they called it—philosophical and legal Darwinism.

Coyote sighed at the breathlessness of it all. Like a fortuitous shortcut to a watering hole, his action had gotten him where he had meant to go all along, only much more quickly, almost as if by accident. But not really!

If Coyote had wound up with worthless goods on his hands, he might consider that it all had been a mistake or a delusion. But the fact remained that when he had taken the man's life, he had gotten exactly what he had wanted all along. That connection between taking life and getting what he wanted decided the question of whether or not the business had been a fluke. On some level, he had known, though he had not known he had known. It was a dizzying paradox.

He wondered, *Does Rabbit know the secret? Probably not. She's a Rabbit, not a Coyote like me. She isn't First Angry, although there was some sign of easy anger there. And she is up to something; I can smell it! A Rabbit like herself, with strong blood, wouldn't be able to resist. Perhaps ... perhaps they were after the same thing, the Coyote and the Rabbit. Well, too late!*

There remained only one problem, one niggling, irritating little detail he had yet to settle. What to do with the body? *What does one do with bodies? Turn the empty bones out or hide them up to be discovered decades or centuries later in their perfect poverty of death?* Hmm. *Did it even matter if anyone saw them?* He wasn't sure.

Confronted by the suddenness of the question, Coyote had perhaps chosen unwisely. But never having killed before, how was he to know? Now that he thought about it, he felt uneasy about what he had done with the body. But he had plenty of time to come up with a better solution, provided things went his way, which they always did.

Being thoughtful by nature, Coyote found himself wondering why it was that when you wounded certain parts, the body fell down dead. Poor design or a brilliant one? And what happened to the man the body had been? Coyote knew the stories and had personal dealings with the gods that ruled over this world and the nether one. A disrespectful lot, those gods, always treating him like a dirty waif. But now that he had their secret, he had become even more like them, knowing life from death!

Yes, I, Coyote, also called First Angry, ... I have stolen murder!

Suddenly, the woman's voice broke in on his thoughts. Burnt Woman with her hesitant voice—barely a voice at all! More like a wisp of smoke rising from her ashes. He had almost completely forgotten about her. He hoped he had not done any of his thinking out loud.

"What are you thinking?" she asked.

Oh, come on. Coyote detested that question and all questions like it. *How are you today? Been up to anything interesting lately? Is there something on your mind?* As if anybody really wanted to know. As if anyone would understand if he told them. *Well, this time I'll tell her, see how she likes it.*

"Murder," he said.

The woman looked distressed. She opened her mouth as if to say something, then shut it.

Coyote smiled to himself. *She'll never ask me* that *question again!*

Twenty-Eight

Early the next morning, Rennie walked over the dig with Danny, Taylor, Raff, and Jack. Alex remained under the ramada with the others.

Caedyn was thoroughly put out with Jack's sudden rise to importance. "What's *he* doing out there?" he growled.

"Helping out," Alex said.

"Helping! How can *he* help?" Caedyn asked. "He's probably the one who did it! Dr. Hanks should have kicked him out of the field school."

Alex lost her patience. "Don't you ever doubt yourself?" she asked. "Don't you ever wonder, Could I be wrong? Am I missing something?"

"No," Caedyn said. "Coach used to say, Doubt is what the *other* team does."

"Hm! That could explain why you miss so much."

"Give him some credit," Marina said. "He gets *half* of what's going on."

"You think it's that much?" Hector asked.

"Why's everybody dissing me? It's not me, it's *him* who's

the problem. But he's getting the royal treatment and I'm getting sniped at."

As the team headed for the middens, Alex ached to see Jack in action. She decided to join the crew chiefs. "I'll be right back," she said. "Hector, you're in charge. Keep 'em in line."

"M-me?" Hector said.

"Why can't *we* come?" Chris asked.

"In a few minutes," Alex answered. "Stay out of Jack's way just a moment longer." She trotted over to the middens.

Jack walked along slowly, watching the ground. When he came to the damaged middens, he drew up and studied the holes. His brow furrowed, then he shook his head. Turning from the holes, he scanned the ground nearby, then widened his inspection to the surrounding area. He bent down, lifted a rock, and removed a crushed aluminum beverage can from beneath it. He studied it for a moment, turning it over and over. He handed it to Raff.

"This is it," he said. "But I don't recognize the sign."

Raff took the can carefully. It was a Coors Lite can.

"I have a real hard time imagining any pot hunters I know drinking Coors Lite," Raff said. "They're not a calorie-counting bunch."

"It's the marker," Jack said. "Everyone who's out doing this has one. It's a way of communicating with other hunters, staking out territory and so on."

"Bag it up," Raff said, handing the can to Danny. "Include the usual provenance information on the bag, that it was found under a rock near the middens. On second thought, put it back under the rock, take a picture, then bag it up."

Rennie said, "Could this be Jep's?"

"Jep doesn't work by himself; he goes out with Arvard," Jack said. "At least, that's how it was last I knew."

"And this isn't Arvard's?"

Jack shook his head. "Nah, they're not beer drinkers. Mormons n'all."

Raff guffawed. "A higher class than your run-of-the-mill, beer-swillin' pot hunters!"

"This is a stranger or somebody new," Jack said.

"Maybe it's someone laying down a false trail," Danny said. "They know you're here."

Jack shrugged. "Could be. But in a way, they don't really care who knows, at least on that level." He nodded at the can. "If they hadn't wanted to leave some sort of message, they wouldn't have left that."

"What about the holes," Raff asked. "One man or more?"

Jack looked at the holes, the frown returning to his face. "That's the weird part," he said. "That's a lot of damage for one man, so I think two, but it could be one man digging like crazy. To me, the pattern just says 'frantic.'"

"What about what they did to my burial?" Taylor asked. "What do you think of that?"

Jack walked over and bent down. Fragments from two or three skulls and several bone splinters littered the grave. He studied the scene a moment. "This," he said, gesturing at the disaster, "is nothing. Nobody was looking for anything here. This is, well, I guess the best word for it is *contempt.*"

Raff slapped Jack's shoulder. "You ought to think about a future in forensics," he said. "We could use a guy like you out here in law enforcement."

Jack snorted. "Right. My daddy'd appreciate that. I'd be a real hit at family reunions."

"Anything else?" Rennie asked. "Is this shovels?"

"I'd say so. One shovel. All the holes are alike. There's no evidence of machinery. If I were to make a guess, I'd say one man with a shovel spent several hours of frantic digging, some of it in the rain."

"What about these back-filled holes?" Taylor asked.

Jack shrugged. "Might not be anything. It could be fill dirt from the other holes."

"Okay," Rennie said. "That's all then?"

Jack nodded. "I'll keep thinking about it. Something might occur to me."

"Appreciate your help, Jack. You done good," Raff said.

"I don't know about that. This might not have happened if I had handled things differently."

"Don't go kickin' yourself. We've got too many mitigating circumstances, so don't rush to take credit."

Jack nodded doubtfully. Alex returned to the students under the ramada.

"Well?" Caedyn asked. "Did he confess?"

Alex ignored him.

"Here's the plan for what remains of the morning," Rennie said, striding up to the ramada. "Caedyn, you and Chris help Danny at his excavation. There's still about a foot of standing water in the kiva. Jack, Hector, Mrs. Hanson, come and work with me in my excavation. Josh and Marina, you work with Taylor on his burial—what's left of it. Alex?"

"Yes'm?"

"I need you to sit down with the F-1's. Document everything that's happened since Saturday morning when we left the canyon. While you're at it, make notes on today's work. Did I forget anything?" She looked toward Taylor and Danny, who shook their heads.

"Let's go then!" she said, stepping away from the ramada. As Caedyn passed Jack, Alex saw them lock eyes. Caedyn scowled. Jack stared back with impassivity tinged with curiosity.

Alex caught up to Rennie. "I hope a real fight doesn't erupt between those two."

Rennie looked in the direction of Alex's nod. "They seem about evenly matched to me," Rennie said. "Except Jack's a little older ..."

"And a lot more burdened by guilt."

"Suggesting? ..."

"That he might think he's got coming whatever Caedyn decides to give him."

Rennie grimaced. "Well, then, we better keep them apart for Caedyn's sake especially."

Alex walked back to the Suburban and took the F-1 notebook from the pile under the back seat. The F-1s were general site notes where, after recording who was on site that day working what excavations, the note writer was free to add whatever wisecracks or personal observations he or she saw fit. Alex found a pen, sat under the ramada, and opened the notebook to the relevant page. She jotted down the date and wrote:

Mending Dig

Something there is that doesn't love to dig,
That sends the storm surge tooth and whirlwind claw
Through tarp and visquine, leaving large and small

A wreck of puddles stretching in the sun.
The work of pot hunters is another thing ...

Then she settled in and began writing in earnest, adding editorial comments as she documented events of the last four days.

She wrote through the morning. At lunchtime, everyone converged on the ramada to eat and rest, then returned to work. Someone left a lunch bag lying on the table. Peeking in, Alex saw it held a banana. She frowned. She had a serious aversion to bananas. She pushed it away and once more spread open her notebook.

A half hour later, she noticed a pickup working its way toward the site. At first she thought Mike and Sharp had returned but, on second glance, realized the truck was unfamiliar. She watched as the vehicle drove slowly toward the ramada and pulled up alongside.

Alex had never met Russell Redhorse, but she knew immediately that the Navajo regarding her in silence was the grand old man himself. Alex returned his look, waiting for him to say something.

With a flick of his eyes, he called her attention to the paper bag sitting on the table. "You got a gun in there?" he asked, eyeing the bag.

Alex raised her eyebrows. The question completely baffled her. She replied off the cuff. "No, it's a banana. But it's loaded."

The old Navajo's eyes sharpened and glittered, but Alex found it impossible to read this response. She stood up. "I'll get Rafferty," she said, retreating.

Raff stood barefoot in muck at the bottom of the kiva,

brainstorming with Danny about what to do next.

"Put your shoes on, Raff," Alex said. "You've got an important dignitary here to see you."

"Aren't those words mutually exclusive?" Raff asked, hardly looking up.

"Important dignitary? Not this time."

"Who is it?"

"It's Russell Redhorse," Alex said, "in the wrinkled flesh."

Raff paused. "Well," he said. "This is a surprise." He hoisted himself out of the kiva. "This is a *real* surprise," he added, hopping on one foot as he strapped on a sandal. He crossed the rubble mounds and disappeared.

Alex decided to stay with the excavation crew to allow Raff and Russell whatever privacy they needed. Presently she heard the sound of a truck driving away.

Rennie said, "Raff's leaving with Redhorse! Now what?"

"Redhorse, hmm ..." Danny said.

"What is it, Danny?" Rennie asked as she sat down and returned to her notes.

"Uh, well ... I have a confession to make. Taylor, Caedyn, and me woke up early and had some time on our hands."

Rennie looked up. "Yes, go on."

"So we went out to the road and we, uh ..."

"Let me guess—you crossed the reservation fence and paid a visit to the shrine," Rennie said.

Bending over a screen full of sludge from the kiva, Caedyn straightened and said, "Wow, that was some guess!"

Danny smiled guiltily. "It was barely past dawn. We didn't think anyone would see."

"So," Hector said, "catch any witches at home?"

"There wasn't *any* good stuff" Caedyn broke in. "No blood-stained altars, no pentangles, no broomsticks ..."

"No bubbling black cauldron? No bottles labeled 'Eye of Newt?'" Alex asked.

"No!" Caedyn exclaimed, disappointed. "Nothing like that!"

"There were human bones like Taylor said, but they looked pretty old," Danny said. "And some dyed feathers."

"And we got all that here, if you count the stiffs in the middens and the feather in the skull by the latrine," Caedyn grumbled.

"Maybe Redhorse showing up doesn't have anything to do with your trip to the shrine," Alex said. "Maybe it's something else. I'm going back to my notes."

Half an hour later, Rafferty re-appeared on site, walking up the dirt road toward the ramada. He headed straight for the water coolers. Hefting one up in the air, he pushed the release button and drank deeply. His arrival did not go unnoticed. Alex could see Rennie crossing the rubble paths and Taylor approaching from the middens.

Raff pulled up a chair and sat down. He noticed the bag in front of Alex, swung the open end around, pulled the banana out, and peeled it. "This yours?" he asked, taking a bite.

"Nope," Alex said.

Taylor arrived and leaned against one of the ramada poles. Rennie sat down in the shade next to Rafferty. "What happened to Redhorse?"

"He dropped me off at the wash," Raff said. "Didn't want to risk coming onto the site again and catching the ghost sickness."

"What *did* he want?"

Raff raised his eyebrows. "Nothing much. He just dropped by to tell us we have witch trouble."

"Witch trouble!" Rennie exclaimed. She and Taylor looked at each other in shock. "What on earth does *that* mean?"

"Wouldn't say any more about it and I didn't push." Raff explained. "He said, 'You got witch trouble.' I asked, 'Me personally or the field school?' He looked toward the site and said, 'All you guys.' That was it."

"That took half an hour?" Rennie exclaimed.

"He heard about the well head, wanted to know if we could fix it. They've got a well near his place on the rez, but they like to know there's backup. Anyway, we talked about stuff like that, about the storm, about his nephew who lost a brand new truck in the flash flood. Just as I left, he said something else weird."

"What was that?" Rennie asked.

"He wanted to know why archaeologists don't get ghost sickness."

"What did you tell him?" Taylor asked.

"I said, 'I don't know—maybe they do.'"

"Wow!" Alex said. "What great material for the F-1 notes!"

Out on the main road, another pickup passed the site. Mike and Sharp honked to let the site workers know they had returned from their trip to Cortez.

Rennie sighed with relief. "Good. Maybe we'll get the water problem solved."

"What do *you* think Redhorse meant by witch trouble?" Alex asked. "I mean, that's pretty serious coming from a traditional Navajo."

"He thought it was important enough to drive over and deliver the message personally," Taylor said. "If you hadn't been here, Raff, I bet he wouldn't have come."

"I dunno," Raff said. "I dunno what he's getting at."

"Maybe he knows who hit the site," Rennie offered.

"If he does, he's not going to come out with it. He did us a big favor comin' over, but he figures the rest is our problem."

"Witch trouble," Alex said thoughtfully. "That might mean that something else is going on besides the pot hunting or something that includes the pot hunting. If we stretch it, it could mean *just* the pot hunting." She paused. "But I think we ought to keep our eyes open for something else."

"Yeah," Raff said. "After all, we've got Harry to figure into this." He looked at his watch. "It's almost quitting time. I'm going to ride out to the well head, see how Mike and Sharp are doing. Go ahead and round everybody up and get 'em back to camp. Todd's going to need help with dinner. I'll meet you back there."

"It's a plan," Rennie agreed.

Taylor nodded. "Thanks for coming and helping out," he said to Raff.

"Yeah, Raff," Rennie added. "Much obliged!"

"You guys staying out here again tonight?" Raff asked Taylor.

"Yep," Taylor said. "And every night for a while." He looked at Alex. "We'll take Caedyn again to keep him in line."

"Right!" Alex teased. "We heard what a fine role model you were."

Taylor lifted his eyebrows quizzically.

"This morning," Alex reminded him. "The shrine?"

"Oh, you heard about that."

"Danny and Caedyn suffered pangs of conscience when Redhorse arrived."

Raff grunted and strode over to his truck. "See you guys in camp later," he said. "There better be something good to eat."

As Taylor and Rennie left for their excavations, Alex tore a page out of the notebook and scrawled notes to herself for when she sat down later to finish the F-1s. Field school members started drifting toward the ramada. She slapped her notebook shut and set it in the Suburban. There was the sound of another vehicle passing on the road across canyon. Wiggins's brown and primer-colored Monte Carlo cruised past the site heading toward camp. He blasted his custom-installed air horn to advertise his presence. The first two measures of *La Cucaracha* drifted across the greasewood flat.

The cook was back. Alex thought it was good only because if Wiggins could drive his Monte Carlo over the roads, then Dr. Hanks could probably get through with the van.

. . . . .

When the field school returned to camp, Alex headed straight for the mess tent, notebook in hand. Since nobody knew yet which details provided clues about what was going on, she figured she would write down everything she could remember. Rennie sat just a few chairs away with her excavation notebook. They kept to their notes in companionable silence while Todd and Bill Wiggins worked in the kitchen.

Caedyn and Chris drove the Suburban into the middle of camp. Opening the vehicle's back door, they lifted out one of the white shower barrels and rolled it over to the kitchen. Wiggins went to assist.

"This one's half full," Caedyn said to Wiggins.

"Good," Wiggins said. "We'll need all of it."

Rennie left her notebook and walked over. "Are the kitchen water containers empty already?" she asked.

"Just about."

"Go easy on it. We don't know for sure when we'll be getting more."

"We don't even know *if* we'll be getting more," Caedyn said.

Suddenly everyone stood still and listened. A vehicle was approaching camp. "Sounds like a car," Rennie said. "Heather, probably."

"Not Hoskers or Hanks," Alex agreed.

Tony Balbo's Honda pulled into the dirt lot. "Oh no," Rennie muttered. "Not him, not now."

Alex felt a flush of alertness as she braced for another encounter with Tony. Two car doors slammed, then Tony and Heather walked into camp.

"Something happen to your vehicle, Heather?" Rennie asked.

Tony answered for her. "Heather was concerned about driving her car over the roughed up roads, so I offered her a lift."

Rennie glared at Tony.

"Damsel in distress and all that," he added.

"Such a gentleman!" Rennie said.

Heather looked pained. "I didn't think I could make it out here alone."

Rennie returned to the table and sat down. "So, how *are* the roads?"

"Not as bad as we thought. My old Honda made it just

fine," Tony said. "I see the van's not here. Does that mean Dr. Hanks has not returned?"

"That's what it means," Rennie said, burying her head in her notebook.

"Is excavation on hold until he returns?" he asked.

"Nope," she replied without looking up.

"Dinner in twenty minutes," Wiggins announced from the kitchen. He peered around a tent pole at Tony. "Are we having guests for dinner?"

Rennie said, "No, we are not having guests for dinner. We're on water rationing, remember? No camp resources are to be spent on persons not officially attached to camp."

"Yes, I'm only unofficially attached to camp, aren't I?" Tony said, taking the rejection in stride. He left Heather standing and entered the tent. Sitting across from Rennie, he said, "But I'm intrigued. Why is the camp's water being rationed?"

"Technical difficulties," Rennie replied. Alex knew Rennie had no intention of discussing the camp's troubles with anyone who didn't need to know, especially someone like Tony Balbo. *Good call!*

Caedyn, however, felt no such reservations. As he and Chris wrestled the barrel around for Wiggins, he blurted out, "Somebody sabotaged the well!"

Tony's eyes shifted back to Rennie, a spark of interest shining in them. "Really?" he said. "Sabotage?"

Rennie threw Caedyn a warning glance. It went unheeded.

"Yeah, all kinds of weird things have been happening, including pot hunters hitting the site. Tore it to bits!" Caedyn stopped talking long enough to help Chris and Bill lift the barrel onto one of the kitchen tables.

"Pot hunters!" Tony exclaimed lightly. "Really! When?"

When Rennie noticed the men hefting the fifty-five-gallon barrel onto the table, she asked crossly, "Why are you putting that in there? Why don't you set it up out back where it won't get in the way?"

The three men paused and glanced at one another. With shrugs, they lifted the barrel and rolled it to the rear of the tent.

Alex's eyes met Tony's. He leaned to one side to look at the floor by her feet and then looked over his shoulder.

"Alexandra," he said, flashing her one of those distracting smiles. "Where's that beautiful bitch of yours?"

Chemicals of aggression shot through Alex's body. She didn't answer, just sat there smiling back at Tony, returning his look—quietly on the surface but inside, weapons were arming. Heather had stood waiting for Tony but now ducked her head and left for her tent.

As if on cue, Kit trotted past, making straight for her water bowl by the open-air table. Danny and Taylor followed her into camp. Alex glanced at the dog and saw that her white shins were muddied. That meant she had been out at the well head with the boys. They walked toward the tent to make their report but stopped short when they saw Tony. For a moment, everybody stared at him in silence.

He took his cue and stood. "Well," he said, bowing slightly. "I won't overstay my welcome." He nodded to the two men, who nodded back. Then he left camp.

Rennie and Alex waited until they heard his door slam and engine start before they let out the breath they had been holding. The car backed up and sped away.

"Where's Raff?" Rennie asked.

"Out at the well head with Sharp and Mike," Taylor said.

"Well," Danny said, "do you want to hear what's going on with the well?'

"We do," Rennie replied. "Is it going well?"

"Well enough," Taylor said.

"Well, well!" Alex exclaimed, laughing.

The two men reported that Mike and Sharp were making good progress in their repairs. Sharp was even making some alterations that would improve the well's usefulness to the field school and to Ernest Brock and his Navajo neighbors.

Rennie breathed a sigh of relief. "Great. How soon till we can get water again?"

"Maybe a couple of hours," Danny said.

"That would be beautiful," Rennie said. "It'll be great to have at least that part of this mess back to normal."

Danny and Taylor left. Once they were out of earshot, Rennie turned to Alex. "*Now* what do you think of Tony?" she asked.

"He did it," Alex answered.

"I believe you," Rennie replied. "What is it you think he did?"

Alex shifted in her chair. "I don't know. But whatever it is, or whatever it's going to be, he did it."

Twenty-Nine

Why is Coyote so smart? How is it he survives, even flourishes, when other animals have a bad time of it, except perhaps for Rabbit? I will tell you.

After the spirits created the world and its creatures, they argued. Some said the animals ought to choose what powers they wanted. Others said no, each animal should take only what was given. The spirits favoring choice argued that if animals chose for themselves, they would have nobody but themselves to blame if things turned out badly. The others said that choice was a power with two faces, one good and one evil, and that giving it to earth's creatures might come back to the gods in a bad way. They could not settle the matter, so they gambled. The spirits who thought the animals ought to be given choice won.

"It is decided," said those spirits. "But to satisfy you others and balance things out, we will shape the powers so that each comes with a weakness equal to its strength. That way, getting choice will not make the animals too dangerous to each other or to us. Now, bring all the animals."

Everyone was brought and seated at a fire. The powers and their matching weaknesses were laid out in little pouches. The spirits told the animals that each one, after choosing its sacred pouch, should not show the contents to anyone. They said that this would be for the animal's own good. Then the animals chose.

Hawk chose a bundle with the power of flight, though such a power made her clumsy on the ground. Deer chose a bundle with the power to leap, although leaping made him visible to hunters. Badger chose the ability to dig, though if he were caught away from his hole in the ground he would be vulnerable to danger. Mouse chose the ability to creep through the grass without being seen, but this made her smaller than anyone except for Ant and Honeybee. Rattlesnake chose to have poison in his bite. This came with a loud rattle that Rattlesnake would have to wear on his tail at all times. So on and so forth.

Coyote hung back during this time of choosing. When the gods asked him which pouch he wanted, he said, "I cannot decide," but in his heart he wanted all the powers. Finally there was only one power left—the power of guile. The other animals did not want it because it smelled bad.

The spirits said, "Coyote, you waited too long. Now there is only this one power left. You must take it."

"If you insist," said Coyote. He took the pouch and put it around his neck. All the other animals moved away from him.

"Hmm," said the spirits. "We wonder if this has worked out for the best." Then they went on to other things.

That night, the animals held a big feast. All the animals ate of the food except Coyote. "Coyote, why do you not eat?" asked the other animals.

"Oh, my belly aches," said Coyote.

Each animal danced, giving in the dance a glimpse of its sacred power. Only Coyote did not take part. "Coyote, why do you not dance?" asked the others.

"Oh, I have a cactus spine stuck in my foot," Coyote said.

After the celebration, all of the animals felt very sleepy. They made beds by the fire and lay down. Only Coyote did not lie down. "Coyote, why do you not sleep?" asked the other animals.

"Oh, the pain in my foot and in my belly keeps me awake," Coyote said.

Soon all the animals were asleep except for Coyote. He lay there waiting for the fire to die, then crept over to the animal lying next to him, who happened to be Fox, and looked in his sacred pouch. He saw Fox's power and Fox's weakness. He took a pinch of the bag's contents and put it in his own.

Next he came to Mouse. He opened up Mouse's pouch and looked in. He saw Mouse's power and her weakness. He took a pinch of the contents of the pouch and put it in his own. Next he came to Frog, then Owl, then Fish. He crept all the way around the circle, stealing a tiny bit from each animal's sacred pouch. Lastly he came to Rabbit.

Pretending to be asleep, Rabbit had kept one eye open watching Coyote. "This is witchcraft," she thought. "I must do something. But what? I am only a Rabbit."

Then she got an idea. Some say the spirits whispered it to her. Others say it was because of the power in her sacred pouch, which was quickness in the brain. As Coyote leaned over and stole from her pouch, she slipped her hand into his pouch and stole from him. Then Coyote knew Rabbit was awake, but it was too late.

Rabbit sprang up. "Wake up!" she cried. "Coyote has stolen from our sacred pouches and knows our weaknesses as well as our strengths! There is danger in this!" All the animals ran, flew, leaped, slithered, or swam away. Coyote was left standing alone with his great hunger.

Coyote sat down and licked his lips in anger. Things had not gone as he had planned, but he knew that as long as he had the bundle around his neck containing a little of each animal's strength and weakness, he would always have the upper hand. When the world changed, as he knew it would, he would survive because he had a pinch of the best qualities of each animal and knowledge of their worst.

There was just one problem. As Coyote shared the qualities of other animals, Rabbit now shared his. "I will get that Rabbit," he said. "I must retrieve that which she stole from me."

Meanwhile, Rabbit opened her pouch and looked in. There was her power and her weakness and, next to it, the pinch of Coyote's power. Rabbit said, "This is guile. Now I see why Coyote did as he did. But what is his weakness?" Though it repulsed her to touch it, she turned the guile over and there, on the other side, she saw Coyote's weakness. It was that he would always think of himself as being better than he was, and that would at times cause him to fail in the hunt.

The gods appeared to Rabbit. "What have you done?" they asked.

Rabbit said, "I saw what Coyote was doing and I did the same. In so doing, I saved others' lives."

The spirits said, "Like Coyote, you have gained greater power and understanding than you ought to have. But as long as you use it for good, you may keep it. There must be someone who can stand up to Coyote, someone who knows who he is. The other animals—some are too rigid, others are innocent, many have no imagination."

Rabbit felt ashamed.

"Now go your way," the spirits said. As soon as Rabbit had gone, the spirits talked among themselves. "That Coyote, he will give them all something to think about, and that Rabbit, she will show them Coyote for what he really is." They felt pleased. "Funny how things work out," they said.

Perhaps you are wondering what weakness it was that Rabbit carried in her sacred pouch. Such wonder is what made Coyote what he is. Few people want to say, "I am like Coyote," but it is no big thing nowadays for one person to try to glimpse another's weakness. It is no big thing for one person to use another's weakness to gain the upper hand.

Thirty

Dr. Benjamin Hanks arrived Tuesday night, two volunteers in tow, and listened to reports of the dramatic events that had occurred in his absence. He did not comment much on what he heard. When Rennie told him that Jack Reed had walked the site looking for clues to the pot hunters' identities, he raised his eyebrows in surprise. But he spent most of the night planning with his crew chiefs how to get the project back on track.

The following morning opened with a business-as-usual tone. Sharp's repairs on the well had worked, so the camp's potable water source flowed once more. Following the recent morning routine, the group drove out to meet Taylor, Caedyn, and Danny, who had spent the night on site.

Summer had come fully into bloom. Light streamed over the site, immersing the workers in a sea of shimmering glare. At 2:30 p.m., Dr. Hanks drove a van load of scorched and exhausted students and volunteers back to camp, then rejoined his crew chiefs and Alex, all of whom were putting in extra hours to try to bring the project back in line.

At dusk, Alex called it quits. Leaving the others to toil in the twilight, she walked the mile up the wash to camp. The first thing on her mind was washing off the day's grunge, then she'd eat a late supper.

As she laid out towels and soap for her shower, she heard snuffling outside the tent. Kit stepped through the flap, upbraiding her with low growls for breaking routine.

"What? Oh, were you worried about me? How sweet!"

Kit leaned against Alex for a good back scratching. The husky's soft, evening-cooled fur felt good against Alex's skin. Kit panted happily, then mouthed Alex's hand in a gesture of affection. Alex stroked the husky as they sat in the tent enjoying a quiet moment together. Then she gathered up her soap and towel and left for the shower, Kit sweeping back and forth across the path.

As she veered toward the women's shower, Alex saw the campfire's glow lighting up the two cottonwoods at the south end of the mess area. Voices rose and drifted away. Standing on her toes to peek over the greasewood, she saw people sitting around the fire. Curious, she moved off the path for a closer look.

Marina, Josh, Chris, Caedyn, and Hector formed a loose circle around the fire, their attention focused on someone sitting further back in the shadows. Alex peered at this person, suspicion rising in her blood. The figure spoke. She cringed as she recognized the voice. The students were paying court to Tony Balbo.

Kit passed the fire and trotted into the mess area. A couple of the students watched her pass but thought nothing of it. For once, Alex appreciated the husky's reputation for independence. Kit came and went as she pleased; nobody would take her presence to mean that Alex was around. Sure enough, they all turned their attention back to Balbo.

"I think it was a dirty rotten trick what they did to the site!" Caedyn said.

"What I don't understand," Tony said, "is why you take this so personally."

Caedyn's demeanor suggested he thought his masculinity was being called into question. "I ... p-personally?" he stuttered.

"Yes, personally," Tony replied. "You behave as if the attack on the site had been an attack on you, on your person, your property, or your ideals."

All this was a bit beyond Caedyn. "It was ... just wrong," he asserted. "It was wrong of them to do that."

Tony chuckled. "Wrong," he repeated. "You're saying the attack on the site was wrong because it was wrong."

"Well, it was," Marina insisted. "You don't know, you haven't seen it."

"So," Tony said, "if I were to see it, I would know immediately that what the pot hunters did was wrong."

"I think you would," Marina said, uncertainty quavering in her voice.

"I think it's a matter of perspective," he said, chuckling.

"What do you mean?" Hector asked.

"Well, think about it," Tony said. "Isn't it obvious?"

The students sat, baffled.

"Archaeologists have the law on their side. If the law, as it is enforced by those in power, comes to the site to judge between you and the pot hunters, it will say, 'Do you have the requisite permit to conduct your business here?' You'll produce the permit, the law will see that all is in order, then it will seek out the others in question. Aside from trespassing, grave desecration, and vandalism, our pot hunter friends will be found delinquent in the permit department, so the law will automatically judge them to be in the wrong. It's a mechanism that's not built on principles that are inherently right, but on the perspective of what is right or wrong in the eyes of the culture in power."

Alex could read dismay and confusion in the students' fire-lit faces.

"How do we know," Hector ventured, "that the principles which determine what is right or wrong in the eyes of the culture are *not* inherently ... uh, accurate?"

"You mean *true*?" Tony asked, stirring the edge of the fire with a stick.

"I mean, they correlate with laws of the universe," Hector said.

Tony lifted his head, then lowered it, smiling. "You mean *true*," he said. "Well, Hector, you're a smart fellow. Think of it. Suppose that tomorrow by some twist of fate the Navajos rise to power and *they* become the lawmakers. How do you suppose they would judge our little scenario?"

"We'd both be wrong," Josh said. "Archaeologists and pot hunters, permit or no permit."

"There might not be permits," Hector interjected. "Native Americans don't look favorably on archaeological activities. They go counter to their beliefs."

"There you have it," Tony said. "The Navajos aren't in power, so there are permits. Where is the right or wrong of it?"

"Are you suggesting," Marina asked, "that if the pot hunters get away with this, they're the ones in power and nobody can say they're in the wrong?"

Tony looked up and wagged his fire-stirring stick at Marina. "That's a very astute question," he said. "What do you think?"

"I think they're wrong whether they're caught or not," she replied.

"The Navajos think the archaeologists are wrong whether they have permits or not, which is to say, whether or not the Navajos have the power to stop them from defiling the burials of their ancestors." Fixing Marina with a bold gaze, he asked, "Knowing this, are you going to stop your work on the site tomorrow? Are you personally going to head up a movement to remove archaeologists from excavations everywhere because Navajos, or even just some Navajos, believe them to be wrong?"

Marina leaned back, away from Tony's ostensible logic. That was the best she could do by way of rejecting his argument.

"Hmm," Tony said, his smile dripping irony. "You see?"

Alex could restrain herself no longer. She stepped out of the shadows. "Professor Balbo is appealing to a very old argument," she said, walking into the firelight and sitting next to him. "It's the 'might makes right' argument, isn't it? Whoever has the might gets to decide what's right. One of the world's oldest rationalizations and very highly esteemed by, well, certain kinds of people."

"Good evening, Alexandra," Tony said, unfazed. "I was wondering when you were going to come out of the bushes."

"And I was wondering when you were going to crawl out from under your rock," Alex retorted.

"Eeee!" Marina squealed.

"Oh, man! This is going to be good," Caedyn said, nudging Chris.

Tony laughed easily. "Touché!" he said. "However, you're misrepresenting me. I suggested only that concepts of right or wrong are dependent upon point of view."

"Hmm, 'point of view,'" Alex said. "As in something is right or wrong depending upon the preference of the individual making the call?'"

Tony nodded. "To put it crudely."

"Okay," Alex said. "That might work in a very basic difference of opinion such as between mom and toddler, where mom is acknowledged as having authority to make the call. But what about situations where different opinions are irreconcilable and the question of who gets to make the call is up in the air?"

"Irreconcilable differences!" Tony exclaimed. "How sad!"

"Here's one that's very sad," Alex said. "Coyote is hungry and has a personal preference to eat Rabbit. Rabbit has an equally compelling preference not to be eaten. Coyote spies Rabbit, Rabbit spies Coyote, and the chase is on. Rabbit is clever and for a time avoids a confrontation, but at last, Coyote corners him in a cave. Now there is only Coyote's preference to eat Rabbit and Rabbit's preference to live. Who makes the call?"

"Well, if they were people and not animals, the law would settle it!" Caedyn said.

"But aren't lots of people murdered in spite of the law?"

Alex asked. "Person A wants to murder Person B, and Person B does not want to be murdered. Coyote wants to eat Rabbit, Rabbit doesn't want to be eaten. How is this dilemma resolved?"

"The person with the biggest weapon and the skill to use it wins," Josh answered. "But that's 'might makes right' again, isn't it?"

"Maybe Rabbit tricks Coyote," Marina said. "Maybe he distracts him long enough to get away or something like that."

"That would mean Rabbit has greater skill in trickery," Hector said. "It could be argued that his greater skill comprises might, then it's still a might makes right situation."

Alex nodded. "You see, Professor Balbo? They're not as stupid as you think." She turned to the students. "Speaking of murder, do you know the formula cops apply when trying to solve one?"

"They look at the evidence at the crime scene and then theorize who might have had the motive, means, and opportunity to commit the crime," Hector answered.

"Yep," Alex agreed. "That formula has the same basic elements as the 'might makes right' principle. The cops look for someone who had the might—the motive, means, and opportunity—to force their view of *right* to the point of causing someone's death. See? Might equals right. Or so some may think."

Tony looked up at Alex. Something about his glance gave her a start. She reacted physically with a slight jump, but the dance and crackle of the flames masked her movement.

"Not all cases of personal preference have such dire consequences," he said smoothly.

Alex recovered. "True. The commercial industry banks on

personal preference. It runs right along to match the tastes of the buying public step for step, sometimes even running ahead to create preferences."

"Sometimes people in conflict with each other go into mediation like in a court of law, but instead of a judge, they use a mediator," Marina said.

"We're not concerned with cases like those," Hector said. "In those instances, the matter of who's making the call is agreed upon by everyone involved. No might is exerted."

Without acknowledging that Hector had spoken, Tony focused on Alex. "Then why choose murder to disclose the flaws of my thinking?" he asked.

"It's an obvious place where your 'preference' theory breaks down and becomes pure *might makes right*. If personal preference *per se* is the determining factor in the outcome of any incident, then it ought to work in the case of murder. Only in murder, two or more conflicting sets of preferences are pitted against each other. Either Coyote murders Rabbit's preference by killing and eating him or Rabbit escapes, which demonstrates that preference in and of itself can't stand as the determining impetus of all human action. When there's no agreement on who gets to make the call, might is often exercised. The question was whether or not you were appealing to the *might makes right* argument, and you were."

Tony reared back. "Well done, Miss McKelvey," he said, his voice dripping false appreciation. "Clever! But while you have perhaps shown that personal preference alone fails as the sole determinant for human law and order ... oh, we are talking about humans here, aren't we?"

"I think so," Alex said. "But who knows?"

"Well then, while you have perhaps shown that personal preference falls short as a regulating principle for society, and while you may have shown that personal preference, when taken to its extreme, could erupt into a might makes right situation ..."

"And a *means, motive, and opportunity* situation," Marina said.

Tony looked at her through the fire. "Yes, perhaps even that." He turned back to Alex. "With all that, you haven't shown any inherent flaw in the principle of *might makes right*. After all, coyotes do track, kill, and eat rabbits—that fact is unavoidably fixed. It's Nature. I can't imagine how you could show that those circumstances should be otherwise."

Alex hesitated, weighing the challenge. "Should I?" she asked.

"I don't know," Tony answered. "Should you?"

Alex laughed. She was aware she was enjoying the confrontation with Tony more than she ought to but felt compelled to keep pushing him. "First of all, I think there is always a difference between how things appear and how they are. Like icebergs. Then there's a difference between how they are and how they could be or maybe even between how they are and how they once were. Maybe when Coyote catches and eats Rabbit, more is at stake than the mere satisfaction of hunger or the survival of the strongest. Or maybe your view that the relationship between Coyote and Rabbit is fixed is too narrow."

Tony laughed. He paused, then laughed again. The self-confidence and drama of the action rattled the students. "This is too quaint," he said. "You're speaking of good and evil, good being the peaceable kingdom with wide open fields of grass and flowers where Coyote can lie down with Rabbit and they chew cud in each other's company forever!"

He jabbed his stick into the fire and probed viciously. Sparks shot upward in the fire's wind, creating a wash of spectacle that winked out just below the cottonwood leaves. "Good triumphs and evil—well, evil has the life crushed out of it. Coyote switches places with Rabbit. A charming and inspiring fable *for the Rabbits!* But look, Alexandra, look! Nothing has changed! We still have a fine case of might makes right! Good triumphs and makes a fine repast of evil!" He turned to her, his dark eyes flashing.

Alex sat for a moment in wonder. While Tony's logic didn't intimidate her, something behind his words did. She searched for the source of the alarm ringing in her head, trying to sort it out from the current of the debate. She said, "I suppose I have no quarrel with the principle of might makes right itself, but with how *right* and *might* are defined. The same thing with the survival of the fittest idea, first cousin to the might makes right principle. The problem lies in our limited and maybe even totally fallacious definitions of *fittest* and *survival*."

"What's fallacious about being eaten and not surviving?" Tony asserted. "Either you die or you don't die. Either you survive or you don't survive."

"That's the question," Alex said. "What is survival, and what makes one fit? Perhaps there's more to it than Rabbit frustrating Coyote's desire to dine on him, and perhaps there's more to being fit than not dying at someone else's hand."

"Or paw," Marina interjected.

"Or paw," Alex agreed.

"Or perhaps there's more to survival than passing on genetic variations which are profitable to life on earth," Hector added.

"Yes," Alex said. "Perhaps there is *much* more to it all than Coyote's and Rabbit's perpetual war."

"You've undertaken a difficult task, Alexandra, and I can't see how you could possibly keep from repeating the work of centuries with the same results: you aren't able to prove anything about anything. It becomes an academic exercise, and when you're done, Rabbit's life remains in peril."

"The way I figure it," Alex said, "proof can be all around, but we're stuck on what we see in the mirror, imposing our own images upon the landscape. The fifteenth-century model of the solar system is a good example. The culture at the time thought so highly of itself that it saw the solar system swimming around it, and when Copernicus suggested otherwise—never mind that his views were only slightly less myopic—well, Coyote tried to eat him. Suppose that's where we are with our own understanding of how things are—stuck in a kind of cultural adolescence, obsessing about our images in mirrors. Suppose there's actually a great window before us through which evidence of God and fantastic landscapes of existence can be seen, but all we're concerned with is our own reflection in the glass."

"There, you've said it," Tony said.

"What? The word *God*?" Alex asked. "I did, didn't I?" She smiled sweetly.

"But it's a supposed God. I'm sure these youngsters sitting here with us, devoting their valuable time and attention to you, would like to hear your proof, not just your suppositions," Tony said. "Well? Does God watch and judge Coyote? Does he bless and inspire Rabbit? Or is it the other way around? Does he bless Coyote and deliver Rabbit up to him? Convince us, Alexandra. Give us proof."

"Proof?" Alex said. "If I'm stuck in the mirror, I can't see the proof. Look at Copernicus. He had a glimpse through the glass, but his contemporaries were transfixed by their own images and fought desperately against what he said he saw." She looked into the fire. "Proof isn't necessary anyway. Isn't it enough that the possibility exists that we're misinterpreting most of what's happening around us? That alone ought to give us something to go on. But it's traditional to resist the momentum or even the desire for the momentum that can be ignited by what's out there. Generations have done just that—wallowed in misinterpretation and invested vast amounts of resources, even waging war, to preserve precious self-images." Alex turned toward Tony, fully facing him. "Besides, if there's one thing I have learned from folklore, it's that just because something hasn't happened doesn't mean it isn't true."

"Meaning?"

"Meaning, among other things, that there are aspects of our lives that do not need grounding in historical evidence or scientific facts, which arise, after all, from human perception. What's truly real is not dependent upon our perceiving it, though it's out there calling, competing against our vanities. Think about it. Maybe there's more going on than we realize, stuff capable of reducing all our facts and evidence, as we put our faith in them, to groundless assertions, half-truths, or milli-truths. You could say that makes them no truth at all, but only the wink and glitter of it in a dark place."

While Alex spoke this last piece, Tony scrutinized her expressions and gestures. He goaded her on. "Poetic," he said.

"And not without effect upon your audience, which we both know is what you're really going for here."

"I don't care what you think," Alex said.

"Of course you care," Tony said, his voice low. "You must care."

"I can't care," Alex snapped back. But as she spoke the words, she felt her inner spiritual guide blush. It was one thing to say she *didn't* care, since what Tony thought couldn't make much of a difference one way or the other in what Alex believed. A twist of the word care to mean something like 'give credence to,' and that much of her assertions was true. But to say she *couldn't* care—that was a lie, a malicious snowball with an icy center thrown in a fit of anger. Of course she cared what Tony thought, she couldn't *not* care. Alex had spoken against herself, and she knew it. But it was too late to take back the words—too late to recant the spell.

Tony's eyes widened. A peculiar expression crossed his face. "Yes!" he exclaimed. "That's it! Why, you're more like me than you want to admit, Alexandra!" He reached out as if to touch her.

In a flash, Alex knocked his hand aside and looked defiantly into his face.

Tony's eyes registered surprise. That winked out, then a slow smile of delight and triumph spread across his lips. He leaned back. Putting his hands on his knees, he shook his head with appreciation—and something else that caused a shiver to seize Alex's spine.

"You've revealed yourself to me, my dear!" he said, rising from the fire. His eyes locked in hers as he maintained an aggressive yet chillingly intimate eye contact. Feeling it a bad idea to allow him to tower over her, Alex stood up with him.

"You have revealed yourself, Alexandra McKelvey!" He turned to leave the fire, glancing at the students as he did. They sat, stunned and speechless, staring at him.

"Well!" he said. "You should all sleep well tonight after those pretty bedtime stories." As he turned away, Alex heard him say something else, something that sounded like *run, Rabbit, run,* following it up with a growling chuckle. As he walked past the mess tent, Alex noticed that Heather sat inside at a table with her notebooks and equipment. Tony didn't even glance at her but walked by shaking his head. They heard one more irony-tinted laugh issue from the dark parking lot, then a car door open and shut. He started the engine, backed out of the lot, and drove off down the road.

Only when he was well away did the stunned group at the fire let out their breaths in a collective sigh of relief. Marina scooted around the fire to Alex. "What a creep!" she exclaimed. "Are you all right? Did he touch you?"

"I touched *him*," Alex replied, feeling irritable.

Chris nudged Caedyn. With a nod and a snicker, he indicated that they should leave. The two young men slipped off into the darkness toward their tents. Josh followed.

"What a creep!" Marina repeated. "What was that all about anyway?"

"I don't know," Alex said, dusting off her shorts.

Marina stood protectively beside Alex. Alex appreciated the gesture but felt the need to get away. More than ever, she wanted that shower. She needed to scrub the burn from Tony's touch off her skin. "Well," she said. "I was on my way to wash up." She bent over and picked up her towel and shook it out.

"Good plan," Marina said. "If you're all right, then ..."

A bit sharply, Alex answered, "I'm fine!"

"Good," Marina said. "I hope he doesn't come back!"

With that, Marina left for the women's side of camp. Hector rose from his place by the fire and approached Alex. He cleared his throat. "For what it's worth ..." he began. "Well, what I mean is ... thanks."

"For what?" Alex asked, surprised.

"For your—what shall we call it—your 'possibility theory'? Not exactly what we're taught in Sunday school, but very interesting!"

Alex chuckled. "Gee, I didn't know you were listening," she said.

"Are you kidding?" he said. "Anyway, thanks."

Alex nodded. She watched him walk into the greasewood, then she turned to make her way out to the women's shower. Another voice softly called her name. Alex stopped and peered into the gloom. Jack emerged from the shadows behind one of the cottonwoods.

"I heard it all," he said. Then he laughed. "I think he likes you."

"Tony?" Alex asked.

Jack nodded.

"Well!" Alex said. "Should I succumb to his charms or play hard to get?"

After a pause, they said in unison, "Play hard to get!" Once more, Alex started toward the shower.

"Alex?" Jack called.

"Hmm?"

"I have just one word for you," he said. He crouched and

picked up a twig, then snapped it between his fingers. "Contempt," he said.

Alex stared at Jack for a moment, struggling for his meaning. She looked in the direction Tony had driven off. Her mind lit up with sudden understanding. "That's right!" she exclaimed. "I think you're right!" Burning with awareness, she turned toward the shower. When she looked back a moment later, Jack was gone.

Thirty-One

Coyote loved games. This business with Rabbit was the best thing to come his way in a long time. He smiled at the shards hanging suspended around his head, pleased to have an audience. "I remember the game I played with Wolverine," he said to the shards. "That one was dangerous. I would have been killed had I lost, but I did not lose. And there was that race with Bluebird. I proved that in a race of wits against wings, wits might still win out. Then there was that contest with Trout, where we held our breaths underwater to see who could go the longest." He chuckled and licked his lips. "I won that one, too."

He smiled. "Rabbit is better because there is something of each of us in the other. Yet there are differences, too. The way her ears lie down flat just before she kicks—endearing, but it gives her away. Foolish to show your mind like that. Her affection for weaker creatures encumbers her. She ought to run with someone with talents equal to her own, someone like ... me." Thinking about this, First Angry remembered a story.

Once there was a family of desert foxes who lived in a den

under a rock. Hunters found them and killed both parents and all the kits but one. The hunters took the kit home and raised it with their dogs. The fox grew up, taking food from the hands of her captors, not knowing they had killed those with whom she belonged, not knowing she was a fox and not a dog. She wanted to hunt the barnyard chickens, but the dogs said, "You must not hunt the chickens."

"Why not?" asked the fox.

"Because it isn't done," said the dogs.

The fox didn't think that was much of an answer, but because she was raised with obedient dogs, she decided not to hunt the chickens even though it hurt her heart. Also, she liked to slip outside at night and prowl the desert. The dogs told her she must not prowl at night.

"Why not?" asked the fox.

"Because that's what wild things do," said the dogs.

As before, the fox did not find this answer helpful. But since the compliant life of a dog was all she had known, she did not prowl but lay by the fire when darkness fell even though the wind whistled from the desert, calling her name.

One night her big ears heard a noise in the barnyard—something new. She crept to the door and looked out. Near the shed where the chickens slept, she saw a shadow slip around a corner. The fox looked over her shoulder at the people and dogs in the house. They had not heard the noise nor seen the shadow. She decided to go and look for herself even though she knew she ought not to prowl at night. Noiselessly she crossed the yard.

She came upon a creature just leaving the barnyard with a chicken in his mouth. He looked like a dog, but there was something different about him. She said to the stranger, "You must not hunt the chickens!" She thought he had simply made a mistake.

The stranger looked at her, dropped the dead chicken to the ground, and said, "Why not?"

"Because it isn't done."

The stranger laughed. "Oh yes it is," he said. "It's done all the time! Who told you it wasn't?"

"The dogs."

Again, the stranger laughed. "That's what you get for listening to dogs," he said.

"But aren't you a dog?" the fox asked.

"Certainly not!"

"Then what are you?"

The stranger sat down and cocked his head. "I have heard of cases like yours," he said. "Come with me."

"Where?"

"Out into the desert."

"Oh, I must not prowl at night," said the fox.

"And why is that?"

"Because that's what wild things do."

Now the stranger looked completely vexed. "I suppose the dogs told you that, too. Never mind, come with me now." He picked up his chicken and trotted off into the desert.

The fox that had been raised with dogs hesitated. She looked back at the house. Then she looked at the dark desert and the stranger disappearing into it.

"Come!" he called.

The little fox strained against the invisible tether that bound her to the house. Suddenly it snapped and she leapt lightly across the sand. "Where are we going?" she asked.

"You will see," said the stranger.

"Okay, but I have to go home soon."

The stranger did not reply but led the fox away from the house over rocks, through streams, over fallen logs. He doubled back on their trail and then picked another direction. The fox began to wonder if she would ever find her way home.

At last they stopped by a pool worn in a smooth stone. The stranger dropped the chicken and called the fox to the water's edge. "You asked me if I am a dog. I am not. Look."

The fox looked in the pool's moonlit waters at her reflection and at the stranger's reflection. She saw that she looked just like the stranger, tawny and lean, with large, upright ears that heard everything. "I'm not a dog!" she said, astonished. "But what am I? What are *we*?"

"We're foxes," said the other fox. "Now you know the truth. Let's eat this chicken and see what else is out there."

"You mean, go prowling some more?"

"Yes! That's what foxes do."

So the fox that had been raised with dogs shared the chicken with the stranger and afterward went prowling with him through the desert's vast silent stones and over its shifting sands. She never returned to the house. The voice in the wind was silenced and her heart no longer hurt.

Coyote remembered the story with satisfaction. It was a good one. *I need only bring her to the pool.* He began to plan just how to do that. "She will thank me for it," he said to the shards.

Thirty-Two

Following another frustrating day on site, the crew returned to camp, labeled artifacts, did chores, ate dinner, and took a few hours off. The chiefs, including Heather, who occupied a chair three down from the main group, sat in the mess tent with Dr. Hanks, laying out plans of attack for the remaining weeks of fieldwork. Rafferty had driven to Bluff to renew his search for Harry Hoskers. Students and volunteers went on walks, retreated to tents, or sat in the mess compound as the evening cool descended.

Still feeling the burn of confusion from her encounter with Tony, Alex took to the wash with Kit. Overhead the luminous cloud of the Milky Way conjured itself from the fading light, the stars' varying degrees of brightness suggesting depth and distance like points on a 3D map. Looking up, Alex felt she was gazing into another canyon, a crack in the otherwise smooth night sky. She felt the tingle of a brisk breeze. The cottonwoods around her swelled and sighed with it.

The walk helped a little. When she returned, she dragged a chair out of the mess tent away from the fire, in the mood to sit quietly in the shadows. Kit lay a short distance away in her dug-out beneath the dripping spigot of the water jug. Todd walked around from the back of the mess tent. Grabbing a chair from the dining area, he carried it over and sat beside Alex.

A few days ago when they had been washing dishes together, Alex had put a riddle to him: "What kind of keys won't fit in a lock?" Dishwashing passed quickly as they played with answers. *Piano keys. Monkeys. Florida Keys.* Todd had said, *Iraqis.*

Now he asked her, "What kind of keys won't fit in a lock?"

Alex liked open-ended jokes. "I don't know. What kind?"

"Honkies," Todd said.

Alex sputtered in amusement. "Really, Todd," she said. "Wherever did you hear such language?"

"I don't know," he said. "School I guess."

"Sounds to me like you've been watching old shows on satellite TV."

"Maybe that's it."

The two sat quietly, enjoying the sights and sounds of camp. Sharp strode up to the fire carrying his guitar. He pulled up a chair and overlaid the usual camp noises with a pleasant stream of music. Like magic, more people flowed out of the greasewood and joined the fire circle.

Strains of *Shenandoah* began, with several voices joining Sharp's. Alex picked up her chair to carry it to the fire circle and, with a jerk of her head, invited Todd to follow. He trailed after. Kit rose from her dugout and trotted over. The singing went on for over an hour. Eventually Sharp stopped and the group at the fire dwindled, leaving only Alex, Todd, Marina, and Kit. Rennie and Dr. Hanks sat in the tent with Heather, who had positioned herself in a corner so that she looked as if she was more or less alone.

Bill Wiggins walked up to the fire and made a big show of looking at his watch. "Nine forty-five, Todd," he said. "Time to hit the sack."

"In a moment," Todd said.

Marina asked, "Anybody know a story?"

"I know a joke," Todd said. "Or is it a riddle?" He looked at Alex.

"What is it?" Marina asked, cautious.

"Nothing bad. It's this: What kind of keys won't fit in a lock?"

And so it went. As Marina wound down a ghost story, Alex's ears picked up a sound coming from the wash. She turned her head and listened. Some dog was barking. She thought it was probably a stray from Old Man Redhorse's spread, then it dawned on her: that was Kit's sharp, high-pitched alarm bark. She looked around the fire and over at Kit's dugout by the table to confirm that she was gone.

"Oh-oh, that's Kit," Alex said, rising from her chair. "Something's happening down at the wash." She pulled a small flashlight from her pocket and set out.

"I'll come with you," Todd said.

Kit's barking grew sharper. As they neared the wash, Todd bent down and picked up stones. "This is not good!" he said, gathering another. "This is not good at all!"

Alex listened to the barking, trying to read it. She noticed an edgy note to Kit's voice—something she'd never heard before. Not that the husky ever did much barking. If she had anything to say, she usually yowled or yodeled. Yet, she didn't sound desperate or panicked. What was going on?

When they reached the wash, Alex turned north, Todd walking nervously at her side, both his hands now filled with rocks. When the barking sounded close, Alex shined her flashlight up the wash. She couldn't help staring in wonder at what she saw.

Several pairs of eyes reflected the light back to her, disks of yellowish spectral sheen. They milled about restlessly. Alex picked out one set that glimmered differently, a pale red instead of yellow. Those pinkish-red lights would be the flashlight's rebound out of the depths of Kit's blue irises. As for the others ...

"Coyotes!" Alex said in a low voice. Todd's body went rigid and a sound of fright escaped his mouth. Alex stood still, watching the dim shapes, wondering what to do. She switched off the flashlight, then whistled low.

"Come, Kit!" she called. "Come on, girl!"

She had no idea if Kit would part company with the coyotes. If the dog decided her new, wild companions were more interesting than her human ones, Alex didn't know that she could do anything about it. She held her breath as she waited for Kit's response.

"Come here, Kit!" she called. Again, nothing happened except that the shadows twisting and turning in the wash receded deeper into the darkness. Suddenly, one shadow separated from the others and trotted straight toward Todd and Alex. Alex could smell the panic rolling off Todd.

Kit's white chest faded into view as she trotted up to them with an unhurried gait. Alex switched on her light to look the husky over. She appeared unscathed. Her tongue rolled jauntily out of her mouth. Alex caught her by the collar, took one last look up the wash and, turning her back on the coyote pack, headed for camp.

It was an extreme act of will on Todd's part to follow Alex's cue. As they walked back down the wash, he wheeled around twice with a sharp intake of breath, stones ready to fly. Alex knew that in his world, close encounters with coyotes could bring bad luck, but trying to protect yourself against that threat by killing them could have an equally bad effect. The boy was not a traditionalist, but some beliefs died hard.

"They're not going to follow us," she said, remembering as she said it that a coyote did follow her once. No need for Todd to know that, though.

As they walked back to camp, neither spoke. Todd veered off and headed straight to his tent without so much as "see ya." Alex let him go.

She passed Raff's truck in the lot, its engine ticking as it cooled. She could hear men's voices and recognized Taylor's laugh—not his merry one, his anxious one. Walking into camp, she found Marina and Rennie waiting at the fire.

"What was it?" Marina asked.

"Coyotes," Alex said. "Down in the wash. They had her surrounded."

"You're kidding!" Marina exclaimed. She looked at Kit and shook her finger at her. "You're running with the wrong pack!" she said. "You belong with us, not with those ... *hoodlums!*"

Kit looked Marina squarely in the eyes and yodeled in defiance. Alex grinned. Kit was never one to be told her business. Rennie said nothing, but returned to the tent with Dr. Hanks, Raff, and the other crew chiefs.

Marina gave Kit a doubtful glance and said good night. Alex looked at the husky.

"You stay here," she said. "No more coyotes."

She could have sworn she saw Kit roll her eyes. The dog padded into the mess area and threw herself into the duff with the tent's shadow, as usual, dividing her into light and dark halves.

Satisfied that Kit would not return to the wash, Alex entered the mess tent and sat down with Rennie.

"Your dog been off baiting the locals?" Rafferty asked.

"Afraid so," Alex answered. "The rabble rouser."

"So, what now?" Hanks interrupted, returning the conversation to the main topic. "You called Mesa Verde and what happened?"

"Steve Henders said he hadn't seen him around, but would ask some people, that maybe he'd just missed him or something."

Taylor and Rennie looked at each other doubtfully. "If Harry Hoskers was at Mesa Verde, *everyone* would know," Rennie offered. "He leaves no head unturned."

Hanks nodded, brow creased. "Haven't you heard anything about him from *anybody*? Down in Bluff? Blanding?"

"Just Fred Stax, his neighbor—the one Harry told he was going to Mesa Verde. Fred watched him load his gear into his truck and trailer and drive away."

Rennie frowned. "That doesn't mean anything. You could stand there and watch Harry ride into the sunset, and the instant you turn your back, he'll pull a one-eighty and head for the moon."

"True," Raff answered. "Still, nobody's seen him since Saturday morning. Usually he drops in to rattle my cage every two or three days, and it's been, what? Five days without a Hoskers sighting? That's downright abnormal."

"And unlikely," Rennie said.

"You two are making me nervous," Hanks said. "Should I be?"

"You should have been nervous from the beginning," Rennie said. "That man's been walking around with a big target on his back." She buried her head in her notebook.

Hanks sighed and gave Rafferty a look that said *What am I going to do with her?* A moment's silence passed.

Then Rafferty said, "I'm driving straight down to Bluff. If Harry's still not there, and if no one has seen him, I'm filing a missing persons report."

Hanks sat stunned. "You mean, you think something really has ha-happened?" he stuttered.

"It's a distinct possibility, given his track record," Raff said. He stood up. "I'll let you know. See ya, Ross," Raff said. "Alex, Danny, Taylor." He nodded at Heather. With that, he left camp.

Hanks glanced at Rennie, who promptly shut her notebook and put it away on the shelf at the end of the tent. "I'm done here," she said as she stalked past.

Alex followed Rennie out to their tent, Kit trotting ahead of them. They lay on their cots for some time without speaking. Then Rennie broke the silence, avoiding the subject of Harry's whereabouts. "Coyotes, huh?" she said. "Kit was romping with the bad boys."

"Don't know what it is with her and coyotes. I think she knew she was in trouble but figured if she ran, she'd be in for worse. So she called for backup. You should have seen her trot out of the middle of that gang, big smile on her face like she was walking out of a game she was winning and there was nothing to it."

Kit lay motionless on the poncho on the floor, but Alex knew she listened whenever her name was mentioned. Alex rolled to the edge of her cot and stroked the dog's back.

"How many were there?"

"Oh, I don't know. It was dark and there was a lot of movement. Not counting Kit's, I'd guess there were at least four pairs of eyes."

The sound of footsteps passing behind their tent alerted them to Heather's arrival. Dropping her voice, Alex said, "Todd was more rattled by the coyotes than Kit was."

Rennie sighed. "Right now I find Todd's reaction to be far more reasonable than a certain other person's tendency to dismiss warning signs simply because he thinks they sound weird."

Weird. The word reminded Alex of the debate she'd been having with herself over whether she should tell Rennie about what had happened with Tony. So far, she had found it difficult to talk about at all, maybe because she didn't understand it herself. Besides, she didn't want to burden Rennie with yet another set of unsettling circumstances. Worry over Hoskers and frustration with Hanks were enough for her to wrestle with.

Others beside Hector had expressed their appreciation for how Alex had stood up to Tony. Marina said that, while she had not understood everything that had been said, someone needed to tell off that snake Tony Balbo.

Alex hadn't replied to that. She didn't feel she had succeeded in telling Tony anything—not anything that changed his thinking. Bristling with triumph, he had been the one to break off the conversation.

His point that she had revealed herself to him—what was that supposed to mean? What had she done? Once more, she replayed the incident in her head. The outstretched hand, the glare—no, the flash—of some insight, something he had recognized but that she herself was unaware of. Had she seen right? Was there admiration or even a twisted intimacy in his deep eye contact? She shuddered. A voice in her head told her that she had somehow put herself at risk.

Then she realized something that made her resent Tony all the more. He had aroused old feelings in her she thought she had left behind when she joined the church—feelings of suspicion and of doubt, of slyness and of cunning ... of enmity! She was maneuvering with Tony like she had done with others in the old days. She thought she had laid those shreds of her old life on the altar—shards of her doubtful heart, broken bones of her willful spirit. Supposedly, the whole works had gone up in smoke. Now here it was, alive and dancing in her soul, aroused just like that—by the presence of a single person.

She felt a wave of misery. For three years she had gotten along on the belief that she had taken care of all old business relevant to conforming to her new life in the church. It had been a vast relief—the process of repenting and starting anew. She thought she had come home. But the dark clouds now swirling in her mind felt far more familiar than the picture she had painted for herself of a safe and neat spiritual home, a place where she could forget the past and be somebody other than who she had been.

Alex turned over on her cot. Why here, in such an idyllic

setting? Why did this person have to arrive and spoil it all? What was she going to do about the strange and—she knew it well enough—dangerous connection forming between them? Should she ignore him from here on out, suppress her nearly instinctual drive to stand up to him, and just let him go about his business? Should she back away from the mystery enveloping them both, linking them in some eerie cosmic dance?

She groaned in frustration. As much as she wanted to do the right thing and be a good person, she knew she couldn't back away. The genie was out of the bottle. She had to accept that and not waste time denying herself or the manipulative stranger trying to gain the upper hand in the game between them, whatever that game was.

"Something wrong?" Rennie asked.

Should she confide in Rennie or not? Alex teetered on the thin edge of the question, then came down hard on the *don't tell* side. "No, nothing. Just ... wondering what's ahead."

Rennie scoffed. "Join the club!"

Questions kept Alex awake for a long time. When she finally did fall asleep, she dreamed that a crowd was accusing her of having done something terribly, horribly wrong. In the dream, she tended to agree with them, although she couldn't figure out what it was she had done or why everyone condemned her.

Thirty-Three

Alex did not have to wait long to hear answers to some of her questions. The next day—another in a series marked by heat and glare—brought with it more frustration as the archaeologists began losing the battle to catch up on their schedule. Believing he could elicit more from his crew chiefs and students, Hanks rode everybody hard. Anxiety bloomed over the site like a drought-resistant summer weed.

Raff arrived to announce that the San Juan County Sheriff's Department had launched an official missing persons search for Harry Hoskers, then left again. The emergency was far too young for anyone to entertain truly unpleasant thoughts, but vague imaginings lurked in everyone's mind.

On her way to the latrine, Alex glanced at the goat skull sitting on the backdirt pile. The big rainstorm of nearly a week ago had undermined it so that the skull had begun slipping down the side of the backdirt pile. The ominous black feather hung from its eye socket by a mere spider's web. It was only a matter of time before a dust devil or canyon breeze whisked it away. When that happened, the skull would look like just another bit of desert detritus.

She shook her head, realizing as she did that she felt the beginnings of a headache. She put her fingers to her temples and rubbed. Like an engine revving, the pain grew. She returned to excavating but within an hour felt quite ill.

"Rennie, I've got to lie down before I throw up," she said.

"What's wrong?" Rennie asked.

"Headache," Alex said, gritting her teeth. "Migraine."

"Need a ride to camp?"

"No, I can make it—I'll take the wash. It's only a fifteen-, twenty-minute walk, and that's about how much time I have before it gets really bad. I'll keep to the shade. I'll try to come back later."

Rennie nodded. "Take all the time you need."

Alex dropped her trowel into the equipment box, took a big drink of water, and walked off the site. When she arrived at the wash, she lay down in the shade until the nausea passed. Then she hiked the wash unsteadily, arriving at her tent, which had only just begun to slip into the cottonwood's shade. Its interior was still hot as blazes, but Alex unzipped the front flap and staggered through, collapsing onto her cot.

No sooner did she lie down than she was struck by the impression that something was wrong. She lifted her head and looked around. Everything seemed in place. She could see no obvious signs of disturbance, yet the impression was strong. Was it a scent or the lingering trace of something else unpleasant or just the migraine playing tricks on her mind?

The pain overwhelmed her. Closing her eyes, she saw strange lights. She sank down, too exhausted to think about the warning impression any more. Remembering she kept painkillers on hand for situations like this one, she sat up to take them, shakily unzipping the back tent flap and two side ones, hoping for a breeze. Then she lay back down and fell into something that vaguely resembled sleep.

Voices woke her some time later. As her attention focused, she realized they were coming from Heather's tent. Alex tried to ignore them but then recognized Tony Balbo's polished tones. Without making a sound, she rolled over and peeked out the open back tent flap.

Tony carried a cooler out of Heather's tent while Heather set up two lawn chairs. He flipped the cooler's lid up and took out a couple of beers, opening one and handing it to Heather. He opened the other for himself. They both settled into the chairs and began drinking.

Alex had seen enough to lose interest. In accordance with the school's standards, the archaeology department was supposed to run a dry camp, but everyone knew there were infractions, especially among volunteers or others not directly tied to the school. Neither Tony nor Heather was enrolled, although the university was surely paying Heather's salary. While Alex thought the indulgence showed contempt for camp rules, she wasn't surprised and really didn't care. She lay back down, the throbbing in her head demanding far more attention than Tony's and Heather's drinking habits.

In spite of her uneasiness with Tony's nearness, Alex felt safe as long he didn't know she was in her tent. She listened to Tony pump Heather for information. She told him work on the site had fallen way behind schedule. He asked what areas of the site were being worked. Heather told him and then divulged information that Alex didn't know. Taylor was opening a meter-wide test trench bisecting the worst part of the pot-hunting damage in the middens. As Tony questioned Heather about the test trench, Alex closed her eyes and drifted off to sleep. Then another voice roused her. It was Todd's. Curiosity overcame discomfort. Quietly, she rolled over and looked out the window.

She saw Tony reach into the cooler, pull out a beer, pop the top, and offer it to Todd. The thirteen-year-old Navajo considered a moment, accepted the can, and drank. Tony stood and offered Todd his chair, sitting down in the dirt at his feet. Heather watched with her usual blank stare.

Alex forgot her headache as she watched Tony ply Todd with charm. He chatted Todd up about nonspecific aspects of camp life. Then he began speaking in confidential tones about the difficulties of dealing with the up-tight whites in the camp.

Todd tried to sidestep the topic. "It's not so bad," he said. "I don't mind." Then he laughed. "Sometimes, it's very interesting."

Tony chuckled, too. "No doubt it is," he said. Catching Todd completely off guard, he said, "Speaking of *interesting*, I heard you had an interesting experience."

Todd froze. Assuming a mask, he looked at Tony as if from a distance. "What do you mean?" he asked.

"Last night in the wash." Tony looked away as if the business were no big deal. Alex understood the ploy. Todd could take up the subject or leave it, whichever he chose.

She hoped Todd would leave it, but he stepped right into the snare.

"What do you mean?" he repeated.

"You know—the coyotes." Tony fell silent, letting another pause do his work for him.

Todd shifted nervously. He forced a chuckle, crossed one leg over the other, ankle to knee, and gripped the arms of his chair. "Yeah," he said, chuckling again. "That was ..."

"Spooky," Tony suggested for him.

Todd didn't reply. Alex wondered why he didn't just leave like he did when he became uncomfortable around her. She watched in surprise as the young Navajo drained his beer. He set the can down on the arm of the chair and got up.

"Another?" Tony asked.

"No, thanks," Todd replied. "I better get going."

As Todd took a couple steps toward the mess, Tony threw out another hook. "It must have been pretty unnerving. With coyotes, you never know what will happen."

"Yeah," Todd said, taking a few more steps.

"The woman with you—what did she do?"

Todd stopped and faced Tony. Although he didn't answer the question, he seemed interested in what Tony would say next.

"Alexandra—Alex. Did the coyotes bother her?"

"What do you mean?" Todd asked.

Alex's neck and shoulder began to cramp. She eased herself back onto her cot and lay there, her whole body prickling with tension.

"You had a bit of a scare when you saw *Ma'i*, didn't you?" Tony said, using the Navajo name for the folk character Coyote. "But Alex—she wasn't scared, was she?"

"I wouldn't know," Todd replied.

"Come on, Todd. She wasn't scared." Tony let this asser-

two hundred and seventy-five

tion stand between them for a moment. "She wasn't scared, Todd," he insisted.

Silence. Alex's heart pounded in her head. *What was he getting at?*

"Do you know why she wasn't scared?"

"Maybe she was," Todd replied, forcing lightness into his voice.

"Do you know why she wasn't scared, Todd?" Tony repeated.

"Okay, why?"

"Because she has strong blood. You know what I mean, don't you?"

Todd didn't reply, so Tony elaborated. "She's a witch."

Todd laughed nervously.

"She is," Tony asserted in a matter-of-fact tone. "I tell you because I know you can appreciate what I'm saying."

Silence. Then, "What makes you say a crazy thing like that?"

"It isn't crazy. That's something I'd expect a white boy to say. You've been brought up to know better."

"I have?"

"Of course." Again, one of Tony's engineered silences fell. "She's a born witch," he said at last. "She came into the world with powers. Isn't it amazing? A bit alarming, too, I would suppose."

Under her breath, Alex whispered, "You've *got* to be kidding!"

"Listen, I gotta go help with supper," Todd said, his voice flat. "You're nuts." There were sounds of footsteps as Todd left, breaking into a trot.

"Her dog, too!" Tony called after him. "The coyotes didn't kill the dog because it's a witch's beast. The dog's got powers too!"

The footsteps faded as Todd retreated from Tony's assault. Alex heard Tony chuckle—almost giggle.

"Why did you do that?" Heather asked, her question shot through with hesitation.

"Why not do it? It's the truth," Tony said, tossing off her reproach with disdain.

"But they were friends ..."

"Women like that have no friends."

"But ..."

"Shut up, Heather. You don't know what you're talking about." Alex heard the threat of rejection in his voice. Sure enough, he said, "Sometimes I wonder why I spend my time with you. I don't know if I even like you."

Heather fell silent.

"Still, there must be something about you I find satisfying."

No response from Heather.

"Have another beer," Tony said. Sounds of a cooler opening, ice rattling, and a pop top tearing off. "Tell me more about this test trench they're planning."

Tony and Heather sat on the other side of the cottonwood for another twenty minutes. If Alex hadn't heard Tony's abuse just moments before or the bizarre interchange he'd had with Todd, their conversation would have sounded like any casual chat about the site's archaeology. At last, Alex heard them put away their chairs and cooler and walk toward the mess area.

Alex lay stunned. She wondered if Tony knew she was in

the tent and had staged the entire scene for her benefit, as she suspected he had the other night at the fire. But no—he hadn't known, couldn't have known. His treatment of Heather assured her of that. Abusive men did not invite witnesses to their private parties. She knew something about how that went.

Thoughts and feelings rolled, fragmented, and flashed. Confusion and anger slid into and out of each other, creating disturbing mixtures, each breaking away as new arrangements of mental struggle broke through. She sat up and tried to get a grip on herself. "He thinks I'm a witch!" she exclaimed softly. "So *that's* what all that was about the other night!"

Suddenly, Alex was glad she had parried his thrust at her, knocked his hand aside before he had been able to touch her. She had touched him in the course of pushing him away, but if she had allowed him to touch her, he would have assumed that she was inviting him into her soul. It was a common theme in folklore: the devil couldn't cross your threshold unless you asked him in.

She felt her head. The pain was gone but she still felt weak and shaky. What should she do now? Obviously, revealing her knowledge of Tony's attempt at provocateuring would be a bad idea. In fact, she couldn't let him find out that she had been in camp at all. She pulled out a water bottle from beneath her cot and took a long drink of warm water. She had to get away before Kit found her or anything happened to betray her presence.

She stuck her head through the tent door and looked around. Nobody in sight. She stepped out and zipped the tent shut as quietly as possible. Then, slipping through the greasewood, she made for the wash. Her plan was to go back to work and then return to camp with everyone else. That way everything would appear normal. Hearing pans clatter in the kitchen, Alex was grateful for once for Wiggins's blundering ways. The commotion provided cover for her escape.

She dropped down into the wash, stopped, looked over her shoulder, and was startled to see Todd standing on the bank, watching. The two of them gazed at each other for several seconds. Alex considered talking to him about what had happened. Todd regarded her silently, standing motionless in a grove of sapling cottonwoods, neither inviting nor discouraging a response. Finally, she decided against saying anything at all and walked off down the wash, giving Todd the freedom to make of her behavior what he would.

. . . . .

Busy with notes, Rennie acknowledged Alex's return to the site with a glance. However, Hector welcomed her warmly.

"Where did you go?" he asked. "We missed you."

Alex heard real affection in his voice and felt grateful for his sincerity. After what she had just experienced, she had begun to wonder if there were any sincere people left in the world.

"Well thanks," she said, patting him on the shoulder. "Had to go find some shade. I wasn't feeling well."

"Oh. Are you better now?"

"I am," she said. "It cleared things up in ways I hadn't expected."

Hector glanced at the sky. Overhead it was an unbroken blue, but in the distance a pillow of white moisture plumped itself above the Abajos. "I think I see a storm brewing up there," he said.

Alex looked toward the mountains. "I think so," she said. "Maybe it will condescend our way."

"We could use a little condensation," Hector joked. "Alex, I don't suppose you know a spell that would give those clouds a nudge in our direction?"

Alex stood stunned for the second time that day. After a moment of confusion, she realized Hector's question was a joke, but combined with the still glowing effects of Tony's assertions that she was a witch, it disturbed her.

"What do you mean?" she asked, realizing as she said it that she sounded just like Todd had when Tony had cornered him.

"I just thought you may have run across some weather magic in your study of folklore and your attention to witchcraft," Hector said.

She studied his face for a moment and noted the slight turn at the corners of his mouth. He was trying to play with her in a harmless way, not at all like Tony's manipulations. She managed a strained smile. Closing her eyes and wiggling her fingers in the air, she chanted, "Partly to mostly cloudy with a 50 percent chance of thunderstorms." She opened her eyes.

"How's that?"

Hector chuckled. "Couldn't ask for more," he said.

Alex relaxed a little. She was beginning to enjoy Hector, especially the funny little personality changes she saw him making day by day. But his innocent question had helped her decide what to do. She would leave the field school to go look for some answers—and maybe for a few good questions, too.

· · · · ·

Raff showed up again that evening to report that no one

had found a trace of Harry Hoskers. Dr. Hanks received the news solemnly. "I'm sure he just went on one of his side trips," he posed.

This suggestion was met by silence.

"I keep coming back to what old Redhorse said that day he showed up at the site," Raff said.

"Redhorse came to the site? What for?" Hanks asked.

"That's right, you weren't here," Raff said. "At the risk of offending the dead Ancient Ones, he made a special trip over, said we had witch trouble."

Hanks threw up his hands. "How come nobody told me this?"

"I guess we forgot," Danny said.

"That's it then," Hanks said. "Something's happened and Redhorse knows what." He turned to Raff. "You have to go talk to him—find out more."

Raff shook his head. "He already said all he's gonna. If I go over and bother him, it'll only make him regret bringing it up."

"What a disaster!" Hanks growled. "That man has been nothing but trouble from the day I met him."

"Are you talking about Hoskers or Redhorse?" Taylor asked.

"Hoskers, of course!" Hanks snapped.

Everyone fell silent.

"Well," Raff said, breaking the gloomy silence. "I gotta get my sorry self back to Blanding. I'll let you know if anything else turns up."

Alex stood. Her car was still at Raff's house where she had left it after the storm. Now she wanted it back. She could wait till tomorrow afternoon—laundry day. But she thought she might break loose before that, maybe as early as tomorrow morning.

"Can I catch a ride?" she asked. "I need to pick up my car."

"Oh, yeah," Raff said. "I've been meaning to get your keys and have my wife drive it out, but with all that's happened ..."

"Why don't you just wait till tomorrow when we go in for laundry?" Taylor asked.

"I just want it back now," Alex replied evasively.

"Fine with me," Raff said. "But you'll have to drive back over the reservation in the dark, you know."

"I know," Alex said.

"Alone," he teased.

"I know!"

"Let's go then," he said.

Alex ran out to her tent to fetch her car keys. Sensing something was up, Kit ran after, keeping a close eye on her. When Alex returned to the mess area, she asked Raff if Kit could ride along.

"No problem. You might need her on the way back to help ward off the skinwalkers. Some of them can run as fast as cars, you know."

"So I've heard," Alex said irritably.

The ride into town would have been pleasant if Alex had not been consumed with her own problems. She petted Kit absentmindedly as the dog rode between her knees. Finally she said, "Things don't look too good for the project."

Raff drove a while before he answered. "No, they don't. I shoulda known." They rode in silence the rest of the way into town.

Alex declined Amy's invitation to visit, thanked Raff for

the ride, and jumped into her old wagon. She didn't relish having to drive back to camp in the dark over those lonely reservation roads and wanted to get it over with.

As she drove, she watched for animals. The whole reservation was open range and cattle and horses frequently lounged on or at the edge of the asphalt. Also, she wanted to avoid hitting other desert dwellers like jackrabbits and coyotes.

Only a few miles of reservation remained when Alex caught sight of a heap lying in the road. She braked and swerved, fighting to keep control of her car. She ran off the pavement and clipped the car's right fender through the sagebrush. Kit was thrown to the floor. The car came to rest with a cloud of dust swirling past the headlights.

Kit jumped back into her seat and threw Alex a look. "Ooawoo-awoo!" she yodeled in complaint.

Alex sat still, waiting for her heart to stop pounding. She looked in her rearview mirror but only saw empty road. She wound down the window and peered out and could just make out the bundle lying a short distance back.

"Sorry about that," she said to Kit. "So what do you think? Should we go back and see what that was or drive like blazes out of here because we don't want to know?"

Kit yipped.

"I'll take that as a 'yes,'" she said. "But yes, what?"

She put the car into gear and turned the wagon around. "Inquiring minds want to know," she said.

She cruised back along the road until the form on the asphalt took shape in her headlights. She studied it from a distance until the jumble made sense.

"It's a body!" she exclaimed. She edged the car closer. The

body didn't move. She flipped open her glove box, pulled out a flashlight, and got out of the car. So far nothing from the heap lying on the road.

"You stay here," she said to Kit, who was sticking her head out the window. "If something bad happens, go for help."

Kit growled, then yipped.

"Fine," Alex answered. "It'll be your own fault then if you end up in a skinwalker Navajo taco."

Cautiously, Alex approached the heap. Except for ubiquitous cricket-song, the night was still. When she got within six feet of the body, a soft, wheezing sound reached her ears. Snoring! Someone was sleeping in the middle of the road! Thinking how near she had come to extending the person's nap forever, Alex strode forward angrily. "Hey there. Hey!" Shining her light over the body, she made out the booted, jeaned, and jacketed form of a Navajo man. She rocked him with her foot.

"Wake up! You're in the middle of the road!"

The snoring shattered and grumbling took its place. Alex shined her light into the man's face and he held up his hand to ward off the beam.

"Get out of the road!"

He pulled his jacket collar up and turned away.

"GET UP!" she yelled. "Go sleep over there!" With the flashlight's beam, she indicated a patch of sand off to the side of the road.

The man glared. Getting to his knees, he picked up the old cowboy hat he'd been using as a pillow and staggered off the road.

"He's drunk," Alex said under her breath, watching the

man move unsteadily across the pavement. "Time to leave."

She trotted back to the car and got in, wasting no time pointing it in the direction of camp. When she had put a couple miles between herself and the sleeper, Alex remembered something a Navajo student at the Y had told her about the reservation having a high rate of hit-and-run accidents. "Some people believe it's because of the reservation's high rate of alcoholism—you know, a lot a drunken driving—but really, it's skinwalkers," he said. Alex had raised her eyebrows. "Really, it's true," he had insisted. "People come across skinwalkers in the roads at night and go out of their way to hit them—get rid of them." But given the events of the last ten hours, Alex hoped she hadn't just seen Todd's future lying back there on the asphalt.

She drove into camp and was greeted by Rennie, Danny, and Taylor. "How was your trip?" Rennie asked.

"Fine," she said. "Except I nearly got me one of them skinwalkers."

The three chiefs looked at her in surprise.

"Or was it a sleepwalker?" she wondered.

Thirty-Four

First Angry entered his den, happy with his new souvenir. He had acquired something of Rabbit's. *How could she be so careless as to leave such personal matter lying about? I burn or bury everything. No one can touch anything of mine. Nobody can touch me.*

He took from his bundle what he had stolen and looked at it—Rabbit's fur, gleaming and dark. For the first time, he noticed that it had red highlights. *Living with those others has caused her to grow careless–that's all. Now I have power over her. Now I can call her to me and she will come.*

Delighted with his own cleverness, First Angry smiled even though no one was around to admire his fine white teeth. Up until now, Rabbit's quickness had made it possible for her to stay out of his reach. No more. *Now that I have this small part of her, she will follow it to me. She won't even know why she comes.* He took a few strands and held them before his eyes. *Oh, oh, oh!*

They were a delight to touch, the water of another's soul to quench his bottomless thirst. He pulled the strands through his fingers, stretching them between his fingertips until they were taut. Fine strands that contained the imprint of her being. He held them up to the light—*more than enough!*

In a low voice, he began to chant.

> *In the beginning, all things were made.*
> *In the beginning, all things were made.*
> *Look at me, I was made.*
> *Look at me, I, Coyote,*
> *I was made, I was made.*
> *I, Coyote, also called First Angry,*
> *I was made, I was made.*
> *The spirits called me from the north, but I did not come.*
> *The spirits called me from the east, but I did not come.*
> *The spirits called me from the south, but I did not come.*
> *From the west I came, where the light leaves.*
> *From the west I came, where life leaves.*
> *The spirits called and I came on thieving feet.*
> *On feet of magic came I.*

He breathed a heavy sigh of satisfaction.

> *Rabbit, Coyote, also called First Angry,*
> *He calls you, he calls you,*
> *Rabbit, Coyote calls you.*
> *As the spirits called him, he calls you.*
> *He calls you, he calls you.*
> *Out of your stronghold you will come*
> *Out of your stronghold you, Rabbit, will come*
> *To Coyote, to Coyote,*
> *To Coyote, also called First Angry,*
> *You will come!*

His mind turning on the power of things, on the power of big things, on the power of little things, on the power that he, Coyote, had that placed him above others, he took Rabbit's fur deeper into his den and placed it among his power objects, the shards that sang for him in their captivity. Now it was just a matter of time.

Thirty-Five

Friday and laundry day dawned. Alex toyed with the idea of excusing herself from field camp. More than anything, she wanted to jump in the wagon with Kit and head out into the desert where she could think.

But during breakfast she studied the grim and determined faces of the crew chiefs. Taylor's usual reserve had intensified ten-fold. Danny looked wearied and withdrawn. Looking at Rennie, Alex nearly cringed. Her mouth was a tight, thin line. Like Taylor, she avoided all eye contact.

Site schedules had been shattered. Excavation suffered if hurried, but little time was left before—before what? Before Harry Hoskers dropped yet another bomb on them? Alex couldn't begrudge the crew chiefs their anxieties.

Only Mike wandered through camp, coffee cup in hand, looking largely unaffected. His survey work was done. The woes of the site weren't really his problem. Meanwhile, Hanks had gone into Blanding to deal with the search for Harry. His involvement made the concern over Harry's whereabouts solid and real.

Alex felt she couldn't just run off, especially without a good explanation. What would she say? That she needed to find out whether or not she was a witch? Perhaps if she said that she had to take care of *personal business,* it would sound common yet urgent enough to get her out of camp graciously. She looked toward the parking lot where her station wagon sat. She longed to whistle to Kit, jump in the car, and just go!

But she couldn't. When Rennie rose and made motions of preparing to leave for the site, Alex stood up, too. Grabbing the daypack holding her water bottles, lip balm, and bandannas, she climbed into the Suburban along with everybody else.

When the group arrived at the site, Rennie approached Alex. "You're working with Taylor today. He's running a test trench through the midden and needs someone with experience to help him. He has to bisect several of the potholes, so it could get messy."

"Okay," Alex said. "Just me?"

"No, I'm sending Chris over. He and Caedyn can move earth fast, but Danny needs Caedyn in his kiva with Mr. Spikes. I'm keeping Hector, and Marina's with me today—she needs experience working floors. Danny and I will split up the volunteers."

Taylor walked up. "Ready?" he asked.

"Sure am," Alex replied.

After collecting Chris, the three of them walked over to the middens while Taylor briefed them. "The test trench will serve a double purpose," he said. "First, we'll look at the layers of occupation; second, we'll document in greater detail the damage an unknown person or persons inflicted on the site."

"Document it? How?" Chris asked.

"We'll run the trench through some holes to see them in the profile," he said. "Then we'll break out our camera and notebooks."

"I don't get it," Chris said. "What difference does it make? What's done is done. We can't undo it."

"You're right, we can't undo it," Taylor explained, adopting his light and polite tone. "Just want to satisfy scientific curiosity. Indulge me, old chap, will you?"

As it turned out, Taylor had already begun work on the trench, although Alex couldn't figure out when he'd had the time. He put Alex and Chris to work excavating in the meter-by-meter square trench and opened the next square meter himself so that they had consecutive meters going simultaneously. Along with excavating, Taylor kept the notes and managed the bagging of artifacts from both segments of the trench.

. . . . .

When the crew returned to camp, they were met first by Kit, her tail matted with burrs, and then by the unwelcome sight of Tony Balbo positioned in the mess tent next to Heather. Dr. Hanks, on the way to drop off notebooks at the cabinet at the rear of the tent, stopped beside him.

"Mr. Balbo," he said. "You seem to have plenty of time on your hands."

Tony returned his look. "I suppose I can't keep myself away."

"I have a proposal for you." Dr. Hanks put his foot up on a chair, leaned on his knee, and waited for Tony's reaction. Fearing the worst, other members of the field school froze in place.

"Let's hear it," Tony replied.

"I hear you're handy with a trowel."

Tony smiled. "Somewhat, yes."

"How about you join the excavation in exchange for meals. We're behind and in desperate need of experienced help."

Rennie slammed her notebooks on the table and stalked out of the mess. Tony watched her leave, then glanced at the others standing there watching. "An intriguing offer. But I fear I'll only be intruding."

"We're running an archaeological field project, not a social club," Hanks replied. "We're struggling here, Mr. Balbo. Why don't you consider it?"

"For the sake of the archaeology involved, sure. I'll consider it."

Hanks nodded his satisfaction. "Good. As a token of my seriousness about this, I want you to stay for dinner." Then he continued on his course toward the cabinet.

As Alex stood feeling slightly panicked about this turn of events, Marina grabbed her arm, startling her. "Do something!" she whispered. "Tell Dr. Hanks he can't let that guy join the field school! Tell him he's ... evil!"

Alex looked at Tony, who caught her glance and nodded to her almost imperceptibly. That instant's eye contact caused Alex to feel violated. A shudder ran through her, head to toe. She muttered, "Man, I've got to get out of here!" And with that, she left Marina standing in the duff staring at her in wonder.

Arriving at the tent, she looked inside. Rennie was nowhere to be seen. Probably she'd gone to the wash to deal with her frustrations. Alex packed while Kit sat on the floor biting the burrs out of her fur. Alex shouldered her hiking pack and picked up her laundry.

"Never mind the burrs, you can take care of them later. Let's go." Kit jumped up and ran ahead of her. Alex ignored Tony as she walked past him to her station wagon. Marina followed, still trying to spur her into action.

"You have to say something! You're the only one who can stand up to him!" she said.

"Not necessarily and not anymore," Alex replied.

"What do you mean, not anymore?" Marina said. "Are you running away?"

Alex opened her car door and threw her pack into the back seat. She stalked around the back of the car, wound the rear window down, and heaved in her laundry bag. "Running away?" she repeated. "I guess I am." She looked at Marina. "I'll be back, though," she said. "I have pressing personal business to attend to."

Marina looked doubtful at this bit of news. "So what are we going to do?" she asked. "How are we supposed to deal with that creep?"

Alex paused to consider the question. She said, "I don't know what you should do, but I know what *I* would do if I were in your place."

"What? Tell me."

"Don't make the mistake of thinking he wants to come to any sort of understanding. Don't let him draw you out like he did the other night at the fire. No matter what he asks, don't feel compelled to answer. The man is not interested in coming to any understanding. He only wants to play with your head and upset, unsettle, expose, and abuse people. Withhold your language—don't invite him in."

"What?" Marina asked peevishly. "What's that supposed to

mean—withhold my language ... don't invite him in?"

Frustrated, Alex searched for a metaphor. "Folk wisdom says that the devil can't cross your doorstep without a very definite, "Please sir, won't you come in?" I don't suppose you've read Goethe's *Faust*? Look, when Tony asks a question, what he's doing is the same as asking if you'll invite him in. Once inside—poof! Total trouble, almost impossible to get rid of. When you try to throw the devil out, he whines, 'But you invited me!' He's only trying to force you to go along with his program. Don't fall for it."

"So uh ... give him the cold shoulder?" Marina suggested.

"Good enough," Alex told her. "Now, I've got a long drive ahead and ..."

"I know. Personal business." Marina looked forlorn.

Alex decided against trying to explain any further. She shut her car door and drove off. As she cruised toward Blanding, she tried to clear her head of the image of Tony's intimate little nod, but it kept playing in her mind, over and over. With that simple gesture, he had once again reached out to touch her, this time with the delicacy of a supposed secret understanding. She felt the intrusion of his intentions but didn't yet understand what they were.

The breathtaking scenery between Monticello and Moab slipped past her eyes untouched. Occasionally she looked off toward a distant sunny knoll but without taking any pleasure in the view flickering past. She struggled to pry Tony's hand out of her soul but, admitting to herself her rising panic, knew that it was too late.

"I wish I understood what's going on!" she said. A slight depression descended on her. Still, she thought, all is not lost.

She had withdrawn from camp and thus from his presence, reducing the effects of whatever spell he sought to cast. She guessed that if she had been completely captivated, she would not have been able to leave. And she *was* on an independent quest for knowledge—knowledge that would, she hoped, give her an edge.

"An edge in whatever the contest is between us!" she said. She laughed as the warm wind from the desert whipped her long, dark hair around her face and out the car window. Kit stood on the armrest of the passenger's door, her head thrust through the partially opened window, ears laid flat by the wind, fur rippling like water.

Alex pounded her steering wheel with her fist. "No! I'm not going to let him get to me. I'm the mistress of my fate." She reached across the seat and patted Kit's flank. "All is not lost," she said. Kit's glance at her was only barely polite.

She stopped in Green River to wash her clothes and refuel. When she unzipped the pocket of the backpack to retrieve her spare hairbrush, she couldn't find it. She looked through the pack. Gone. "Oh, no!"

Did Todd believe Tony's assertion about her being a witch? If he did, maybe he had stolen the brush for a Navajo Shooting Ceremony, a ritual where a personal item of a witch is stolen and then shot with arrows, rocks, or bullets. Within days or weeks of the injury inflicted upon the item, the witch is expected to sicken and die or to be driven out.

Alex didn't think shooting ceremonies and other unwitching rituals were very effective means for ridding a community of witchcraft since, for the most part, they merely reversed the roles of victim and victimizer. She had argued once in a paper that witchcraft is perpetuated in the very activities meant to eliminate it.

Was it possible that she was the target of a Shooting Ceremony or had she merely lost the brush and not noticed it until now? She laughed. "Maybe *that's* why I left the field school in such a hurry!" she said to Kit, who was dancing with impatience to get out of the car. "Driven out by a Shooting Ceremony!"

Kit yodeled at her.

"You watch yourself," Alex cautioned. "As it goes for the witch, so it goes with her familiar."

Thirty-Six

As night fell, Alex headed across the desert toward Vision Canyon, making her way at anywhere from five to thirty miles per hour depending on the degree of washboarding in the road. She watched the sky as she drove, orienting herself by the stars' pinpoint signposts.

She said to Kit, "It must have been neat to be at sea, steering by the stars. Imagine figuring your position off other places and even other times."

The husky gave her one of her looks.

"Oh, am I *boring* you? Sorry!" She took a closer look at her furry gray and white companion. "Just what kind of poetry *do* you have in your soul?" she asked.

Kit gave a low, throaty growl, then stood up on the armrest and leaned out the window to sample the night air and snap at moths.

"Oh," Alex said. "That kind."

Alex had never driven this remote stretch of desert alone so late at night, but keen with adventure, she pressed on until she found the next turn-off. She parked the station wagon on

Vision's rim and switched off the headlights. Moonlight glazed the slickrock for miles around.

Recognizing where they were, Kit leaped to the ground and immediately began to sweep the area, her fur a magnet for moonlight. Alex leaned against the car, trying to clear her mind.

As the moon set, the stars hung strikingly low and bright and the air held that peculiar mixture of pre-dew breezes, warm and cool strands of air raveling and unraveling. Stillness gathered around her, interrupted only by the wind brushing past her ears.

She walked to the rim of Vision Canyon and followed the lightfall down its walls as far as she could see. She sat in the sand, releasing a long breath, realizing for the first time that she had been holding it in. True relief untied hidden knots, and she felt her body take up a different rhythm.

As if in greeting, a sound rose from the darkness at the bottom of the canyon—a laugh with a lilt, falling in cadence for several notes. A canyon wren, tricked out by the last of the moonlight, singing into the field of stars fluttering overhead. The call broke off. Alex walked back to the car. She poured water for Kit, rolled out her sleeping bag over its insulation pad, and nestled in, but for a long while, the stars held open her eyes.

· · · · ·

When she woke at sunrise, she squirmed out of her sleeping bag, stood up, opened her car door, and draped the bag over it to dry off millions of pinprick dewdrops that had bloomed on it during the night. When she turned to face the dune at the canyon rim, her attention snagged on a weird image.

Standing on the dune's crest, back-lit by the sun so that all features receded into shadow, was a squat figure. The specter maintained absolute stillness on two short, thick legs that rose into a torso dominated by a barrel chest. On its shoulders balanced a heavy black head adorned by a headdress from which protruded two curving horns.

The apparition snatched away her breath. She swept her understanding for an explanation of the thing. Stuttering thoughts retrieved only ancient names—*genius loci, numen, Kokopeli,* the chief one being *shaman.* She seized on this last. *Shaman.*

She stared harder. The form possessed the shape she imagined a shaman dwarf would have, distorted and eidolonic. She wondered if she were hallucinating, but she couldn't think of a reason the image facing her across the distance would not be real. The prominent horns moved slightly. She squinted, trying to make out features, but the face she knew must be there remained hidden in shadow.

She froze in an idea that this shaman had come to speak to her, to reveal something of the highest importance. She trembled, considering her worthiness. Was all right with her? Then she remembered why she had come, and she knew *all is not right.* She panicked at the thought that the thing on the dune knew this, knew of her trouble over that man. She was troubled and dark. Surely the shaman would know this. The thought that the visitor would judge her unworthy and leave without delivering its message provoked stabbing desperation.

Don't go, she thought. She whispered it: "Don't go!" Suddenly her rational side kicked in. She blinked. No! This couldn't be happening. There couldn't really be a holy man on the hill, calling her to attention across the ringing silence.

And yet ... the electricity crackling between her and the figure on the dune was real. If it was imagination, it was imagination's highest flight, an arrow sprung from a wild bow, piercing years of experience. Whatever Alex thought she knew trembled for its existence.

Where was Kit? Did she see the thing? Alex turned slowly to look. From the corner of her eye, she could just make her out in the brush beyond the car, sniffing bushes. Kit hadn't seen.

Alex's slight movement stirred the figure on the dune to action. Suddenly it shape-shifted, doubling in size as another form broke from the shadow chrysalis standing before her. Two legs multiplied to four. A horizontal spine writhed out of the vertical dwarfen one, then out stretched a broad flank, catching the sun across its surface, glowing golden. Polished black tines and a long-muzzled face with widely set black eyes and black facial markings re-formed from the headdress-crowned head. When the transformation was complete, a pronghorn buck stood broadside, staring. He bounded twice, then stopped and looked over his shoulder to see if she would follow.

This all happened so quickly that Alex's mind hadn't been able to keep up. The buck looked at her for several seconds, nose, eyes, and ears taking her in. He bounded two times again, paused, and when Alex made no move to pursue him, walked at a leisurely pace up along the ridge of the dune and disappeared over its crest.

This had been by far the best trick light and perspective had ever played on her. Alex stood there astonished, playing the scene over in her mind and feeling a slow burn of wonder spread head to toe. Once more, in a meeting with *Other*, her being had been shaken up and her bare psychological bones rolled out across the sand in one of the desert's games. Although she felt bested, she also felt better for it. In concert with the metamorphosis of the figure on the dune, she too had broken through. In the immediate wake of the experience, her wings remained wet and crumpled and she felt vulnerable and exposed. *Nevertheless*, she thought as she made motions of preparing breakfast, *nevertheless life, with its sudden gifts of creation and un-creation, is good.*

· · · · ·

Still feeling the heightened sense of awareness the mirage had ignited, Alex shouldered her pack and hiked into Vision Canyon. Kit scrambled down the trail ahead or over attractive obstacles beside it, destroying any chance of seeing wildlife beyond the pronghorn shaman, although that certainly had been enough.

They arrived at the bottom of the canyon just before noon and set a leisurely pace up the wash, stopping to watch the antics of insects scurrying off the rapidly heating sand. Then they threaded their way in and out of every alcove or cleft 'til they arrived at the Theater of Gods. Alex didn't plan to stay long. The pronghorn incident had given her what she had come for. Her appearance before the pictograph panel was a mere formality.

But the panel seemed to have other ideas. It chattered away at her, every detail of the rock canvas clamoring at once. She let her eyes wander the mural. Once again, the Warring Ones caught her attention. As before, the two men struggled, one's spear poised to thrust into the other. Alex had no idea whether this image of murder about to be committed had been intended by the artist or was something she brought to the picture. It could be that the spear was aimed across the second man's body at a bighorn sheep to the rear of the herd.

Then her eyes rested on the two skull-headed figures standing off to the side watching. She could not avoid connecting them to the Warring Ones. Like devils tarrying to receive their due, they kept their vigil, awaiting the decisive spear thrust, a thrust that would never come. The figures had stood for centuries, the upraised spear frozen in the air, and the murder, if that's what it was, uncommitted.

The scene called to Alex's mind one of the world's oldest murder dramas: the story of Cain and Able. The biblical version had it that Cain, a farmer, made God an offering of his crop. The Old Testament suggests that God was not pleased with this offering for reasons that are somewhat obscure to the reader. Thus, Cain's reaction of slaughtering his shepherd brother, whose offering of sheep had been accepted, seems a disproportionately bad one, making the crime's motives appear to be jealousy and rage.

But in another version of the story, Alex had found a more complete explanation for Cain's murderous behavior. This version told how Cain had loved Satan more than God, implying that an unwholesome state of mind had tainted his offering. Then as Cain had sulked over God's rejection, Satan approached and divulged to Cain the secret of mortality—a secret that's not so astonishing today, but back at the beginning of the world when no one had died and men were said to have lived hundreds of years, grasping it required a grand stretch of the imagination. Once Cain heard it, he reveled in it, saying, "Truly I am ... the master of this great secret, *that I may murder and get gain.*" So Cain killed his brother and then celebrated the atrocity, singing, "I am free; surely the flocks of my brother falleth into my hands."

Alex could only guess what effect Abel's spilled blood had on the Earth, whose innocent soils soaked it up. And life's blood has spilled into the Earth from similar tragedies since, shafting and fanning as the great secret is whispered ear to ear. Scripture, folktale, or something else altogether, the story's truth had for Alex far-reaching implications. For one thing, she could see how Abel's blood could stand as the original byproduct of exploitation from which all other pollutants take their nature and form.

She wondered if God had stood by like the two specters in the panel and witnessed the deed. Or perhaps, this being the first murder, Cain had left Abel's lifeless body on the open ground or had only clumsily concealed it. Generations of murderers and their methods of stealth and concealment would pass before detection of such crimes would require as much cunning as the committing of them. Thus, the first fruit of the terrible secret may have lain out where everybody could see it, completely obvious.

Obvious. Alex pictured it, a poorly concealed crime whose motive had been to get gain. Abel's body lying in full view, a mysterious scene to anyone unfamiliar with what had happened and why.

At that instant, Alex's mind reeled from the blow of a horrible insight. "Oh no!" she cried. She stared at the panel, a sickening realization shattering the spirit in which she had approached this sacred place. The chatter she had first perceived had been scores of voices speaking at once, all pointing toward one thing. In her mind's eye, she witnessed a scene that shook her to her core. Suddenly, she knew precisely where Harry Hoskers was and how he had fared. It was obvious.

Thirty-Seven

Coyote stepped from his den and looked up at the sky. He could feel that she was approaching. Rabbit was about to arrive. But he had to admit, she had taken longer than he had expected. And running like that! Unanticipated. *Where had she gone?*

No matter—she was coming back. She always did and always would. It was old, what was between them. It had always been this way between Coyotes and Rabbits. Say what she would, in the end, it didn't come down to what she *hoped for,* what little stories she told herself in her dreams, but what *would be.*

Now we will see who is inspired, won't we? Now we will see whom God favors—the Rabbit or the Coyote. He sniffed the breeze. *Still smoky. Too bad about the fire! Well, never mind, it's still Coyote's game.*

He hummed softly, then sang to himself:

> *Out of your stronghold you will come*
> *Out of your stronghold you, Rabbit, will come*

He went over everything. Was all prepared? Of course! He, Coyote, also called First Angry, also called—other things—always kept the needful at hand. He was always ready. *Timing is everything!*

This game he played with Rabbit had broken the boredom he had suffered for so long. She engaged his attention like—well, he didn't think he'd ever experienced anything like it. Her wide green eyes, growing sharp at the sight of him. Her voice, with its haughty music. *Hah, Coyote! You there, just you try it! Try to catch me! My blood is strong!* Their twin minds, their twin hearts.

She'd said it. *I can't care.* Music to his ears.

Yes, he, Coyote, knew just what she meant. He had learned early in life that one mustn't care. Grandfather Rattlesnake, with his great, venomous fangs, taught little Coyote not to care. *Thou shalt not care* was one of the commandments of hell. If you cared, you lost your power. If you cared, you couldn't do what you had to do to survive. If you cared, others could take what you cared for and hold it over you until you fell on your knees and begged.

Coyote spat as he thought about all this. It would be different with Rabbit. Except ... he knew that she did care. He saw how she guarded some of the others. He'd seen it at the fire. A guard Rabbit! That really was something new. *I wonder how she does it—care, yet meet me, Coyote, step for step?*

If he were really going to do this right, he probably ought to find a way to get at her through them. That would be the purest practice of his art. That, or discovering her weakness and using it against her like he did with Burnt Woman.

But no, what he'd done with Burnt Woman wouldn't work

on Rabbit. She was too ... too ... *Well, she knows those tricks. She's been there before, but unlike Burnt Woman, she didn't stay.*

Then a thought hit him that consumed him with wonder. *Was caring a power or a weakness with her?* Until now, he had always considered it a weakness, but after dealing with Rabbit, he had to wonder. *Has she found some magic that makes it strong? At the fire, it was like a wall. I only just managed to slip over it.*

He shrugged. She had strong blood. She knew some magic he didn't. He had strong blood, too. He knew some magic *she* didn't. That was all there was to it.

Thirty-Eight

As she drove across the tabletops of the Colorado Plateau, Alex saw smoke rising over a distant mesa. Consumed with her own worries, she thought nothing of it. It had been a bad year for brush fires. As the field school had come and gone from Blanding, they had seen pillars or clouds of smoke standing on the mesas. They imagined a rancher and his hands or a group of Navajos or a contingent of fire-fighters immersed in yet deeper pools of heat as they struggled against fires on summer days already aflame with sunlight. Sometimes the field school could see the flames and live coals pulsing against the desert night, the whole fiery complex drawing the eye as music draws the ear.

As Alex wound along the route to the field school, the cloud of smoke swung first to one side of her line of sight, then to the other, returning always to the middle of her windshield. As she neared camp, its field of movement narrowed. Haze filled the view. She began to get a very bad feeling.

Within ten miles of camp, she passed two police cars and a small fire truck heading back toward town. They motored across the reservation at a leisurely pace, obviously returning from a job rather than driving out to it. A mile from camp, the odor of burned vegetation filled the car. She stepped on the gas, rounded a bend, and was forced to slide to a stop at a roadblock just over the Navajo Nation's border. A single White Mesa police car sat at the roadblock. White Mesa was the Ute Indian reservation just south of Blanding.

A big Ute got out and approached Alex. He wore a baseball jersey and cap. A gun belt rode low over his cut-offs. "Hi there," he said.

Alex leaned out her window, peering ahead, but a bend in the road cut off everything from sight but the haze. "What's going on?" she asked.

"Brush fire," he said. "Where you headed?"

"To the field school up there," she said. "Is that where the fire is?"

He didn't answer. "You belong to that field school?" he asked.

"I do," she said, as if speaking a vow.

"What's your name?"

"Alexandra McKelvey," she answered.

The big Ute thought a moment, then nodded. He looked into the car. Kit sat quietly in the passenger's seat, panting lightly, returning his gaze. "Nice dog," he said. He swept the visible contents of her wagon with a quick glance, then stepped back. "They're expecting you," he said. "Go on in."

Alex sped down the dirt and gravel road, adding a plume of dust to the haze. She was relieved to see that the cottonwood sheltering her tent stood green and untouched, as did the big trees sheltering the mess tent. She passed the edge of the fire where the black wasteland left off and the barely spared grease-wood, rabbit brush, and sage began. A small fire truck sat at this border, keeping watch over the smolder. But the camp was intact. She turned down the side road and rolled into the lot next to a sheriff's vehicle.

Jumping out of the car, she trotted into camp, Kit sprinting ahead. Rennie, Marina, and Hector, wearing sweat-laced layers of dust and ash, hurried to meet her. The air was bitter and smoky. Piles of personal gear lay in heaps, gathered in preparation for evacuation.

"Oh, thank goodness!" Rennie exclaimed. "We were worried something had happened to you!"

"You were worried something had happened to *me!*" Alex returned. "What about you? Is everyone okay?"

"Mike's up in Moab for smoke inhalation. Sharp's with him—some burns. It's precautionary. We expect them back tomorrow. Everyone else is okay."

"The fire broke out after a minor thunderstorm," Hector said. "There's a theory that lightning struck a tree down in the wash."

"It spread real fast!" Marina added. "I wasn't sleeping after the storm and smelled smoke. The flames were easy to see in the dark."

"Marina raised the alarm," Rennie said.

"When did you get it out?" Alex glanced toward the mess tent. Under its eaves, Dr. Hanks sat with Taylor, Caedyn, Chris, and a sheriff's deputy.

Rennie looked at her watch. "About half an hour or so ago, officially," she said. "The wind changed, and that saved the camp. Then it dropped off completely. Help arrived and so on and so forth."

"Good," Alex said. Then she grabbed Rennie by the arm. "Come out to the tent," she whispered. "We've got to talk."

. . . . .

At Alex's insistence, Rennie also coaxed Taylor from the group sitting with the deputy and brought him to the women's tent. All three sat in the smoky interior, the crew chiefs listening as Alex began to explain her theory about what had happened to Harry Hoskers.

She hadn't gotten far when Taylor interrupted. "The deputy was just saying that Hoskers's truck and tent trailer were found out on Mustang Mesa dumped over the side of a canyon."

"Oh my gosh!" Rennie said.

"Who found it?" Alex asked.

"An oil and gas survey crew."

"Did they find anything else?" Rennie asked.

"Nothing. It had been there probably since the storm. The tracks had been washed away and there was no trace of Harry." He paused. "Those who specialize in these things suspect foul play." He frowned a moment, then added, "Oh—and some ranchers reported the presence of a flashy black C-J type Jeep in the canyon around that time."

"A black Jeep?" Alex shook her head. "That doesn't fit, but it doesn't matter. Look, we have to get to the site."

"Why?" Rennie asked, nervous.

"Because that's where the answers are."

"At the site?" Rennie asked in amazement. "What are you talking about?"

"I'll show you!" Alex said. "Please, let's just go."

Rennie stood up to go, but Taylor remained sitting on

Rennie's cot, his expression doubtful. "The cops want us to stick around camp," he said.

"Why?" Alex asked. "Because of the fire?"

Taylor hesitated.

"Is it because of the fire, Taylor?" Rennie asked.

"Well ... there's some indication it wasn't a lightning strike."

"Deliberately set?" Alex said.

"There's a possibility," Taylor replied.

Alex nodded. "I'd say there's a *big* possibility."

Rennie turned to her. "Well, tell us what you've got."

"I'll tell you on the way to the site," Alex said. "Let's get going!"

Taylor stood. "What'll we tell Dr. Hanks and the local law?"

"Just say we're going out to check on the site," Alex said. "Won't that sound reasonable?"

"In the wake of an arsonist's attempt on the field school and the site being hit by pot hunters, I'd say it does," Rennie answered.

The three went back into the main section of camp and extracted grudging permission from Dr. Hanks. "But stay together!" he called after them as they ran for the truck. "And don't do anything foolish!"

"If we decide to do anything foolish, we'll let you know," Rennie called back. "That way you can get in on it!"

· · · · ·

Twenty minutes later, Alex, Rennie, and Taylor stood at the end of Taylor's test trench, shovels in hand. A mild breeze sifted what was left of the day's heat. The sun stood on the western mesas, balancing there on the thin edge of its disc. A few cumulus clouds drifted out of the north, sailing into the cross-currents of the approaching sunset.

The two women and the man standing on the middens paid little attention. Their anticipation had been aroused, but not by anything as innocent as the coming sunset. They stared in silence at the largest hole in the ancient trash heap, one that the person who had attacked the site had taken the trouble to back-fill.

Alex shook her head to clear it of the impressions filling it—impressions of the mindset of the person who had done this thing, violating not only those who had lain buried for centuries but native cultures in general. Not to mention the blow struck against those whose interests linked them to the site such as archaeologists. Such as *these* archaeologists.

"I don't like how this feels," Taylor said. "If you're right, then this is a crime scene, and we're out here mucking around ... "

"If I'm right," Alex argued, "this has been a crime scene since last week, beginning with the storm and then with us tramping over it since then. Not to mention what damage your trench has done. Besides, we don't know it's a crime scene yet."

"We ought to talk to someone ..." Taylor began.

"Come on!" Alex said. "Nobody's going to believe us until we've got something to show."

"We can expect what happened following the pot hunting of the site," Rennie said. "Nobody showed the least interest until Harry disappeared ..." Her voice trailed off and she looked at the two holes. "But what will we say if there *is* something? I mean, about how we happened on it?" She crouched and stared at the mounds.

"I don't know," Alex said. "How about, we were ... documenting the extent of damage in the middens by ... uh, excavating one of the holes ... to see how deep it is, or something." She waved her hands in frustration. "I don't know! There must be some reason archaeologists would do something like this. You're the archaeologists! *You* think of something!"

Rennie's brow furrowed. "We could say that we decided to finish documenting the midden damage, which we haven't had time to do up 'til now ..."

"I'm still not convinced we need to do this," Taylor broke in. "This is just a wild hunch and Hanks will have our hides ..."

The trio heard a sound in the brush behind them. They turned and froze, staring at the greasewood. There was a rustle, a flash of white, and Kit trotted out, face and legs ash-smudged. Panting heavily, she looked up into Alex's face to see if she would be chastised for breaking rules and following them to the site. The moment for it passed. Thirsty from the trip she'd made to join them, she stood over Alex's pack.

Taylor and Rennie looked at Alex. "I guess I forgot to tell her to stay," Alex said, shrugging. She opened her pack and took out a water bottle, pouring Kit a drink in the palm of her hand. "You were saying?" she said to Taylor.

"I was saying we don't have any proof that this is necessary ..."

"Proof," Alex said. "There's proof and then there's *proof*." She dried her hand on her jeans. "What about what Old Man Redhorse said about us having witch trouble?"

"Yeah, but ... that could mean anything."

"It doesn't mean *anything*," Rennie said.

"It means deprivation of vital resources or death," Alex

said. "Redhorse was warning us—warning Raff, anyway—that someone had designs upon our lives or the life of one of us or upon resources valuable to us or ..."

"All of the above," Rennie filled in.

"Yes, or all of the above, including our ideals, beliefs, you name it. Then there's the damage to the well-head, the fire ..."

"Hitting of the site itself," Rennie added. "She's right, Taylor. There's something here and someone is trying to keep us from finding it."

"Gee, I don't know," Taylor said.

"Oh my gosh! Look at Kit!" Rennie exclaimed, her voice pitched with shock.

Alex and Taylor turned to look at Kit, who stood on the nearest back-filled hole. She pawed at the earth, lowered her head, and cocked it to one side, her whole body rigid. She gave a low growl that rose at the end to a whine—a sound Alex had heard her make only one time.

"She's doing what she did at the alcove," Alex said. She looked at Taylor.

He stroked his mustache with his thumb and forefinger. The look in his eyes sharpened. He glanced at his test trench, which was on a dead-on alignment with the pothole Kit stood on and within only a few days of excavation.

Oddly, Alex relaxed. Her point had been driven home. She walked over to Kit and put her arm around the dog, scratching her chest and pulling her in to comfort her. Kit pulled away and left the middens, seeming to lose interest in the whole business. Alex let the dog go and looked up at Taylor. "Well?" she said

Taylor said, "*I'll* dig." He set to work with the shovel, carefully studying the dirt in the filled-in hole as he did. Alex and Rennie stood nearby watching.

He dug with extreme care, feeling his way along with the shovel and his expert sense for changes in the soil, levering off shovel after shovel of dirt. Each one counted. Each shovelful removed a layer of concealment that had buried an obvious secret.

Dusk had just begun to fall when Taylor stopped digging. He dropped the shovel. Pulling his trowel out of his back pocket, he knelt down and began scraping back the soil, shifting aside pot shards and burned animal bone. The ring of the trowel's metal blade changed as it struck something with less resonance than fired pottery.

With his hand, Taylor brushed away the dirt, revealing the arc of a slightly worn cloverleaf-cut vibram boot heel. He sat back on his haunches and looked up at the women. There was a tacit agreement to proceed. Taylor troweled along the edge of the sole, revealing the base of a leather upper. He cleaned the heel with his trowel until the insignia stood out.

Timberland, it read. Clearly not a brand favored by the Anasazi. But Harry Hoskers had worn Timberland boots. They'd gone well with his expensive jeans and T-shirts advertising trendy nightspots in the California-Hollywood time zone. Harry had made a few token gestures to fit in better with the Colorado Plateau crowd, but there had been some vestiges of his previous life he had not been able to discard.

Until recently.

Thirty-Nine

There is something ludicrous about murder, something about its excesses and gross wastefulness that points to its absurdity as a solution to personal problems. Just step back a little, look beyond its shocking reminder of mortality, put aside your consuming urge for reprisal, and you will see it—how the disjointed nature of the act exposes the murderer's underlying impotence.

Shakespeare was aware of this. *Hamlet* belabors the point, as by the time the play ends, bodies litter the stage, two as the result of plots gone wrong and one, Hamlet himself, dead from a death wish. King Claudius suffers overkill as he's forced to drink poisoned wine and then is stabbed to death with a poison-tipped sword. Even before this, the play's body count is high, with one death occurring off-stage before the play even opens.

Alex was aware that *Hamlet* is usually classified as a tragedy, but there were at least a few who thought of it as a black comedy. After all, in *Hamlet* so much time, energy, and life's blood are wasted and in the end there's nothing to show for it but the waste itself. Reminiscent, in a way, of slapstick.

Alex thought Harry Hoskers's death was tragic but that it also contained elements that were grotesquely comedic. On one hand, his death was a sad loss to the project, which he had sustained with his powerful, if misdirected, energy. And, Alex thought, who knows, maybe the connections that run between people are deep enough that even Harry Hoskers had brought something delectable to the table. On the other hand, Harry had played a foolish game and wound up entombed in his own midden, the next burial in line for excavation. Somebody's idea of a sick joke.

Although the Deeppockets project had come to an end, in a manner of speaking, the Hoskers Project continued. Responsibility for Hoskers and his site passed from the hands of the archaeologists and into the hands of the San Juan County Sheriff's Department. Since the body was discovered right off the edge of the reservation, the Navajo tribal police came over for a look. It was decided that excavation would continue only insofar as was necessary to remove Harry from his midden, and the police personnel were handling that. Archaeologists would attend in an advisory capacity, standing on the law protecting archaeological sites from any threat of damage and destruction. Hanks permitted only himself, Taylor, Danny, and Rennie on site to keep an eye on their individual work areas.

In the excitement and confusion that followed the discovery of the site owner's body, no one had thought to contact Danny. Sunday evening, he arrived at camp with six volunteers, the largest group to date. They were not even allowed to stay the night. Considering that the murderer was still on the loose, and in light of the various acts of sabotage committed against the field school, the students were told to pack up and prepare to leave.

Sunday passed, Monday afternoon arrived. Alex sat with her musings at one of the tables set up outside the mess tent, surrounded by depressed students, Mike, Sharp, and Josh. Dr. Hanks, Taylor, Rennie, and Danny were out at the site.

Heather moved quietly around the table, supervising what would probably be the camp's last artifact washing and labeling session. Since the police had taken over the site, the only site-related work that remained to be done was labeling the artifacts and keeping up the notes.

Sharp sat cleaning the tread of his boot with his pocketknife. Suddenly he said, "Who'd have thought it. Old Harry was with us the whole time. Only he *wasn't*. He was dearly departed."

"Perhaps his ghost is mingling with those of the Ancestral Puebloans on the site," Hector said.

"Maybe he's taken up the ghost bongos," Chris said.

"Ghost *drums*," Marina said. "Not bongos."

"So, is the closing of the field school a sure thing?" Josh asked.

"Yes, tomorrow," Marina said. "That is, us little ol' students and volunteers will have to leave." She looked at Alex. "The big chiefs are staying."

"Just to break camp, clean up, and keep watch over the site until the cops finish," Alex said. "Once they release the site, we'll backfill the excavations."

"You'd think the local constabulary would want us all to stay," Hector said.

"Why?" Marina asked.

"Technically, we're suspects in Mr. Hoskers's murder. The authorities have only begun their investigation. Matters of motive, means, and opportunity remain to be explored." He glanced at Alex. "They have yet to determine who had the might to force their misconception of right upon the unfortunate Mr. Hoskers."

Heather passed by, her face completely closed. Alex decided to risk a question. "What are *you* going to do, Heather?"

Heather's eyes darted toward Alex but stopped short of looking directly at her. She shrugged.

"Seen Tony around?" Alex asked. She tried to make the question appear a casual one, but at the mention of Tony's name, Marina glanced across the table at her.

Heather hesitated.

"I mean, does he know we're breaking camp?" Alex continued.

"I don't know," she said, shrugging again.

"Think you'll see him in time to tell him?" Alex asked.

Again, the shrug. She set bags of artifacts on the table. "These are the last of them," she said.

"These may be the last bags of artifacts that ever come out of the site," Josh remarked.

"Unless you count body bags," Sharp said.

Bill Wiggins, who had walked over to fetch warm water from the barrel in the low-burning campfire, guffawed at this comment.

"Then there will be the evidence bags," Alex added thoughtfully, "to be stored until they're pulled for analysis."

"Yeah," Mike said. "Just like *we* do it."

Hearing a vehicle approach camp, Alex looked up.

"Is that Dr. Hanks and them?" Marina asked.

Alex rose from her seat. "I hope it's not the police coming to ask more questions." Kit, lying in a dugout, lifted her head, stood up, and shook out her fur. Alex guessed the dog recognized the engine noise, which meant that the crew chiefs and Hanks were returning.

Sure enough, the Suburban and pickup swung into the lot. Everyone walked over to meet them, but Hanks got out and waved them off. "We can't discuss what we know, so don't ask," he said, sweeping past. He dropped off his notebooks and headed for his tent. Rennie got out of the Suburban, Taylor and Danny from the pickup.

"You okay?" Alex asked Rennie.

"Yeah, I'm all right," she said. "It looks like we're going to lose the site along with Hoskers, and that gets to me, but ..."

A thought occurred to Alex. "What *does* happen to the site now that Harry's done with it?"

"I don't know. I'm sure the police are looking into that very question."

"Hm, maybe it isn't over yet. Maybe the project will somehow continue."

"I doubt it," Rennie said. "Moneywise, Harry Hoskers was the driving force. I can't see it going anywhere from here. Besides, the police think ..."

Suddenly aware of the group gathering around, Rennie jerked her head toward their tent.

"I need to take a shower. Walk with me to the tent."

"Hey, no fair!" Caedyn said. "We want to hear, too!"

Alex and Rennie headed for the more isolated stretch of greasewood in the women's area. "Looking at where the questions are going," Rennie said, "it seems the police think the site itself might be a motive for murder but don't know exactly how. They asked if anything of value was buried there."

"Well *duh*, what with whole pots and who knows what under that dirt," Alex said.

"On the other hand, everyone knows Hoskers had plenty of shake-hands-with-the-right, stab-you-with-the-left associates."

Alex shook her head. "I don't think that's it."

"No?"

"No. It has something to do with the site."

"Another thing the police are wondering is if maybe Harry visited his site on the way to Mesa Verde and caught the pot hunters ravaging it."

"All possible," Alex said. "But there's the question of how his truck and camper got all the way out on Mustang Mesa. If the killer moved them, why? And what about the killer's own vehicle? How did the killer get to the site and then back from Mustang Mesa?" She stopped and looked at Rennie closely. "How *did* Hoskers die?"

Rennie looked around. "You didn't hear any of this from me," she said.

Alex nodded.

"Well, it appears he was struck at least one deadly blow from behind with a metate fragment, probably while he was crouching down, possibly to look at something on the ground. We found it today in another one of the back-filled potholes." They were at the tent now. They stepped in and sat on their cots.

"That old grinding stone that's been lying on the middens?"

"That's what Taylor said," Rennie answered. "A weapon of opportunity."

"Indicating the murder was not premeditated." Alex shook her head. "But I don't see it," she said. "Harry Hoskers confronting someone and getting hit from behind?"

Rennie dropped her head into her hands. "The police suggested there might have been a couple of people involved ..."

"Jack said only one," Alex interrupted.

"Yeah, well–Jack's not a homicide detective."

"That could be an advantage," Alex replied.

As if something sharp had suddenly pricked her, Rennie stood straight up, her face drawn.

"You don't look so good," Alex said. "Are you sure you're all right?"

"I don't want to talk about this anymore," Rennie said. "I'm going to take a shower."

"Good idea," Alex said. Rennie grabbed clean clothes and stuff for her shower and left.

Alex sat alone in the tent's heat, her mind flitting back and forth between vague impressions and wild thoughts. Suddenly, she lifted her head as something intruded on her thinking in a way she didn't understand. It was like a light had switched on in her mind and was slowly growing brighter or like a distinctive sound rising above some tumbling thoughts. Light, sound, or something else, it was clear and compelling. Suddenly, more than anything, she wanted to go for a walk.

She left the tent and hurried toward the mess, passing the women's shower on the way. Rennie's towel hung over the side. Water trickled lightly from the barrels.

Entering the mess area, she looked for Kit. The dugout be-

three hundred and twenty-three

neath the water spigot was empty. Looking toward the mess tent, her eyes caught Todd's. The Navajo boy dropped his gaze. Alex swept the work area with a look. No Kit.

"Where's my dog?" she asked Jack, now sitting alone at Heather's table.

Jack looked around. He shrugged. "Don't know," he said. "They went on a water run. Maybe she followed the truck to the well head."

Alex sighed impatiently.

"Something wrong?" Jack asked.

"No," Alex said. "I'll catch up with her later." She walked toward the road.

"Where are you going?" Jack asked.

"For a walk," Alex threw back over her shoulder.

"Be careful!" he called.

· · · · ·

As she walked, heat pressed in on her from all sides. Her dark hair absorbed the sun and she wished she had brought her crusher. Reaching into her pocket, she took out a scrunchie, pulled back her hair, and twisted it up into a ponytail. Then she took off the white bandana she was wearing on her neck and tied it over her head.

The image of Harry Hoskers's boot sole protruding from the midden resurfaced in her mind. Poor Harry! She hadn't known him well and hadn't liked what she did know of him. But there at his midden graveside, staring down at his boot, Alex had found the question of whether or not she liked Harry to be irrelevant. The same was true of the question of whether or not he had brought this fate upon himself. She figured a dead person regained some of the innocence he had at birth and Alex did not feel inclined to hold any of Harry's misdeeds against him.

However, there was another person involved, someone Alex felt a mix of emotions over, none of them good. In her mind, Alex called this person the Violator. By violently wrenching Harry from this world and thrusting him into the next, the Violator had committed not only an unlawful act, but one in which he had moved against the personal world of Harry's intentions and desires. But it didn't stop there, for in destroying Harry's ability to live in accordance with his world view, the Violator had also made attempts on the lives of those connected to Harry, including everyone in the field school. And who knows how far the shock waves from such violence spread out or to what heights they rose.

Perhaps the best way Alex could counteract the effects of the deadly attack on her friends was to bring everything out into the open. Maybe it was possible to counter-balance the whole terrible business by revealing the Violator's identity and intentions. If she could set into motion a new chain of events, maybe healing could begin, both on individual and community levels. The question was ... how?

When she was within a quarter mile of the site, she took a power pole right-of-way and headed up the side of a mesa. After following this rough trail a short distance, she left that too, making her way up a talus slope.

She turned around to see what Kit was doing, then remembered that Kit wasn't with her. Without the husky's energy and keen senses to back her up, Alex suddenly felt naked. She stopped, wondering if she should return to camp. Shading her eyes, she looked at the top of the mesa. Its call sounded loudly in her soul. Against her better judgment, she resumed her climb. She knew now she was heading for Cliff Kiva if she could find it.

She reached the mesa top in under an hour. Brushing off her hands, she walked along the rim, looking for the cairn that marked the kiva's entrance. She stopped and took in the view. The dig was easily visible from this mesa rim. She wondered if they could see her. Probably not unless they were looking with binoculars, and why would they be doing that? Once more, she set off to find the kiva's entrance.

. . . . .

A little while later, she sat down on a rock beside the marker. A slight breeze cooled her overheated skin. She listened. Except for the grind of a cicada's call and the drone of an airliner flying west, the day was as quiet as it was bright. She wished she had brought water. She gazed out over Big Wash canyon. Her nearest obvious neighbors were the minuscule figures searching the site for answers explaining Harry's final state, but she had the strangest feeling she wasn't alone.

Her eyes wandered to the dirt at her feet. A few marks in the sand caught her eye. She bent down for a closer look. Footprints. She stood up and searched the ground. Boulders and stones on and around the rim offered firm surfaces for anyone wishing to travel without leaving marks, but ... Alex had the impression that whoever had made these felt no real concern over leaving them.

As she thought about what the footprints meant, her heart began to pound. Weeks had passed since the field school had hiked to the kiva. Someone else, however, had been making use of the remote and infrequently visited site. Thoughts tumbling, she wondered if the police had been up for some reason, but—*no*—wishful thinking. No one had mentioned the kiva to the police. No one had had any reason to. Furthermore, it was well-hidden in miles of mesa rimrock. Unless you knew what to look for, you wouldn't know it was there.

Plain common sense told her to run. A word to the cops at Deeppockets that there was something out of the ordinary on the mesa across from the Hoskers murder site and they'd be up in a breath. It wouldn't be her problem, it wasn't her problem. All she had to do was turn the matter over to the authorities. She could keep to the edge of this whole, rotten business— on the safe side of the edge. No one would blame her for not taking risks.

She took a breath, then dropped over the mesa edge and slid down the scree to the kiva's mouth. She knew she was invisible to the workers at the site—a speck lost among the mesa's jumble of stony detail and roughly folded shadows. Cliff Kiva might be within view, but its location and its size compared to the rest of the mesa endowed it with privacy. Alex considered the kiva's appeal to the person she sought: it was an odd mix of the obvious and the obscure. Near enough to observe the movements of the field school with a good pair of binoculars, far enough away to afford concealment, if only temporarily.

She paused, listening. No sound issued from inside. Adrenaline dumping into her bloodstream, heightening her senses and causing her hands to shake, she entered the fissure–corridor that led to Cliff Kiva's chamber. Her legs went weak.

"Ooh—don't do this now!" she said. She pressed the palms of her hands against the rock walls to steady herself. A few short steps inside and the fissure gaped below, the walls parted like the lips of a sleeper. A draft rushed up, startling her. She realized that her own breathing was as rapid as Todd's the night he had confronted the coyotes.

"I guess that's what I'm doing, isn't it? Confronting the coyotes." Every few steps, she paused to listen. Silence. When she crossed what she thought to be the corridor's halfway point, her steps faltered. Still time to turn around and run. *Maybe.*

Another deep breath and she pressed on. When she came to the edge of the drop-off, she halted. As rubbery as her knees felt, she wasn't sure she could make the jump. The shaft gaped below her, a ragged drop varying in width and in depth. Somehow, she had to summon strength for the two- to three-foot leap.

At least now she could see that the chamber was empty. Rather than providing relief, this fact aroused fears of being trapped. She looked back over her shoulder at the entrance. Like a window in a high-rise, it had as its only view the blank and unending sky.

She took three deep breaths to steady her nerves, then leapt the dropoff, landing safely on the other side. There she saw, leading to and from the hole opening into the fissure behind the cavern, tracks made by the same boot that had imprinted the dirt at the mesa's rim. Other than that, the chamber showed no signs of use. Alex crouched at the fissure's entrance and listened.

It was the strangest thing! From inside came a clinking noise like that made by wind chimes. Her curiosity piqued, she leaned closer. What in the world could be making such delicate sounds? Someone tapping on stone? An Anasazi ghost playing a phantom instrument? *What?*

She dropped to her hands and knees and peered through the hole. Pieces of pottery dangled from rock overhangs, tied there with jute cords. Some shards were arranged in mobiles so that, when the breeze stirred, they clinked against each other lightly. Other artifacts sat on rock shelves or had been wedged into cracks.

Overcome by wonder, Alex dropped her guard and eased through the hole, landing on the fissure's rough floor. She approached the nearest dangling object and suspended it on her palm. It was a dazzling specimen of late Pueblo pottery. A black, labyrinthine pattern decorated the shard's white slip. It had been cleaned so that the pattern achieved nearly its original gloss and elegance. A hole had been drilled through one corner and a jute cord had been tied to it with a simple knot. She let the shard go. It swung away, clinking as it struck the rock wall.

She looked around at the gallery of displaced objects, taken like quotations out of the context of their original story and forced into this bizarre one. On a ledge nearby lay a painted jug handle. Alex picked it up. A series of black dots and thin lines marked its spine, distinguishing it as another striking example of a one-of-a-kind piece. She set it down, tapping it back into position.

Similar objects dangled around her head or sat on overhangs, decorating the passage not only visually but musically. Alex inspected several more pieces until it became obvious that the devil lay not in the details here, but in the overall pattern. All of the items were in some way flashy stand-outs.

Alex fought twinges of appreciation for this strange setting. She knew that some would argue that the fissure had been made beautiful. Some would say that showing through in arrangements of ceramics and music played by fluttering shards —removed, no doubt, from Deeppockets itself and maybe even from the project's artifact bags—was the consciousness of an artist. But another voice whispered in Alex's brain, *there be madness here,* a play on the phrase written on old maps where knowledge of the world left off and the realm of dragons and monsters began. She felt this even though there was nothing sinister or threatening about the objects themselves.

She came to the bend in the passage, turned, and followed it to the dead end. There she found something out of the ordinary even for this outlandish showroom—a set of keys. She plucked them from their grotto.

They were attached to a ring with a sterling silver replica of a Pueblo III pottery shard. An artistic piece in its own right, something about it seemed familiar. Alex thought back. In her mind's eye, she saw the keys tossed into the air. They landed in someone's hand in a store—no, the minimart in Blanding. Then she remembered the keys landing in Harry's hand. She turned the silver shard over. It bore the artist's name and an inscription: *To Harry from Tamara.*

"Now, *who* is Tamara?" she whispered. Keys to a Chevy hung on the ring. Alex guessed they were to Harry's truck. Also attached were a post office box key and a couple of house keys.

She set the keys back on their shelf, then looked up. The buzzard's wing still protruded from the rock shelf overhead. "I'm surprised *that's* not decorated, too," she said. But then her eye caught sight of an object lying next to the wing. "What's that?"

She felt for finger-holds to hoist herself up. She faltered

trying to find a foothold, then pulled herself slightly above eye-level of the shelf.

Her missing brush lay beside the moldering carcass of the buzzard, dark strands of her hair looping through its bristles. The shock of seeing it there and the realization of what its presence meant caused her to lose her grip. She slid down the wall, crumpling to her knees on the floor. Then came a fight to control panic.

Now she knew the truth of her situation. She'd gotten in way over her head by coming to the kiva alone. But maybe there was still time to get out! She got to her feet and staggered back through the passage, stirring up music from the dangling ceramics as she pitched through them.

She heaved herself up on her belly and wriggled through the fissure's entrance onto the chamber floor. When she had squirmed halfway through, she suddenly realized that she was not alone. On eye level, which at the moment was floor level, she saw a pair of hiking boots. Above the boots, jeans. Stiffened by fright, she looked up, but found it difficult to follow the legs all the way to the face she knew was there.

Tony Balbo crouched down beside her to make it easier for her to look at him. "You've come at last, Alexandra," he said. "I've been waiting for you."

Forty

"Permit me to help you up from that awkward position," he said, taking her arm. When he touched her, Alex felt a wave of nauseating panic. The edges of her vision faded. *No,* she thought. *I can't faint! Not now!*

Struggling for control, she refocused. Every second lost to hysteria would only deepen her disadvantage. Her struggle to stay alert was so intense, she felt sure she was giving off chemical signals or that the electrical field around her body was shooting off sparks. Maybe her aura had gone kaleidoscopic. Surely Tony would smell, taste, or see her fear.

If he did, he didn't let on. He waited in a gentlemanly manner until she responded, pulling herself the rest of the way out of the hole and getting up onto hands and knees. She lost heart at the strength she felt in his arm as he lifted her. When she was on her feet, he turned her so that she faced him. She tried to avoid eye contact without betraying her fear. She wondered which proverbial choice her instincts would make—flight or fight.

Oddly, something in her cast off both. She adopted a complete submission to her circumstances. This was due in part to the split second appraisal of her options. Trying to run away down the kiva's cleft corridor was impossible. The risk of injury or worse was too great.

Turning on Tony and trying to fight him seemed futile. For one thing, he probably expected such a move. The strength in his gesture of helping her up confirmed that she wouldn't win a struggle. So she stood there, fighting panic so that she could face him in some other way. He released her and stepped back as if to appraise her condition.

"But you seem distressed!" he said. "Come now, where's that cool defiance with which you so piqued my interest?"

Alex felt a stab of self-condemnation. She *had* deliberately drawn his attention, hadn't she? As her powers of speech began working again, she looked into his face. "It's there," she said.

He smiled. "So I see." In a conspicuous gesture, he looked around and then peered out through the corridor. "And your bitch? I can hardly imagine you came without her."

"She was gone when I left camp," Alex said. "So I did come without her."

"Perfect!" he said. "Saves me some trouble." He stepped away, then a thought seemed to hit him. "But do you suppose the absence of your creature will diminish your capacity?"

Alex wondered what in the world he was talking about, then remembered. Tony thought she was a witch, or so he had said. His question referred to what he thought to be her familiar. "No," she said. But in her heart, she knew that Kit's absence did indeed weaken her position.

"Hmm. Well, come sit down," he said, walking to the boulders lining the rim of the balcony. She felt surprise at how little of an attempt he made to restrain her. No doubt, he, too, had considered her choices and knew how limited they were. "We have a lot to talk about, don't we?"

He sat on a boulder and gestured for her to take the one next to him. Feeling that she had nothing to lose, she obliged.

"Tell me," he said. "Your opinion would be of the highest value to me. What did you think of my little gallery? Beautiful, isn't it?"

Again, Alex had to make a choice: truthfulness in answering his question or deception. She paused to think. Well, since he so admired her cool defiance ... "No, Tony, it is *not* beautiful," she said. "Clever, maybe, but not beautiful."

His face fell. "I thought you of all people could appreciate it," he said, looking at her from beneath hooded eyes. "I thought that as an artistic expression, it worked."

"A lot of art is clever," Alex said. "But it isn't beautiful. Your 'effort' works in the way a lot of art works—as a monument to violation." She stopped, waiting for his reaction.

A smile spread across his face and his eyes went wide with delight. He giggled. "Well, my dear," he said, "you are nothing if not adept with language. I saw that the other night at the fire—you are a sophist *par excellence*. Far more clever than I with words." He leaned back and crossed his legs at the ankles.

Again, Alex felt surprise. His body language expressed ease with her presence. He didn't seem to understand that at the first opportunity she would try to escape. "A sophist!" she exclaimed.

"Yes, of course."

Thinking out loud, she said, "You mean that I'm not interested in truth or reason, just in winning verbal games."

He nodded. "That's it."

Alex rolled her eyes. She decided to cut to the chase. "So, why did you kill Harry?" she asked. "I mean, there must have been something of his you wanted that he stood in the way of your getting."

Tony bit his lip. "You tell me," he said.

"I don't know," Alex replied.

"Of course you know."

"I don't."

"What do you take me for?" Tony yelled, rising to his feet and leaning over her. "You know as well as I do! Don't try to play your games with me, Alexandra! I know you for what you are—*better than you know yourself!*"

As suddenly as his rage had flared up, it dissipated, leaving Alex staring in astonishment.

He sighed. "Come now, Alexandra," he said, his voice returning to its croon. "I would think you'd appreciate my understanding of your soul. I never thought I'd ever meet anyone like you. Who does? Only the very fortunate or those destined to."

Alex considered the two forks in the conversation: Tony's motive for murdering Harry, and Tony's assumptions about Alexandra, which if pursued, would provide clues to what he planned to do with her. Alex decided to return to the first path.

"Harry had something you wanted," she said. "Probably something to do with the site." She nodded at the gallery. "Seeing your little collection in there, one might assume you are a pot hunter and that you've been collecting evidence like a miner collects ore samples ... evidence that leads you to believe that somewhere beneath Deeppockets lies a fortune in pottery and other valuable artifacts."

She paused, looking at Tony for his reaction. He sat as still as a rock, dark eyes returning her look, a very slight smile playing on his lips. "Go on," he said, as if listening to an amusing story.

"But that's not it," Alex said. "A small—or large—fortune in illegal pottery is nothing compared to something else you hoped to gain. I think you've got a shrine in there," she said, gesturing at the gallery. "A place of incantation, of concentration. There's something else about the site you desire, not the money. The shrine is only a temporary house for your lust."

"Oh, lust is such an ungainly word," Tony protested. "It reminds one too much of even more unpleasant words that it rhymes with: dust, rust, crust. I liked the other word you used—*desire*—much better."

"I think lust will do," Alex retorted, thinking his rage would erupt again.

But he only laughed. "Whatever you like, my dear," he said. "Go on."

Alex felt confused by the man's unpredictability. What should she do? She decided to press her point. "I think you ascribe some power to the site itself or think of it as some kind of focal point for your own power. Whatever the case, you became obsessed with Deeppockets, perhaps because of Harry's cavalier attitude toward it."

"The man was a complete idiot!" Tony said. "*You* saw it, I know you did. That site is such a delicate and wondrous place, a riot of energies, a garden of ..." He searched for a word. "... of *significance*. Harry stomped over it like one of Brock's brutish bulls."

Alex was incredulous. "That's good coming from you!" she exclaimed. "As if killing Hoskers and then stuffing his body in the middens isn't the height of desecration!"

"Just a bit of irony, Alexandra," he replied, as if from modesty. "I'm sure Harry appreciates it. You'll agree that he was looking for something of that sort to happen. I merely gave him what he wanted—a violent death, the culmination of his efforts. Then I added a few touches of my own."

"You mean, making it seem like pot hunters had hit the site as a cover for the real crime. Burying Hoskers where the Ancestral Puebloans buried their dead. Burying him on his own property, right beneath the feet of those in his employ ..."

"The list does go on!" Tony said. "How about the one where he gets to be excavated like one of the burials around him! That's my personal favorite."

"Oh, let me guess," Alex said. "The Coors can ..."

"Ah, I'd forgotten," Tony said. "His own. He preferred Heineken or one of the other imports. Coors Lite was one of his attempts to fit in better in San Juan County. It was already in the truck, just waiting to be recycled. A nice touch, don't you think? After all, he was little better than a pot hunter himself. So many ideas came to me like that." He snapped his fingers.

"Only things went a little awry," Alex said. "I don't think you actually planned to kill Harry, but something happened that made you decide it had to be done right then."

"That's quite a leap," Tony said, nodding. "What makes you think so?"

"You tried to drive us out. The damage to the wellhead,

the fire—you were concerned someone would find him. That concern became real when Taylor decided to run a test trench right through the midden where Harry lay. Then you had to get us out because you had committed an off-the-cuff murder, probably your *first* murder, and you had been clumsy and caused yourself a lot of problems you thought you could solve if only we weren't in your way. Seems a bit awkward. I would expect you to be more deliberate than that. But ... what did he say that caused you to jump the gun?"

"He answered a question," Tony said.

"Which was?"

Tony paused, glancing at the hole in the back of the cavern. "Did you see the keys?" he asked.

"Yes," Alex said. "Who is Tamara?"

"It's not TA-mar-a., it's Ta-MAR-a," he corrected her. "Although, it may have been TA-ma-ra at one time. She's a redhaired beauty, a cross between a new age priestess and ... how do you say it? A jock. She's in great condition, a runner, into archery and dressage. Owns a thoroughbred stallion named Hoskers' Edge. Quite a striking woman, if a bit of a fraud."

Alex put together the inscription on the keys with the implications of Tony's words.

"Harry's significant other? Nobody knew ..."

"*I* knew," Tony said. "She's in Telluride. He never invited her over to see this side of his life and she never asked, though she wanted to. She wanted so very badly for Harry to include her in his big adventure. She considered forcing him to choose —either let her come or bye, bye, Harry. But she was a good girl and choked it down, kept silent, put up with his lone ranger excursions even though it made her feel neglected."

"Obviously, you knew a lot about their relationship," Alex said. "Why didn't anybody else?"

"You know Harry," Tony said. "He didn't think it was relevant to what he was doing here. I'm sure it just never came up."

Alex paused, trying to sort through this new information. "So, how did you know?"

"Saw them together in Telluride," he said, "late last fall." He shrugged at her look of doubt. "Dr. Hanks was right. I *do* have a lot of time on my hands."

"So, you, uh, comforted poor Tamara?" Alex asked.

"I did. She was seething over the relationship, suspected that another woman might be frustrating her plans ... all kinds of unworthy thoughts, not exactly in line with one endowed with new age spiritual awareness. Like I say, she's a bit of a fraud. I saw her just recently ..."

"Before or after you killed her boyfriend?"

"Before," Tony replied, his tone light. "She'd about had it, wondered if I thought she should end the relationship. I believed she was interested in making more of ours. You see, up until recently I was only her confidant."

The disgust Alex felt flowed over into her tone. "What about Heather?" she demanded.

"*That* pathetic creature," Tony said with a dismissive wave. "She got what she wanted. Heather had a bad relationship with her father and, like a lot of women who grew up with that problem, has one of those sad attractions to abusive men. I merely stepped in and satisfied it for her."

Alex could barely contain her anger. "You became a sadist to her masochist, then abandoned her?"

"Exactly. It's what she expected."

"And what did you get out of it? Information about the site?"

"That's it," Tony admitted without a sign of conscience. "And access to it, or so I'd hoped. Dr. Hanks finally invited me, but it was rather late in the game."

"And you had already taken other steps," Alex said. "So, about Tamara ..."

"Ah, yes. Well, she likes me, you see."

"You mean, she has some weakness you're exploiting!" Alex said. "But what's the connection to the site?"

"I asked Harry what would become of the site if anything happened to him."

Alex nodded, remembering how she had asked a similar question. "And?"

"He really did care deeply for Tamara, in his way. Unknown to her, he made out a will and, on a romantic whim or maybe for other foolish reasons, left the site to her."

Suddenly Alex got it—the whole, ugly scenario. "You already had some control over her, and now you knew that on Harry's death, she would have control of the site."

"You're right, it was rather a spontaneous act on my part to move forward so quickly. I hadn't intended to do him any injury at all until that opening appeared and it all came to me." Tony became agitated. "It was hard to forget how he invited that pot hunter to the site and all the other ways he endangered it."

"Including trying to get it into the park system," Alex said, her mind reeling.

"Leaving the site to Tamara! How useless is that? One way to think of it is that what happened was meant to be." He began pacing the chamber. "Our meeting that day was unlikely. He got a flat tire on his trailer out by Mustang. I stopped to help, and he invited me to ride along with him to the site, told me of his impending trip to Mesa Verde. Then he answered my question straight out, told me Tamara would inherit the site upon his untimely death. The metate was right there at my feet. You know the rest."

"He didn't know about your acquaintance with Tamara," she posed, feeling ill.

"He could have known, would have known if he had been paying attention. But Harry tended to focus on the wrong things."

"Yeah," Alex said. "He totally missed the metate poised to smash into the back of his skull."

Tony sat back down, curiosity showing in his eyes. "I hope I haven't intruded too clumsily upon your own interests in the site," he said. "If I have, I want you to know I think there's room for two."

Alex sputtered in shock and dismay.

"Ah, perhaps I have intruded," Tony responded, completely misreading her. "Then what is *your* suggestion?"

Alex found this turn in conversation completely dumbfounding. Dazed, she said, "I have no designs on the site."

Tony laughed, the lilt of it ringing through the chamber. "So you say, my dear," he said. "Very well, it can wait until you feel more comfortable with me."

Alex had the feeling she had just said she didn't want to play, only to have that taken as the next move in the game. "What do you mean, when I become more comfortable? They'll come looking for me."

"Not for awhile," Tony said. "They only found Harry so soon because of you. Am I right? I'm sure you had your own reasons for that. But who's going to know where to look for *you*?"

"They'll start looking soon—maybe they have already. How long do you think this hide-in-plain-site trick is going to work, especially when people start looking for a field school student lost in the desert?"

This thought gave Tony pause. "It's all in the timing," he said. "In how long it takes people to do this or that, to think of this or that. But where you're concerned, perhaps I ought to go down and see if you've been missed. After all, I can't imagine you would want to be found, not after all that's happened between us."

Alex felt a cold draft blow up from a deep, dark cavern in her brain. "What's happened between us?"

"Why, you came here because I called you. You saw your hairbrush in there?" He gestured toward the entrance to the fissure.

"Yes, I saw that," Alex said. "And I thought that's what it meant. But I didn't come here because you called me! That's absurd."

"I don't think it's absurd," he retorted. "Other cultures don't think it absurd. Some go to great lengths to make sure that no personal items or residue are available for such rituals. And then," he said, bending down, picking up sand and letting it run through his hand, "there's all this recent business with DNA, growing new organs, and so forth. It seems that any given cell may contain something that is essentially you, with all of its strengths and vulnerabilities. That includes, of course, that matter by which you may be summoned forth."

"Maybe I came here for my own compelling reasons," Alex snapped back.

"What might those be?" he asked. "Ah, let me guess—something to do with your feelings for those ignorant, up-tight, self-righteous creatures you associate with."

"They aren't ignorant, up-tight, or self-righteous. Not compared to you! But you're right. It is about them. I'm surprised you can see that."

"Of course I see it. That's how I drew you out at the fire that night. I knew you wouldn't offer anything to me directly, but if it were a matter of defending someone else ... well, you *let it all hang out,* as they say."

Once more, Alex sat stunned, then cursed herself for walking into the exact trap she had warned Marina to avoid.

"At any rate," he said, looking up, "I think it safe to say that you're here because you want to be and because I ... well, I blush to say it."

"Say it," Alex said.

"We have an intimate understanding." He stood and brushed off his hands. "And we have a common interest."

"I told you I don't want the site!" Alex screeched. "How stupid can you be? I don't want the site and there are a lot of cops working on this thing. Sooner or later they'll find the will and ..."

Tony reached into his back pocket and pulled out an envelope. He handed it to her. She looked at him, took it, and removed the papers from inside. *Last Will and Testament* read the scroll across the top. It was an informal document, signed with Harry's flamboyant script. She looked up at Tony, startled.

"I have his keys," he said.

"Someone will know ..."

"I doubt it. Harry Hoskers did not have what you would call a lot of foresight," Tony said. "I doubt anyone has the slightest idea."

"How will you ..."

"I don't know yet," he interrupted. "Some opportunity will present itself. Oh, Tamara gets the house in Bluff, too, but I don't know what she'd want it for. She's got trendy written all over her, and neither the site nor the house are quite up to the current fad—not by her standards, anyway."

Alex stood silent, completely taken aback. It didn't matter what she said or did. Words twisted up in the machinations of Tony's mind, meanings writhed, tortured.

Measuring her look, he said, "You're thinking about it. Good." He reached into another pocket and pulled out baling chord. "Now, I must go down and pay a little visit to the camp. If you'll put your hands behind your back ..."

"I thought you said I was here because I wanted to be," she said, eyeing the cord.

"I know you are here because you want to be, but I don't think you know it yet. Turn around, please."

At a loss for options, Alex complied. He bound her wrists firmly. Alex could feel the nerves along her spine prickle as his breath touched the back of her neck and his fingers brushed against her skin. When he was done, he turned her around to face him. She met his eyes. The feeling of vulnerability was nauseating.

"It really is an honor to know you, Alexandra McKelvey. I've wanted to meet you—or someone like you—all my life. I look forward to our continued association."

Looking into his face with its chilling beauty, Alex remained silent. She couldn't think of a reply or even a reason to speak. Her meanings transformed completely in the dark chemistry of his soul so that he heard, not what she said, but what he believed must be said. With a jolt, she realized that Tony Balbo had no concern whatsoever for truth or reason. He perceived himself as having power, and so he could make things mean what he wanted them to. Remembering their fireside chat, she suddenly saw just how right she'd been about him. *Of course, might makes right.* Too bad she'd missed a thing or two.

She tried one last time. "You've got it wrong, Tony," she said. "I'm not what you think."

Tony raised his eyebrows. "You most certainly are," he said. "Can it be you don't know it? But maybe you're a raw talent, an *ingenue* in the art. What an opportunity! Let me spell it out. You are a born witch, my dear."

Alex tossed her head defiantly. "I'm not."

"You are," he asserted. "I believe you are not aware of it, though. Or perhaps you've noticed but haven't yet accepted it. Let me guess, you have dreams about flying, don't you? Ah, hit that one, didn't I? Yes, and how about an uncanny ease with animals? A generous *je ne sais quois* that attracts others? Well, I can testify to *that* one. My dear Alexandra, you shouldn't fight it, and there's nothing to be ashamed of. You are what you are and I am what I am. We have a natural affinity for each other." He turned away from her, making for the corridor.

"I'll return shortly," he said. "We'll leave tonight. I have a nice Jeep ..."

"A Jeep!" Alex exclaimed, remembering the reports that ranchers had seen a Jeep in the canyon around the time of Harry's disappearance. "A *black* Jeep?"

He stopped, surprised. "Yes," he said. "Although now it seems I may have to do something about that. Apparently it isn't my little secret anymore."

"What about your Honda?"

"What about it? You really can't expect me to do the kind of roaming I do in a banged-up Honda. Hondas are expendable, but a good, four-wheel-drive vehicle is invaluable. It's my reliable trail horse."

"You really are a skinwalker," Alex said under her breath.

"Speak up, Alexandra. It's not polite to whisper."

"You're a skinwalker!" she said. "You put on different skins to work your nastiness, both psychological skins and metal skins."

Tony didn't answer but gave her a wry glance. "I'll be back soon," he said, leading her to a rock and seating her. "Make yourself comfortable." And with that, he crossed the drop-off and disappeared down the corridor. The entrance darkened at his passage, then re-filled with light.

The loneliness of the place closed in on Alex. She felt an uncomfortable mix of relief and deep disappointment—relief that Tony was gone and disappointment that she hadn't done better in dealing with him. She tugged at the baling string. It held firmly.

How in the world had she gotten herself into such a mess? "Must have gone wrong somewhere," she muttered. Good girls didn't wind up in caves with their arms tied behind their backs. Good girls didn't attract the attention of the Tony Balbos of the world. Or did they? Well, if the good girls really were being good, what would the Tony Balbos want with them anyway?

For once, Alex wished she'd listened to all the advice people had given her about not wandering in the desert alone, especially from her mother, who was fond of telling her that you never know what kind of weirdos you might run into out there.

Forty-One

Minutes passed, an hour. After that, Alex stopped trying to keep track. She wondered what Kit had done when she had returned from the well head or wherever she'd been and couldn't find her. She thought over Tony's proofs about her nature, which naturally, he had greater insight into than she had. She satisfied her anger by methodically rejecting his arguments and told herself that she did not at all enjoy having someone admire her because he thought she was a witch.

She peered down the corridor, sizing up her chances of negotiating the fissure with her hands tied. She could see no point in trying unless either maiming or death was more desirable than Tony's company. Well, maybe they were, but she wasn't willing to resort to such drastic measures yet. Tony showed no signs of inflicting imminent harm, but what if he had merely donned another of his skins in response to cues he had picked up from her? Perhaps he was letting her see what he thought she wanted to see in order to accomplish his ends. Just another of his manipulations. Why should she believe herself immune to his enchantments?

Her religion taught her that if she found herself in a difficult place, with no apparent way out and all personal resources exhausted, she ought to pray. She had been taught that if she prayed, inspiration would come and she might even be delivered miraculously.

That was the basic teaching, but Alex's mind always had to explore the *what ifs* of any situation. What if you had gotten yourself into trouble through your own foolishness and were getting more or less what you deserved? What if God was testing you?

She had never put much stock in that last question, but she reviewed it out of habit. What could God possibly gain from testing anybody? The satisfaction of seeing a person pass or fail? Somehow, that seemed beneath him. And how in the world did we develop a model for God's actions toward humans based on one of the most frustrating aspects of school, the one that caused every child the most stress and, in some cases, the most shame?

Now let's be fair, Alex told herself. She understood that the God's test idea was supposed to be about building character; but to torment herself, she sometimes took it a step further: what if the situation you were in *was* the answer to your prayer or to someone else's prayer? *Hm, what's been in my prayers lately that could have brought this on?*

She looked at the roof of the cave and said, "The real question is, what am I supposed to do now?" A breeze brushed against her and somewhere outside a raven croaked. Other than that, her question floated unanswered. As she shifted position on the rock to relieve a numbing in her rear, a sound from the kiva's entrance startled her.

Rocks and dirt showered over the entrance. There was a clatter of tumbling stones, then a form appeared in the entrance—an animal! Alex leaned forward for a better view. It looked like a coyote! For a moment, Alex's inflamed consciousness imagined it to be Tony, metamorphosed completely into his skinwalker form.

The animal growled, then made a wonderful sound—a long, high-pitched yodel that Alex recognized at once. It wasn't a coyote, it was Kit!

Kit looked over her shoulder as another form appeared, a human one. It bent down and peered through the tunnel. Alex sat still, wondering what was going on. A voice said, "Go on then." The husky bounded through the corridor, running along the ledges and tunnel walls. She leaped the dropoff and landed in the chamber, bounded over, and threw herself against Alex's legs. Alex nearly toppled from the happy impact. The husky looked at Alex quizzically when she didn't grab or pet her. She yowled, the sound rolling around the chamber.

"Sorry, girl," Alex said. "I'm at a disadvantage." She turned her attention to the figure coming down the corridor. It was a smaller one, not Tony or any of the crew chiefs. Backlit by the corridor's entrance, the form was unrecognizable. She waited until the figure reached the dropoff and stopped. Alex stared in wonder. "Todd!" she exclaimed. "What are *you* doing here?"

"I could ask you the same question," the boy said, looking around the chamber warily. When his eyes rested on her, they were filled with distrust. "Your dog came back to camp," he explained. "She looked for you. I seen you leave and then I seen her leave camp on your trail. For some crazy reason, I followed."

Alex could tell from the look on his face that she'd have to speak carefully to him. Otherwise, he might just leave her to what he thought to be her well-deserved fate.

"I'm glad you did," she said calmly. Todd peered at her. "What's wrong with your arms?" he asked.

"They're tied," Alex said.

"Tied," he repeated. "Huh! Who did this to you?"

"Tony Balbo," Alex said.

Todd leaned against the corridor's wall, thinking. "Why would he tie you up?"

Alex saw no reason to mince words. "Because he thinks I'm a witch," she said.

Silence filled the cavern. Alex bit back the urge to explain further. No matter how long it took, she had to wait for Todd to ask—if he would. Otherwise, he might just think the better of coming and beat a hasty retreat, leaving her in her predicament.

Finally he said, "Why would he think you are that?"

"Because *he's* one," Alex said. "And he can only see himself in others."

Todd looked down, sizing up the dropoff. With a leap, he crossed it. He crouched and studied her like a wary animal. "*Are* you one?" he asked.

"One what? A witch?" she said. She could tell from his silence that it was indeed the question. "No," she told him firmly. "I'm not."

Kit lay at Alex's feet, looking at her by turning her head nearly upside down over her back.

Todd's eyes traveled around the chamber again. "But if you are ... one of those ... you'd tell me you weren't, right?"

Alex was getting really weary of such impossible logic. She'd gotten it from Tony and now she was getting it from Todd. She bit her tongue and maintained her patience, staring at her shoes. This must be the same dilemma women standing accused at witch trials had faced.

"Not necessarily," she answered. "What would I say if I *weren't* a witch and you asked me that question?"

He looked confused. "I see what you mean," he said. "But can you prove to me you aren't?" He looked at her hopefully.

Alex considered long before she answered. "No. I couldn't prove it to Tony and I can't prove it to you. But I have a suggestion," she offered. "Why don't you go, leaving me tied up. You have to get out of here anyway before Tony comes back. Go back to camp. Tell them where I am. Tell them what's going on." She drew in a breath and then let it out in a long, tense sigh. She knew her next words were a huge gamble, but really, there was no other way.

"Or don't," she said. "Keep what you've seen to yourself if you prefer. You make the choice. Would a witch do that, Todd —let you choose? Just leave before Tony gets back or you'll be in danger. He's a skinwalker; he'll kill you."

"Why?" Todd asked.

"He killed Harry Hoskers. He did it to get Deeppockets. Your being here will pose a threat to his plan and he'll have to get you out of the way. You don't have to be a witch to figure that out. Now get out of here."

Todd hesitated, then stood, deciding to test her word. He started down the corridor.

"Todd!" she called out.

He turned to face her.

"Just—just *please* take Kit with you," she said. "Tie her up so she can't come back."

"Okay," he agreed.

"Kit, get up!" Alex ordered. "Go on, go with Todd!"

Kit looked at her, confusion flickering in her blue eyes.

"Go on!" Alex yelled. "Get out of here!"

Kit rose to her feet, hesitant.

"Come on, Kit," Todd said. "Let's go."

The husky turned to follow Todd, looking back at Alex.

"Go on!" Alex urged. "Git!"

Todd started through the passage ahead of Kit.

"Todd!" Alex cried.

He whirled, agitated.

Alex lowered her voice. "Let Kit go first or she might trip you up."

Obligingly, Todd stepped aside.

Alex said, "Okay, girl—go!" The dog flew off down the corridor and Todd turned to follow.

"Uh, Todd?" Alex said. He turned back, frowning. "Your footprints?" she said. He brushed out the prints in the dust on the chamber side of the dropoff and left through the passage.

· · · · ·

Time crept by. Alex wondered what was taking Tony so long. Had the police stumbled upon some clue he neglected to conceal and then caught him? If so, would he tell them where she was?

After thinking about it, she realized that probably he had needed to come up with some ruse for showing up at the camp without a vehicle since he wouldn't risk driving the Jeep. And then maybe something had detained him. She half hoped so because the chances he would run across Todd leaving the kiva would be reduced.

But what if that was the delay? What if he came up the mesa at the same time Todd was going down or met him on the road and became suspicious ... "Oh," Alex groaned. "I hope not."

. . . . .

More time passed. The light in the chamber grew dim. At last, Alex heard the telltale clatter of stones as someone approached the kiva. A lone figure appeared, silhouetted in the entrance. It was Tony. He leapt the dropoff. The look on his face told her that whatever had happened at camp had satisfied him.

"Ah, thanks for waiting for me," he said, smiling. "I apologize for the delay, but some things can't be rushed." He walked over and sat next to her on the rock. "Wouldn't want them to suspect anything, would we?"

"*Please* untie me," Alex said. "My hands are numb."

"Not yet, Alexandra. I will loosen the knot, though."

She stood and he worked at the baling cord. Feeling rushed back into her hands.

"There!" he said. "Better?"

Alex nodded.

"Well!" he said, sitting again on one of the balcony stones. "That took some forethought on my part. Please sit down." He gestured for her to join him.

As Alex measured the distance between Tony and the edge of the balcony, a wicked thought crossed her mind. If she rushed him and kicked him in the chest, he might lose his balance and ... As her mind followed through the rest of the thought, a wave of shame sickened her. At this point in the game, nothing had occurred to suggest the need for doing anything so terrible. She looked at him, wearied by her lack of options. He returned her gaze, then looked over his back at the cliff's edge as if he had read her mind. He smiled. Again, he patted the rock beside him. She shrugged and sat down.

"All right," she said. "Tell me."

"I told them the radiator in my old Honda had gone dry a mile north of camp and could I impose upon the camp's water supply? Ms. Ross asked why I hadn't just gone to Brock's spread, which was closer. I said the place was posted every eight feet and I didn't want to get shot. Ms. Ross seemed disappointed by that missed opportunity." He chuckled. "That young lady, the very pretty one, hovered about throwing me looks of profound distaste. I stopped to talk with that Heather creature and remarked that I didn't see Alexandra around. Nobody seemed the least bit concerned about you except for that fellow who keeps to himself. I seem to remember hearing he was from a family of local pot hunters."

"Jack," Alex supplied.

"Yes, Jack. He said you had gone for a walk and was surprised I hadn't run into you."

"What did you tell him?"

"That maybe you'd gone the opposite direction or left the road. The important thing is that no one thinks you're missing." He paused. "I thought you'd like to know that you haven't caused your friends any concern yet." He laid his hand on her shoulder. "That Navajo boy, though—something was going on there. Oh, and I thought you'd like to know your dog is tied to the table by the cottonwood. That's a bit strange, isn't it? I thought you had issued strong orders on that subject."

"Maybe she got into trouble," Alex posed, trying to keep hope out of her voice.

"Anyhow, I think we ought to move. If we leave now, we'll have several hours start on any search effort ..."

"How do you think you're going to get out of the canyon without being seen?" Alex asked. "The authorities are already looking for a black Jeep."

"The right-of-way roads," he answered. "That's how I come and go around here—by those or other obscure paths with the coyotes." He stood up, giving her shoulder a squeeze. Alex fought hard to keep her fear-threaded repulsion or whatever she was feeling under control.

"What about your gallery," she asked, keeping her voice level. "Don't you want to dismantle it?"

"No. I'll leave it for the police to find, with a couple of exceptions, of course. Just to give them something to puzzle over."

"Your fingerprints are all over those shards," she said.

"No, they're not," he said. "But *yours* are. What do you think they'll make of that?" He touched her under the chin. "I'm going to bring the Jeep around so you won't have to walk so far. I have water and food, which you no doubt need. When I return, we'll see about removing your bindings." He turned and approached the dropoff.

What came next happened so quickly it shocked Alex. Tony was in mid-leap across the dropoff when another form came hurtling down the corridor. The two collided just as Tony landed on the other side of the shaft, knocking him off balance. He yelled and hit the wall, clawing at its surface in a vain attempt to keep from falling. Alex realized then that the other form was Kit. Dog and man went down in a blur.

Tony disappeared from sight immediately. Horrified, Alex watched as Kit's front feet caught the very edge of the cleft, legs splayed wide, head and neck craning as she tried to counterbalance the force of gravity pulling her into the shaft.

"Kit!" Alex screamed. "*Kit, get out of there!*" She lunged from her rock as if to grab Kit by the legs or scruff of the neck—with her teeth, if necessary—but tripped and fell heavily onto her side. She twisted around so she could see what was happening.

Kit slid backward, her nails losing their grip on the hard-packed surface of the floor under the dust. Alex gritted her teeth as she watched. She could imagine the dog's back legs working, trying to find or make a toehold—anything to give her leverage. Would she find it in time? The huskey shifted her front legs, seeking a better grip. She found it. With a groan of effort, she heaved herself up over the edge and shot out onto the floor of the chamber. Then she spun and danced back to the shaft.

"WOOO–OOO!" she complained down into the hole. For one crazy moment, Alex flashed to a cartoon of Roadrunner leaning past the edge of a cliff, sticking out his tongue and bleating "Meep meep!" at the hapless Wile E. Coyote, who was in the process of taking another plunge.

Alex let her face fall into the dirt, relieved Kit had survived the accident. Then the husky was beside her, pushing her nose under her arm. The dog yodeled again, but weak from shock, Alex couldn't respond.

In just a few seconds, everything—*everything*—had changed. She could hardly believe it. Was it over? Was it *really* over? She forced herself to look up, expecting to see Tony climb out of the shaft, his face livid with rage. But the dropoff's rim remained empty. A startling silence filled the chamber. She strained her hearing to pick up any sound. There was only Kit's light panting.

She couldn't bring herself to roll over, exposing all those soft underparts to whatever danger might await. Again she steadied her breathing and listened for a sound from the shaft. None came. Was he dead?

Slowly, slowly, she rolled over, then with effort sat up. Folding back her legs, she managed to get up on her knees. Then she did hear a sound, a low moan, as if someone were regaining consciousness. She jerked herself around to face the shaft and froze, but Tony did not rise out of the shaft and lurch toward her.

The noise echoed around the chamber like moans from a ghost. Then came other sounds: grunts of effort and frustration, the rattle of falling stones, a cry of pain. The cry caused hope to leap in Alex's soul. She looked toward the hole, straining to hear through the loud and fast beating of her heart.

"Alexandra," Tony hissed between rasping breaths. She didn't answer.

"*Alex!*" Tony roared. Alex heard agony in the voice, yet there was command as well. All the same, she thought she knew what his calling her meant. He was helpless and suffering. Alex's wrists might be tied, but Tony Balbo had fallen completely under her power. A wave of complicated emotion rose in her.

"So it's *Alex* now," she said, her voice rife with sarcasm. A surge of victory and wild freedom mixed with the loathing she felt for the man.

"Pain forces brevity," he gasped. He cried out, racked by a wave of it. It was several seconds before he could speak again. "Alex ..."

"What," she said flatly.

"You're still there," the voice gasped. "Good."

Alex listened to Tony's labored breathing and caught herself smiling. She thought she ought to feel shocked by how much satisfaction she took from his suffering, but she didn't feel shocked or ashamed—not one bit. Under the circumstances, who would blame her?

"I ... aha ... need your help," Tony said raggedly.

At these words, a terrible, powerful wrath flooded through Alex. *He needed her help!* He, a creature with a lust for power so great he had killed someone in an attempt to satisfy it, *he* needed help! She imagined freeing herself and leaving him in the crevice to let the rot that had already overrun his soul devour the rest of him. Yes, leave him in the jaws of his fate like a rabbit in the teeth of a coyote! He deserved every moment of his pain and suffering.

"Sorry!" she cried, giddiness pitching her voice. "My hands are tied!" She nearly giggled at her little joke.

Tony's response was too weak to hear. Curiosity and excitement overcame her. She scooted on her knees to the shaft's edge.

"What did you say?" she asked.

"I said you have to help me." His voice was barely a whisper.

"Hah!" Alex exclaimed. "Not by *your* logic, I don't!" She leaned over the edge as far as she dared and looked down on him. He lay wedged between the walls, out of reach even if her hands hadn't been tied. He winced at the shower of sand that fell in his face as she shuffled at the shaft's edge.

"No, by mine you don't," he agreed between raw breaths. "But by *yours,* you do."

Forty-Two

Alex didn't know what happened. She thought maybe *she* had fallen into the crevice. She felt the ground beneath her give way and the world spin past. She shut her eyes and braced for body to strike stone, for bones to shatter, for teeth to be knocked out of her mouth, for the world as she knew it to end. *This is it*, she thought. *This is how it happens. Oh God, let it be quick.*

The last words she would ever hear in this world—Tony's words—rang over and over. *By mine you don't, by yours you do.* Why did he have to say that? Ringing repeatedly in her mind, the words sounded like a taunt, one child jeering at another. *Nah, nah, nah-nah, nah! By mine you don't, by yours you do.*

The stupid thing was, his words did break her heart, just as if she were a silly, over-sensitive child. They weren't even true, yet they shattered her. They *ought* to be true, but weren't. *Why weren't they?*

Nah, nah, nah-nah, nah!

Because I've done no better than he. And that's why the words hurt so much—because they were *supposed* to be true. The superiority she felt to this Violator, to this black villain, had been built on her belief that she lived in harmony with a wholesome sense of responsibility to her fellow beings that Tony did not and perhaps could not feel.

Yet for a brief moment, her desire to see him dead or suffering according to what she thought he deserved—or as Tony would put it, in culmination of his own efforts—had given her a glimpse of what it meant to be Tony Balbo. In fact, she had become Tony Balbo *if only for a moment.* But it had been quite enough to stain her with thoughts of his blood and to cause her to realize that if Tony deserved death or punishment for being who he was and doing what he did, then maybe she did, too.

Still bracing, still tense, she waited for the great crush, the last breath. *Why is it taking so long?*

True, she hadn't killed anybody or caused suffering, not like he had. But she had *thought* him dead, *thought* him suffering. Long ago—like maybe last year—Alex realized that the distinction the world made between doing and thinking did not bear up to close scrutiny. The heart and mind were the ground from which all living sprang, so who could determine where thinking left off and doing began? *For as he thinketh in his heart, ...*

Didn't I know this already? I thought I did ... That she should realize her mistake on a heart-breaking level at the end of her life felt like a disorienting plunge itself. Her soul choked on regret. *God, forgive me! Everyone, forgive me! I thought I knew, but I didn't. Oh, what else don't I know? There must be so much!*

Well, she thought she had known that, too. But now she *felt* a bottomless lack of understanding. Her own words came back to mock her: *I think there is always a difference between how things appear and how they are. I think.*

She hadn't understood anything, not even her own words! As she faced the death of everything she believed about herself, the walls in her mind seemed to grow transparent. The world rushed in on her with astonishing detail. She was swept up in some kind of force, like a flash flood, except instead of water she rode waves of energy and sensation, of pure vitality. Yes! Rather than feeling choked and breathless, she felt quickened.

Swirling forces, like countless rivers and tributaries, touched hers. Hungrily, she traded waters with them. Animals, plants, even things thought of as not being alive—stones, dirt, clouds, the sun, the moon. Something was happening between them all.

Wow! It rippled like light, like lightning—what she felt running between herself and all things. She could see and hear the combined striving of matter and vital force rising like a song or an expanding radiance. It grew until it swallowed her up. Sudden heat flashed through every corner of her being until she thought she might burst into flame. But the fire was not threatening. Like the earlier sensation of being caught in a flood, the burning added life rather than took it.

She relaxed. In the face of the bounteous economy of creation, she accepted her ignorance. Yes, she was ignorant, but she knew now that she was in a bright, brimming garden that called to her to walk more deeply in and join in a glory of dance. *Is this it—death? It feels so-oo good!*

As if from far away, she heard a man's voice: "Alex ..."

She ignored it. She had to make a choice—continue in the

burning or retreat to a cooler place. The experience was so wonderful, she couldn't think of a single reason not to let it have its way with her except that she had never experienced it and had never heard it spoken of. Did her friends talk about it at school? No. What about at the pulpit in church? There she had heard language that approached it, but language that was only a shadow of what she now felt. Usually, it was spoken of as some sort of spiritual grail drifting in an unspecified place in the unimagined future. The experience was unscripted. As such, it could be frightening.

But instead, she felt herself yielding to some inner map that she trusted. Her mind calmed. For some reason, she remembered her dream about flying and the feelings she had experienced while airborne. This, too, felt like that—a form of power or virtue that heals and cleanses and reorganizes the disorganized.

Again the voice, this time from even farther away: "Alex."

If this is dying, let me die forever! But at once, she understood that she had to go back. The burning began to subside.

Slowly, she became aware of a mild breeze on her face and a sense of stability. She realized she was no longer falling. No, she wasn't falling at all. Nor was she in pain, except ... *there's pressure on my knees. And ... my shoulders—they ache! Also ... I'm trembling ... all over.*

"Alex!" a voice roared, startling her. She jumped into her senses. Still, it took a moment for her vision to open. Cool lights rebounding from stone led her slowly back into the world. As the familiar sound of Kit's panting faded in, she realized that, not only had she been momentarily blinded, she had been deafened, too.

And there she was, still on her knees at the edge of the shaft. She hadn't fallen and she wasn't dead! The burning still clung to her like dying embers. She was shaking, barely standing up to it. But here she was, right back where she started, her wrists still bound, and ... was *he* still there?

Tony. That's whose call had intruded on her quickening. But he was also the reason for it! *Okay–maybe not the reason, but the catalyst.* Alex stared down into the shaft, trying to focus.

"Alex ..." Tony hissed. He moved. Stones clattered as they fell from around him and rattled down the shaft's walls.

Suddenly Alex felt a surge of intoxicating pity. That swelled into something more natural than pity and far less bounded. She realized then that not only must she help Tony, but that her desire to help him formed the whole yearning of her soul, regardless of the risks involved.

"I'm here," she said, blinking. "But I don't know what to do. I need to get help, but I can't get across this hole with my hands tied."

"Think of a way," Tony said.

Kit trotted to the edge of the shaft, sending down another shower of sand. Tony tried to turn his head but couldn't.

"Back, Kit," Alex said. "Get away." She backed off, too, then extended a leg in an effort to rise from her knees. She was stiff and sore from having her hands tied and felt weak all over. It took a couple of efforts, but at last she succeeded in standing and steadying herself. She looked around, seeking a solution to the problem of her tied hands. She spotted a ragged edge on a boulder over by the balcony. She went to it and sat, working herself into postion until she could touch the baling cord to the teeth of the makeshift saw.

"Huh!" she said. "Why didn't I think of this before?" She paused as a thought hit her. "Maybe he was right," she whispered. "Maybe I *did* want to be here." She scraped the cord against the rock's edge. "But I don't want to be here anymore."

"Alex!" The desperation in Tony's calls was increasing.

"I'm here!" she called. "I'm working on it."

She was aware that Tony's position was precarious. He might slip out of the stony grip holding him and plunge the rest of the way down the shaft. Or his injuries might be severe enough to kill him. She might have only a few minutes. She sawed awkwardly at the cord. In a moment, she felt something give. She stopped and tested her bonds. They still held but not as firmly. She resumed sawing, doubling her efforts.

Kit paced around the chamber, anxious to be off.

"Go lie down," Alex told her. Kit milled a bit more, knowing that Alex was in no position to enforce her command. Eventually the husky threw herself down into the dust with a grunt of irritation.

Minutes passed. As Alex concentrated on trying to saw through the baling cord, she lost contact with Tony. Suddenly she realized she hadn't heard a sound from him for several minutes. "You still there?" she asked.

"Unh."

"Hm. Sounds pretty vague."

Probably he was having trouble staying conscious. What could she do for him while she struggled to free herself? She had some fuzzy idea it was important for him to stay conscious—that is, it was important to remain conscious if it was important for him to live. She didn't bother with the ironies of the situation. What to do? Well, what did one do for liars, thieves, and murderers? What did one do for anyone in Tony's position? Throw him a rope.

Alex took a breath. After a moment, she said, "Okay, Tony—it's up to us. We have to work this out. Try to pay attention." She recited:

A bunch of the boys were whooping it up in the Malamute Saloon ...

Her voice bounced from her efforts to free herself, but in the natural echo chamber of Cliff Kiva, it made its impression. As she recited, she had an uneasy feeling that the lyrics were weirdly appropriate. "Oh, listen to this part, Tony. Sound familiar?

There's men that somehow just grip your eyes, and hold them hard like a spell;
And such was he, and he looked to me like a man who had lived in hell ...

She paused to catch her breath. Sawing while at the same time dredging up old poems from memory took effort.

"Were you ever out in the Great Alone, when the moon was awful clear ...

"Ever been there, Tony? In the Great Alone? Huh, I'll bet that's where you have your pizzas delivered."

There was something else in the lyrics about music that meant "hunger" and "stars," but she couldn't remember. That was as much as she could muster about Dangerous Dan. What about other poems? Any others rattling around in her memory? She knew that there were, but in the urgency of the moment, they eluded her.

What about a joke? *Is it wrong to tell jokes at a time like this?* She answered her own question: *Who cares?* She addressed the crevice. "I've got one for you. A ship full of red paint and a ship full of blue paint collided off the shore of a deserted island. What do you think happened to the crew?"

She listened for a response. None came.

"Well?" she asked, sawing at the cords.

Again, silence.

"You think you're so smart," she said. "Give up?"

"Never!" he rasped.

Never. Something about the tone made the word sound like a threat. At the very least, Alex heard defiance in it—a shout against the universe. Evidently, she'd hit a nerve.

She wondered once more if she was doing the right thing in trying to help him live. How did you deal with a witch without becoming one or without becoming his victim? It was an age-old question and one not often discussed even in cultures that acknowledged witches.

"You're back! Remember the question? Ship of red paint, ship of blue paint, collision, deserted island. What happened to the crew? I don't want you to strain yourself, so I'll just tell you. They got *marooned.* Get it? Red paint, blue paint, *marooned?*" She tested her bonds—almost there. "I don't tell that joke to just anyone. You should feel honored."

What else? What else? What about singing? Hymns didn't seem to be the thing—at least, not the traditional hymns she'd learned in church. She couldn't think of a single one appropriate to the situation. But a few lines from *Ode to Joy* she'd learned in a high school German class floated up in her memory—a testament to rote learning. She decided to throw them into the pot.

She said, "Brace yourself, it's for your own good." She sang robustly, just as she had in German class all those years ago:

> *Freude trinken alle Wesen*
> *An den Brusten der Natur,*
> *Alle Guten, alle Bösen*
> *Folgen ihrer Rosenspur*

And that's how, when the rescue party arrived at the mouth of Cliff Kiva, they happened to hear singing issuing from the throat-like corridor of the old Anasazi sacred place.

Forty-Three

That following spring, Rennie and Alex stood at the bottom of Vision Canyon, looking up at the sky. The first stars of the spring constellations were pushing through fields of twilight like crocuses through snow.

"It's getting dark," Rennie said. "Should we do it?"

Hands on hips, Alex looked up at the canyon rim. "I've wanted to do a night hike into or out of this canyon ever since I found it."

"What if we lose the trail?" Rennie said.

"Don't worry. If we get off the trail, Kit'll put us back on."

"Then let's go!"

They shouldered their packs and started down canyon. Finding the head of the trail and slogging through its deep sand proved to be the easy part. When darkness fell, the cairns marking the trail became hard to distinguish from background jumbles of stones. Parts of the trail crossed slickrock where there were no tracks to follow, and sometimes the two women had to stop and search or else wait for Kit to come looking for them. Once when the husky did have to double back, she gave them a look that said, "Losers!"

"Give us a break!" Alex retorted.

Kit yipped and turned her tail to them and they followed her back to the trail.

"She's not going to lead us off any cliffs, is she?" Rennie asked.

"Why would she do that?"

"Oh, I don't know. Maybe to lighten her load?"

Alex gazed after the dog, feeling the usual wave of affection and wonder. Growing up, she'd had several dogs in her household—all docile, obedient *I only live to serve you* types. *You are my world and my joy* types. Dogs who loved easily and perhaps too much. She hadn't even known a creature like Kit existed—one that challenged her right to the title of dominant species.

"Yes, sometimes I wonder myself," she said. "Kit doesn't appear to have an atom of the 'loyal servant of man' genetics found in your basic beagle. Couldn't ask for a better desert dog, though."

"Her choice of boyfriends seems to be outside of the box, too," Rennie said.

Alex felt Rennie was insinuating something but let it drop. They worked their way up the trail, enjoying the puzzle. Finally they made the rim where Alex's station wagon waited.

"We made it!" Alex said. She and Rennie gave each other high fives. Kit danced around, sharing their excitement or maybe demanding credit for getting them out alive. Alex set out water and food for the husky, then she and Rennie made supper and sat eating it in silence, enjoying Vision Canyon's evening ambiance.

Finally, Rennie said, "What did you think of that last day of field school?"

Kit came up from behind and pushed her nose under Alex's arm, flipping it up so she could lie down beneath it. Alex scratched the dog's chest.

"You mean how Hanks finally got around to firing old Wiggins?"

"Yeah, on the *last day!*"

"Too bad it took Wiggins wrecking the pickup to finally provoke Hanks," Alex said.

"Well, Hanks was never around when we had to deal with the sanitation issues."

"And then Rafferty showed up in camp with Manny Smith, brother of the guy running the trading post down canyon."

"The guy who actually built that shrine across from the site, yeah. After all our fantasizing about it, it turned out it was just a homestead he built decades ago, only he ended up in a boundary dispute over it with the Navajos, so he decorated it with feathers and old bones stolen from an Anasazi burial to keep them away."

Alex said, "Remember how someone dumped Kool-aid into the water barrel for Hanks's last shower?"

"Oh, that was too funny," Rennie said, laughing. "Couldn't have been Taylor, could it?"

"Of course not. Taylor said, 'It's all part of the curse.'"

The quiet settled between them. Then Rennie shook her head. "There I was worried about Harry sabotaging the project and an even bigger threat than Harry was out there lurking."

Alex weighed the question of whether or not she was ready to talk about Tony. The whole business still unsettled her, and she had a strange but unsupported feeling that it wasn't over. Besides, she didn't quite know how to put into words what had happened between her and Tony. Would anybody understand?

Her bishop hadn't. Alex had gotten the impression that if he could have put her on probation for her part in the drama, he would have. But he hadn't been able to find any commandment she'd broken except ... except that somehow she still seemed bound up in the business. *And I am,* Alex thought. *I am still bound up in it.*

Rennie broke in on her thoughts. "Has anybody told you what happened in camp that day?"

"Huh? What day?"

"You know what day."

"Oh, *that* day."

"Don't you want to know?"

Alex wanted to know but had been afraid to ask. In lieu of answering Rennie, she sipped her hot chocolate. Eight months after the Cliff Kiva incident, she still felt shy talking about it! For one thing, she had begun to wonder. That day in the cave—had her spiritual ecstasy been real or was it something off-plumb of sane? A flood of faith and a sense of the infinite had overwhelmed her. *I thought I was dying, for heaven's sake.*

Had the whole thing been just another desert mirage? At the time it was happening, it seemed right. It had seemed to be a rapture of insight that wasn't too far off some of her other experiences. In other ways, though, maybe because she hadn't heard much talk about such things, it seemed just weird.

"Why don't you let me tell you?" Rennie asked. "Here. Now. Then you'll know."

Will I? Alex wondered. After a moment, she nodded.

"Good. Well, it all started with Wiggins complaining about how unreliable his kitchen help was and asking if any of us had seen Todd. About then Todd shows up leading Kit, his belt looped through her collar. They looked like they'd been running. When Jack saw them, he got suspicious, especially when Todd tied Kit to the table under the trees. Everybody knew how you felt about that sort of thing, and seeing Todd do it tipped Jack off. He began to hover."

"Hover?"

"Yeah, around Todd. Asking questions. Todd put him off until suddenly he turned to Jack and asked him a question."

"What was it?

"He asked Jack—are you ready for this—if he thought you were a witch!"

Alex felt grateful for the darkness covering her blush. "And Jack said?"

"Jack said he didn't know much about witches, but he supposed there were two mistakes you could make. One is to think that someone who isn't a witch is one, and the second is to think that someone who is one isn't." Rennie's tone was slightly bemused. "This make sense to you?"

"A little," Alex said, smiling.

"Anyway, get this. Todd told Jack he thought he'd made both mistakes. Jack asked him why he had tied up Kit. Todd said if she wasn't tied up, she'd go somewhere Alex didn't want her to go. Jack said, 'Where's that?' And Todd said, 'Let her go and find out for yourself.' Then he went and talked to Hanks, and the next thing we knew, Todd quit the field school."

"I heard that part," Alex said. "With Todd gone, Taylor thought that we were all just hours away from death by food poisoning."

"But while Todd was off talking to Hanks, Tony shows up carrying an empty anti-freeze jug. Something about his radiator story sounded fishy, but then everything he said sounded fishy."

"So, who turned Kit loose?" Alex asked. "Or did she just take matters into her own paws and free herself?"

"After Tony left, Jack got me, Danny, Mike, and Taylor together. He said we might be interested in seeing where she went if we turned her loose."

"And then?"

"Jack untied her, said 'Find Alex, Kit!' and man, she took off like a rocket. We made the mistake of trying to follow on foot. Eventually we figured out she was headed for Cliff Kiva, but she got there with at least twenty minutes on us."

"Is that all!" Alex exclaimed. "It seemed longer than that."

"Yeah, to us, too." Rennie slapped her thighs. "I still can't believe I missed all the warning signs. I thought Tony was just some big jerk."

"How could you have known?" Alex said. "You ever seen anything like that before?"

"Like what?"

"Him." Alex felt uncomfortable repeating the name, but what was there to fear now? "Tony. If you've never really seen it before, how can you know what it is when you do?"

"*You* knew the moment you laid eyes on him." Rennie peered at Alex over the rim of her hot chocolate. "I was there, I saw it. Without even knowing his name, you were ready to roll right over him. So, how did you know?"

Now Alex really squirmed. She and Rennie were good friends, but Alex had never really discussed her past with her.

Actually, her past couldn't explain how she *felt* about Tony, how he engaged her attention and energies on a deep level. How it seemed like she knew him, though before that summer, they'd never met. And then there was the event in the cave—how he had sent her over the edge, so to speak. No, her past wouldn't explain it. Rennie was sharp. She had probably guessed that something else was up.

As if she had read Alex's mind, Rennie said, "Want to talk about what happened between you two in Cliff Kiva?"

The question transported Alex back to the strangest moment of that very peculiar day. As she had stood watching rescuers extract Tony from the crevice, she was struck by the sense that she had reached the end of a hazardous journey, one in which she had come upon new and startling ground. That in itself was not so unusual. But never in her wildest dreams would she have imagined that someone like Tony Balbo would partner her on a spiritual trip. Had she understood that making such a trip was necessary, she certainly wouldn't have chosen him as a traveling companion. Would Rabbit seek out Coyote's company on such a journey? She would have expected a soul as hostile as his to sabotage such an undertaking or that at some point she would have had to flee him.

A little irony-tinted chuckle escaped her as she realized something. Rabbit didn't have to seek out Coyote's company. Where Rabbit was concerned, Coyote was always there or already on his way, crouching low in the brush or keeping to the shadows, seeking out Rabbit. In large part, Coyote *was* the journey.

She sighed. It wasn't that she didn't want to tell Rennie what had happened and how she felt about it all, she just didn't understand it yet herself.

Rennie gave her a way out. "Too bad we couldn't have just said a magic word and changed Mr. Balbo into a toad."

There it was again—the witchcraft theme! Alex smiled. Oddly enough, talking about the affair on that level seemed safe and interesting. "You know—when I was on my way to ..."

"Fall into his clutches?" Rennie offered.

Alex felt a wave of embarrassment. "You once used the phrase 'call him out.'"

"That's right, let's go with that. When you were on your way to *call him out* ..."

"Yes, when I was on my way to do that, I called him the Violator. Somehow I felt it reduced him to something dark and negative, but when I saw him down in the shaft, and after my own ... well, when I saw him there, and after some of the things he said to me, it seemed all wrong ..."

Alex paused. She hadn't meant to get so close to the heart of her experience like that, but suddenly, there she was.

Rennie reached over and gave her knee a reassuring squeeze. "It's okay. I think what you did was brave. Weird, but brave. And I mean *weird* in a good way."

"Well, I look back at that now, at my attempt to use a word that made him manageable, at least to my poor thinking, and now I think, no. After all, that's what *he* did—reduce people to bite sizes, to the things they had lost and to their mourning ... to what made them vulnerable."

Alex lifted her hot chocolate and sipped it. "Now I think the focal point for change doesn't lie outside like that. You know, *abracadabra,* and ..."

"Is that a real word?"

"Abracadabra? Yes, it's Latin. It's over two thousand years old. People once thought that written on a magical shape and worn on the body it could heal or prevent illness."

"But now it's just your standard word for bringing about a magical change."

"Right."

"Okay, so you were saying, 'focal point for change doesn't lie outside us,' *abracadabra*, and your enemy gets hit by lightning or his pet hamsters rip out his throat ..."

Alex laughed. "Maybe this does sound silly."

"No! Please, go on!"

"Well, maybe our focus for change shouldn't take the form of acts of force directed at others. Especially common acts of language, such as, well, name-calling, which seems to me now to be some sort of magical act, like casting a spell. Exposure to Tony brought home to me that I need language that changes *me,* moves *me* more deeply into whatever it is that's going on out there." She gestured at the sky. "If I can get that language—language that changes me—then the risk I'll become like him reduces."

"You mean that you'll become stronger than him?"

"No, I mean that what it is about him that's so dangerous—his attempt to make everything over in his own image—becomes less of a threat to me." She took another sip. "Did you hear that funny question Taylor threw out there when Tony was still trapped in the cleft?"

"No!" Rennie said. "Tell me!"

"Here's Tony Balbo, murderer of Harry Hoskers, wedged six feet down between two walls, being crushed between a pair of stone hands like he was a little black gnat, and Taylor leans over and asks him this really silly question—only it turns out it wasn't so silly. He did it to provoke Tony and help him stay conscious, but it got me thinking."

"What did he say?" Rennie asked.

"He said, in his annoying fake British accent, 'I say, ol' chap, is *Tony* short for *Anthony?*'"

"I can guess what Tony replied to that," Rennie said.

"Oh—don't!" Alex chuckled. "Not good for the mind. Anyway, like I said, it got me thinking. I figured that Tony probably was short for Anthony or maybe Antonio, something like that. I wondered what that name meant. Then one day, I looked it up. It means *priceless, inestimable.*"

"I wonder if he knew that," Rennie offered. "He certainly acted like he did."

"Yes, but it occurred to me that I had no right to mess with a name like that. 'Tony' was at least good enough for him, or at any rate, better than anything I could come up with."

Forty-Four

Coyote studied the bars on his cage. He was not impressed. After all, he was Coyote, also called First Angry, also called ... other things. He was more than he appeared. *They think they can hold me. Me! First Angry! I will stay only as long as it suits me. Timing ... timing is everything!* Coyote understood that the ability to determine the future lay in how well one understood the past. He knew all the old stories, especially the ones about himself. One applied exactly to this situation.

All the other animals thought Coyote was too much trouble. They said that Coyote never learned. They said he did the same bad things over and over. They decided they would be better off without him. The animals dug a pit and caught Coyote in it. Then they gathered at the pit's edge and looked down.

"Now that we have caught him, what do we do with him?" they wondered.

Skunk said, "Make Coyote say he is sorry for the bad things he has done."

The animals thought this good. Since Eagle had such a piercing voice, they chose her to talk to Coyote.

Eagle said to Coyote, "You have caused too much trouble. You must say you are sorry for it."

Coyote said, "If I apologize, will you let me out?"

"Yes," said the animals.

"I am sorry," said Coyote.

Something about what Coyote said did not sound so good. Confused, the animals stood at the edge of the pit.

"I am *very* sorry," said Coyote.

Still the animals hesitated.

"For all the trouble I have caused," Coyote added.

Now the animals felt unhappy. What Coyote said did not fix things like they thought it would. They didn't know what to do. Weasel saw a chance to get rid of Coyote once and for all, which would be a good thing for him personally. "If we turn his bad magic back on him, he will go away," said Weasel.

"What do you have in mind?" asked Antelope.

"If we fill the pit with water, he will drown and be dead," said Weasel.

"Would that be a good or bad thing?" asked Antelope.

"It would be a good thing," said Weasel. "With Coyote dead, things will go back to how they were."

The animals decided that the way life had been was better than how it was now, so each carried an olla filled with water and poured it over the edge to fill up the pit. But Coyote drank all the water. The animals looked down and saw him there still alive, his belly big and round. "Waiting around in this pit all day made me thirsty," he said. "Thank you for the drink."

"What now?" the animals asked Weasel.

"Build a fire and push it in on his head," said Weasel. "He'll burn up and die."

The animals built a huge fire. When it was good and hot, they pushed it on Coyote's head. But Coyote was full of the water they had poured on him. He raised his leg and put out the fire.

Now, the animals became very angry. "He won't die!" they said.

Weasel thought hard. After a moment, he said, "I know! Each of us must fetch a rock and throw it on him. He will be crushed and die for sure."

The other animals were doubtful. "He has a way of getting around things," they said.

Weasel said, "What can he do this time? Rocks are rocks."

"Yes," said Coyote, from down inside the pit. "Rocks *are* rocks."

Each animal found a rock to throw at Coyote.

"Get ready to throw," said Weasel.

The animals were just about to throw their rocks when the Spirits appeared. "What are you doing?" the Spirits asked.

"We are going to kill Coyote," said the animals.

"Why?" asked the Spirits.

"Because he steals from us and bothers our women," said the animals.

The Spirits said, "Do what you will, but if you kill Coyote, you will destroy balance in the world and bring disharmony and sickness upon yourselves."

The animals looked at the Spirits.

"We mean, more than you have now," the Spirits said. "Can living with Coyote among you be so bad?"

Weasel raised his rock to throw it down on Coyote. The rest did like him.

The Spirits said, "If you kill Coyote, who will you have to blame when things that go wrong? Think about this."

The animals thought about it. Then they threw their rocks into the pit.

"Ooo! Ow!" yelled Coyote.

The animals felt encouraged by these sounds. They said, "This time it's working!"

Soon the pit was filled with rocks, large and small. Then the sun went down. "Hey, Coyote!" the animals called. "You there!" They listened to the pile of rocks. No sound came from it. "Hah! It is done!" said the animals. "Now things can go back to how they were."

The animals celebrated Coyote's death. The celebration lasted well into the night, and at the end of it everyone slept soundly. When they woke in the morning, they were astonished to find that, while they had been sleeping, someone had switched their tails. Turtle now had Rattlesnake's tail, Fox had Bobcat's tail, Eagle had Trout's tail, Deer had Lizard's tail, and so on and so forth.

Since everyone knew that Coyote was dead, the animals blamed each other for the trick. As each animal tried to get back its tail, all fell to fighting. Then someone noticed that Weasel's tail had not been switched. "Look at Weasel! He must be the one who did this!"

"No, no!" cried Weasel. "I didn't!" Weasel feared for his life. Just as the animals were about to lay hands on him, Rabbit, who had been away, returned to the village.

"What's going on?" she asked.

"We killed Coyote, but Weasel is up to Coyote's old tricks!" the animals said.

Rabbit said, "What do you mean? I just saw Coyote on the trail running away."

"No, that isn't possible," they said. "Coyote is dead." They explained how.

"Hm," said Rabbit. She helped sort out the trouble with the mixed-up tails, then went to the pit to see for herself. The others went with her.

"You will see," they told her. "You will see that he's dead."

But when they arrived at the pit, they found the stones they had thrown on Coyote had been made into a set of stairs leading from the bottom of the pit to the top, and no Coyote. "Boy, those are really nice stairs," said the animals.

They put a roof on the pit and lived in its chamber, which was cool in the summer and warm in the winter. They wove inside and sang there, and on one of the chamber's walls, they painted a picture showing what had happened with Coyote and their tails and how he had given them this new place in which to live. The last figure in the pictograph was Coyote running away, laughing.

Coyote chuckled. *That's how it was, and that's how it will be.* But until the time came, he had to do something to make his life in the cage interesting. The trick was not to die of boredom waiting for the grand moment to arrive.

He pulled an envelope from inside his clothing. He took the scrap of paper from inside and unfolded it. Once more, he read it. It said, *I am not the kind of woman who writes to felons. Stop trying to contact me.* It was unsigned, but Coyote knew full well who it was from. He chuckled.

He said, "My dear, you are *exactly* the kind!" He returned the paper to its envelope and tapped the letter against the palm of his hand. Then he brushed it across his lips. "Coyote and Rabbit! A match made in heaven." He picked up a pencil stub and began writing.

My dear Alexandra, you've answered at last. I've been waiting for you.

He had known all along that she would answer him, just as he'd known she would come to the kiva. She couldn't have resisted then and she wouldn't be able to now. It was very old, what was between them, and if he knew anything at all, he knew that what mattered was not those pretty stories she wanted to believe, but what *is*. The rhythm of the dance they danced came out of the Earth and rained down on their heads from the stars. It beat in the blood like drums. It was deep magic. They had no choice—no choice at all—but to dance it to the end. Together.

Many thanks to Charmaine Thompson, Heritage Specialist for the Uinta National Forest, for her friendship and archaeological advice (any mistakes in archaeological fact are mine, not hers); to the independent citizens of Montezuma Canyon (you know who you are); to Ron Priddis, my editor at Signature Books, for pointing out where my words went wrong; and to all other friends, family, and associates who encouraged me and provided insight and inspiration. Finally, I am boundlessly grateful for the bright and tireless support of my husband Mark, always there to throw notional ropes when I stepped in creative quicksand.